Girls of Summer

C.E. Hilbert

Dedication

To God...Thank You.

1

Keep moving. Don't look.

With the steady pace of a metronome, Charlotte Dixon's pointed-toe, four-inch heels clicked against the dusty concrete floor. Swiping through emails with each step, Charlotte maneuvered the maze of cars, orange pylons, golf carts, and piles of sand in the underground walkway that connected the Beaufort Bombers executive parking to the offices of Watershed International. Straining to stay absorbed in the far-reaching demands of her new job, she refused to allow the controlled chaos in the garage to tug her backwards in time to when her five-year-old self raced through the place in sneakers and a stained Bombers T-shirt. Back then, her hand had been always snugly locked in her father's wide, rough grip.

Tightening her fingers around her phone, she artfully avoided the burn of happy, sun-soaked days that tried to lure her into deeper memories. She had neither the time nor the inclination to wallow. No longer was she the little girl who thought her father walked one step behind God. Today, she was a full-grown woman running into a future with Watershed Industries, and her father's God would have to catch up to her.

Like a well-timed ballet, the doors to the elevator opened. Sliding into the rectangular box, she pressed the button for the fifth floor. With a jolt, the elevator chugged upward. Charlotte's eyelids immediately sealed tight. Breaths came in short spurts as she braced her hands on opposite carpeted walls. Pressing her left palm firmly into the coverings, she clutched her phone in her right hand, burrowing the overpriced metal and plastic into the seventies shag. Counting backwards from one hundred, she fought against the rising bile in her stomach. *Eighty-seven, eighty-six, eighty-five…*

The pace of her counting was steady. Counting was a salve to her hatred of small spaces designed for death. The elevator shuddered. Her knees buckled, almost tumbling her forward. As the doors creaked open, Charlotte sucked in a lung-filling breath. With a whistled exhale, she strode down the hallway, shoulders locked, back straight—her focus on the wide, glass reception desk at the opposite end of the hall.

Work waited.

Work was a gift.

Work pressed out fear.

Work equaled escape.

No Pain. No memories. Just the daily grind of running a multi-national company and a Double A baseball team.

Easy.

"Good morning, Miss Dixon."

"Good morning, Bridget." Offering the perfectly polished twenty-four-year-old assistant a quick nod, Charlotte reached for the neatly bundled stack of mail in the letter tray. With a rapid sift, she recognized most were in plain envelopes forcing her to open each one before discarding. *Ugh!* She hated dealing with the details. If she could only trust her assistant to eliminate the unnecessary, but in the last six weeks, Bridget had appeared to be more interested in gossiping in the break room than deciphering a priority.

After too many heart-wrenching break-ups with former employees, or what her MBA cohort referred to as "firings", Charlotte created a self-imposed rule. Every new hire had two months either to rise to the challenge or self-exit. Until the associate reached the eight week mark, Charlotte purposely remained aloof to avoid emotional entanglements during the evaluation period. Bridget had two more weeks. Sadly, Charlotte could almost feel the pink slip sliding through her fingers onto her assistant's desk.

Intent on sorting her mail, Charlotte barely lifted her gaze as she closed the few steps to her office.

"Miss Dixon," Bridget's soft southern drawl stopped her.

"Yes, Bridget?"

"There're two gentlemen waiting to see you."

Charlotte glanced towards the low white leather chairs in the reception-waiting area. Both were empty. *Ten...nine...eight... Breathe, Charlotte. Patience is a gift you can always give.* "Bridget, where are they?"

"Oh, since you were late, I thought they'd be more comfortable sitting in your office."

Charlotte nodded and continued toward the cracked door to her office. Pressing open the frosted glass door, she found two black suits waiting for her.

The first suit, wrapped around a man with a nearly shaved head, sat in one of the chairs. His ankle was propped against his opposite knee and his lips curved into a subtle smile. Despite the austere black suit, his soft and rounded ruddy cheeks—enhanced by the twinkle in his eye—calmed her agitated spirit. No harm awaited her with him.

Suit number two barely contained a significantly taller and leaner man than his counterpart. He rested a broad shoulder against the bank of windows spread across the length of her office. His black suit stretched across his wide back. His vision was likely filled by the view of the ball field dressed for winter. Whether she was in danger with suit number two was too soon to tell.

"Gentlemen," she plopped the mail on her desk. Sliding onto the white leather, high back chair, she crossed her arms loosely around her middle. "I hear you wanted to chat with me."

Suit two turned.

Charlotte's stomach tumbled. Reflexively she clutched her flat waist, hoping to stop the fall. *Danger ahead.*

He was more than a tall suit with a wide back. He was nearly perfect. Military short, high and tight haircut. Shoulders so thick they stressed his jacket to near-ripping as he placed a hand in his pocket. Almost black, wide-set eyes locked with hers. His square jaw could use a razor.

Her tummy splashed to a puddle. *Stupid weakness*

for a sprinkle of stubble.

"Miss Dixon, my name is Special Agent Dylan O'Neal." The balding gentleman reached his hand across the desk, offering her a smile and a flash of his shiny badge. "This is my partner Special Agent Murphy. We're with the FBI."

Every hair on the back of Charlotte's neck stood at attention. Her stomach rolled on a wave of nausea, washing away the tingle of attraction. "FBI?" She hoped her voice hadn't quivered with the three little letters. Those three letters had caused her to wake in a cold sweat five out of seven nights a week for the last eight months.

"Yes, ma'am," Special Agent O'Neal answered. "We were hoping to ask you a few questions regarding your art gallery."

"The gallery?" *They knew. How could they know? Had Remy turned her in? Had her mother?*

She glanced toward Special Agent Murphy who was leaning his Olympic-swimmer-worthy shoulders against the window. With his arms linked across his chest and gaze narrowed, his body seemed to scream accusation. She swallowed against the threatening reemergence of her breakfast of black coffee and steel-cut oatmeal. Yanking her focus from Murphy, she forced her breath to slow. *In. Out. In. Out. You've got this. You've been breathing since the doctor slapped you on the bottom and called you a girl. Breathe, Charlotte.*

"Miss Dixon," O'Neal tugged a small leather notebook from his pocket, flipping several pages, his kind smile pouring through her.

She latched on as if it were a lifesaver thrown from a sinking ship.

"You opened your gallery five years ago; is that correct?"

"Yes. I opened the gallery a few months after I finished graduate school."

"MBA from Stanford?"

"I received both my graduate and undergraduate degrees from Stanford."

"Kind of a long way to go for a New Yorker, don't you think?"

Charlotte shrugged. "Stanford has one of the best business schools in the country."

"But your undergraduate degree is in Art History."

"Yes. I like art. That's why I opened the gallery. Combined two of my passions. Business and art. " She reached for the bottle of water on her desk. Tipping the drink against her lips, she fought against consuming the whole bottle in one swallow. She set the half-finished bottle on a leather coaster shaped like home plate and shifted her gaze to Special Agent Murphy. "I'm sorry, but do you mind telling me why you're here? I can't believe the FBI is this interested in the education of a U.S. citizen. Hundreds of students graduate from Stanford every year. Are you interviewing all of them?"

Murphy shoved away from the window, closing the distance to her desk in two strides. Wide palms stretched against the glass surface. He leaned forward until only a breath separated them. "Why did you have

Remy Reynard audit your books eight months ago?"

Charlotte's heart hammered, the beat reverberating through her body. Her tongue transformed into a piece of wet cardboard. All the moisture evaporated in her mouth. Reaching for her water, she tried to recall the prescribed answers, prepared months ago when Remy gave her the report on her business, but her mind was a clean sheet of paper. She closed her eyes and wished the God her sister spoke of so highly would show up and snatch her from the chair.

Save her from the FBI.

Save her from her mother.

Save her from the lonely, self-imposed, isolated life she had to lead.

Opening her eyes, she stared straight into the deep gray, maybe green—but definitely not black—eyes of Special Agent Murphy.

Time was up.

All the plans concocted over the last few months were for nothing. With the FBI involved, she'd never know the truth. She'd never be free. Never be safe. She opened her mouth to answer, but the ring of her cell phone halted her confession. Glancing at the screen, her heart warmed. "Excuse me one moment, gentlemen." She swiped the screen to answer the call. "Hello."

"Hey, darlin'." The slow, southern drawl of Remy Reynard washed over her clearing away her initial fear that her best friend had turned her into the FBI. She could trust Remy.

But only him.

"Haven't heard from you in a while."

"Darlin', you know me. I've got too many irons and not enough fires."

She smiled.

Remy was always...well, Remy. Ever the charmer, Remy was her only friend from her childhood years in South Carolina. Her true confidante. And in more ways than she could count, he was her savior. She loved him. He loved her. "So, what can I do for you?" She swiveled, forcing the agents to watch the back of her office chair and giving her some of the precious space she craved.

"It's not what you can do for me, but what I can do for you."

"Naturally."

"Darlin', have you had any unexpected visitors?"

"Yes, in fact, I'm afraid I have company in my office at the moment."

"Well, we always like company in the South, don't we? Do you think they'll be visiting long? I was hoping you might join me for lunch at that delightful little fish house along the river you like so much."

Remy knew she hated fish.

She'd become violently ill when she was six years old, and the last meal she'd eaten was his mother's fried catfish. It was the last time she'd eaten anything from the water.

His news couldn't be shared over the phone. "Why sure. I do love that little fish spot. I don't believe my meeting will take too much longer. How about we meet around 11:30?"

"Sounds good, darlin'. You have yourself a good meeting. Don't talk too much. You know how men hate to hear you drone on and on."

"Yes, dear. I'll see you at 11:30."

"Bye."

She swiveled the chair to face the agents. The few minutes reprieve built her wall of courage and determination. The FBI wasn't about to stand in the way of her getting to the truth. She needed to remain detached. Being reserved wasn't a federal offense. Other measures she intended might be, but she would cross those bridges if and when she had to take action. "I'm sorry about that interruption. Now, you were asking why I had Remy review my books." She shifted her focus to Special Agent O'Neal whose tender heart shined in his eyes. "Remy's an old friend. We've known each other since we were children."

He nodded to her. "You were born here, in Beaufort County."

"My father lived his whole life in South Carolina. As did every other Dixon since Colin Shaunessy stepped off the boat in Charles Town centuries ago."

"But you were raised in New York by your mother?" Murphy asked, his voice returning to an intense neutral as he slid onto the chair beside O'Neal.

If you could call it being raised. "Yes, but I spent most summers in South Carolina until I was a teenager."

"What brought you back to South Carolina, now?" O'Neal asked.

"My father passed away two months ago, and left Watershed, and all its interests, to my sister and me. I needed to relocate to fully understand the business and adhere to the terms of the will."

"But you hadn't spoken with your father in several years; isn't that correct?" Murphy's eyebrow lifted. "Why would he leave you a multi-billion-dollar business?"

"I don't believe my relationship with my father is any of your business."

"I disagree."

She tore her gaze from Murphy and settled on the cherubic face of his partner. "If you don't have any other questions, I have to ask you to leave. I have a very busy morning."

O'Neal nodded. "Unfortunately we do have a few more questions, Miss Dixon. But we shouldn't take up too much more of your time."

She sighed. Waited. And, hoped the face of non-interest she'd perfected throughout her early adulthood reflected the complete opposite of the nervous dance party twisting in her belly. *Just a little bit longer, Charlotte. You can do it. Stay cool. It's best for everybody.*

"Back to your gallery. As you said, you asked your old friend Mr. Reynard to audit your accounts. Why?"

"I needed an audit. I trust him." The subtle encouragement and open kindness she saw in O'Neal's eyes, stirred her deep seeded need to share even a little of her burden. "The gallery started very small. I barely made enough to pay my mortgage on the building, let alone eat more than peanut butter and jelly sandwiches. But, two years ago the gallery hosted a show for Lex Markov the same month he was tapped to design the cover of *Sibling 5's* latest album. The publicity of designing for the hottest group in the country caused his show to explode. Everyone in the city wanted a ticket. The gallery went from being an unknown to *the* place to find the most cutting edge artists. I had more business than I could handle on my own. I was turning away truly talented artists because I didn't have the time or the room to show their work. I had to hire some additional hands. Within six months of Markov's show, my staff was nearly a dozen people, including stringers who scouted different artists. I bought the building beside the original gallery so I could expand. Everything moved so fast, I wasn't able to properly keep track of accounts." She gave O'Neal a soft smile. "I went to business school, I should've known better, kept better records, but everything expanded beyond my capacity. I called Remy and asked him to audit the books, as a favor, to be certain I was covered. I was worried I had missed some taxes or something. Accounting was never my strong suit."

"An old friend completing your audit doesn't sound very official," Murphy said.

She ignored the pull of Murphy's gaze, keeping her focus on O'Neal. "No, I imagine it doesn't. But I was embarrassed. When I started, I was determined to run the gallery without any assistance. I wanted to prove to my family I could do it without any help, but I was drowning in my own hubris. I knew Remy would be discreet. And he'd be honest. I figured any uncrossed 't's' could be fixed without my family being aware."

"You didn't want help from your family?" Murphy challenged.

More than he could ever know. "That's correct."

"But your mother started working at your gallery two years ago. Didn't she refer Markov to you?"

Heat burned a path up her neck. Her exposed collar bone felt like a flashing red neon, *"Guilt Lives Here"*. "Yes, she did. But I'm not certain that is relevant. Her husband passed away, and she needed a distraction from the pain she was enduring over the loss of her spouse." The partial truth almost sounded whole to Charlotte's ears. Almost.

Murphy leaned forward in his chair causing the metal frame to creak. "You don't think the timing is a bit odd? Your business skyrocketed at the same time your mother came into your employ?"

"No, I don't." Or at least until eight months ago she hadn't.

"Your mother is first generation American, correct?" Murphy continued with the questions.

"Yes, on her mother's side. However, my grandfather's family has ties to the Mayflower, but what does my mother's lineage have to do with Remy's audit?"

"Your grandmother immigrated to the U.S.."

"Yes, but again, I'm not sure why you want to know about my grandmother. As I said, my family was not financially involved with the gallery." At least she hadn't intended for her mother to be connected. Remy had discovered her mother's potential intimate connection with the gallery's finances—the non-paper trail kind.

"And your grandfather owned fifty-one percent of Beckford Mercantile at the time of his death, correct?"

"Yes, but again, what does Remy's audit of the gallery have to do with my grandfather or grandmother?" Charlotte's stomach twisted into a pretzel. She refused to think her grandparents had any connection to the irregularities Remy had uncovered. Mama, on the other hand…unfortunately the connection was too easy to assume.

Agent Murphy rested his elbow on her desk. "And, you're also aware after your grandmother's death, fifty percent of your grandfather's holdings will go to your mother and fifty percent to you."

She nodded. "And, again, Agent Murphy, what does that have to do with the audit of the gallery's books?"

Murphy leaned closer. His eyes narrowed.

A knock sounded on her door. Before she could respond, the door swung open.

Filling the doorway was all six-foot-three inches of Mac Taylor—the undeniably handsome thorn in her side for the last two months. And she'd never been happier to see him. "Mr. Taylor, did we have an appointment?" She hoped he would demand her presence in whatever meeting, stand-up, or round-up he had scheduled for the morning. She deplored meetings, but this morning, she would give her favorite designer jeans and heels for one of those painfully depressing stock-ledger reviews he forced her to attend.

He barely glanced at the two FBI agents, before shifting his dark brown gaze to her. "We have a stand-up in Arthur's office to discuss the progress of the systems conversion on the West Coast, and then we have the scouting report to review from last week's winter ball round-up. The coaches and scouts are meeting in the team conference room at ten-thirty, but if you're too busy to care about the team, or the business, please continue on with your little conversation." His top lip twisted to a snarl. "Wouldn't want to distract you with real work." He pivoted and strode out of her office.

"Gentlemen, I am sorry to cut this discussion short, but as you heard, I'm apparently late for a very important date."

O'Neal closed his notebook. "Miss Dixon, I'm sorry we've disrupted your morning." He reached inside his jacket and pulled out a business card. "Special Agent Murphy and I'd like to continue our conversation at a later time. Would you be so kind as to have your assistant call us with a convenient day?"

She hoped she hid her shocked relief. She didn't care what made them stop their questions—even if it was Cranky-Pants Taylor. Reaching for the card, she stood and then walked to the door. "I'll have Bridget set up time in the next week or so. With the holidays, it may not be until the new year."

O'Neal shook her hand. "That'll be fine. If we have

any urgent questions, we'll get with you sooner."

They walked to the elevator. With a swish of the metal doors, they were gone.

The tension twisting at her shoulders released. She glanced at Bridget, handing her Special Agent O'Neal's card. "Tell Mr. Taylor I'll be a few minutes late to the stand-up and please contact the agents to set up time to finish this um...meeting." She closed the door. Her body felt like mushed spaghetti as she slid to the floor. Tears raced down her cheeks. Breaths puffed through her lips in short spurts.

Time was running short.

She had to know the truth. Or die trying.

2

Murphy and O'Neal exited Watershed Industries using the scenic route through the Double A ballpark, the pride of the small, tightknit community of Colin's Fancy, South Carolina. Nearing the end of the calendar year, the field was covered with a protective tarp, saving the grass for the warm days of spring.

Murphy's long strides quickened closing the distance to the exit. Anger fueled each step.

"Man," O'Neal hollered. "You've got to slow up or I'll be running on my chubby stumps."

Murphy glanced over his shoulder. His partner, slightly pudgy and barely five-foot-six, was nearly skipping to keep up with him. Chuckling, he stopped, leaned his shoulder against the fence and waited for Dylan. "Dude, you could stand to run once in a while. What if we're in the middle of a sting and we have to chase down a criminal?"

"That's why I have you, Cade. You're like half bionic. You can chase him down, and I'll drive the car and cut him off." He shrugged, slowing his gait to a stroll.

"I risk my life and you stay in the car like a grandma? What do you bring to this partnership, Dylan?"

"Sensitivity," he said. Patting Murphy on the shoulder, the two exited through the side gate, nodding to a security guard on their way to the dark blue government issued sedan.

Murphy slid behind the wheel and cranked the ignition. The decrepit vehicle likely wouldn't pass any EPA regulations, but it made it from zero to seventy in under sixty seconds—all he could ask of a car. Gliding into the surprisingly heavy early morning traffic, he changed lanes and merged onto the parkway for the hour-plus trek back to Charleston and the regional office where the partners were temporarily assigned. Today's hundred-and-twenty-mile round-trip tour of the South Carolina low country hadn't met his expectations. Not even close.

He was hoping the surprise visit would set Little Miss Perfectly Coiffed Dixon into a tailspin, but she'd deflected their questions like a pro, which only fueled his frustration. He'd lost his cool, not something he was known to do. Self-disgust planted itself on his shoulder and chirped in his ear.

After two solid years of tracking the spider web of the New York branch of the *Bratva*, Russia's answer to the Mafioso, he'd thought today was the day. The day he could stop searching for clues and start closing the shackles in the name of Lady Justice.

He'd presented the potential of Charlotte Lucya Dixon as a possible witness or co-conspirator to the Assistant Director, convincing the AD a temporary reassignment to Charleston was necessary to break the case. Although he and Dylan had been in Charleston for less than twenty-four hours, he'd strong-armed O'Neal with a mixture of guilt and will. Confronting Charlotte Dixon as soon as possible would make their case.

After the last thirty minutes, he regretted not listening to his levelheaded partner. Dylan had been right. Cade's desire for justice in this case ran too deep. He needed to stuff his emotions into the pit he called a heart. Seal them away until he heard the clink of the jail doors lock behind the last *Bratva* slime ball.

He changed lanes. The winter sun shined through the windshield, warming his hands and soothing his spirit. He relaxed his grip and leaned back into the seat, stretching his legs as far as the cramped sedan would allow.

"Take the next exit." Dylan ordered, breaking the nearly fifteen minutes of silence.

"Why?"

"Don't question, Probie. When have I ever steered you wrong?"

Cade lifted an eyebrow, but flipped the turn signal and eased into the right hand lane, turning onto Kean Neck Road.

O'Neal was silent for a few minutes. "Turn right on Witsell."

The backcountry roads were lined with rows of gnarled trees and pockets of plowed fields ready for planting in the early spring.

Cade had the sinking fear that Dylan was leading him to a barren location so he could give him the overzealous lecture he deserved. Dylan didn't yell often, but when he did, he could peel the paint off an iron bridge. Not that Cade didn't deserve the lecture, nearly shouting at a suspect/witness this morning; but he would never let his partner know it. He hated admitting when O'Neal was right.

"Turn onto Half Moon Island Road."

He turned the car onto the road, the tires slipping against the gravel path. "Where are you taking us, O'Neal? I think we're far enough for you to scream your head off at me and not even a seagull will hear. I doubt they have discovered this swamp yet."

"Relax. No yelling, Probie." Dylan glanced back at his phone and stroked his finger against the screen. "You're looking for a gravel road to the right, maybe another hundred yards."

"You know we're on a road with gravel?"

"Just slow down and look for the gravel road on the right."

Less than a minute later, the road appeared. If he hadn't slowed the car, he would have missed the turn-off. He eased down the narrow path shaded by hundred-year-old live oaks and magnolia trees meshed together to form a tight fence on either side. The path abruptly ended in a muddy mix of sand and gravel. A wall of trees blocked their forward progression.

"Now what, 'O captain, my captain'?"

"Now, we hoof it." O'Neal popped the glove box, reached inside for an evidence bag, and pressed a button to release the trunk. "Grab your boots. This will be messy."

"Where are we going?"

"We're about to do some heavy eavesdropping on one Miss Charlotte Dixon and Mr. Remy Reynard."

Throwing his backpack filled with evidence bags, water, and a clean pair of shoes over his shoulder, Cade struggled to keep up with Dylan. "What do you mean, 'eavesdrop'?"

Dylan winked. "I mean listen without being noticed."

"Listen to what? They are supposed to be meeting for lunch at some restaurant."

"Yes. She loves 'that little fish spot', doesn't she?"

Cade stopped and a grin pulled at the corner of his mouth. For the last two years, he had researched everything he could find on Anastasia Bickford-Dixon-too-many-last-names-to-hyphenate, and her only child, Charlotte. Charlotte was once asked about her childhood in a *New York Times* art section feature on her gallery. She talked about her favorite spot where her father's property and her best friend Remy's properties met. They liked to fish on occasion, but she never kept anything she caught because she hated the taste of fish. She had called it 'the little fish spot'.

"How did you figure it out?" Cade asked, matching his strides with Dylan's as they pressed through the trees.

"Well, Probie, that's why I'm the senior agent."

Today would be the day. Charlotte Dixon and Remy Reynard were conspiring about something. He just hoped the something they discussed would be the key to locking away the terror of the *Bratva*. "Lead on, oh, wise one. Lead on."

3

Ignoring the shouts of Mac Taylor, Charlotte rushed down the hall, bypassing the matchbook sized elevator. One trip a day was her limit. Opting for the equally frightening metal grate staircase leading to the garage, she forced her gaze to her feet rather than the gaping abyss in the darkness below the narrow stairwell. Sweat pooled at the base of her neck, threatening to streak down her back. Her clammy palms slipped on the slick railing. Her fears were starting to overcome her. She needed to find a therapist in South Carolina. Long distance with Dr. Julianna wasn't helping anything but the need for better deodorant. Hearing the faint din of footsteps behind her, she glanced at her watch and quickened her pace.

Time was running short to get to the back forty where the Dixon and Reynard family plantations were separated by a winding creek. Where Remy would be waiting to tell her how much trouble she was facing.

Charlotte slammed open the heavy metal door and sucked in a deep breath. Stepping into the wide garage, she scurried through the orange cone obstacle course as fast as her four-inch heels and pencil skirt would allow. Pressing the unlock button on her key fob, she waved to Mr. Croix, the groundskeeper. "The new dugouts look great, Mr. Croix. You'll have to give me a tour tomorrow." She took another step toward her car.

BOOM!

The blast threw her ten feet backwards into a concrete pillar.

Her head cracked against the corner. The ringing in her ears rivaled the time she'd sneaked to the top of the bell tower of St. John the Baptist in Charleston at noon. A warm sticky substance oozed down the side of her cheek.

The garage skewed in her vision.

Two Mr. Croix's sprinted toward her with fire extinguishers in their hands.

The blaze evaporated to a smolder in seconds. Billows of smoke filled the garage.

Pressing her hands against the ground to stand, knives seemed to stab her palms. Pain radiated up her arms. Nausea rolled from the pit of her stomach and burned her throat. She dropped her hands in her lap, lifting her gaze to her smoking car, and saw two Mac Taylors racing to her. "Aww man, not him," she muttered. And the world went black.

~*~

Mac sprinted toward Charlotte. Fear jolted adrenaline through his system. He shouted at Croix to call 911 as he slid to her in a move he'd last used heading into home for the Bombers nearly ten years earlier.

Ignoring the tear he felt in his knee, he gently

shifted Charlotte's head forward to inspect her wound. The gash was at least four-inches long but didn't seem too deep. He reached into his pocket, yanked out a handkerchief and pressed the clean linen against her head. With his hand firmly supporting her neck, he tried to assess her other injuries. Most appeared to be superficial, but he would feel much better when a paramedic, or better yet, an Ivy-League-educated doctor made an assessment.

He glanced across the garage where Croix and two additional groundskeepers were valiantly spraying down the car that now looked to be in more of a smolder than threatening flames.

What happened?

Had Charlie "You-Can-Call-Me-Charlotte" Dixon's car really exploded? In Colin's Fancy, South Carolina? A town so small it didn't even make it on the Beaufort County map. He shook his head, glancing at his temporary patient. If she hadn't left the scouting meeting in such haste, after making a stink last week for not being included in the winter meetings or the two-day jaunt to Puerto Rico to watch two new potential pitchers, he would never have chased after her.

Racing down the back entrance to catch her, he'd heard the explosion before his feet hit solid pavement. The blast had shaken the walls like a tuning rod. With little thought, he'd smashed open the door to the garage and watched in horror as a blood-soaked Charlie slid to the concrete.

In the past two months, he'd dealt with her

tantrums, fits, and demands, but the moment he saw her helpless and in need, he wanted to rush her to safety. When his beloved employer and mentor died two months ago, he'd known his greatest challenge in life would be to endure the twelve months Bentley Dixon's Last Will and Testament required of his daughters.

Each stood to inherit nearly a quarter of a billion dollars if they could "cordially" co-lead Watershed International and all of the subsidiaries under its control—including Bent's prized acquisition, the Double A baseball team, the Beaufort Bombers—for one little calendar year. Within twenty-four hours, Mac was convinced that Charlie "You-Can-Call-Me-Charlotte" was ignorant to the definition of the word cordial. Despite spending her first six years and summers until she was twelve in South Carolina, Charlie Dixon embodied every stereotype associated with the privileged upper class. She was pushy, demanding, and was aloof with nearly every employee with the glaring exception of the groundskeepers and baseball support staff. With the men and women who made the ballpark shine, she was the sweetest Southern belle he'd ever encountered. The kindness she desperately tried to keep behind her hardened shell was what kept drawing him to her. For the sake of Bent, Mac was determined to crack her hardened exterior and help convert the man's prodigal daughter into the legacy his dear friend deserved.

The wail of a first responder siren drew him from his thoughts.

Alarms echoed off the garage walls. The ground trembled under his legs as an ambulance squealed to a stop beside the smoking car. Two medics rushed from the cab.

Mac brushed Charlotte's hair from her face. The cut above her left eyebrow had stopped bleeding. But the bruise spreading from the cut's center would require Charlie's deft hand at cosmetics in the coming weeks.

"What do we have?" One of the medics asked as he squatted beside Mac.

"I think she was thrown about ten feet or so with the explosion. She has a large gash on the back of her head and on her forehead, but I don't think she's broken anything. There's a bunch of cuts and scrapes that I can see. She passed out a few minutes ago." His breath slowed.

The first medic snapped plastic gloves on his hands as he glanced down at Charlie. He nodded to his partner who jogged back to the ambulance. Kneeling opposite Mac, he ran his fingers down Charlie's body. With swift precision, the medic secured a neck brace to stabilize her. He shifted his gaze. "Sir, you'll need to let her go so we can do our job."

Mac swallowed past the thick lump in his throat. "What about her head?" He heard the firemen spraying down the last embers of the car, but he couldn't pull his focus from Charlie. She still wasn't moving.

"Let me take a look." The lead medic slid his hand under her head, replacing Mac's own hand. Glancing at the wound, he yanked a roll of gauze from his bag. With the calm of experience, he wrapped her injury, handing Mac the bloodied handkerchief.

The second medic rolled a gurney to a stop. The two men worked efficiently strapping Charlie to the spine board to move her to the ambulance.

Mac stood as they raised the gurney. The medics' voices were low as they shuffled toward their ambulance. "Where are you taking her?" Mac hollered.

"Memorial. Do you want to ride with her? Are you family?"

Mac shook his head.

"You can follow us."

Above the din of the firefighters and the arriving police cars, the slam of the ambulance doors ricocheted through the garage. Mac crumpled his now bloody handkerchief in his tightened grip and watched until the vehicle disappeared. Pivoting, he ignored the shooting pain coursing through his knee and jogged to the staircase, hoping to avoid the police. If they started asking questions, he'd never get to Charlie. And he needed to get to her. He didn't have time to question why. He just needed to be with her.

4

Charlotte blinked. The pain of bright lights seared her vision. Involuntarily, she snapped her eyelids closed. Beeping pierced the fog cloaking her brain. With force rivaling a heavy-weight squatter, she opened her lids into a squint. Through blurred vision, she recognized the sterile, white walls of a hospital room.

She tilted her head to the side. She must be hallucinating.

Stretched out in the chair beside her bed was Mac Taylor. His chin, with a day's growth of salt and pepper stubble, rested against his chest. Normally pressed and crisp, his white dress shirt looked as if it had been yanked off of the floor of a seventeen-year-old's room. A seventeen-year-old who'd held someone bleeding in his arms.

Whose blood was it?

Snippets of the explosion flashed through her mind with warp speed. Had anyone else been near her car? Tears trickled down her cheeks. The thought someone else may have been injured today overwhelmed her. The tube attached to her arm tugged against the bed, triggering an alarm.

"What?" Mac shot to standing, knocking a water

pitcher to the ground. Reaching for Charlotte's hand, his eyes reflected the worry in his sleep-husky voice. "Are you OK?" He rested his hip on the edge of the bed.

She nodded.

"Are you crying?" He reached forward to touch her cheek.

She jerked her hand from his and wiped her cheeks. "I'm fine. I pulled my IV out. The tears were a reflex."

His eyebrows drew tight emphasizing the deep crease at the bridge of his nose.

The door opened and a nurse, nearly as wide as she was tall, shuffled into the room. "Are you OK?" she asked.

Mac moved from the bedside as the nurse squeezed between the bed and the chair. She glanced at Charlotte's arm. "Why did you pull out your IV?"

"I didn't do it on purpose."

The nurse lifted an eyebrow and shook her head. She extracted a pair of gloves and quickly replaced the IV, resetting the alarm. "Don't be so careless, Miss Dixon."

"When can I leave?"

"When the doctor releases you. But if you keep yanking on your IV, you'll be with us through the new year. Sleep tight." The nurse scooted out through the doorway.

Charlotte released an audible sigh. She shifted her gaze to Mac, who was leaning against the wall, his hands shoved into his pockets. "You don't need to stay," she said. "I'll be fine."

Stepping toward her, he rested his hip on the edge of her bed. "I know you'll be fine. You're always fine, Charlie."

"Charlotte." *Charlie.* She hated how her father's nickname for her warmed her aching heart.

"Yep, see. You're always fine." He chuckled. "But I promised Georgie I'd stay here until you were ready to go home."

Charlotte narrowed her focus. "Georgie was here?"

Mac nodded. "And your Aunt Savvy, Mellie, Remy, and Georgie's friend, Cole."

"Who?"

"That senior analyst in finance who's been helping Georgie understand the business."

"Why?"

"Why? Why were they here? Why were they here when their relative and friend was rushed to the hospital–unconscious, after her car exploded less than thirty feet in front of her? Why? Your family was worried. I was worried." He patted her hand. "Worried people come to the hospital."

Trying to ignore the warming blush she felt creeping up her neck and cheeks, she glanced through the crack in the curtains where the hint of streetlights spangled against the dark sky. "How long have I been asleep?"

Mac glanced at his watch. "About fourteen hours. You were in and out for a while, but they sedated you to help with the pain."

"I wondered why I didn't hurt."

"Miracle of modern chemistry."

"Why did you stay? Here, I mean? If I was sedated, I didn't...don't need a babysitter. That's why they have nurses."

He moved away from her bed, but stood nearby. "Charlie...Charlotte, you were knocked unconscious. By an explosion. In your car."

"So?"

"So?" He shook his head. "So? You could've died. Someone could be trying to kill you."

Her whole body went rigid. "Why would someone want to kill me?" *Other than the obvious reasons known only by Mama and the men with slicked back hair and shiny suits.* "Are you sure it wasn't just some faulty wiring? The car is pretty new."

"New cars don't just blow up. The sheriff and the FBI already have their investigators looking into it."

"The FBI?"

He nodded and slid his hands in his pockets. "Special Agents Murphy and O'Neal came by earlier. They might still be loitering in the waiting room. If you are up to it, they probably would like to talk to you."

She bit down on her bottom lip. Searing pain shot through her body as a trickle of metallic salt filled her mouth. But, she was thankful for the sting. The ache stopped anxiety from engulfing her. Closing her eyes, she willed the pooling tears to stop.

Control.

She needed to maintain control. And, she desperately needed a viable reason for the explosion.

Any reason to shift the focus away from reality. But most importantly, a reason rectifying her mistake of the day: Talking to the FBI. She'd made so many errors in judgment in the last year. Today's message was loud and clear. Somehow *they* knew the FBI had paid her a visit. She was being warned.

Silence was golden.

Sharing was deadly.

5

Georgie Dixon scrolled through her favorite social media site. The smiling faces and well curated photos of friends and barely acquaintances did little to calm her worry as she sat vigil for her sister Charlie.

Err, Charlotte. One day she would remember her half-sister deplored their father's nickname for her. Rubbing the heel of her hand against her damp cheek, she tried to stop the seemingly endless stream of tears that had started when she'd received the panicked call from Mac explaining Charlotte was injured and he was headed to the hospital.

Hours ago, the doctor told the family Charlotte would be OK. Her sister needed rest, but she would likely be released the next day. There was nothing more Georgie could do for Charlotte, but despite agreeing that Mac should be the one to stay with her, because the FBI seemed to be shadowing her sister's every move, Georgie couldn't leave.

They were sisters. Sisters stayed. Sisters supported each other. Sisters protected each other. Even if they had been separated for the majority of their lives, Georgie felt an inexplicable connection with Charlotte.

From her lone chair at the end of the hall, she glanced toward the waiting room where the two FBI agents sat. They'd arrived just before the doctor's positive update. But, when the others left the hospital, Georgie chose to remove herself from the Special Agents' line of sight. She didn't know what they wanted with her sister, but she wasn't about to unintentionally incriminate Charlotte by nervously chatting with the two men who had kicked off the Watershed gossip mill.

Gossip spread like infield dirt during a windstorm at the Watershed offices. Georgie heard about the FBI's visit to Charlotte's office before the two agents had left the building. She wondered why the FBI agents were talking to Charlotte. And why hadn't Charlotte told her sister? Sisters were supposed to share everything, but not Georgie's sister. Rather than confiding in her, Charlotte had ignored Georgie in the two meetings they both attended that morning, fueling even more questions in Georgie's mind.

She wasn't alone in her curiosity. By mid-morning nearly every conversation in the office seemed to be speculating guesses as to why the FBI had visited Charlotte. As Charlotte abruptly left the scouting report with no excuses, the head of baseball operations jokingly guessed Charlotte had only joined the meeting to avoid talking with the "Feds". The group, a mix of rough-talking, former journeyman ballplayers and coaches, spent the next few minutes theorizing what crime Charlotte could have committed to have the FBI on her corporate doorstep.

Their imagined indictments ranged from turning a Fed to stone with a single look to causing another's ears to bleed with clipped words from her Yankee mouth. Each crime was more ridiculous and defaming than the last. Georgie should have stopped them and defended her sister, but in the moment she froze, agreeing with the men by means of her silence.

Their mean-spirited guesses suddenly ended when the main building felt as if an earthquake had rumbled the ground beneath them.

How could Georgie have known the tremor she felt nearly killed her sister? The same sister she had allowed a room full of arrogant men to slander. The memory of their words continued to burn in her spirit.

By the time Georgie was able to extricate herself from the sheriff's deputy's initial questions, streamers of yellow crime scene tape were wrapped around the executive lot. The space seemed to transform from simple lined parking spots, to a veritable forensic playground for a half dozen local crime scene investigators in under an hour. Even with only a quick glance at the accident scene, the image was seared in Georgie's brain.

Several hours later, as Mac instructed Savvy, Mellie, Cole, and Georgie to leave the hospital, the picture of the parking garage continued to flash in her mind. She walked with her aunt and friends to their waiting cars, but she couldn't leave. She may have missed the opportunity to defend her sister to a room full of toxic jocks, and she may not be able to do anything for her medically, but she could stand in solidarity outside her room. And so she did.

Entrusting Savvy and Mellie to her friend Cole,

she trudged up the four flights of stairs to the backdoor entrance of the hall where her sister was sleeping. She chose a single seat three doors down from Charlotte's room. From her vantage point she could watch the still lingering FBI Special Agents. The fact the spot was likely hidden from Mac's view should he leave Charlotte's side was an added bonus. She had known him most of her life and he would be furious if he knew she'd stayed behind.

Scrubbing her face with her palms, she leaned back into the chair feeling the weight of exhaustion drape over her.

Holy Father, please protect Charlotte. You know what she needs. Please, Father God, grant her safety and health. Show me how I can help her. Please Father.

"What in the name of all that is holy and right in this world are you doing here?"

So much for a good hiding spot. "Hi, Mac."

"Georgiana Dixon, I told you to go home with Savvy and Mellie. Why are you still in this hospital?"

"I am an adult, not a little kid. You can't tell me what to do." Of course to her ears she sounded more like a fourteen year old than a woman of twenty-four. Perhaps a little stomping would emphasis her adulthood.

"Not an answer."

"I couldn't leave. I tried. I really tried, but something made me stay. You know what I mean. You have brothers. Could you leave if they were in the hospital?"

Kneading the small tendons connecting his

shoulders to his neck, Mac's body seemed to deflate. "Slugger, I wanted you to leave because I don't know why the FBI is so interested in your sister. Or why her car inexplicably imploded. Or whatever it is your sister has been hiding. What I don't know far outweighs what I do. I can't protect either of you if I don't have as many of the facts as possible, and until I have the facts could you please help me out and do what I ask?"

Adding to Mac's pile of worry was not her intent. He was right, as usual. No one really knew what was going on with Charlotte or her involvement with the FBI. They had no idea what kind of dangers could be waiting for any of them. "I will leave, but you have to promise you will tell me everything. I'm so worried about her, Mac. What could she be involved with that would cause the FBI to come to our offices. The FBI, Mac. The F...B...I..."

"I know. I'm worried, too. But speculating isn't getting us anywhere. When Charlie is ready to share, she will. And until she is, it's my job to keep you both safe. Now, I need you to leave down that back staircase I should have been smart enough to realize was there waiting for you to be sneaky."

He snatched her into a quick three pat hug and then stepped back. "Promise me you will go straight home. You can't do anything more for Charlie. At least, not now."

With a nod, Georgie turned away. She would leave the hospital, but she would find a way to help Charlotte. She would defend her sister against whatever the FBI threw at her. She only hoped they didn't have any change-ups in their arsenals.

6

Cade Murphy absently scanned the contents of the hospital's fourth floor vending machine, amazed a place promoting health and wellness would supply slow death in shiny wrappers. Although he appeared to be weighing his options between sweet and salty, the glass of the vending machine allowed a perfect reflection of Georgie Dixon, Charlotte's younger sister. With all of his research, he knew the half-sisters were more than estranged, so he was more than curious when he saw her not so stealthy return up the back stair case fifteen minutes after a grand exit with her family. Why was she sitting vigil for a sister she barely knew?

"Buy me a candy bar. I'm starving." Dylan barked from behind the pages of the two-week-old magazine he was scanning while they waited to question Charlotte Dixon for the second time in less than twenty-four hours.

Cade tossed a power bar he'd pulled from his suit jacket, hitting O'Neal squarely in the chest.

Dylan picked up the rectangular package and turned it over in his sausage fingers. His face twisted in a grimace. "This is not candy."

Cade dropped onto the well-worn seat beside his

partner. He draped his arm over Dylan's shoulders. "Dude, you need more candy like a kid going to the dentist to get seven fillings. Eat something healthy for once."

"You and the healthy stuff." Dylan grunted as he read the back of the package. He ripped open the foil with a snap, chomping a generous bite. "Ugh. This tastes like glued sawdust."

Cade chuckled. "How would you know what glued sawdust tastes like?"

"Taste bud imagination. It's an acquired skill from watching so many cooking shows."

Shaking his head, Cade pushed back the sleeve of his jacket to reveal his watch. 1:15 AM. Three hours in the waiting room. His patience was rapidly fraying. Lifting his sleeve to his nose, he grimaced. The stench of sweat, sewer, and sludge made for a heady aftershave. He recognized the remnants of their failed trek through the swamp yesterday afternoon, the stakeout that wasn't when neither Reynard nor Miss Dixon showed. He wanted and needed a break in this case.

With every memo he typed and every evidence bag he logged, the demand for justice pounded through his body. The tentacles on this investigation stretched from drug trafficking to human trafficking. The money laundering he was convinced Miss Charlotte Dixon and her mother were facilitating was merely the cherry on top of the wretched sundae.

He wanted justice. Justice for all those who were lost. Justice for the ones who were lost even today, locked in basements, shipped across the ocean, or strung out on the latest drug cocktail. He'd lost his brother and his fiancée to the horrors of drug abuse, and if he had the opportunity to cut off one of the dangerous snakeheads supplying the drug pipeline he would gladly swing the saber. If he took a few other corrupt activities with the blow, he would celebrate all the louder.

A crumpled wrapper hit him in the face, and he jerked his head to the right ready to curse Dylan. His partner nodded toward the corridor where he noticed the beautiful Georgiana Dixon was no longer sitting vigil. Instead, Mac Taylor, lead counsel for Watershed International, walked toward them filling the hall with an air of defeated exhaustion. With his bloody shirt, he looked less distinguished than yesterday morning, but nearly seeing the death of one of your company's owners could shake even the strongest of guys.

Both agents stood and closed the gap to him.

Taylor ran his hand down the length of his neck, kneading the connection at his shoulder. "Gentlemen, I'm sorry to have kept you waiting. I was hoping Miss Dixon would be up to talking with you tonight. I'm afraid she's been in and out since the doctor told us she was stable. She's coherent now, but cranky." His lips lifted into a twist of a smile. "Which, all things considered, is a good sign, since cranky is her normal disposition."

Cade took a step closer but felt the weight of his partner's hand on his shoulder.

"We only need about five minutes." Dylan said.

"The local CSI team has finished collecting evidence at the garage. However, initial discovery points to a bomb being planted in Ms. Dixon's car. The sheriff's forensic team took her car and will be evaluating it in their lab. We won't know for sure all the details for a few more days, but unfortunately, the evidence points to an attempt on her life. Only hers.

"The team thinks the explosion was designed so the structural damage in the parking garage was limited and no other car caught fire. If the preliminary forensics are confirmed, this type of work is extremely specialized and rarely used. Ms. Dixon should be worried. Someone is trying to send her a very loud message. We're hoping she might have an inkling of who would want to take her life.

"Although the local sheriff's office will be lead on the case, he has requested that we aid in the investigation. He was aware of our earlier conversation, and so he asked if we could follow up with your client."

A crease formed at the center of Taylor's forehead, deepening his frown as he listened to Dylan. The underlying implications were clear to both Cade and Dylan, but could this corporate attorney fully understand what potential danger his client was facing?

Silence hung between the three men.

Other than the frown, which could have easily been his resting face, nothing beyond tense exhaustion exuded from the corporate lawyer. He simply nodded and turned toward Charlotte's room.

7

Charlotte stared through the tiny crack between the drapes into the clear night. She longed to be home, to be in her own bed with its fluffy down comforter and mound of pillows. She didn't care that the home she longed for was now in South Carolina rather than New York. Based on the day's events, she was grateful for the distance from the city. The destruction possible in New York was far more deadly.

Sucking in a deep breath, she acknowledged she needed to make a new plan. And, she needed the help of the best planner she knew.

She needed Remy.

Even though she couldn't fully wrap her mind around the disaster boiling around her ready to explode, or rather, explode again, he would be able to help her understand the severity of the situation.

Her mother's choices had created enough landmines to span the infield of Yankee Stadium, but Charlotte didn't have a manager or even a third base coach to give her signals on where to run.

The door creaked snapping her attention from tomorrow's worries back to today.

Mac's wide frame filled the space. Ignoring the tug at her heart, she forced her face to reflect what she hoped was a blank canvas.

"The FBI agents wanted to talk with you. Are you up to it?" he asked.

No. "Do I have a choice?"

"Nope," Special Agent Cade Murphy shoved Mac out of his way.

His partner followed behind him. Special Agent O'Neal's cheeks were flushed and his gaze beckoned to her with kindness; the complete opposite to his chisel-featured partner. O'Neal shuffled toward the end of her bed and gave her a slight nod. "How're you feeling?"

"Like I slammed my head against a concrete wall. How should I feel, Agent O'Neal?"

Mac moved to her right side and placed a gentle hand on her shoulder. The subtle heat emanating from his touch was impossible to ignore. She was too tired to fight the soothing comfort of his warmth to her spirit. "Charlotte, the agents need to do their jobs. Let them ask their questions. Try to limit your comments to the facts. That should help their investigation. Isn't that correct, gentlemen?"

The two agents simultaneously nodded.

"Well, this shouldn't take long. I don't know or remember anything."

"Ms. Dixon, sometimes the littlest detail—a detail we think is totally irrelevant—is the key to breaking a case," O'Neal said. He drew a tiny leather notebook from his jacket pocket. "Why don't you start with your day? We saw you early yesterday morning. What did you do after we left?"

Charlotte's throat felt like worn sandpaper, and she reached for the cup on the tray. She slurped the remaining contents through the bendy straw. With a shaking hand, she lifted the plastic pitcher to refill the cup.

From his relaxed position leaning against the corner, Murphy's narrowed gaze honed in on her.

"Thirsty?" she asked, tilting the cup in his direction.

Folding his arms, he shook his head, but remained silent.

"The day was pretty normal," she said. "As you know, after you left, I met Mr. Taylor for a stand-up, and then we had a scouting review on a couple pitchers we are considering coming out of Puerto Rico. I had lunch plans with a friend and had to leave the scouting meeting early. I went to my car, clicked the key fob, and then everything went black."

"Did you talk to anyone outside the meetings or on the way to the garage?" O'Neal asked.

Charlotte nodded. "On my way out I confirmed with Bridget that she would make an appointment for us to meet again, since you requested it. And I spoke to Mr. Croix, our chief groundskeeper, as I was heading to my car."

Murphy stepped out of the shadow. "Did you hit the button on your key fob before or after you talked to Mr. Croix?"

She closed her eyes trying to recall the moments before the explosion. "I think"—she opened her eyes and glanced from Murphy to O'Neal—"I think I did it while I was talking to Mr. Croix. I was rushing because I was late, but I wanted to be sure to mention something to him about the new dugouts. He treats the grounds as if they're his backyard, and the ballpark sparkles under his care. I wanted to make sure I thanked him. Maybe I paused for a second? I don't know. But I always push the button before I get to the car. I must have pushed it early...right?" She glanced up at Mac, uneasily grateful his comforting hand was resting on her shoulder.

"I don't know, Charlie." He shrugged. "I heard the explosion, slammed through the door, and saw you on the ground. Mr. Croix might know. Is the timing of when she pressed her key fob important for the technicians?" He looked at Murphy.

"Whether the explosion happened before or after could be the difference between whether someone wanted to scare you, hurt you, or kill you."

8

Cade's thoughts pinged off the walls of his mind as he stared out the passenger side window. The mysteries of the last twenty-four hours were piling on top of each other, and he was having trouble sorting the pieces of dirty laundry.

He glanced at the dashboard clock as they merged onto U.S. 17N back to Charleston. Nearly twenty hours earlier he and O'Neal had been squatting in the marshes and dense woods bordering the Dixon and Reynard properties waiting for the best friends to meet at their "little fish spot". Up to his knees in pluff mud and putrid muck, he had been certain he was only hours away from the break he'd been anticipating for two years. Now, he and Dylan were headed back to the field office to file paperwork chronicling the day's activities; another futile day in a string of fruitless efforts to crush the *Bratva*.

Charlotte Dixon was the key.

He knew in his bones she would unlock the steel door he'd been pounding since he'd lost his brother. He didn't know whether she was an unwitting accomplice or entrenched as deeply as the generations that had come before her, but she was his best entry into crippling the organization that destroyed his life.

He'd been an agent for nearly ten years, applying to the academy while he was still in law school at Ohio State. And over the last decade, his life had been consumed with seeking justice. Justice for the life he hadn't been able to live.

The quiet road clicked by as he tried to determine the next avenue to continue with the case.

O'Neal had risked his reputation and a cushy promotion to follow Cade's hunch from the elite of the Upper East Side to the Low country, and Cade was determined not to let his partner down.

"Hey, Murph," Dylan said, interrupting Cade's fruitless thoughts. "You want to share before you put creases in that face of yours?"

Cade twisted to look at his partner and was once again grateful for his longtime mentor. Dylan was only five years Cade's senior in age, but had years on him as an agent and seemed to have the wisdom of a ninety-year-old. They'd been in sync from the first moment Cade was assigned to O'Neal. Externally they appeared to be divergent, but both had an innate sense of justice.

"None of it makes sense."

"What? The uptown princess-slash-art-gallery-owner who now runs a baseball team in South Carolina, whom you also believe is living a double life as a money laundering, third generation, Russian Yuri whose car happened to explode today? I don't know why you would think that doesn't make sense."

"I know it's a stretch. Charlotte Dixon's record is as clean as snow. Maybe she's not a sleeper agent. But her mother's...Stasi's is like a patchwork quilt sewn together with illegal gambling, the no-fly list, enough husbands to field a basketball team, lost years, and more shady friends than the worst defense attorneys. And of course we can't forget the grandmother."

Dylan changed lanes. "Who could forget the grandmother?"

"Alla." Cade shook his head. "Alloochka 'Alla' Antonov Bickford. Immigrated during the height of the cold war. No one would have suspected the beautiful, sweet, Russian, former ballerina with her precious accent and her excellent table manners of being anything other than the loving housewife, mother, and grandmother she professes to be."

"All that time, you really think she was a sleeper, spying on her husband and his company's advances, including contracts to feed soldiers?"

"Who would have ever thought that food stuffs for domestic military bases could be the back drop for this kind of a case?"

"Grandma Bickford wasn't even on the radar of the CIA or NSA until her daughter got mixed up with Markov and Little Odessa."

"I have a hard time believing Alla was a spy." Cade yanked the grandmother's photo from the bulky file on his lap. Her high cheekbones looked sharp enough to cut glass, but it was her deep-set eyes that drew him in and made him want to tell her all of his troubles. "She looks like the sweetest of grandmas. As if she wants to make a batch of pierogis and give you a glass of milk."

"Naw, Murph. That's your Ukrainian grandma in Cleveland. I don't think old Alla spent a single day in the kitchen after she married good old Cyril. He's old school Park Avenue money. Her fresh-off-the-boat routine played perfectly to his blueblood arrogance. I'm sure the old guy never suspected his devoted wife was doing anything other than taking tea at the Russian Tea Room."

"Maybe she wasn't." Murphy splayed a few of the dozens of photos he'd accumulated of Alla and her daughter, Stasi. They were sharply stunning women. Somewhere in her late eighties, Alla was a remarkable beauty with her shock of white hair coifed and twisted at her nape. He ran a finger across the lone photo of all three generations. The women shared the same high cheekbones and deep-set eyes shouting their heritage, but that was where the similarity seemed to end. From his interviews with her, Stasi was unlike her coolly distant daughter. Stasi used her beauty as a weapon to lure men, twisting them to her will until they were defenseless to her demands and needs. He understood Stasi. She was predictable, following the patterns of her social class, which allowed for easy intelligence gathering without raising suspicion.

But not her daughter. Charlotte was an enigma to him. She was as stunning as both generations before her—however the familial resemblance stopped at the high cheekbones and deep-set eyes. She stood only an inch shy of six feet and was lithe from years of disciplined running. She rarely wore clothing not custom designed or from a couture showroom. Her education was top notch and despite his poking the previous morning, she was an outstanding young businesswoman who had a track record of success. Romance was the one area she seemed the least like her mother, providing few romantic entanglements that could be used as leverage.

Flipping pages in the thick file, he scanned summaries he could recite nearly verbatim. Charlotte Lucya Dixon—born to Anastasia "Stasi" Bickford and Bentley Dixon. Raised in South Carolina until the age of six when she was abruptly swept away to New York to live with her mother and maternal grandparents. She attended a litany of boarding schools—hauled back to NYC after each of her mother's tumultuous relationships ended. Her choice of university spoke silent volumes. Stanford was nearly three-thousand miles from her mother's home and influence. Beyond her education and the start of her gallery, the trail of Charlotte Dixon was nearly silent—the opposite of her mother.

The vibration in his pocket drew Cade's focus. On the other end of the call, his superior clipped through her standard litany of update questions, before pausing. Cade sucked in a deep breath.

"Murphy," Senior Special Agent Cavanaugh's voice, tinged with her Bostonian heritage and a near constant state of disappointment in her subordinates, echoed through his ears. "I realize this is a passion project for you, but the U.S. government doesn't have ocean deep pockets. You and O'Neal have one month. Not a single day beyond. Understand?"

"Yes, ma'am. I believe we're close."

"So you said when I allowed momentary insanity to inspire my signature on your temporary assignment papers."

"I appreciate your confidence in this case." Cade swallowed against the rising ball of anger scorching his throat.

"Don't kiss up, Murph. It doesn't suit you. I can hear the vomit you are choking back by trying to be solicitous. Just do your job and make us both look stellar."

The line clicked dead as Cade opened his mouth to respond. "Nice to chat with you too, Agent Cavanaugh."

"She actually said 'good bye' to you?" Dylan questioned.

Cade threw his phone on the dashboard. "What do you think?"

His partner chuckled, rumbling in his belly. "She's a character."

"That's one way to describe her."

Shutting down the conversation, he bent his head and stared at the scenery sweeping past his window. He was close. He could nearly touch the answer. But, he only had four weeks. Special Agent Surly was about to be introduced to one Charlotte Dixon. She would see how the Federal government played hard ball.

9

Dragging a soft down pillow over the back of her head, Charlotte tried to drown the bright sounds of praise and worship music beating against her brain. The effort was as effective as using tissue paper to stop an avalanche. She rolled to her back, pulling the pillow with her. Lifting her phone from the charging pad on her nightstand, she raised it just above her face and swiped her finger across the screen, revealing the date and time: *December 31, 6:47 AM.*

Each day she was able to mark off her imaginary calendar moved her one step closer to completing the terms of her father's will and placing the necessary distance between herself and her new housemate—her half-sister, Georgiana. She grabbed the pillow, suctioned it to her face and screamed with all the power in her lungs. Pain reverberated from the stabbing headache—partial residue from crashing head-first into a cement pylon mixed with frustration laced with fear for her family due to her current living conditions. She couldn't wait to get away from South Carolina and back to her normal life. Back to New York.

New York.

Her heart melted at the thought of shopping on

Fifth Avenue, the beauty of Rockefeller Center at Christmas, her airy loft in So Ho and her art gallery—a curated mix of canvas and artisan pieces. But they, along with good food and civilization, were all out of her reach for three-hundred and twenty four more days. If she survived.

"The difference is whether someone wanted to scare you, hurt you, or kill you." Special Agent Murphy's analysis of her situation drove shards of fear through her body, piercing the last illusion of security, fortifying her need to uncover the depths of her mother's treachery. Could her own mother be behind the explosion? She released a sigh and tossed her pillow across her queen-sized bed.

A knock interrupted her thoughts. Flopping her head to the side, she groaned, "Come in, Georgie."

The door squeaked, and a mass of curly, dark blonde hair entered the room. The hair topped a heart-shaped face stretched with a permanently dimpled smile. Georgiana "Georgie" Dixon plopped on the end of Charlotte's bed, sliding her legging clad legs under her.

"Morning, sleepy-head." She patted Charlotte's leg. "How're you feeling today? How's the noggin?"

Charlotte rolled to her side, away from Georgie. "It's not even seven. Why are you awake...and in my room?"

"Aw, don't be silly, Charlie. It's New Year's Eve. We've lots to do. Aunt Savvy is expecting us by eight."

"It's Charlotte...not *Charlie*."

"Sorry. I'll remember. I promise." The weight

shifted on the bed as Georgie moved to stand. The soft shuffle of padded feet across the hardwood floor barely lifted over the wailing of upbeat Christian Rock bellowing into Charlotte's room. "You'll want to get up soon. You know Savvy doesn't like to be kept waiting. Remember last week for the Christmas party?"

"I would think a stay in the hospital would give me a reprieve."

"One would think, but then most don't think like Savvy. By the way, Bridget dropped off some mail for you yesterday. I left it on the dresser."

The door clicked behind her sister, blissfully muffling the sound of songs of praise. Charlotte's mind floated back to a week ago and the party Savannah "Savvy" Dixon Boudreaux had thrust upon her.

On Christmas Eve, Savvy recruited relatives Charlotte had not seen since she was twelve years old to reacquaint her with their Southern ways. Countless cousins, coupled with an inordinate amount of gravies, fried vegetables, and heavy meats left her with a desire to hide behind the loveseat she'd favored as a five-year-old when her parents would be in the heat of a typical Tuesday evening shouting match. She'd resisted the urge to disappear and opted for drawing on the art of mindless chit-chat, a craft she'd perfected through decades of cocktail parties, fundraisers, and art shows. As much as she had dreaded the party, the evening was a beautiful event—one she was certain Savvy could have accomplished with little input. But their aunt insisted both she and Georgie be present for the set-up and tear-down of the Christmas party. And now, the looming New Year's Eve bash.

Charlotte rolled and sat up, dangling her legs over the edge of the bed. A wave of nausea crashed through her body, making her thankful she had avoided the macaroni and cheese Georgie had waiting for her when she returned home yesterday evening from her stay at Memorial Hospital. She glanced over her shoulder at the clock. She had one hour to pull herself together and be ready for a day of Savvy, Georgie, and the unending exuberance the two ladies exuded. Charlotte's feet hit the ground. *Game on.*

~*~

Charlotte's guttural groan wafted over Georgie tiptoeing down the hallway. With a sigh, Georgie opened the cabinet above the sink. Neat rows of main house cast-off coffee mugs stood like striped soldiers ready for their next mission. Reaching for two mugs, she slid them next to the coffee maker. The gurgle of the machine ricocheted off the walls of the cramped, galley style kitchen in the guest house. But Georgie couldn't focus on the deep, bold flavors. She rubbed her temple, wishing she had an answer for how to reach Call-Me-Charlotte. For how to fulfill this near compulsive need to protect her sister. The sister who had zero inclination to share any of her worries or pains with Georgie. And Charlotte had more than a single serving of pain. Pain draped around her sister like a vintage wrap-dress. Pain that had little to do with her concussion.

Since their father's death, the two relative strangers began sharing one of the former plantation outbuildings that had been transformed into a guest cottage. Their living arrangement was courtesy of Daddy. A very blatant stipulation in his will.

His two daughters needed to live and work together for one calendar year to fully gain access to their inheritance. Georgie didn't care about the money or the company. Fulfilling Daddy's last wish was the main reason she was percolating coffee for two, as well as fending off verbal strikes bright and early. But if she were honest, her daddy's last wish was not too far from the long ago buried hope of her own.

When she was small, she desperately wanted a relationship with Charlotte, her glamorous, older half-sister from New York City. She used to imagine late night phone chats and Sunday dinners after church. When she was barely a girl, Georgie created an entire imaginary world just for her and her older sister. By nine years old, she locked away her fantasy sister when the real one dismissed her with little more than a nod at her mother's funeral. After returning to the family home for the wake, Georgie retreated to her favored hiding spot, a nook behind the love seat in the main salon, unwilling to allow Charlotte to witness the pain she'd caused. She hid until she heard her sister walk out the front door and out of her life. Until a few weeks ago.

Georgie was now a twenty-four-year-old woman, but she wanted to honor her father's last request. He longed for his daughters to know each other; to be friends, not just blood relations. And, as with so many aspects of her relationship with her father, he made his wish into a challenge: live with each other for one year and gain a fortune neither daughter could spend in two lifetimes.

Success was fundamental to her father. Daddy taught her from a young age the skill and tenacity required to win games and contests of all kinds. From baseball to board games, Bentley Dixon instilled a love of winning in his youngest daughter that drove her to victory, even when she didn't want to play.

With a tentative sip of her coffee, she glanced down the hall toward Charlotte's bedroom. "Daddy," she said. "This might be one game I can't win."

10

Two hours later, Charlotte and Georgie faced each other in silence. Their mutual quiet underscored the melody of party preparations. Seated on the wide benches flanking the original kitchen table of the main house, they wrapped silverware in neat packages made of linen. The pile of silverware-and-napkin burritos was already on the high side of fifty with an endless basket of loose antique forks, spoons, and knives waiting to be swaddled in the decades old fine squares.

Charlotte plunked another tight package onto the growing pile and tried to drown the chatter of Aunt Savvy and Savvy's best friend, Mary Ellen, or Mellie as she was known by her friends. The two directed the catering staff to create an elaborate tasting menu complete with a full array of Low Country delicacies, including oyster casserole, shrimp and grits, and lobster Savannah.

Savvy and Mellie laughed and worked together in a choreographed dance longer than fifty years in the making. Charlotte's heart twisted with a strange tug, and she dropped her focus back to the silverware and cloth. The menial task was a welcome distraction to her pounding head. Despite the searing pain, her mind couldn't help swiping through flashes of her "accident" enhanced by the bombshell Remy had shared upon her return home.

After further audit, Remy had discovered a definitive link between her mother and the inexplicable money transfers flowing through the gallery's accounts. Based on Remy's find, the evidence pointed to her mother stealing money from the gallery and Charlotte's own pockets. Remy *feared* Mama was laundering money through the gallery but had not yet found proof. Charlotte had thought so as well and she didn't have to think too hard to guess for whom her mother was willing to risk breaking the law, but could Mama also be willing to order her daughter's death? Her mother was many horrible things, but a murderer? No, Charlotte couldn't, wouldn't, believe that of her.

The clank of silver against silver drew her out of her worry and back to the task at hand.

"You're doing a nice job," Georgie's voice was slow and softly southern.

Snatching loose silverware sets from the basket, Charlotte plastered a smile across her lips. "Well, I'm sure my BA in Art History and my MBA are being used to the fullest by twisting ancient forks and knives into bundles so hordes of relatives I can't keep track of with the best family tree can stuff their faces."

"Hush, Charlie!" Savvy snapped. Her aunt's fiery nature was the polar opposite of Georgie's sugary sweetness. "You better watch that tone, young lady. I don't care how hurt you are. I'll not have your sassing while you're sitting at the breakfast table of generations of great Southern ladies and gentlemen.

Not even a concussion is an excuse for rudeness."

Charlotte dropped the silver she was wrapping. It clattered on the table. "Yes, ma'am." Best not to correct her aunt for the hundredth time that her name was Charlotte.

Aunt Savvy nodded. In her early sixties, although she only admitted to forty-nine, Savannah Boudreaux was five-feet-two inches in heels. Her perfectly coiffed, white blonde hair was teased into a bob just under her chin, and her face showed barely a wrinkle beneath her expertly applied cosmetics. She was the widow of the town's beloved veterinarian and sister to Charlotte and Georgie's father, making her royalty in Beaufort County. After Georgie's mother, Delia, passed, Savvy and her then-living husband, moved into the house to help Savvy's brother raise her niece. She was a perfect surrogate mother to Georgie, but Charlotte often felt as if Savvy missed her calling as a drill sergeant.

Savvy's ruby red lips stretched into a wide grin as she slid onto the bench beside Charlotte. "Girls, these look fabulous. I can't thank you enough for helping Mellie and me pull this little party together." Savvy's voice slowed to Georgie's Carolina pace drawing out the word party to *pawh-tee*. "We are so far behind with all of the cooking. We just never would've gotten to a little detail like wrapping the silver. And y'know how hard it is to balance a plate of shrimp 'n grits with loose silver in your hand." Her stiffly sprayed bob barely moved as her head shook in a shiver at the apparent horror of a guest having to simultaneously handle both food *and* silverware.

Georgie gently laid her latest wrapped bundle into the stack and nodded. "Yes, ma'am. Used to be Daddy's biggest point of contention at a party. He said he loved the silver all wrapped up tight so he could stuff it in his pocket and keep his hands free so that he could plate up all the food." A shadow crossed low over Georgie's eyes, a lone tear streaked down her cheek.

Savvy slid her hand across the table and squeezed Georgie's fingers.

Charlotte dropped her gaze as her own vision blurred. She couldn't put a name to the myriad of emotions she had experienced over the last forty-five days, but sadness over joyful memories of her father definitely wasn't one of them. Beyond baseball, most of her memories of her father centered on the front door and it closing behind him.

Grabbing a handful of silver and a stack of linen, she refocused on her task. Busy hands were critical for surviving the rest of the year. Busy hands made for a quiet mind and a quiet mind equaled a silent mouth. Busy hands. Quiet mind. Silent mouth. She needed the trifecta to accomplish her goal and earn the much-needed money waiting for her next November. Without the money and the answers she hoped Remy would continue to uncover, she wasn't sure she could return to New York. And she would never truly be free.

The weight of the room and the mix of nostalgia laced sorrow made breathing difficult for Charlotte, causing her head to scream for relief. She desperately wanted to run outside to suck in the crisp, late December air. She needed to escape from this place.

She'd loved Colin's Fancy when she was a child. It was idyllic; filled with sticky summer days and baseball filled nights. But the joy she felt ceased when her mother dragged her out of this house and the quirky traditions when she was barely six years old. If her father hadn't insisted on annual visits each summer until she was a teen, she probably wouldn't have any memories of the plantation or the communities that treaded on the edges of the property.

Not all her memories of Colin's Fancy were tainted by her mother's abrupt exit. There was her fourth birthday when she'd read her first book aloud to her father. The Christmas when she was three and they walked through the front door after the midnight service to find Santa had delivered dozens of presents. The 4th of July when she was twelve and Tyrone Jolley had leaned forward under the weeping willow and awkwardly smacked his lips to hers for her first real on-the-lips kiss while fireworks exploded over the river. And she had her memories of Delia.

Her stepmother had treated Charlotte as if she were her own daughter. Delia had loved her unconditionally, established boundaries, and enforced discipline—three things her own mother could never give. No, not all memories of this house and this place were sullied, just most of them.

Colin's Fancy was the echo of her parents' fights meshed with the image of Delia's body, decaying with cancer and ultimately, mangled and lifeless after an unexpected car accident. Her heart twisted as she remembered her longing to live here with Delia, her Momma D. But her mother's stranglehold on her choices and her father's decision to focus on his business rather than his daughter had kept her from the woman she loved most. She thought of how excited she was when she finally had a baby sister, and then how angry she became when she knew she needed to exclude herself from her dream family. Yep, this place was a regular parade of mixed memories, good and bad. She lifted another set of silverware and made quick work of tightening another bundle.

Savvy patted her hand. "That's my girl. Do you remember wrapping silver when you were maybe four or five years old?"

Charlotte didn't respond. Savvy had been playing the *do you remember when...* game for the past six weeks, and each time Charlotte lost.

"Oh, you were so cute. All of that dark hair twisted in braids. You came bopping into the kitchen and Mellie and I were prepping for....Mel what were we making when Charlie first helped with the silver?"

"Charlotte..." Charlotte said with a sigh.

Mellie wiped her hands on a black-and-white dishtowel. Her dark brown eyes sparkled with a long-ago memory that seemed to flit to the front of her mind. Her skin was a shade darker than burnt caramel without a single line or blemish. With the exception of a few extra pounds, she looked just as Charlotte remembered.

She slid in beside Georgie. "Well, I believe that

was an Easter dinner. My Gerald was stationed in Japan, and Bent had invited me and my boys to stay in the guest house y'all are bunking in now. Anastasia was in New York visiting your grandparents, but your daddy insisted you stay for the egg hunt."

Charlotte's stomach rolled and twisted at the mention of her mother. Any story involving her mother and Colin's Fancy couldn't be good. She loved the woman, but Charlotte rarely liked her mother.

Savvy laced her arm through Charlotte's and squeezed. "Oh, I remember now. You came toddling down dragging that old raggedy doll and asking if you could help. You were so sweet, missing your momma and tired of waiting for your daddy at the front door." Mellie shook her head. "Both my boys were sitting right here, twisting and rolling away, clanking silver like they weren't priceless antiques. You pulled yourself up on the seat next to Wilson and grabbed a pile of silver and started rolling. You didn't say much, just listened to my boys talk about baseball and the new coach. You had to sit on your knees just to have both arms above the table, but you beamed bright enough for boats in the bay to make it all the way up the Beaufort River."

Savvy nodded. "You were the cutest little thing. I just knew you'd grow up to be a true Southern stunner. Too bad you went and ruined that glorious dark hair." She patted Charlotte's head, ran fingers through ombre locks, and pursed her lips. "You could be so much prettier if you just tried a little. Don't you think your hair's a little contrary?"

Georgie giggled. "Aunt Savvy, I love Charlotte's look."

Mellie smiled. "I agree. Not all women can pull off that hairstyle."

"*Hmph,*" Savvy shook her head as she scooted out of the booth and began chastising one of the sous chefs hired for the party.

Georgie's giggles grew and she rested her cheek on Mellie's shoulder. "Oh, Mellie, I think you just won an argument with Aunt Savvy."

Mellie patted her cheek. "Well, I don't know about that…"

The chimes announcing a new visitor interrupted the conversation.

"That's probably one of the boys bringing the extra glasses. You two girls keep chatting. Does my old heart good to see the two of you together. Your daddy is grinning from ear to ear in heaven right now." She shuffled out of the seat and disappeared through the doorway.

Charlotte lifted her gaze to Georgie and stared into crystal blue eyes identical to her own. Her heart twisted. "Georgie…umm…"

Georgie shrugged. "It's OK."

Charlotte wasn't sure what was *OK,* but she felt a shift in her; a shift into something hazy and unclear.

Muffled voices echoed through the entryway and filtered into the kitchen, growing louder with each second. One voice was an octave deeper than Mellie's southern drawl.

Dropping her unwrapped silver, Georgie shot up

from the table and raced to the entryway. "Mac!"

Charlotte felt her insides tumble to her knees and her shoulders drop ten inches at the mention of her father's right-hand man. Mac "I'm-Too-Handsome-for-My-Own-Good" Taylor.

Mac Taylor was the man her father had entrusted with his business, his baseball team, and his daughters' lives. For better or worse, he was her warden, her keeper, and her oligarch for the next eleven months. She wanted to hate him and his dictatorial ways, but in the hospital, he had been her savior.

The memory of the FBI agents' interrogation stung her bruised and battered mind. Her frame involuntarily shook at the thought of the cycle of questions from Agent Murphy and his steely gaze that made her want to divulge every secret she ever had, beginning with the candy she stole from her Babushka's pocketbook when she was eight to the entire ordeal with her gallery and her mother's likely criminal activity. And yet, one glance into Mac Taylor's soft, chocolate brown gaze gave her the strength she needed to remain resolutely vague.

She couldn't deny her inexplicable attraction to him, and a month ago she would have rather jumped into a vat of vinegar after shaving her legs than admit he was kind. But after the other night her heart had softened towards him. And yet, anything less than business formal with Mr. Taylor was a disaster in waiting. She would learn to control the butterflies in her stomach which started when he spoke, entered a room, or his name was mentioned. A little discipline and hard work, and she would be able to be in a room with the handsome lawyer without a single shuffle from her butterfly army. She could do it. She just needed to focus on anything other than the all systems meltdown she experienced when she was within a ten foot radius of the man.

She shifted her attention to her wrapping, forcibly ignoring the gushing Georgie. Silver clanked as she drove her hand into the basket and snatched a handful of cutlery, dropping them onto the wooden surface with a dull clunk. She wished Mac would have stayed away. Why did he need to meddle in her already overcomplicated family? Didn't he have one of his own? Did he have any idea what his mere presence was doing to her fragile control?

The sweet chatter of her sister churned her stomach. Georgie treated him as if he walked on water. But he wasn't that special. He was just a man. A man with a chiseled jaw, dark hair graying at the temples, and eyes the color of espresso. Yep, just a man.

She barely noticed him.

Glancing up, she caught sight of his thick arm linked through Georgie's. The knife-spoon-fork combo slipped from her hand, hitting the table and flopping in a jangle of dissonant tings against the tile floor. With a sigh, she scooted from the bench and knelt to retrieve the flatware. As she reached for the base of the fork, a long-fingered, tan hand grasped the tines.

Her gaze locked with deep, dark brown. Swallowing hard against the lump in her throat, her lips tightened across her mouth. "I've got it. You can let go. No need to rescue the fork."

The corner of his mouth lifted softly, revealing a single dimple in his right cheek. "Just trying to help," he said, with a soft wink.

They stood simultaneously, their arms brushing lightly. The hairs on the back of Charlotte's neck stood tall. With a dry swallow, she shuffled around him and plopped onto her seat.

Sliding onto the bench across from her, Mac was followed by her sister, who snuggled into his side. He draped his arm over Georgie's shoulders, squeezing her close. "How're you feeling?" he asked Charlotte. "How are your hands? Your head? Any residual headache from the accident?"

With a shrug, she dropped her focus to the table and yanked another set of silverware from the basket, and began bundling. "Nothing that could keep me from making sure half of Beaufort County has free hands."

She could almost feel the shake of his head.

"I see your attitude wasn't wounded."

Charlotte dropped her bundle onto the stack and slid off the bench. "I think we have enough silver wrapped." Heaving the basket with napkins and silverware from the table, she moved toward the doorway. "I think I'll see if they need help with the flowers. If not, I'm going back to take a nap. Seems you have everything under control here." She glanced over her shoulder. "Welcome, Taylor. I'm sure these ladies are glad you're here."

11

Charlie walked through the doorway that connected the kitchen and the main dining room. The natural sway of her hips with the added weight of the basket filled with silverware bundles drew Mac's attention to her long, lean legs. The twist of his gut in reaction had him shaking his head. *She's technically your boss, Taylor. No unmentionable thoughts. God's always watching, and He's probably given a little window for Bent to glance through as well.*

He cranked his neck and kneaded the small space connected to his shoulders. He rarely felt tension in this kitchen. The giant room held the same cozy warmth he'd experienced in his own mother's kitchen during childhood, but Charlotte had the ability to turn the loveliest of situations into an exercise in angst. The last six weeks had been a lesson in managing chaos in all areas of his life, the most tumultuous having just walked from the room. Prayer had become an even more necessary staple for him. Bent often professed the difference a few minutes on his knees could make when facing an insurmountable obstacle. Hurricane Charlie would more likely generate hours on Mac's knees, and he wished he could ask his mentor for advice on how best to navigate the storm.

Mac's grief was nothing compared to Bent's "blood family", but he struggled every day to work without the old man yelling down the hall at him. He expected Bent to pop in for lunch or call after hours with excitement humming through his voice at the discovery of a new pitcher or business opportunity. Mac had not had the space to grieve the loss of his mentor and friend. Not fully.

Bent had entrusted him with the running of his business and the execution of his will. Mac was trying to fulfill all his best friend's final requests while maintaining a professional distance, but Bent's estranged daughter was making his longed-for aloofness nearly impossible.

She seemed to attract trouble with the consistency of flies finding the honey pot; the exploding car was just one of many events that spelled trouble with a capital "C".

Savvy slid onto the bench Charlotte had vacated, and patted his hand. "Just ignore her. She woke up on the wrong side of the bed six weeks ago and couldn't find the right side if she was Sherlock Holmes." She glanced over her shoulder toward the empty doorway. "Guess she has more Stasi in her than we ever thought."

He shrugged. "She should get at least a partial pass because of the accident. Slamming your body into concrete could not lead to a positive attitude in the best of people."

Georgie tensed. Her mass of dark blonde curls seemed to droop with the mention of the explosion.

His heart twisted in pain for his adopted kid sister. Mac first met Georgie when she was twelve. Lopsided pigtails topped a heart shaped face as she followed her dad to the practice fields. Her kindness and innocence was as pure today as when she was tiny and coached Mac on his throw to second, claiming his hop "could use a little work". He wished he could ease Georgie's pain. She was desperately trying to keep everything in balance—her grief, her career, her relationship with her sister and even her aunt. Mac needed to find a way to help her while dealing with Charlie. The balance was a teeter-totter ride he wasn't enjoying.

He tucked Georgie into his side. With a loud smack, he kissed her forehead. "Don't worry, Slugger. Charlie will be just fine. And Sheriff Camby and the FBI will figure out what happened."

Georgie dropped her gaze to the table, her finger tracing an unseen pattern along the smooth surface. A single tear landed just to the left of her hand.

Lifting his gaze to Savvy, he tilted his head to the side. She nodded, rising from her seat, wordlessly telling him most of the story he already knew.

"So," he pulled Georgie tighter to his side. "Why don't you tell me what the deal is?"

Her whole body shook against his side with her silent weeping. Stroking her arm, he let her cry and waited. Patience had served him well as a boy sitting up with his prize lamb when she fell ill, as a catcher bouncing around the minor leagues hoping for a shot at "The Show", and as an attorney across the table from a worthy adversary. He could wait out a few tears.

Georgie sucked in a shaky breath. Leaning her elbows on the table she rested her chin in her cupped hands tilting her head to meet his gaze. Still damp, the crystal blue depths reflected raw agony. "I don't know what else to do, Mac," Her voice broke just above a whisper. "I thought after Thanksgiving, you know, those first few weeks, things would naturally get better. But they haven't. I think they've gotten worse. You were in Ohio, and I didn't want to whine, but Christmas Eve was awful. She was awful. And now this explosion...this....bomb? Why would someone attack her or anyone at Watershed? Do you think she's in danger? Is the whole organization? Will we be able to convince her to stay? She has to stay, Mac. It's Daddy's last wish. But why would she stay if someone is trying to blow her up?"

A shudder chased through his body. The sheriff had confirmed today that the explosion was indeed caused by a bomb. He didn't want to think about the bomb. He couldn't process the thought that Charlie could have been killed. He blocked the what-if thoughts from his mind and shifted his attention to what he could control. He'd wondered about the Christmas Eve party a week ago. He'd flown home to Ohio before Christmas so he'd missed the annual Savvy Dixon Boudreaux Blow-Out. The party should have been a great way for Charlie to acclimate to the family and the social scene of Beaufort County. Of course, that would've been too easy. "Tell me what she did on Christmas Eve," he prompted. Anything to divert from the talk of bombs.

She twisted on the bench, pulling a knee to her chest as she faced him. "She was terrible. You could feel how much she hated everyone and everything. And this is her family, Mac. Can you imagine? She looked down her nose at the party like it was a third-rate redneck hoedown rather than the elaborate ordeal Savvy throws every year. I'm not one much for parties, but Savvy knows what she's doing. I can't imagine a party planner in New York could do any better." She nearly spat when she said the name of the city.

Mac nodded, recognizing the venting he would endure. For over a decade, Georgie had used his shoulder for her tears and her frustration, and she was just beginning to crest the wave.

With hands twisting and curls bouncing, Georgie proceeded to describe Charlotte's conduct during Savvy's much lauded annual Christmas Eve party.

Mac's stomach burned, and he felt a sharp pain at the base of his neck as she shared Charlotte's snub of local politicians, extended family, and her father's close friends. Mac got an image of lithe Charlotte draped in a skimpy black cocktail dress holding up a wall in the main living room with her lips pursed, forehead scrunched, and focus narrowed as all of the Dixons' wide range of acquaintances tried to woo her. And she had probably flicked them away with her sharp words as though she was swatting flies at a picnic.

"The worst was Auntie Darla, you know, Momma's former sorority sister who lives in Mobile but visits her family every Christmas and still comes to

Savvy's little soirée?"

A vision of teased, unnaturally red hair the size of Alabama, and rouged cheeks scorched his mind. "I remember."

"Well, she came to the party and was trying so hard to be cheerful and upbeat. She felt so bad she missed Daddy's funeral. She went straight up to Charlie and asked all about New York and her little gallery. She chatted her up like they were at a Sunday social. And Charlie looked at her with *that way* she has. You know the look I'm talking about?"

"I know the one." He'd been on the receiving end of the look more times in the past few weeks than he cared to remember.

"There's Auntie Darla chattering away, her hands waving, when Charlie takes a sip from her glass and says, 'Darla where does one find that particular shade of red your hair is colored? I don't believe I've ever seen such a color outside a crayon box.' Can you believe?" She tossed her hands wide.

Although Mac thought Charlotte's description was fairly accurate, that was the type of thought not meant to be spoken aloud. He guessed Charlie missed the lesson in Sunday school. "Unfortunately, yes I can. But you can't judge her for what she says or by the morals your parents raised you with, Georgie."

Her mouth dropped open, and she laced her arms over her chest. "We had the same father, Mac. She was raised with the same morals I was…or mostly was."

He ran his hand lightly over her long curls. "No, she wasn't." With a sigh, he dropped his hand to the table and twisted on the bench to face her. "She didn't have your dad in her life the way you did. And she certainly didn't have Sav or your Uncle Rayburn or Mellie or your church. She had a mother who, as far as I can tell, used her love as a thing to withhold if Charlie didn't perform to her expectations. And a distant father, who chose his life over a life with her. She didn't have what you had...have, Georgie."

Her eyes closed. Dropping her forehead to her folded arms, she released a long deep breath.

Silence lingered between them, cushioned by the clinks and clangs of the catering staff.

She was processing the frustration of the past few weeks. Her anger toward Charlotte was likely a manifestation of her grief. Anger was one of the steps. There were five, or so he'd been told when his mother died. He was a lawyer not a psychologist. He couldn't remember them all, but he was certain of anger. Georgie definitely was experiencing anger. And, he imagined Charlotte was experiencing some anger of her own. Women. Why couldn't they punch it out and be done, like men?

Lifting her head, she propped her chin on her knee and tilted her head to the side. "It's not fair."

"What's not fair?"

"Why are you always right?"

He felt the corners of his mouth tug. "Taylor curse. I'm the oldest, so I'm always right. My brothers hate it."

Her crystal eyes rolled. "OK. What am I supposed to do about my older sister?"

He wanted to tell her to yell at Charlie and tell her she was being a snobbish idiot. He wanted to tell Georgie to haul off and sock her sister in the jaw—a method that had worked well with his brothers a time or two. But he knew the answer Bent, his own dad, and The Lord wanted him to give. "Love her," he whispered.

"She makes it super hard."

"Well, love isn't supposed to be easy. It's like hitting a hanging curve ball; if it was easy everyone would do it."

"Seriously," she said, with a shove to his shoulder, "is everything baseball with you?"

He stood and offered a hand to help her stand. "God gave us baseball so we would have an easy way to talk about the hard things in life."

Stepping toward him, she wrapped her long arms around his waist and laid her head on his chest. "I'm glad Daddy put you in charge. He chose well. You are a man after his own heart."

He patted her back three times and lifted his gaze heavenward. *I hope she's right.*

12

Sweat pooled on Charlotte's chest, and beads raced down her back. Her feet pounded the gravel and dirt path connecting the main road to the plantation grounds. Running in December in South Carolina didn't offer the same fear of frostbite as winter runs in New York.

First tick in the positive column for South Carolina.

And, although running with a diagnosed concussion likely wasn't doctor approved, she clung to the hope her greatest love would grant the calm continuing to evade her. Running had been her outlet since she was first sent to Connecticut for year-round boarding school. On the winding, weed-filled paths around campus, she'd found a sense of calm when her personal life was a mass of twisted emotions and emptiness.

Through her teen years and into adulthood, running had been her constant companion. When her mother remarried for the fourth time, when Momma D died, when her mother accused her of flirting with one of her step-fathers, when her father ignored her, and when she ignored her father's dying request, running had never failed her. She could push herself through bruised toes, swollen feet, pulled hamstrings, and sore backs, because by mile four or five she would achieve peace. A clear mind filled with nothing but the pain of her body as a reward. Yet, after several miles along what could only be described as a barren, backwoods country road, she wasn't any closer to the bliss of an empty mind.

Her abhorrent behavior over the last few weeks played like a newsreel in her mind, and one little car bomb couldn't excuse a devastating stack of terrible conduct. Charlotte wanted to blame her behavior on the strained situation, the unspoken fear of what lay outside of her control or even her living conditions, but the reality was she was being a brat. She was *being* her mother. And she never wanted to be any version of Anastasia 'Stasi' Bickford.

Not ever.

Rude. Overbearing. Entitled. Her mother was the textbook definition of a person with whom Charlotte didn't want to associate.

Technically, her mother worked for her, but the salary was paltry, and she had preferred to play ostrich with Mama's bookkeeping rather than confront her. Even before she'd asked Remy to intervene with an audit, she'd suspected her mother was skimming money, but Remy's recent discovery exceeded even Charlotte's worst expectations of her mother.

One week before her father's death, Remy delivered the results of the initial audit. Charlotte's suspicions were correct. Her mother's paychecks were more frequent and fuller than they had agreed. But he also found irregular lump sums coming into the gallery—dollars way above the average price of the pieces she sold and often connected to artists her mother "discovered". The command to come to South Carolina for the funeral and the reading of the will had given Charlotte the reprieve she needed.

Until the FBI dropped by for a chat.

And her car exploded.

And Remy confirmed her worst fears.

She slowed her run to a lazy jog, the gravel turned to a muddy path as the guest house came into view. The white clapboard, three-bedroom house was almost a mile from the main house, far enough away to feel separation, but close enough for Savvy to drop by for coffee. The driveway was a worn path off of the main gravel road, quilted with mossy grass and dying weeds. Her final steps were muffled as she rounded the wraparound porch to the front entrance.

A scream caught in her throat, her hand rushing to her chest, at the sight of long denim clad legs dangling over the edge of the porch. Her gaze roamed up the legs to the broad chest stretching a taut, well-worn flannel shirt. She locked her gaze with the watchful eyes of Mac Taylor. A lump replaced her scream.

Why did he have to look as if he stepped out of an outdoor living catalogue? She always went a little melty when she saw a man in a wooly plaid shirt and a days' growth of beard.

Extending his hand, he offered her a bottle of water. "You've been gone awhile." He patted the porch floor beside him. "Why don't you take a load off?

Catch your breath."

She greedily sucked back half of the water. "Thanks." The porch was a bit higher than her hip forcing her to hop to sit beside him.

He nodded. "Thought you were taking a nap?"

Her breath slowed, and she lifted her shoulders with a shrug, "Wasn't tired."

"So you ran for over an hour instead? Doesn't seem like good therapy after being released from the hospital less than sixteen hours ago. Can't imagine running is a good idea after a concussion."

The screaming in her brain confirmed he was probably right, but she would never let him know. "Why do you care?"

He shifted to face her, leaning his back against the weathered column supporting the porch. "Let's not forget who sat with you during that entire hospital stay."

She ignored the warmth spreading through her stomach. "No one asked you to stay."

"You're welcome."

"Thanks, but as you can see"—she spread her arms wide—"I'm doing just fine."

His gaze followed the length of her body. "Yeah, your outside looks OK."

Wrapping her arms tight over her belly, she scooted against the opposite pillar and crossed her legs at the ankles. "We've established I'm fine. You can go. Unless there's something else you want to discuss."

"Just thought you might want to talk about why you are being abhorrently rude to your sister, aunt, and the entire county."

Heat burned her cheeks, and her stomach churned at the accusation that mirrored her own self-conviction. Lifting the bottle to her lips, she tried to muster the strength to fight the charge, to justify her behavior, but she couldn't. Sure, she could rationalize her actions and words by explaining her mother's deception or sharing the pain she was trying to understand over her father's death. She could make Mac understand, but then she would have to explain, to share what was in her heart—and that was something she wasn't willing or able to do. With him or anyone. Sharing equaled weakness. Weakness wasn't Russian. And as much as she wished she could deny it, today, she was definitely Russian to her core.

Licking the final drop of water from her lips, she crushed the bottle in her hand. The crackling of plastic echoed through the stillness of the December afternoon. She slid off the porch and moved to step around him, hoping if she ignored him, he would go away. The tactic had worked flawlessly with every other man who'd ever been in her life, including her father. Her jogging shoes squeaked with each step until her hand rested against the door.

"Never thought you were a coward."

She glanced over her shoulder. "What are you talking about?"

He flipped his legs onto the porch and stood. "You've been a brat. You know it. I know it. Everyone knows it. But you won't own up to it? You want to ignore the fact you've been a horrible person to your sister and your family. That you've acted like a fourteen-year-old sentenced to a summer at her grandparents in the middle of the backwoods without access to the Internet rather than a woman in her thirties who has been handed a multi-billion dollar business on a platter. Do you care about anyone but yourself? I never met your mother, but you certainly have given me a picture of what she must be like."

She whipped around, closed the two steps between them, and poked her finger into his chest. "Listen here. You may be my warden, but you don't get to pass judgment on me. I can act however I want. As you pointed out, I'm in my thirties. I can be a jerk to whomever I choose. You might control the purse strings, but you don't control me." Her anger puttered to a stop. Slumping against the door, she felt the first exhausted tear trickle down her cheek. *No! Not tears. Anger. Please, let me stay angry.*

Anger was easier.

Anger was justified.

Anger at her mom for ruining her business, setting her at the cliff of financial and possible legal ruin.

Anger at her father – there weren't enough therapy hours on the planet to work through her resentment and anger over their relationship.

Even anger with her current situation—living with her twenty-four-year-old sister and away from her home in Manhattan.

All these should definitely grant her an inkling of annoyed irritation.

And, nearly being killed in the parking garage of

her building should allow for a fit or two.

But, no. She had to go all teary-eyed when one man called her a coward.

Her shoulders started to shake, and her breaths came in short spurts. This crying jag would be a doozy.

"Hey." Mac placed his hands on her shoulders. "Are you OK?" In the space of a breath, his voice melted from ice-cold litigator to compassionate friend-savior.

A subtle tremor zipped from her stomach to her heart. Shaking her head, she stepped away breaking the tender contact and reclaiming the space she needed to breathe. She sniffed back tears. "I'm fine. It's just been a long couple of days. And, apparently my jog didn't do its job." Lifting her gaze to his, she rolled her shoulders and wrapped her arms around her middle.

He leaned against the wall. Crossing one ankle over the other, he lifted a single thick dark eyebrow.

"What?" she asked.

"You tell me."

She swallowed against the lump in her throat, wishing she had another bottle of water. "Nothing to tell. I'm a woman. I can cry if I want to."

"You don't seem like a crier."

She released a sigh, shoving her hand through her damp hair. "Well, looks can be deceiving."

He shook his head. "I've known criers. Some are my best friends. Your sister, she's a crier. You," he said, as his gaze stayed pinned to hers, "not so much."

His frank perusal sent a wave of shivers down her spine that had little to do with cooling down after her run. "Can we discuss this later? Maybe when I don't have to twist myself into Savvy's image of a New Yorker turned Southern belle in,"—she paused, glancing at her running watch—"well, in less time than I had to get ready for the Christmas party when I looked, and I quote, 'Lahck a little refugee from funeraw camp'."

Her southern sounded like a bad comedy impression of a Civil War bride, but she brought a laugh out of Mac. Suddenly, she felt lighter. The load weighing on her only minutes before seemed cut in half.

"She actually called you a refugee from a funeral camp? What is funeral camp, exactly?"

A smile tugged at the corner of her mouth. "I can't even imagine. I assumed it was some weird southern thing I didn't know about. I'll be the first to admit it's beautiful down here, but I often feel as if I've been dropped onto a whole different continent."

"When I first moved here, I felt like a fish out of water. I grew up in a small town, but I'd been playing ball for OSU for nearly four years and was accustomed to the pace of a bigger city. I found my way." His gaze locked with hers. "You'll find yours."

Her stomach twisted. Was it really possible for brown eyes to twinkle?

"Any word from the FBI? The sheriff called me this morning to confirm it was a bomb."

Her heart quivered. She'd been trying to block the who, what, when, and why bomb situation from her mind because no matter what scenario she conjured, every option led back to her mother. And that was one secret no number of heart-melting twinkles of Mac Taylor's chocolate eyes would ever rip from her.

She refused to bring anyone else into the circle of catastrophes she'd created. Remy was likely one too many. She could handle the helping of retribution she was receiving. What she couldn't live with was someone else's blood on her hands, particularly this thorn in her side she was beginning to treasure. "Haven't heard a word," she said. "And I imagine it'll be something silly. Some prank by someone who wanted to get my attention. Someone who is mad we traded Tony Lowery." Her chuckle sounded stilted to her.

"You have to take this serious. There's no way to know who's behind this stunt. They could try again. Do you want me to arrange for some security here and at the offices? The sheriff can't offer the manpower, but we certainly can to keep you safe."

She wiped a bead of sweat off her forehead. "That would be a waste. I'm sure we're fine. Just an upset fan. Drop it, OK? We have a party tonight. Celebrate the New Year. You don't want to make Savvy angry."

His forehead scrunched into a mass of waves. "I don't know, Charlotte. This seems serious."

"Let it drop. Please. Just for now. I promise, I'll call Special Agent O'Neal after the party."

"Promise?"

She thrust her pinky finger toward him. "Pinky promise."

He chuckled as he wrapped his pinky finger

around hers. "Deal."

"Well, if I don't get a shower, I won't find my way anywhere but onto Savvy's 'bad' list." She turned.

He stepped toward her, and her heart quickened. "I'll let you go." He laid his hand gently on her shoulder. "But, we still need to talk. I'm not letting this drop. Not the accident *and* not how you're treating your family. There are a little less than eleven months left in the terms of the will. You can't keep fighting against everyone around you. You have to start trusting us."

"Yep, I get it. We'll chat. Later." She slipped inside and shut the door behind her. If she'd turned around, viewed the same kindness in his eyes that she could hear in his voice, she would have fallen into his arms seeking the comfort she'd never found but always wanted. She needed to be strong, to keep her guard up. She couldn't risk showing vulnerability. Not now. Not ever.

~*~

Mac stepped back quickly to avoid losing his nose in the door. Releasing a sigh, he shoved his hands in his jean pockets and started the long walk to the main house and his car.

What just happened? He'd gone to the guest house to rip into Charlie and protect his self-appointed little sister, but instead found himself wanting to comfort her. The same feelings of comfort and care had nearly overwhelmed him while he sat vigil by her hospital bed and now they returned with the same consuming need pounding through his spirit.

He couldn't explain or even rationalize the compassion tipping on obsession he was experiencing for Charlie Dixon. He didn't like Charlie. Or rather, he didn't want to like her. But since he saw her lying helpless in the garage, his feelings toward her had been rapidly changing her from adversary to...he didn't know what exactly, but based on his heart's rapid turn he had a pretty decent assumption those feelings were not temporary.

The estranged daughter of his surrogate father had been nothing but an irritant these past few weeks. And before Bent's death, she had been the only person in Bentley's life who brought a cloud of sadness into his world. From the time of Bent's diagnosis with lymphoma two years ago, he'd tried to reach out to his eldest daughter, but she'd blocked him at every turn.

With each effort, and each time she ignored him, Mac had grown angrier. When he finally came face to face with Charlie at the funeral, he wanted to rail at her, but seeing her pain had pricked at his heart. His desire to chastise Charlie transformed into a need to save her. In their first encounter, Mac felt God had given him a mission to ease her pain. But after the explosion in the parking garage, he wasn't sure he was equipped. Seeing her small and broken in the hospital bed, his want shifted to a near desperate need to protect. He wasn't even sure who she needed to be protected from.

Could he save Charlie without losing himself?

13

"And then Bent shoved Savvy in the pond! Can you believe?" Billy Jack, a second cousin twice removed, snorted as he recalled a story from her father's childhood.

Charlotte watched him. He stood nearly two feet away from her and yet, his shaking, round belly brushed her hand in jolly excitement. His breath, laced with tobacco and something oddly sour filled the tiny space.

Taking a small step backward, she plastered a perfected cocktail party smile across her lips. "Funny story. Thank you for sharing. I'm sorry, but my aunt has asked me to keep drinks moving, so if you'll excuse me?" Before he could stop her escape with more anecdotes, she slipped from Billy Jack to her newfound sanctuary—the kitchen.

Clanging pans and swift moving catering staff greeted her. The chaos was a welcome reprieve from the near constant stream of relatives and family friends who wanted to kiss her cheek or "squeeze the stuffing out of her." She glanced at the clock above the sink. At least three more hours left until the New Year rang and revelers would find their way off the grounds. She could almost feel the light weight of the down comforter she was loathe to leave this morning.

The breakfast nook was empty, and she slid into the seat she had vacated earlier. All the muscles in her neck and back seemed to ooze into the booth. She closed her eyes and rested her throbbing head against the wooden frame. Slowly releasing a sigh, her mind began to argue with her heart about returning to the party.

Savvy would track her down, ready to foist on her some third-cousin-seventeen-times-removed-from-her-grandmommy's-side. A part of Charlotte welcomed the distraction of long-lost relatives. While the party whirred, she could ignore her new reality of enemies circling. Before yesterday, she only had to deal with one known adversary, but now she not only had to deal with invaders from the north, she had the added adventure of skating around the FBI as well. A few more hours of Savvy's little shindig was looking better and better.

"Penny for your thoughts?"

The rich baritone slid through her like hot cider on a cold New York night. Her eyes opened and locked with deep brown warmth. "Are you following me?"

"Naw, I came in to sneak some cold roast beef from the fridge." He pointed to the white bread sandwich on the table in front of him.

"Not enough southern goodness out there for you?"

He chuckled. "My palate is out of practice. I was away from Colin's Fancy for nearly ten days." He lifted the sandwich and chomped a manly bite.

"So instead of eating the elegant spread, you steal leftovers?"

With a shrug, he swallowed his bite. "You can't beat cold roast beef. It was my favorite treat as a kid. We had roast beef once a month, and then I would get crank-up sandwiches for every lunch the following week."

Her head tilted to the side. "Crank up?"

"It was a kind of roast beef salad—mayo, some pickles, celery, and something I've never been able to nail down. It was one of the comforts of my childhood. And I was the only brother who liked it."

"You got all the crank-up to yourself?"

"Not an easy feat with two brothers who could eat double their body weight on any given Sunday."

Leaning her elbow on the table, she cradled her head in the palm of her hand. "I can't figure you, Taylor."

Swallowing another bite, he wiped his mouth and leaned back against the booth. "What's to figure? I'm a simple guy. Simple food. Simple clothes. However, my job's not so simple at the moment." He raised a single eyebrow. "But I suspect that, too, will make itself a little more manageable in the near future."

Leaning back against the bench, she laced her arms across her chest. "You think?"

He nodded. "Yep. I do." He lifted the sandwich to his mouth. "So, back to my original question, penny for your thoughts?"

With a shrug, she bit her lower lip. "Not thinking of anything in particular."

"Then why are you hiding?" He ate a bite.

She sat straighter. "I am not hiding."

"Liar. I saw you with Cousin Billy Jack. Does his breath still smell as if he smoked twelve packs of cigarettes and chewed on old sweat socks?"

She felt the muscles relax at her neck. "That's an excellent description."

"Not hiding. But self-preservation?"

"Something like that."

"You can't hide forever, you know."

"I know. It's just a little…much."

"I would've thought you'd be used to parties. Didn't you do the whole Manhattan socialite thing?"

She shrugged. "But, those guests didn't regale me with story after story of my father when he was a child or a teenager or just starting out as an adult or last year at this party. Pretty much, every cocktail party I attended in New York was 'your daddy' anecdote free and not a single person was twice removed from being a full relative."

"I can see why that might be hard. But aren't you curious?"

"Curious about what?"

"Curious about your father," he said. "Talking to all those second and third removed's might give you some insight into Bent. You might find he isn't the villain of your story after all."

"Thanks for the counseling, Freud." Scooting out of the booth, she glanced over her shoulder. "However, I think I'd rather take my chances with the party than listen to any more about my daddy issues." She took a step away from the table. "Enjoy your crank."

He took her wrist in his hand. "You can't get away that easy."

"Please, let go of me."

Mac released her wrist. "I gave you a pass this afternoon. But, we still need to talk about how you've been treating everyone. You have to start trusting us."

"Is that nice act just an act, Taylor?" She kept her voice low, trying to control the wave of guilt mixed with anger that seemed to want to swallow her whole. "Do you want me to confess how horrible I've been to Georgie and Savvy? You want me to talk about my father? You want to shower me with more waves of guilt than the Palms Isles beach? Don't worry. If that is your end game, I already beat you to the guilt washing punch, and I don't need more from you. I can't deal with it. Not today. I have to get through the next three hours. Smile plastered across my face. So if you'll excuse me, I'll find another third removed cousin." She pivoted, pushed the connecting kitchen door and walked into a wall of conversation thick with Southern drawl. Charlotte shoved her argument with Mac and her worries away. No matter how right she knew Mac was, she couldn't face the why behind her behavior these past few weeks. Instead Charlotte would do what she did best. She hid in plain sight.

Stretching her lips into a broad smile, she dove into the party.

14

Two hours later, leaning against a pillar supporting the archway connecting the formal dining room to the expansive sitting room, Mac watched Charlie work the room. She efficiently replaced the dry glass of Bent's cousin Merle with a fresh drink while chatting with Merle's wife Lydia—likely about her beloved cats Wiley, Scratch, and Tippers. Mac had been cornered by Lydia last 4th of July and spent the better part of an hour listening to the crazy antics of the motley trio. To Charlie's credit, she appeared enthralled by the story, but he noticed she changed the direction of the wait-staff's circulation, had the shrimp and grits refilled, and directed a steaming cup of coffee into the chubby paw of Billy Jack.

She was good. If he wasn't so frustrated with her, and confused by his own feelings, he would take her a glass of water with lemon—her beverage of choice—and a well-deserved compliment.

"She's good."

Mac shifted his attention to the diminutive blonde standing to his left and nodded. "Seems to be in her element."

Savvy laced her arm through his. "It's more than being comfortable in a large party. She clearly has orchestrated many of these events in her life. She likely took the responsibility instead of relying on her mother."

He patted her hand resting on his forearm. "Not a big fan of Anastasia?"

Her blood red lips pursed to a tight pucker. "That woman caused my baby brother Bent more ache than twenty heart attacks. She was a train wreck when she lived in Colin's Fancy, but what she did to that poor girl makes my stomach turn."

"What do you mean? What did she do to Charlotte?"

"She denied her the opportunity to grow up with family who loved her. Stasi used Charlie as a weapon to wield against Bent rather than loving her the way a Momma should."

"I thought Charlotte chose to stay with her mother."

"She did. Not that the witch gave her much of a choice. When Charlie decided she wanted to live with Bent and Delia, she was twelve years old. Georgie was a baby, but she loved being a big sister. Charlie wanted to help Delia. She loved Dee like she was her own mother. I don't know exactly what transpired between Charlie and Stasi when she went back to New York that Labor Day, but she was never allowed to spend the summer in South Carolina again. Not seeing his daughter nearly broke Bent, but I think the pain must have been worse for Charlie. She didn't just lose her daddy, she lost the only woman who ever put her first. Delia was Charlie's mother in all the ways that count.

When Dee was diagnosed with cancer, Charlie would make secret trips to visit her at the hospital. Bent and Georgie never knew. I don't know why Charlie wanted to keep it a secret, but she had her reasons. I've never told anyone. I only know because I happened to see Charlie leaving Delia's room one Saturday afternoon and I asked Dee about it. She asked me to keep their secret, and I have until now."

"And you don't know why Stasi didn't let Charlie move to South Carolina?"

"I would place money on meanness."

"I don't think I follow."

"That woman is as mean and squirrely as a hungry, rabid dog cornered in a back alley. She'll do anything. I think she revels in causing people pain. She loves to destroy. I'm surprised she didn't come to Bent's funeral and dance on his grave."

"She sounds lovely."

"I'm exaggerating, but not by much. I'm not surprised Charlotte is the way she is, rough and tight on the edges. She's had to protect herself her entire life. An awful way to grow up. And now all this business about her car exploding. The poor thing just needs some love and care."

"Savvy, you don't think her mother had anything to do with her car, do you?" Mac's stomach twisted at the thought.

"No...I don't think so." Savvy shook her head. "Stasi's crazy. Vindictive. Meaner than a rattlesnake. But I don't think she would intentionally harm her daughter, physically, I mean. The harm emotionally has already been done. And besides," she said, clearly thinking about it. "What possible motive could she have to blow up her daughter's car?"

15

Georgie sidled up to the right of Charlotte as her older sister directed a server toward a group of empty-handed guests. Sliding her arm through Charlotte's she rested her head to her sister's shoulder. "You do this very well. I was watching Savvy earlier tonight, and I can feel how impressed she is with you."

Charlotte shrugged, effectively extricating herself from her sister's embrace. "It's not a big deal. Mama and Babushka threw parties of all sizes and arrangements. I was always in charge of the staff. Baba said it was because I could speak the best English, but in reality I think she was afraid my mother would scream until the servers scattered like mice."

"Is your mother really that awful?" Georgie took in Charlotte's stiffening shoulders. "I'm sorry. Savvy's always telling me every thought in my head doesn't need to be expressed through my lips."

Charlotte turned and gave her a soft smile. "You're fine. My mother is difficult, but she's still my mother. You know the old adage, I can make fun of my family, but watch out if you do. I guess no matter what she does I'll always be protective."

Georgie brushed a non-existent hair from Charlotte's shoulder. "I understand." She turned toward the din of the party. "Savvy and Mellie really pulled another fabulous party together."

"Yes," Charlotte nodded. "Of course I'd have liked a vegetable that still held its nutritional qualities, but I can't argue the food is tasty, if not healthy."

"It's Low Country cuisine. Nutritious is a relative term. Now delicious, that's one we all can get on board with."

Charlotte chuckled as she rested her shoulder against the wall.

"Are you tired? Is this all too much after your accident?"

Charlotte shook her head. "No. I really am fine, except for some bruises and a headache I can't seem to shake."

"You had us so worried. I can't imagine how something like that could happen to your car. It's practically new. Daddy said you should never trust foreign carmakers."

"Georgie, almost every American car is made outside the U.S.A. Most 'American' cars are really Japanese."

"Well, regardless. I can't imagine how your car went boom." Georgie watched her sister's face, hoping to gain some semblance of a clue as to why the explosion happened, but Charlotte's gaze was blank.

"I need to go check on some things. Would you mind following up with the two servers who're supposed to be cycling through the library and the music room? I haven't seen them in a little while." Without waiting for an answer, Charlotte stalked toward the back of the house.

Georgie closed her eyes and leaned against the spot vacated by her sister.

"Hey, Slugger, did you strike out again?"

Without hesitating, she stepped into Mac's wide embrace and let her surrogate big brother ease her ache.

"I stuck my foot in my big ol' pie hole again."

His chuckle vibrated against her ear. "Sounds painful. How'd you manage it?"

Stepping away from him, she shrugged. "I don't know. I complimented her on how well she's running the party and then out of the blue she started talking about how difficult her mom is. I may've offended her by saying her mom is awful, but then as I tried to shove my ankle out of my mouth, I tried to get her talking about the accident. And poof, she ran off in the opposite direction."

"No wonder she ran away. She probably couldn't understand a word you were saying what with your mouth full of ankle, foot, and toes."

With a single eye roll, she sighed. "I'm so worried, Mac. Do you think someone is deliberately trying to hurt her? Cars just don't blow up."

He patted her head, making her feel twelve again and he was the starting catcher for the Bombers. "Georgie, I don't fully know what's going on. The sheriff called earlier –"

Wind whipped through the entryway, flittering Georgie's skirt and snapping her attention to the front door, open wide to the brisk December night. Three guests, one woman and two men, stomped into the foyer. Money seemed to drip from them as they handed their coats to a waiting server.

Georgie bristled at their abrupt entrance. Not because they didn't belong, but because they did. "I can't believe she's here."

"Who's 'she'?" Mac whispered, matching Georgie's tone.

"Anastasia. Stasi, Charlotte's mother."

~*~

Charlotte lifted a finger to her lips and let the chocolate sauce tingle her taste buds, soothing some of the rough spaces scratched throughout the evening. She should have told Georgie about her car, at least what she believed to be the whole story. She should have told her the reason the FBI showed up at their offices. About her mother's gambling debts, the apparent money laundering, all of Remy's discoveries. Georgie was her sister. She deserved to know. And Charlotte longed to share the burden. Sisters shared secrets and helped each other through difficult challenges. At least that's what every movie, magazine article, and sappy holiday special had shouted at her for the last three decades. Charlotte desperately needed a sister at the moment, but all she had was a roommate. By necessity.

She couldn't confide in Georgie, not completely. Not that Charlotte thought her sister would share any information that could put her in danger—or rather, more danger—but she was worried simple knowledge could place Georgie in harm's way. She may not be experienced at being an older sibling, but she was responsible for protecting her little sister. No matter what happened, she wouldn't put Georgie at risk. Instead she kept her at arm's length, choosing to hurt her feelings than make her a bullseye for mental and physical pain.

The catering staff weaved in and out of the stacks of glasses, plates, and empty tureens, transforming the grand kitchen into cramped quarters. She scooted around two waiters and dropped onto the bench in the breakfast nook.

Charlotte desperately wanted to flash backwards six months or six years. She wanted to go back to before she knew about her mother's activities, to go back to when she could let go of her need to seek her mother's approval, when she could still hug her daddy and tell him she loved him. She sank deeper into the corner bench, gasping for air as the guilt growing with each day squeezed her heart. Tears burned wet paths down her cheeks, and she knew her thick mascara would darken the trail, but she couldn't care anymore.

The last few months crashed around her with the force of a hurricane. She rested her head on her folded arms, and tried to block out the cacophony of dishes, plates, and servers swirling around her. But as much as she wanted to drown in waves of self-pity and regret, she had hostess duties. The horror of Savvy or Georgie tracking her down, or worse, Mac Taylor, and seeing her state of self-pity had her swiping at her cheeks.

Mac Taylor. Or rather, Francis MacAllister Taylor, Jr. confused and enthralled her. For weeks, he had been fighting her at every turn, reminding her she was the unwanted prodigal daughter. But if he didn't want her here, why had he been so protective and supportive with the FBI? Pity? Regret? Misguided chivalry?

Regardless of his motives, she had gratefully hidden behind his shield. With all Remy had discovered, she couldn't afford to be fully transparent with any law enforcement until she spoke with her mother, confirmed her suspicions or maybe, just maybe, found the errors in Remy's logic and proved Mama's innocence.

Hope burned in her belly. Swallowing against the lump lodged in her throat, she closed her eyes. Stasi was not one to be dealt with trivially. And hope very rarely held a legitimate chance in her mother's orbit. Charlotte would need a clear plan and a full understanding of the implications surrounding her mother's activities before she approached her.

Drawing a cleansing breath to fill her lungs with the tickle of cinnamon-laced oxygen, calm settled into her bones. Steady and fortified, she was ready to circulate and socialize. With determination she opened her eyelids, and her gaze locked with the inquisitive focus of her self-appointed protector. "Did Savvy send you?"

The corner of Mac's mouth lifted in a soft grin. "Nope, Georgie. We had a few unexpected guests." He slid his folded handkerchief across the table.

Matching his smile, she wiped her cheeks, leaving dark stains on the crisp white linen. "Sorry."

"No worries, you keep it."

Rolling her shoulders, she twisted the marred cotton in her hands. "Who's throwing the balance off at the party? Don't tell me. Special Agents Murphy and O'Neal showed up?"

"Yes, but I don't consider them unexpected since Savvy invited them at the hospital while they were waiting for you to wake up."

Her head fell softly to the side as a chill raced up her spine. "Who came uninvited, Mac?"

"Your mother arrived about five minutes ago flanked by two of the roughest looking gentlemen I've seen outside of a few roadhouses I went to when I was in the minors."

Chills twisted into a wave of burning nausea. "Stasi's here?" She couldn't soften the quake in her voice.

He squeezed her clenched fist. "She can't do anything to you, Charlie. She probably just wanted to check up on you after your accident."

"How would she have known about the accident? I didn't tell her, and I know Savvy wouldn't call her even if she was on fire and Mama had the only bucket of water." Scooting off of the bench, Charlotte shook her head. Her mother was here. Motherly concern was never the answer when Stasi was involved. The only logical reason was to finish the job.

16

The cackle of her mother's laugh burned a laser strip through Charlotte's body.

Draped in a sequin and crystal encrusted gown, a size too small for her curvaceous frame, Anastasia Bickford-Dixon-Mallory-Stenson-Shaw glittered like a neon light in Times Square. Mama liked to be the center of attention and clothing was one of her favorite spectacle driving methods.

Thankfully, Savvy had corralled Stasi to a corner in the blue salon, well away from the stares and gossip of the partygoers peppering the main floor of the house.

Charlotte slowed her pace. Mac was right about the two men with her. Every edge needed weeks of sanding. Sucking in a breath of cinnamon-scented strength, she stepped into the room. "Mama, what brings you to South Carolina?"

Stasi stood with her arms extended. "*Malyshka*! Let me look at you. I heard about your awful accident, and I had to see that you were OK." She dragged Charlotte into her stiff-armed embrace.

"Mama," Charlotte whispered. "How did you know about the accident?"

Stasi patted her back, sliding her long-nailed hand

to Charlotte's neck. "I know everything. Everything." Stasi stepped back, softly brushed her fingertips across the thick bruise on Charlotte's forehead, and kissed each of her cheeks with an Upper Eastside smile plastered across her lips.

"Where are you staying, Mama?"

"With you, of course. After all, I came to see you."

"You know I'm staying in the guest house with Georgie. There's not enough room."

"Well, then certainly your aunt can find a little room for me." She turned toward her former sister-in-law.

Savvy looked past Stasi and locked gazes with Charlotte. In the space of a heartbeat, her aunt's solidarity washed over Charlotte.

"I'm so sorry, Anastasia, but it's the holidays. You know how Colin's Fancy gets overrun with house guests. We don't have a single pillow or towel to spare. I'll have Tori call the Butler Inn. I'm certain they'll find a place for you and your...umm...associates to rest your heads for the evening. But, please be certain to get your fill of good, Low Country cuisine before you leave."

Stasi's face pinched and relaxed. "Well, it seems tonight is too full of *other* relatives to deal with your mother, Charlotte. I'll be on my way. I wanted to ensure you were well. You look well enough. You will come to visit me tomorrow for tea, yes?"

Charlotte felt a solid hand squeeze her shoulder, and she gratefully relaxed into Mac's seemingly omnipresent support. "Yes, Mama. I'll see you for tea tomorrow. But as Savvy said, please enjoy some food. It's been a long time since you've dined on Low Country delicacies. I'm sure some of this place holds fond memories for you."

"Oh, Charlotte, you know the refined palate can't appreciate this...cuisine."

"Well, it's your loss. Mellie's okra is about the best thing I've had since I left Manhattan."

"*Hmpf.*" Stasi leaned in to kiss her daughter. "We have much to discuss," she whispered in Charlotte's ear. "You shouldn't have ignored the request. Closed the accounts. You are not in charge. Remember who is mama. Don't think I didn't notice the two FBI agents attending your aunt's party. I would hate to think my blood is sharing stories outside of the family. Remember who you are."

Charlotte tried to control the tremors even as they wracked her body. She touched her lips to her mother's cheek. "Mama, I know. How could I forget?"

Stasi lifted a single eyebrow, her gaze reflecting a statement of force Charlotte had known since childhood. "Well, *malyshka*, we shall be off. I look forward to tea tomorrow." She flicked her gaze to Savvy. "So good to see you, Savannah dear. I see you are still enjoying the wealth and station of your younger brother even after his passing. Impressive, as always."

"Mama, please don't. Not here. Not now." Charlotte pressed her mother's shoulder, angling her toward the exit. "I will see you tomorrow." Charlotte followed her mother and the woman's two goons through the foyer to the front door.

Stasi twisted to kiss Charlotte's cheek. "Tomorrow we shall celebrate the New Year and all of the possibilities. We have so much to catch up on, *malyshka*. So much. Do not be late."

~*~

Cade popped a cheese straw in his mouth as he watched mother and daughter embrace at the front door. Charlotte's body language screamed fear and Stasi's answered with determined anger. He wondered what mother had whispered to daughter and why Charlotte seemed genuinely surprised by Stasi's arrival.

The two goons with Stasi were well known associates of Anton Dorokhov. He recognized the two enforcers even without the not-so-subtle nudge from Dylan as the partners observed the mother-daughter reunion. Stasi coming to see Charlotte flanked by Dorokhov's men was circumstantial evidence gold in the investigation and gave Cade one additional piece of leverage against Stasi.

Charlotte held onto the door as Stasi and her security detail disappeared the same way they entered. Her frame tremored, just barely noticeable, as Charlotte closed the door with care worthy of the finest set of crystal glasses. His mind must be playing tricks on him. Even bruised and nearly blown up, Charlotte Dixon seemed to be made of icy cold steel, and yet, she clearly seemed to fear her mother.

The din of the party had lowered to subtle whispers as all eyes and conversations had shifted to the exchange between mother and daughter. The crowd seemed to be waiting for a speech from Charlotte. The breaths of the party collectively held unwilling to miss what Charlotte would say about her mother's unexpected arrival and equally dramatic exit.

Mac Taylor, who seemed to be Charlotte's own personal superhero, laid a hand on her shoulder as she turned to face the waiting party goers. Extending her lips into a wide mouthed smile, she engaged what Cade could only describe as a giggle. "Well, you never know what you'll experience at a Savvy Boudreaux fête."

Her gaggle of relatives chuckled and turned back to their various conversations, all of which Cade was sure were now focused squarely on the reintroduction of Stasi to their quiet circle.

Shoving against the door, Charlotte caught Cade's gaze. He wondered if she could read his mind and the litany of questions popping into his brain. Her smile wavered and her shoulders dropped, as she started to close the gap between them, but Taylor stopped her and whispered into her ear.

"What do you think his lawyerly advice to her is?" Dylan asked.

"Plead the Fifth?"

The newly minted dynamic duo wove the short distance to Cade and Dylan. Cade couldn't help noticing the comforting arm Taylor laid over Charlotte's shoulders. Her cheeks blushed two shades deeper than normal cosmetics and Cade would have been blind not to notice the tilt of a smile on the stoic Charlotte Dixon's lips. *What was really going on between those two?*

As was becoming her annoying habit, Charlotte extended her hand to O'Neal, effectively ignoring Cade's existence. "I'm so glad you were able to attend Savvy's party. I had no idea she invited you, but I'm thrilled she had her charming wits about her in the hospital to extend the invitation."

O'Neal's eyes twinkled as Charlotte's hand slid into his. "Miss Dixon, this party is beyond my wildest expectations."

Man, could Dylan lay it on thick.

"Yes, well, Savvy does know how to throw an exceptional event. Even if it's on the heels of her Christmas blow-out."

"Well, we appreciate the invitation. Don't we, Murph?"

Enough of this dance... "That was your mother."

Charlotte blinked twice and she gave a little cough. "Yes, that was Mama. How did you know?"

"She's kind of hard not to hear." *Come on, Charlotte, give me something. Prove to me you aren't a lying, cheating, snake like your mother.*

"Well, Stasi's never been accused of being subtle."

"Why didn't she stay?"

"I'm not sure that is relevant to you, Special Agent Murphy."

Mac placed his hand on her shoulder. "I think Special Agent Murphy is interested that your mother came to check up on you. Is that correct?" He nodded his head toward Cade.

Charlotte shifted her gaze between Cade and Taylor. Cade had to stifle a chuckle at her almost awed expression as she had to look up at both men. He couldn't imagine the towering beauty had looked up at many people in her life. Cade widened his stance and crossed his arms over his chest. Let her worry a little more. If his size intimidated her, so be it.

"Well, I was surprised she came down to check on my wellbeing. My mother is not traditionally concerned with such things. And she did swear a few decades ago to never again travel south of the Mason-Dixon Line, so you can imagine my surprise by her visit. But, as any daughter would be, I am thankful to have my mother's concern."

"Certainly," O'Neal interjected. "I think Murph and I were just shocked to see your mother, considering all of the excitement encompassing New York at this time of the year."

"As I said, your surprise is equal to mine, Special Agent O'Neal." Charlotte smiled. "But if you don't mind, I'd rather focus on this amazing party and celebrating the incoming year." She glanced at the clock on the mantel in the main parlor. "We only have a few minutes remaining of this year, and I will be grateful to leave it in the past. May I get either of you a beverage so you can toast the new fortunes of the coming year?"

"Well, what do we have here?" Remy Reynard seemed to appear out of thin air.

The forensic accountant whose involvement in the audit of the art gallery was the catapult to Cavanaugh allowing Cade's and Dylan's temporary assignment to Charleston, was dressed too formally in a classic tuxedo for the low country cocktail party gathering. He kissed Charlotte's cheek, tugging her to his side in a casual embrace. "Are y'all trying to exacerbate my poor dear's throbbing head with more questions she can't possibly answer?"

"Mr. Reynard, I didn't expect to see you this evening. I thought you were engaged at a fundraiser in Charleston," Cade said.

"Well, aren't you a clever Yankee? I was a co-host at a little fête at an inn on Battery. Charleston society does feel the need to make every social occasion have significance." He winked at Charlotte. "But, I would be remiss if I allowed this New Year to roll in without celebrating the long awaited return of my dearest friend. I've wished for this day since she abandoned me for the debauchery and delights of the North."

Mac shuffled back from the group, tugging at his collar as he left without a word.

Charlotte's gaze followed the attorney until Taylor disappeared from the room. Their budding romance could either be the crack Cade was looking for or Taylor could become a thicker wall than one Charlotte Dixon had already erected around herself.

Turning back toward the group, a smile stretched across Charlotte's lips that didn't quite reach her eyes. "Gentlemen, my aunt will be mortified, we are only fifteen minutes from midnight and you are drink-less. I will be right back."

"I'll help you," Cade said. He could play Dylan's game. He wasn't as good at it, but Cade was known to have a little charm under his tough exterior.

Cade followed her as she wove through dozens of relatives all asking about her mother's arrival, "bless her heart". With each inquiry, she bobbed her head, but kept moving, forcing Cade to nearly run to keep up with her pace. At the back bar, she ordered for all three men and included a club soda with a lime for herself. His research was correct. Charlotte Dixon didn't drink, because if she did the stress of the last few days, and especially the last hour, would have caused even the most stalwart teetotaler to contemplate a drink or two.

"You shame me and my training at Quantico. Can you run a mile in those stilettoes?" he asked.

She flipped her chin toward him. "Don't you already know? You seem to know everything else."

"Fair enough."

Sighing she twisted and leaned her elbows on the bar. "Why are you here, Agent Murphy?"

"It's Special Agent Murphy, and your aunt invited me."

"No, why are you in Colin's Fancy? Why are you in South Carolina?"

What could he say to her without revealing that she was one of the prime suspects in his case against the *bratva*? "Your gallery came up in the line of an active investigation. Special Agent O'Neal and I are following a lead."

She locked her gaze with his. Her clear blue eyes

held more questions than he could decipher. Was she really her mother's daughter or was she simply an unwitting pawn in a game her mother had been playing for decades? Would he be able to earn her trust? What would it take to crack the ice of Charlotte Dixon?

The bartender tapped her shoulder forcing Charlotte to break her stare. Clutching two of the drinks in her hands she nodded toward the remaining glasses and Cade obliged, lifting his and Dylan's drinks.

"Well, I hope you've discovered my little gallery doesn't have anything to hide," she said as they walked back to Remy and O'Neal.

"And, how do you explain your car exploding?"

Shrugging, she winked. "Unhappy accident?"

Unhappy accident? Was she insane or just a good actress? "Miss Dixon, most people wouldn't refer to totaling a sixty-thousand dollar car with such nonchalance."

"Well, I guess I have more important things to worry about. The last few months have put the little stresses of life in perspective."

"Again, I wouldn't refer to bombs at the office as a little stress."

"Nor would I. I am thankful that no one was seriously hurt." They slowed their pace as they approached the waiting men. "But, I am certain that the explosion is nothing more than a fan displaying his distaste for some recent trades."

"Seems a bit of an extreme explanation, don't you

think?"

Remy chuckled as he took his drink from Charlotte. "Oh, my dear Special Agent Murphy, nothing about sports in the south is considered extreme. You should see this place during football season. Charlotte, I almost forgot. Savvy stopped me as I made my way in and asked me to have you check on the final celebratory moments for the midnight extravaganza." Remy glanced at his watch. "You better skedaddle or Savannah Boudreaux will have my hide. And it is such a nice hide I would like to keep it through the New Year and beyond."

17

Charlotte shoved open the French doors leading to the side porch off the kitchen. Sucking in the cool damp air, she mentally logged another tick in the debt column of her friendship with Remy. He always seemed to know when she needed a reprieve. And like her own guardian angel, he always found the means to make her need a reality. Wrapping her arms around her waist, she heard the countdown to midnight begin.

Ten...

Her thoughts went to her father. *Oh, Daddy, what you must think of me? I'm so grateful you didn't have to see me like this.*

Seven...

Are you with Delia again? Is your God real? If He is could He help me? I don't know what to do.

Four...

Can He send someone to save me from this mess of a life?

Shivers followed the soft touch of a broad hand on her bare shoulder. She turned and stared into the inviting gaze of Mac Taylor. Without a thought, she stepped forward and wrapped her arms around his waist, reveling in the warmth his body exuded.

He reached between them and tilted her chin up

with a finger. "Happy New Year," he whispered. His lips barely grazed hers, but the touch ignited her like every firework exploding on the Eastern seaboard.

He broke the connection, but gently caressed her cheek, brushing off a tear she was unaware she'd shed until she tasted the salty remnant on her lips. Her vision locked with his, and the tender gaze acted like a knife cutting the slender connection between them.

She stepped from his embrace, placing breathing distance between them.

What just happened? Was he an answer to the prayer she'd prayed? Had her absent father heard her from beyond the grave? Was his God that quick to respond? "I'm sorry," she whispered.

His eyebrows knitted together. "Why are you sorry, Charlie?"

She clenched her jaw. "It's Charlotte."

"OK, *Charlotte*. Why are you sorry?"

She turned her back to him and stared into the foggy, blackness of midnight. "I shouldn't have hugged you. I..." She couldn't find the words she wanted to say without revealing the confusion in her weary heart.

"You've had a tough couple of days. It's the holidays. No need to explain."

She squeezed her eyes closed against the uncontrollable tears burning to be set free. The warmth of his breath slid over her, fighting against the chill of the mid-winter night.

Feeling him move behind her on the centuries-old porch boards, she wrapped her arms tighter across her middle. She wasn't sure if she was conserving heat or trying to avoid reaching out to grab him to her.

"Charlotte, we didn't do anything wrong."

"I know," she said, focusing her gaze into the distance, no longer black with night, but hazy with an orange glow. Panic shot through her. "Mac, do you see that?" She pointed in the direction of the guest house.

"Yes...is it what I think it is?"

"If you think it's a fire in the guest house, then yes, it's exactly what you think it is. Call 911." With no thought but saving her home, she raced down the side steps, ignoring his shouts chasing her.

Orange and yellow flames dashed up the large pine trees marching on either side of the guest house. Charlotte guessed her new home was only minutes from being engulfed.

Running to the decrepit shed, she sought the small garden hose she remembered hung on the side. She aimed the spray toward the fire and began to pray again, a habit she unwillingly was acquiring.

"Charlie!"

Shouts rang above the crack of the fire. The growing rumble of feet racing from the main house reverberated under her, but she wasn't deterred from trying to save her home. In the moment of terror, she couldn't lie to herself. It was her home. She needed to protect the only place to hold that precious title since she was five years old.

The trees were too quickly being devoured. They wouldn't be able to keep the fire from spreading throughout the entire grounds. In desperation, she aimed the hose toward the house, but she was fighting a losing battle. How long would it take to get a fire truck and crew here? How could this have happened?

"Charlie!"

She turned at the sound of Georgie's shout. A dozen partygoers lumbered through the yard weighed down with buckets behind her sister.

Tears scorched Georgie's cheeks as she ran to Charlotte's side. "Oh, Charlie! You can't stay here. You could be hurt."

Charlotte shook her head and focused her attention back to the building, catching a glimpse of a water brigade passing buckets up the line to douse the pine trees. Dozens of relatives, whose names she really needed to learn, stood stalwart as they passed bucket after bucket. The line of family must have stretched the mile back to the main house out of view.

The wet sting of tears streaked down Charlotte's cheeks.

Savvy shouted in the distance ordering the family into straighter, tighter lines. "This won't do, folks. Remember how we lost the carriage house in '85 because we couldn't get a decent relay of water. I won't be responsible for the same folly."

A chuckle quelled Charlotte's sentimental tears. Her aunt, still perfectly coiffed, ordered the family like a five-star general.

She jumped at calloused fingers wrapping around her shoulder. Shocked by the touch of Mac's hand, she quickly relaxed at the gentle expression of concern stretching across his face.

"Let me try for a little while." He reached for the hose and continued the steady stream.

Watching his determined stance as he confidently showered the house with her tiny garden hose, she wanted to lean into him. She didn't care that the thought was insane and the idea of being close to him made him a potential target. She just knew she needed some of his endless supply of comfort and strength.

The echo of sirens in the distance shot a zip of relief through her and drove a unified cheer from the fire-fighting party-goers.

Within moments, two fire trucks and an ambulance whipped into the driveway, spewing gravel. The firefighters moved with efficiency and grace as they quickly squashed the remaining flames.

The trees were charcoal, but the house was saved. Her home was still her home despite the smoke and fire damage she guessed waited through the front door. Lifting her gaze toward the smoke-filled night sky, she offered a silent "thank you" to the God Georgie kept sharing. Maybe He was answering her prayers? Charlotte enfolded her sister in the tightest hug of her adult life. They both cried, as Charlotte gave in to the fear and panic that, a moment earlier, had threatened to swallow her with the fire.

"You saved the house," Georgie whispered.

Charlotte shook her head. Why had she suddenly cared so much about old lumber and walls?

~*~

Georgie held tight to Charlotte. "You're a hero."

Her sister stepped out of her embrace. "I didn't do anything."

"Don't shrug this off, Charlie. You saved the house."

Charlotte shook her head.

"Yes, you did," Georgie said, forcing her sister to make eye contact. "Most people wouldn't run toward danger. But you did. All to save our home."

Charlotte's icy gaze could have frozen the fire with significantly less effort than the family's brigade moments earlier. She turned her back to Georgie, focusing on the skilled efforts of the firefighters.

Georgie bit the inside of her cheeks to stop the flow of tears she could feel brimming. She twisted away from the dimming fire, knowing she would need to once again play hostess to the dozens of relatives now chattering amongst themselves.

"Let her be, Slugger."

She stepped into Mac's brotherly embrace. Her tears streamed, dampening his shirt where her cheek tightly pressed. "Why does she do it?" Georgie shuddered.

"She doesn't want to be vulnerable. She's spent the majority of her life steeling herself from potential hurt. After experiencing ten minutes with her mother, I'm surprised she allows herself to feel anything."

Georgie sighed and stepped from Mac's comfortable hug. "I know you're right. I just want her to want to be my sister. Why can't she give just a little?"

"I'd say the hug I witnessed, and her desperate need to save your house, your home with her, are steps in the right direction."

She shifted her gaze from Mac to Charlotte's back. Her sister stood ramrod straight, alone against the world. "I want to help her feel as though she's a part of the family not *a* part. You know?"

He ruffled her hair with his fist. "Trust me, she feels part of the family. She just doesn't want to admit it."

Georgie glanced over her shoulder and noticed the shorter of the FBI agents talking to Billy Jack. "Mac, I know they are trying to help, but I don't feel right about federal agents asking questions. I don't know what happened tonight, but I think we need to figure it out before we get outsiders involved."

He nodded. "Are you sure?"

"Yes."

"I'll take care of it." Mac walked the gentle slope toward Billy Jack and Agent O'Neal.

A chill raced up Georgie's spine as she glanced toward the skeletal remains of the trees she had dreamt under when she was a preteen. What a blessing no one was injured.

Remy's arm wrapped around Charlotte's shoulders. Her sister visibly melted into Remy's side. Georgie's stomach burned and her chin jutted at the obvious comfort her sister was willing to accept from a friend rather than family. Why couldn't Charlotte find the same easy peace with her own sister? Why was their relationship a constant battle?

Swiping at a stray tear, Georgie focused on the firefighters and lifted a silent prayer of thanks for their tireless efforts. Her eyes slid shut as she concentrated on being in the presence of God, seeking His comfort in the midst of the chaos surrounding her. With a deep breath, she felt the intangible quality of her heavenly Father's arms wrap tightly around her. The comfort she longed to feel enveloped her. *Oh, Lord, I thank You for all that You have accomplished here tonight. Bringing dozens of people together to rescue a building, seems like such a minor item in the grand design of this world, but I know You have an eternal purpose for this accident. I pray You would forgive my sin of envy and help me to see the wonderful gift of Remy's and Charlotte's friendship. I want so desperately to be a part of her life I have a difficult time remembering she had a life bigger than what the two of us could have together. Help me to be grateful for the time we have rather than begrudging the time we don't. Holy Father, help me to be consumed by You rather than be consumed by need or want. Help me to see You in the midst of the worries of this life. If I am not intended to be a conduit of Your grace to Charlotte, help me see who is in need of knowing Your love and grace. Help me to be a shining light for You to that person so that he or she might come to know You. Thank you so much for loving me in spite of all of my failings and flaws. I pray, Lord, that You might help Charlotte find the same kind of peace that I feel with You. Lord, hear my prayer.* With a soft sigh, she opened her eyes to the focus of the interrogation-worthy stare of Special Agent Cade Murphy. "Can I help you?"

"Were you praying?"

She shrugged. "It's only appropriate. God saved my home. A thank you seemed the least I could give."

"Firefighters saved your house."

"Yes, but who put them there if not God?"

"Then who started the fire?"

She paused. Lifting her gaze to his shadowed eyes, she tried to see past the hard exterior of doubt. "Special Agent Murphy, God uses all things, good, bad, and ugly, to His glory."

His snorted response shot her hand to her hip. "You don't believe God is in control?" she asked.

"Chaos is in control. And all we can do is try to tame it."

"*Humpf*," she grunted, swiveling away from him.

He chuckled. Sliding up to her side he bumped her hip with his. "Didn't mean to hurt your feelings."

She whipped her head and narrowed her focus. "Trust me, you didn't hurt my feelings. I have zero skin in this game."

He lifted a single eyebrow.

"What?"

"Georgiana, I believe you always have skin in the game. You seem like a woman who doesn't know how to avoid being emotionally invested."

"You don't know me."

"Darlin', it's my job to know you."

A chill raced up her spine. She wrapped her arms tightly around her middle. "What's that supposed to mean?"

He matched her stance. "I'm a professional profiler. I literally get paid to know you."

"Show me."

"Show you what?"

"Profile me, Mr. Big-Shot Special Agent Man."

"Mr. Big-Shot Special Agent Man?"

"Whatever," she poked him in the arm. "Show me your super-duper profiling skills."

"OK," he said, rubbing his jaw. "You are emotionally available to everyone you meet, but this causes you to be perpetually wounded. You seek approval and comfort from the older women in your life because your mother died at a very young age. You did, and continue to do, nearly everything your father wanted you to do, even when you hate it, such as...let's say running a baseball team when you hate sports."

Her jaw dropped. "I don't hate baseball. I—"

He raised his hand, gently pressing his fingers over lips. "You asked. Let me finish. I hate being interrupted."

Anger burned in her belly, but she clamped her mouth shut.

A smirk lifted his lips. "Where was I?"

She sucked in a breath and tightened her grip on her middle.

Tilting his head to the side, he said, "Can you take it?"

She narrowed her focus. "Bring it."

He chuckled. "OK. You have a deep unwavering belief in God that drives you, but it also misguides you because you can't see people are inherently evil. They'll always hurt you. You desperately want your sister's approval. You're intensely creative, but you've kept that part of you hidden because it is the one piece of you that you are most afraid to have criticized. You paint because you love the idea of creating a space of warmth and beauty. But you also paint because it allows you to release pent-up anger, resentment, fear, and self-loathing. You want to please your father, and because of that you will continue to deny your creative self to focus on business and baseball, two things you hate." Shoving his hand in his pockets, he rocked back on his heels. "How'd I do?"

A mixture of warmth pricked with icy fear floated through her. With the exception of her age, hair color, and weight, he'd completely nailed her. How could he know her so well? They met exactly two times, once at the hospital and once tonight. Was he a mind reader? She sucked in a breath. "Not bad. But I do love baseball."

He lifted his finger and tilted her chin. "No, you don't. You've just done a great job convincing yourself." With his light touch, her icy fear melted to a puddle of slush in her belly. Swallowing against the knot in her throat, she opened her mouth.

"Murph..."

They both turned at the sound of his partner's voice.

Special Agent O'Neal and Mac were walking up the slope.

Stepping back, Georgie broke the intimate connection. A sudden chill coursed through her frame. Instinctively, she scrubbed her arms to stave off the overwhelming cold.

"Murph, we should head back to Charleston. The locals have this covered." O'Neal said with a nod toward a deputy sheriff who was talking to one of the firemen.

Scooting to stand beside Mac, Georgie sucked in a breath calming her nerves.

He leaned close. "Everything OK?"

Unable to push words through the growing knot, she nodded.

"I'm so sorry about the fire, Miss Dixon." Special Agent O'Neal offered. "But it sounds as if the firefighters will have you walking around inside to see the internal damage by tomorrow afternoon."

"You talked to the firemen?" Georgie asked Mac. "Do they know what started the fire?"

Mac's brow drew tight. "No. They'll have an officer from the State Fire Marshal out here first thing in the morning to investigate for arson. No one will be getting into your house for a while, I'm afraid."

"Arson?"

With a gentle squeeze of her shoulder, Mac smiled. "It's routine. They'll hopefully be able to dismiss the fire as nothing more than an unfortunate cigarette from a party guest."

"I guess that makes sense." She turned to Murphy and O'Neal. "Gentlemen, I'm sorry your experience at a Colin's Fancy party was cut short and filled with such drama." She extended her hand to O'Neal. "I want to wish you a Happy New Year."

Releasing the agent's grip, she swiveled and

pasted what she hoped appeared to be genuine smile on her lips. "Special Agent Murphy, Happy New Year to you, too." Her fingers slipped into his and were quickly enveloped by a long lean grip. Warmth emanated from the connection and the chilly air seemed to sizzle around her.

He held her hand a moment longer than appropriate forcing her gaze to meet his. "Happy New Year, Georgie," he whispered. "Please call me Cade. Special Agent Murphy sounds as if you're my witness or something."

She felt the knot in her throat thicken, forcing a matched tone of his whisper to press through her lips. "OK. Cade, Happy New Year."

With her hand still in his oversized grip, he lean forward slightly and brushed his lips to her cheek. "It's traditional for friends to give good wishes with a kiss. And we are friends, aren't we, Miss Georgie?"

A breath puffed from her lips as he stepped back and released her hand. Her whole body was ablaze. She was certain if she looked down, she would see streaking patterns of light streaming across her chest.

Cade shoved his hands in his pockets and nodded his head to Mac. "Happy New Year, Mr. Taylor. I'm sure we'll be seeing you soon."

Georgie's gaze locked with the steel green depths of Cade Murphy's eyes. A soft sigh slipped through her at the tilt of his smile. What would this New Year bring?

18

"Remy, I know Mama did this. Or her goons. Somehow I know she's responsible." Charlotte sipped warm apple cider, chasing her bitter words with the sweet flavor. Huddled under layers of afghans and comforted by the creak of the back porch swing, she stared into the moonless night, hoping it would settle her zipping mind.

"Darlin', you don't know anything."

"Who else could it be?"

"Bad wiring in a house that used to be a shed?"

"Rem, no matter how much I've complained about my accommodations, you and I both know the guesthouse was modernized to meet the dreams of the best designers on the planet. Every amenity exists, or existed, in those four walls. Most people in this country would think they won the lottery if they called the guest house home."

"OK, so not bad wiring. Maybe one of the guests or a staffer wandered out there and dropped a cigarette? You know how stiff Savvy can be about smoking near the main house."

"It was Mama, Remy. She's so mad at me. I could feel it when I saw her. She would never have set foot in South Carolina if I hadn't taken her name off of the accounts. She needs money, and when Stasi needs something she will stop at nothing to make her needs a reality. I can't believe she's behind the accident..."

"You mean the bomb that could have killed you? The explosion that happened to coincide with Anastasia's removal from direct access to your bank accounts. You mean that accident?"

Charlotte waved her hand, ignoring the fear laced worry that grew every time she heard the word bomb. "Maybe, I don't want to believe it. But tonight she could have hurt someone else. She could've hurt Georgie. I'm afraid she won't stop until I'm no longer a problem. And I brought you into the middle of this. Remy, what if she does something to hurt you? I would never forgive myself."

"Sugar, you know I'm too charming to be at risk. And I could've stepped back the instant I knew what was not quite what. This is my choice. So hush with all those worries. I love you. I would do anything for you."

"Even put yourself in the crosshairs of a crazy Russian-American socialite desperate for money?"

"Even that. Friendship runs deep."

"Friendship runs deep. I love you too, Remy." She kissed his cheek.

"OK, enough of the gooey." He twisted to face her on the swing. "For argument sake, let's say you're right, and Stasi or one of her lovely associates set the fire. Don't you think it's about time to get the authorities involved? They're clearly suspicious of something or they wouldn't have come to your office before it blew up."

"The office didn't blow up, just my car."

"Details."

"Details are important. Missing the details is how I ended up in this mess. If it wasn't for you..." A tear streaked down her cheek, burning a warm path.

"Aww, sugarplum. Don't worry. We'll figure out your crazy money-laundering momma and her whacky drug lord, bomb-making friends. Every family has problems. Yours just might be a little extra special."

"Do you really think I should say something to the FBI?"

"Yes."

Remy and Charlotte turned at the deep timbre of Mac Taylor's voice.

How long had he been listening to them? What did he know? "Mac, this is a private conversation," Charlotte said.

"I think we're beyond private conversations, Charlie. Your car was blown up and now your house, a home you share with your sister, was set on fire. What are you not telling me?"

"On that note, I need to find my momma and make sure she has a ride home. Happy New Year, darlin'." Remy leaned forward and kissed Charlotte on the cheek. "I'll talk with you tomorrow."

The echo of Remy's wingtips trailed in his wake.

Tugging the blankets under her chin, Charlotte stared into the dark and smoldering night, unable to make out the firemen she knew were still ensuring no embers might reignite and cause further destruction. She wondered if she could hire them to tamp down the rapidly spreading blaze she called her life. The flames were so hot, she wasn't prepared to discuss the chaos of her dysfunctional life with anyone, let alone perfect Mac Taylor and his broad-shouldered, confidence-oozing self. His weight dropped the swing two inches as he sat beside her, yet she resisted turning to him.

"Give me a dollar."

"What?" She shifted to face him.

"Give me a dollar. Hire me as your lawyer."

"I'm in a cocktail dress on the back porch wrapped in a pile of blankets because my house almost caught on fire. Not a dollar bill in sight."

"Very well." He stretched his palm out to her. "We'll do this the old fashioned way. Take my hand."

"Why?"

"I'm about to become your attorney."

"Taylor, did you inhale too much smoke? You're already my attorney."

"I'm Watershed's attorney. With one shake of the hand, I'll be your personal attorney and anything you tell me will be privileged."

"Anything?" A small burst of hope flickered in her heart.

"Anything."

She lifted her hand from under the mound of blankets and slid her palm towards him. His fingers enveloped hers; his touch heated her better than the weight of a thousand blankets.

His gaze captured hers. With a gentle squeeze of

his hand, he became her confidante. "Tell me. I promise we'll find a way to fix it."

19

The rhythm of Mac's encased fists against his heavyweight bag paced with the thud of his rising heart rate. When he'd returned to his row house in the early hours of the New Year, sleep evaded him. A pot of coffee, a thirty-minute session with the bag, and the winding story Charlie had shared with him continued to tear at his soul. Lives destroyed all because of a selfish need for power and unmatched greed. How could a mother treat her only daughter with...

Whack! Whack! The heavy bag twisted.

The supposed money laundering Remy uncovered was likely the source of the FBI interest, but with all Charlie had revealed, he couldn't be too cautious. Maggie, his brother's fiancée, had an Uncle Jack. Before six this morning, Mac left Maggie's uncle a message for help. Jack Ramsey and his connections with the government and law enforcement were shrouded in layers of classified files and undisclosed locations, but Mac prayed Jack would know what options they had, both legal and sketching around the edges.

Behind the din of wall speakers, the shrill of his phone stole his attention. Ripping off his gloves, he answered the call on the second ring.

"Happy New Year!"

The singsong of his brother Sean's and Maggie's voices floated through the phone. Mac responded in kind, cradling the phone between his shoulder and ear. They chattered about the past week and the early stages of wedding planning. Gulping a half a bottle of water in a single swallow, he barely registered the couple's words in the midst of the happy glow emanating through the phone.

"Sounds great." Mac said, when a pause forced his side of the conversation.

"Hey, Mags," Sean said. "Why don't you go wake up Joe? I'm sure he'll want to wish his big brother a Happy New Year."

"All right." Mac heard Maggie's soft smile. "I hope this is the most spectacular year for you, Mac."

"You too, Maggie-girl."

"What's up?" Sean's voice came through clear with the slight edge of his police steel.

"What do you mean?"

"Jack woke me a little before seven this morning wanting to know why my brother is asking for contacts within the FBI's organized crime division."

Mac heard a screen door slam through the phone.

"Do you want to explain to me why a corporate lawyer is asking for a contact with the FBI? Why you are calling the closest thing I have to a father-in-law before sunrise and seeking dangerous favors?"

Releasing a sigh, Mac downed the remainder of his water bottle. "I have a situation. I need some advice. Not a big deal. Jack seemed amiable over Christmas. I didn't think it would be a big deal. Tell him not to bother." The crinkle of crushing plastic sliced through Mac's apartment. He tossed the empty bottle in the recycling bin as he padded to the oversized black leather sofa in his street-facing living room.

"Organized crime? Two words that always spell big deal."

"I didn't want you to get involved," he said. Sitting on the couch, he gazed through the wide window with a view of the ballpark lights four blocks in the distance.

"How'd you think I would stay uninvolved? You called Uncle Jack."

Kneading the small space between his neck and shoulder, Mac sighed. "Sean, I shouldn't have called Jack. I really can't tell you what's going on. Attorney-client privilege."

"A phrase every cop on the planet hates almost as much as 'not guilty'."

"Hey, you're the one who wanted to chase all the bad guys. I can't help it if sometimes the bad guys have good lawyers."

"Is this one of those times?"

"Do you think I would represent a criminal?"

"Is her last name Dixon?"

"Let it rest."

"No. You're my brother. I love you. You wouldn't let me deal with all the O'Donnell stuff by myself. I'm not letting you face whatever those Dixon sisters are dragging you into by yourself. Bentley Dixon asked too much of you with those women."

"I appreciate your support. And if I think you can help, I have you on speed dial, but for now, I think Jack is a better resource. Can you just trust me?"

Silence was the closest thing to an agreement Mac received, before their younger brother, Joey, snatched the phone from Sean and wished Mac a Happy New Year.

"Will I see you before I report to spring training?" Joey asked.

"I'm not sure. But regardless, I'll be in Florida for a few weeks with the scouts. You better be on your game or you'll wind up riding pine in the Carolina League rather than snagging pop-flies in Minnesota." Mac stifled the circuitous lecture he'd given Joey nearly every day he was home in Ohio for Christmas. "Do the time in the gym and stay away from Marshal Smith. Trouble seems to follow him. And you don't need any extra help finding trouble. Why not catch up with Jessup? He was always a better influence. Bet he can still beat you running the forty."

"Yes, Mom." In many ways, his twenty-six-year-old brother hadn't matured past sixteen, and both Mac and Sean took turns bailing him out of an endless cycle of trouble. Since the end of baseball season this fall, he'd been nursing a shoulder injury and non-physical wounds neither Mac nor Sean could uncover. Joey, with his string of bad choices, was often the main subject of Mac's prayer life. And he once again lifted a silent prayer to the Lord for his baby brother and the healing he could only receive from the great Healer.

"Just do what you need to do to get back to

playing form. I can't imagine your manager will want to deal with anymore of your...extracurricular activities."

"I hear you. Between you, Sean, and Jessup you'd think I needed rehab or something."

"I'll back off if you promise me you'll show up to Florida in shape and ready to play."

"Deal. Now tell me the truth. Will gorgeous Georgie be in Florida in March?"

"Don't even think about it, Sprout."

"What about the chilly one? Will hot Charlotte be scouting players, too? Maybe I'll need to play in the minors to get my shoulder back in shape. Wouldn't mind looking at either of those pretty girls of summer for a few months."

"Girls of summer?" Mac couldn't help the chuckle at Joe's tweak to the 'Boys of Summer' term for ballplayers. "Sprout, forget about Charlie and Georgie. Focus on your shoulder, your game, and getting your life out of the tabloids, and into a church bulletin. Get your life in order and maybe the Good Lord will send you a nice lady to keep you on the straight and narrow."

"Jealous, big bro? You have your eye on one of the delectable Dixon sisters? Did the Good Lord finally send you a damsel to rescue?"

20

"Charlie?" Georgie's voice was barely a whisper above the creak of the guest bedroom door. "Are you awake?"

Charlotte glanced at the antique clock on the bedside table. She had slept exactly twenty-seven minutes. "I'm awake." Shoving herself up, she rested against the headboard.

Georgie folded her long body onto the end of the four-poster bed. "The arson investigator just arrived." Georgie tugged her zip-up hoodie tight around her chest.

"Did he say how long it would take?" As Georgie repeated the arson investigator's rundown, Charlotte's mind wandered to her confession to Mac. Why had she told Taylor anything? He was the last person who could help her. Or was he? He'd listened to her, and his face had reflected concern, without judgment. But how could he not be condemning her today? Every minute she stayed in South Carolina, she placed everyone—her sister, the team, the entire company—in danger.

Her mother's arrival last night was all the proof Charlotte needed. Every whispered accusation she'd imagined and heard, had to be true. Stasi surely didn't come all the way to South Carolina to check on her daughter's well-being.

And in less than six hours, Charlotte needed to calmly have tea with the woman who likely tried to have her killed not seventy-two hours earlier. The person most likely to have set fire to her home. The person who used her business like a personal ATM.

Her mother.

Charlotte had to confront her mother with what she knew. Today. She couldn't wait a moment longer. Beyond the gallery and the risk of prison, too many lives were in jeopardy. She needed to confirm the theft, the money laundering, the car explosion, the house fire. All of it. Her mother's not-so-secret connection with Anton Markov and the *bratva* needed to be exposed.

Even if exposure triggered the demise of both Stasi and Charlotte.

Puffing a breath, she focused on her sister. Even weary from sleep Georgie was the stunning image of Delia. Dishwater blonde curls, tamed into a wayward bun, framed her heart shaped face and lightly freckled cheeks. Her only link to their father was the Caribbean-ocean colored eyes both sisters shared.

The wall of ice Charlotte had built around her heart twenty years earlier— a wall to shield her from the pain of loving her sister, her father, and Delia and not being able to be with them—had been slowly melting since the funeral and now stood as nothing more than a moat of cloudy water. "I'm sorry, Georgie."

"Why are you sorry? It's not your fault. Savvy invited so many people last night anyone of them could have accidently started a fire wandering around the property with a cigar or a candle. Praise God no one was hurt."

Charlotte swallowed a confession. No matter how much relief she felt sharing the burden with Mac, she couldn't risk anyone else knowing. Not before she knew what to do. Mac was convinced he could help. Remy, too. But she refused to put anyone else she loved in danger. Especially not sweet Georgie. Not after everything Charlotte had given up to keep her baby sister safe. "I imagine Savvy needs some help cleaning up."

Georgie nodded and slid off the bed. "The caterers took care of the dishes and everything last night, but furniture needs to be moved and Christmas needs to be de-Christmased throughout the house. The big cleaning crew will be here tomorrow, and Savvy would hate for them to really have to clean anything."

"I'll be down in a few minutes."

"OK. I'm sure Savvy will appreciate the help." Georgie left with a click of the door into its frame.

Charlotte flipped to her stomach. A tear tilted down her cheek. Lifting a silent prayer to the God of Georgie and their father, Charlotte asked for a day of peace to start the New Year.

Just one day.

A whole year would be pushing the limits of even a benevolent deity.

~*~

Five hours, twenty boxes of Christmas decorations, and a hot shower later, Charlotte smoothed her black and white checkered pencil skirt under the diminutive oak table in the Rose and Thorn Inn's breakfast room. Nearly all the tables of the quaint inn's dining room were filled with patrons in various states of high tea consumption. A special celebration on a special day.

Delicate towers of tiny sandwiches, cookies, and bowls laden with clotted cream and jellies crowded every clear surface in the room except for Charlotte's table. She knew better than to order prior to her mother's arrival. Cold tea to Stasi was tantamount to declaring war.

Charlotte sipped her water, crossing her legs at the ankle, and kept a discreet eye on the door. She'd left Remy two voicemails this morning, hoping to have him meet with Mac and her so they could best strategize how to approach the FBI. But her normally chatty best friend, whose phone was perpetually cupped in his palm, had ignored each of her calls. She tapped the edge of her phone as the rumble of vibration notified her of a text. Swiping the screen, she read the message from Remy.

Happy New Year. Unexpected business engagement in DC. Will call when I'm back in town.

A slight calm washed over her. If Remy was out of town, neither her mother nor her compatriots could hurt him. She could call him later to gain his insight into the best approach with her three lettered friends. The farther away from her, the safer he was. Now if she could only figure out how to keep Georgie safe. And Mac. And Savvy. And...

"That table is unacceptable."

The shriek of her mother's voice permeated the small dining area, bouncing off the walls, sending shivers, and chilling Charlotte to the core. Standing, she lifted her handbag and closed the few steps to the reception area and her mother's tantrum.

"I cannot sit in the open. I insist on the private room I requested."

"Ma'am,"—the manager stepped from behind the reception desk—"I do apologize for any confusion. Give me a moment, and I will see if we can't free up the blue room." His heels clicked against the wide pine floors as he rushed down the hall.

"Mama." Charlotte kissed Stasi's cheek. "I see you've made an impression as always."

"Well, I've never been treated this poorly," Stasi said, fanning herself. "I'm sure that horrible woman you call aunt arranged for this appalling experience."

"Mama, it's a table for tea. It's not as if you've been locked in a POW camp for the last six months without access to water."

"Well, it might as well be." Pivoting on the soles of four inch stilettoes that allowed her to see nearly eye to eye with Charlotte, her mother's gaze scraped the length of Charlotte's body. "Was this the best you could do?" she said. "You look as if you are going to a funeral, *malyshka*."

Well, at least she and Savvy agreed on something.

"I had little choice in what to wear, what with the majority of my clothing damaged. I'm certain you heard about our misfortune last evening. I had to borrow this from Georgie."

Her mother flipped her hair over her shoulder and glanced down the hall past Charlotte. "Ahh, here's the silly manager."

"Ma'am, your private tea is set. If you'll follow me."

Charlotte bit her cheek as she followed her mother down the narrow hall and into a twelve by twelve room lined with toile wallpaper in robin's egg blue on three sides. Floor-to-ceiling windows afforded a breathtaking view of the English-style gardens and pond along the back half of the property, comprising the fourth wall.

"To your specifications, ma'am. I do apologize for the confusion." The manager offered with a sweep of his arm.

Stasi barreled by him, assessing the room and contents. "It will suffice."

Gracing the center of the room was a round table with a single ornate leg support. The table was flanked by two high-backed chairs upholstered with a flowered fabric complementing the wallpaper. Mini sandwiches and cookies dominated the table. Two delicate, wide mouth teacups were set before each place with small ramekins of orange peels, cinnamon sticks, and cloves. Matching tea pot and plates completed the elegant presentation.

Clearly, the elevated place-setting was dictated by Stasi. High tea wasn't something with which to be trifled. And although most teas in the United States were more British than Russian, Babushka drilled the necessity of traditional tea into the fabric of Stasi's life from the time she was small, and repeated the lessons once Charlotte came to live in New York. The Bickford women compromised on the food, but rarely on the cinnamon and orange accompaniments.

Charlotte preferred coffee and sandwiches made on full slices of bread. The process of a "cup of tea" and the memories associated, churned waves of repulsion within her stomach.

Stasi glanced to the small bell—a requirement at all meals—and nodded. "We'll ring when we need you," she said, with a wave of her hand sending the manager scurrying out of the room. "Sit, *malyshka*. You cannot take tea standing. One would think you'd been raised in this backwater town."

Charlotte slid onto the chair opposite her mother. With automatic precision, she lifted the tea pot and served Stasi before adding tea to her own cup.

"The youngest must always serve their elders. This is the way. You take care of those who come before, malyshka. This will make you good daughter. Good granddaughter. Good woman. Serve others. Always serve family first. Never forget."

Her grandmother's wisdom. Her grandmother's demands.

She lifted the cream to her mother, but Stasi shook her head, stirring with a cinnamon stick before raising the black tea to her lips for a tentative sip. "So, tell me of this unfortunate incident at that house."

"Mama, you know about the fire."

"Your house caught on fire? Why would you think I would know of a fire, *malyshka*? I was thrown from Savannah's house like a common beggar. No room? *Pft*. That woman just wanted to embarrass me last night. And you allowed her to make me look *cmexa*? A fool? In front of *those* people? You are no daughter. You are a traitor." She slammed her hand on the table; the teacups clanked in their saucers and cookies rattled across the plate.

"Mama, settle down."

Half standing, her mother leaned across the table, a hair's breadth from Charlotte.

"Settle down! You want I should settle down? You do not tell me how to feel or behave, little girl. You do not tell me anything. You are the child. I am the mama. Don't you forget. You forget? We will make you remember." Her narrow eyes flashed to black. Her cheeks flamed pink, darkening on pace with the vein beating in her neck.

Charlotte sucked in a shaky breath, her heart vibrating against her ribs. "Mama, I could never forget I'm your child." She reached her hand across the table, stroking her mother's clenched fist. Soft physical touch was the only defense against Stasi's mood swings. A lesson Charlotte had learned too young.

Swiping her hand across her forehead, Mama slid back into her chair with a nod. "See how you make me behave. You always were a temperamental little girl.

Throwing fits to get her way. Now. Eat your food. Drink your tea. We are celebrating the New Year."

Charlotte lifted her cooled teacup dragging a sip past her taut lips.

"*S Novym Godom, malyshka!* Happy New Year, baby girl." Her mother's red painted lips smiled wide as she snatched a triangle sandwich from the tray. With a small bite, she patted the corner of her mouth. "This will be the best year ever. You shall see. Mama will take care of everything."

Charlotte smoothed the napkin on her lap.

Mama dolloped thick cream on a petite scone. She seemed to be calm. Calm was very rarely a good sign with Stasi.

"How long will you be staying in South Carolina?" Charlotte reached for a crust-less cucumber sandwich. Not eating at tea was paramount to treason.

Dabbing the corner of her mouth, Mama finished chewing before answering. "I'm sure you wouldn't want me to rush our visit. After all, I have nothing to do."

"Of course not. If you're here, who is watching the gallery?"

"I closed the gallery for the holidays. I thought that would be as you wish. You've taken my access to the accounts away. Pulled my artists. What could I do?" She shrugged. "I told all of your employees to enjoy their long break with their families."

"But Mama, the holidays are our busiest time. With tourists. Gifts. We need the money to keep the gallery open."

Mama drew a delicate sip of tea. Setting her cup on the saucer, she stretched her hands long against the white cloth. "What do you care about keeping the gallery open? You cut me off from the funds needed to pay artists, to pay the bills, to pay staff. How could you possibly care about the gallery?" She spoke in a low controlled voice, sending fear rippling through Charlotte.

"Remy or I could release funds. You can still write checks. Remy recommended we have two co-signers for the time being. Just while he finishes the audit." Charlotte bit the corner of her sandwich, hoping the terror threatening to engulf her remained concealed from her mother.

"And you expect me to jump through hoops like a dog at a circus to do you a favor?"

"Of course not, Mama. I appreciate all of your help. But the gallery needs to stay open. It's my livelihood. My business."

"*Pish.* You will have your father's money. Money that should have been mine years ago. You can fund the gallery for decades. You can fund all sorts of projects. Give gifts."

"I can't funnel money into a failing business, and if I don't have clients shopping for art that is exactly what the gallery will be. A failing business."

"Do you question me? Didn't you put me in charge? Didn't you beg me, 'Mama, I have to go to South Carolina to honor my father's wishes. Please take care of the shop.' I have a life. I have needs. But you don't care about me. You are always take. Take.

Take. Take. I give because I love you. I'm your mother."

Drawing in a deep breath, Charlotte smiled. "Yes, I did ask you. Thank you. If you think it best the gallery close for a few weeks, then I'm sure it is the best choice." She stretched her hand out to her mother.

A small candle of hope burned for Mama in Charlotte's heart. For all her mother's self-indulgent actions, Charlotte could not fully reconcile her mother with the criminal activity Remy discovered. Perhaps Mama had been used. Coerced. Perhaps she was innocent. Charlotte knew in an instant what her wish for the New Year was.

"Well, then my darling, you must trust your mama." Her red tipped fingers stretched across the table, clutching Charlotte's hand. "You know I will always do what's best for family. A lesson you clearly haven't learned yet. But you will. I just need to find a few more ways to instruct you. Unfortunately, sometimes lessons to children require pain. It is biblical; spare the rod, spoil the child."

Beads of sweat popped against Charlotte's forehead. Hope slipped from her heart.

The grip of Mama's hand over hers cut off circulation. Visions of the explosion and the fire fought for center stage in her mind. Had the tragedies been inflicted by strangers? Or were they a mother's lessons?

21

A light drizzle slid down the cloudy window of Cade's motel room five miles from the field office in Charleston. He rotated his neck, popping the joints. Shifting his focus from the dismal New Year's Day, he punched the passcode on his phone. A picture of Georgie and Charlotte Dixon staring at the smoldering guest house filled the screen, Georgie's arm draped around Charlotte's sagging shoulders.

The care Georgie gave Charlotte, care her sister openly rebuffed, was surprising. From all his research, he knew the sisters were barely acquaintances, but the buffet of stories he heard the night before painted a painful picture.

With all he and O'Neal had discovered through casual conversation over okra and oysters, Georgie should despise Charlotte. The stories ranged from how Charlotte treated their father during his advanced cancer to the years of unreturned letters and spurned offers of reconciliation. And now, Charlotte was back in Colin's Fancy set to acquire half of their father's estate. Money Georgie clearly deserved more than Charlotte, just ask any one of the dozens of relatives ready to share their opinion. Yet, he had visual evidence, both on his phone and burned in his brain, of the generous spirit Georgie offered to her sister. If he hadn't seen the unabashed love displayed before his own eyes, he would have doubted the sincerity of the photos. Scrolling on his phone, the photo he'd snapped of Stasi and her "friends" came into view.

Stasi's unexpected arrival was a pleasant turn in the case. He knew going straight to Charlotte to question her about her gallery was a risk, but a calculated one already paying dividends. He couldn't be certain the fire and the car bomb were directly related to Stasi and her presumed illicit connections, but the timing was too coincidental to infer a mere happenstance. Guilt bubbled against his excitement over the case advancements. He hated that anything he did may have caused the violence, but thankfully, no one was hurt.

Whether Charlotte was knowingly in league with her mother's dangerous game or was simply a pawn on the board was still unanswered. His decision to interview Stasi's daughter generated the sparks he needed to confidently move forward with his investigation. Guilt, or no guilt. He would keep pressing to discover the missing pieces to the puzzle.

A thick pounding against his door snapped his attention from the photos.

"Open up, Murphy," Mac Taylor bellowed.

Cade slid the case folder under the bed, closed the screen on his phone, adjusted his shoulder holster to secure his weapon, and opened the door.

"Mr. Taylor. Did you swing by to wish me a Happy New Year? A phone call would've sufficed."

"Let us in, Probie." Dylan said, peeking into the open doorway. "Mr. Taylor was just sharing some delicate details about your beloved case. I thought you'd like to know before I call Cavanaugh." Dylan pushed past Cade, but Taylor was slow to move. He hesitated at the threshold, rain sliding down his face and shoulder.

Cade extended his arm toward his cramped motel room.

Taylor silently accepted the invitation.

Without waiting to be asked, Dylan snatched a bottle of water from the mini-fridge and began recounting Taylor's story between gulps.

"Slow down, O'Neal, or you'll be the first known case of a Special Agent drowning from a water bottle."

Dylan slouched in one of the four unmatched set of chairs circling the scarred corner table. "Cade, this story is too much. I've always believed your theories, but hearing what Mr. Taylor shared…"

Cade dragged one of the chairs from the table and straddled the seat. Crossing his forearms against the backrest, he narrowed his focus on Taylor who stood barely inside the door. Water still rained down his frame, creating a puddle around his feet.

"Take a load off, Taylor," he said, extending his hand to the empty chairs, hoping his tone held a congenial welcome his mind couldn't conjure.

While Dylan recounted the story, Taylor remained stalwart and silent. Witnessing the protective defense Mac Taylor used at the hospital to shield Charlotte from interrogation, and the care he'd displayed at the party, Cade wondered if Taylor could be trusted.

The stern lawyer was likely falling under the spell of Charlotte Dixon and would do anything to deflect attention from her. Cade needed to determine if Taylor was a concerned citizen or merely a besotted suitor. "Your story's pretty fantastic, don't you think?" Cade asked with a lift of his eyebrow. "Based on our research, you don't know Miss Dixon very well, and yet you expect us to believe she shared this dark secret...secrets, with you? And she wanted you to share them with us? We've only known you for what? Two, three days now? What makes you think we believe you? Why didn't Miss Dixon come to us directly?"

Taylor didn't budge from his spot against the wall. "I spoke with Jack Ramsey. He said I could trust O'Neal."

"Kind of a few steps from a lowly field agent to one of the highest-ranking national security officers." Cade could only imagine the connections Taylor had if his first phone call was to Jack Ramsey. He lifted a shoulder toward Dylan. "How'd he even know who you are?"

Dylan rolled the bottle of water between his hands. His focus dropped to the table. "I worked a kidnapping case with Ramsey early in my career." He offered no further explanation.

The room fell silent except the slash of rain beating against the building.

Cade nodded, knowing his years of training kept his face from betraying the swirl of questions about his partner's unknown connection to one of the legendary figures in national security. Ramsey's exploits in covert operations had been rumored to be the framework of a popular movie series. "So, O'Neal comes highly recommended. What makes us certain that Miss Dixon isn't just playing the odds?"

In two strides, Taylor closed the gap between them, slamming his hands against the table, rattling the silk flower centerpiece. "Listen. I'm done. I'm tired. And I am scared out of my mind. I am terrified one or more people I love will end up in a body bag. I'm choosing to trust you, despite my better instincts. Charlie's life is on the line, and she needs all the help she can get. I'm here asking you to help me save her. Are you in or are you out?"

22

The mist of the late afternoon rain, gave Georgie the sense she was in a distant world filled with wonder and glory, helping her forget the trials of the past week...weeks. Her inner child could almost see angels gliding above the fog rolling across the winter plowed fields. Snuggling into her fleece lined raincoat, she slogged through the thickening mud as she approached the tightly woven white pines and magnolias edging the property her many times great grandfather won as part of a card game when he first arrived in the Colonies from Ireland.

Georgie loved to hear the fantastic stories of Colin Shaunessy. How he stood near this very spot and felt as fancy as a member of the peerage, and gave his land the name Colin's Fancy so every generation would know exactly how he felt that first day. She knew Savvy and her father had exaggerated the tales of his exploits and glossed over the less savory aspects of their lineage. But she loved her roots and she prayed one day Charlotte would come to love them with equal passion.

Plucking a dried hydrangea blossom from the ground, she turned down the gravel path toward the guest house. She'd walked the exterior with the lead investigator as the inspectors worked through the inside. He thought they would be able to make a claim on the destroyed contents with the insurance company by the time their offices were open tomorrow.

She sucked in a deep breath as the charred exterior came into view. Twirling the flower between her fingers, she maneuvered the fifty-foot grass and mud-patched path to the porch stretching the length of the tiny house.

Living in the guesthouse had been her idea. When her father announced the codicil to his will requiring her and Charlotte to cohabitate for one year, she knew they would never achieve the sibling intimacy her father desired in the main house. Too many nooks and too many relatives would give Charlotte ample opportunity to ignore her. The guest house, with its sweet dormers and single bathroom, was the perfect answer to developing immediate closeness, if only in proximity at the beginning.

Those first few weeks with her sister tested every part of her Christian charity. Charlotte sneered when Georgie smiled. She ignored dinners, locking herself in her room for hours. Then she'd leave with Remy, but never invited Georgie along. When Charlotte was difficult, which was often, Georgie recounted one of the last conversations she had with her father. *"Patience, Georgie. Charlie will need more patience than you've ever given anyone or anything in your entire life. But a relationship with your sister will be worth the fight. Love her. No matter what she does or says. Just love her."*

If she closed her eyes she could still smell the

awful mix of ammonia and decay permeating her father's final days. No matter how many bouquets of peonies, Daddy's favorite, she ordered, their pungent aroma wasn't enough to snuff out the fragrance of death. And no matter how hard she tried, she wasn't able to crack the wall of ice his beloved Charlie erected between them.

The floorboards of the porch creaked under her thick, knee high rubber boots. Brushing soot off the window, she glanced inside.

The couch cushions were strewn across the floor and several small holes were visible in the walls. Turning from the damaged living room, she slid against the porch wall and sighed. Restorations on the guest house may not be complete until their year was up. How was she supposed to connect with her sister in a ten thousand square foot former plantation?

"Knock, knock."

She brushed away the spilling tears before lifting her gaze to the generous smile of her friend, Cole. At just under six feet tall, he was lean with what her aunt referred to as patrician features: high cheekbones, deep set eyes, and a thin nose. Cole was the only friend she'd made at Watershed since she'd been forced to take an active role at the company. He'd only started a few months before her father passed, but Cole took his death harder than most of the other employees. She'd requested he work with her as an interpreter of sorts. After four years at Savannah College of Art & Design she was amply qualified to design a new jewelry line or even paint a mural in the center of town, but understanding anything with numbers was beyond her capacity. Cole was one of her father's financial analysts and knew the mechanics of Watershed better than most. In only a few short months, she'd come to depend upon him not only for his business sense, but as a confidante.

"Hey, what's wrong?" he asked, squatting in front of her. Concern marred his forehead.

"I just realized we'll likely be months before we can move back into the guest house."

"Is that so bad? One bathroom between the two of you couldn't be easy. There's like seven in the big house. You'll have your space and Charlotte will have hers. Easy."

Her lips lifted, but the smile left her heart cold. "I don't know what I'll do, Cole. My father's dream was for Charlotte and me to become true sisters. Over the last few weeks we've been little more than roommates, but at least we had to interact every day. I'm afraid when we move into the main house we will barely see each other in passing."

"Have you talked to her about how you feel?"

"What am I supposed to say?"

"How about, you love her and you want to spend time getting to know her?"

Georgie snorted. "Why didn't I think of that? Oh, right, I did when I invited her to dinner nearly every night since she moved to town. Or when I asked her to go to church with me. Or when I asked her to go with me to some of the Charleston galleries. And with every invitation she said no."

"But it seemed like you were getting closer."

"Maybe...last night she was too upset to be guarded and..."

"And...what Georgie?"

"She hugged me back."

He squeezed her hand. "That's encouraging."

With a sigh, she gave him a sideways smile. "It only took two major tragedies in less than seventy-two hours for my sister to initiate human contact. Super promising."

He chuckled. "I heard her mother showed up. How did she handle her?"

"How'd you hear about Stasi?" With the exception of Mac, no one from Watershed had been invited to the New Year's Eve party. Savvy had insisted for years that both her father's employees and his friends should have the ability to enjoy major holidays without the subtle strain of work talk floating from corner to corner.

"One of the servers lives in my building. She told me it was quite the entrance."

"For all of Charlotte's difficultness, her mother is about a thousand times worse than Charlotte on her worst day."

"Whew...that bad?"

"And Charlotte had to have tea with her today. I've only been living with Charlotte a short time, and she's afraid of nothing, at least from what I can observe. But one look from her mother and I was amazed she didn't evaporate into thin air." She shook her head. "Enough about my sister's crazy mother.

How was your New Year's?"

"It was fun. Set off some fireworks. Nothing too fancy."

Glancing at her watch Georgie cringed. She'd told Savvy she would only be gone about an hour and she was twenty minutes past her hour. Standing, she brushed off her jeans. "I need to head back to the house."

"Do you mind if I keep you company? I parked near the house but figured you'd be out walking in the rain."

"That predictable, huh?" She slid her arm through his.

"Artist. Broody weather. Fits."

"Not everything is an equation."

Wrapping her chilled hand in his long-fingered warmth, he squeezed. "Georgie, everything is problem solving. A plus B always equals C."

They strolled in companionable silence. The drizzle's shift to rain had them quickening their pace.

"Let's cut across the creek." Georgie said, slipping her arm from his. "We'll shave five minutes off the walk."

Hopping from slippery stone to stone, Georgie straightened her arms to either side for balance. With one leap her boot slipped against the rock, and she splashed back into the murky water.

"Georgie!" Cole shouted, hustling to her.

She laughed, reaching out her hand to his. "I don't know what I was thinking. I'm not graceful on those rocks when they are dry."

Clasping her fingers around his hand, she placed her opposite hand behind her for leverage. But her hand didn't find the muddy bottom of the creek where she used to collect tadpoles and crawdads. Instead her fingers slipped over the ridges of what felt like tuxedo pleats.

Twisting in the creek, she looked behind her. A scream stuck in her throat.

Just above the surface was the bloated, beaten face and body of Remy Reynard, still dressed in his New Year's Eve tuxedo.

23

Charlotte's heart sped as she turned her car down the magnolia lined drive connecting the main road with Colin's Fancy. Two local police cars, three state highway patrol cars, and one unmarked car lined the circle drive in front of the main house.

Georgie!

Thrusting the shift of her rental car into park with a jolt, she grabbed her handbag and rushed up the wide front steps. With a hip thrust, she scooted through the doorway and stifled a scream when she saw Special Agent Murphy.

"Ms. Dixon. Where've you been today?" he asked with a lift of an eyebrow.

"Tea with my mother. Why are you in my house? Again."

"Ms. Dixon?"

Charlotte pivoted at O'Neal's gentle voice. It seeped through her bones calming her racing spirit.

"Special Agent O'Neal, why is half the Beaufort County sheriff's office parked in the driveway? Is Georgie OK?"

He nodded. "Ms. Dixon, I think we should go into your study and have a little talk." He glanced toward his partner with quick lift of his chin.

"Can I see Georgie first?" She wanted to stuff the words back into her body. Outward caring caused destruction in her world.

"Georgie's fine. You can see her in a minute. We really need to speak with you in private."

"I'm sorry. A parade of police makes a lady concerned. Whatever you need will have to wait a minute. I want to see my sister." She pressed past him, her heels echoing oddly through the house. "Georgie?"

"Charlotte?"

Her sister's broken voice floated from the kitchen and Charlotte closed the few steps to the swinging door.

Huddled against her friend, Cole, in the breakfast nook, Georgie's ashen face was streaked with tears.

"Georgie? What happened?" She slid onto the bench on the opposite side of the table.

"Oh, Charlie. I'm so sorry...so s-s-sorry..." Her voice trailed behind choking tears.

She reached across the table and Charlotte clasped her hand. With soft strokes, she tried to sooth Georgie's distress. Shifting her gaze to Cole, she attempted to gain unspoken answers.

"Charlotte," his voice shook. "I mean, Ms. Dixon, there's been..." Visibly swallowing, he lifted his arm from Georgie, laying his palm over the sisters' clasped hands.

"Is it Savvy? Is she OK?" Charlotte swiveled her focus between Georgie's flood of tears and Cole's blank stare. "What's going on?" She yanked her hands from the pile. "Why is every law enforcement agency within a hundred-mile radius camped out on the front lawn? And why do the two of you look as if your best friend just died?"

"Charlie, honey."

Charlotte twisted in her chair at the welcome sound of Mac's low voice. The sight of the day's growth of beard sprinkling his jaw and his warm brown gaze settled the acid boiling in her stomach. "Mac, please tell me what's happening."

He closed the few steps and dropped to Charlotte's eye level. "Darlin', it's Remy."

"What's Remy?"

He clasped her hand in his. "He's in the hospital, sweetheart. He's in pretty bad shape. He's at Memorial. He's in a coma."

A sharp bolt of ice ripped through Charlotte. She yanked her fingers from Mac's grasp. Bile threatened to leap from her body as the kitchen tilted to the left. She shook her head. "No. You're wrong. He texted me this morning. He had to go to D.C. for work."

Fumbling for her handbag, she tugged her phone from its compartment. Swiping the screen with shaking fingers, she pulled up the text. "See? He's fine. You're wrong. Remy's fine."

Mac slid her phone to Cole. Grasping both of her hands, he forced her to raise her gaze to his. "Charlie, I don't know who sent that text, but Georgie and Cole found Remy in the creek this afternoon while you were at tea. The police think he never left the grounds after the party. They aren't certain if he fell and was knocked unconscious, or if..."

"If...what, Taylor?" She sucked back the tears threatening her vision. Remy couldn't be hurt. What if he died? He was her lifeline. He was the only one who knew the whole truth. *He knew the truth.* Tears swamped Charlotte's vision. Her breaths shallowed. "No...no...it can't be true. Not Remy. Not Remy..." She lifted her gaze to Mac. "It's my fault. Mac, it's all my fault."

He snatched her to his chest, absorbing her sobs. He whispered, but nothing broke through the hum filling her mind as her mother's words zipped through her mind. *I just need to find a few more ways to instruct you. Unfortunately, sometimes lessons to children require pain.*

"Mac, she did it. It's all my fault."

"What's your fault, Ms. Dixon?" Special Agent Murphy's thick voice cut through Charlotte's grief. "If you are in some way connected to Mr. Reynard's accident, you should tell us now."

"Miss Dixon is clearly shocked by the news of her best friend." Mac's tone turned lawyer. "She needs some fresh air. You will excuse us." He tugged Charlotte to stand, clamping her to his side and giving her little choice but to go with him.

Before they could step onto to the back porch, O'Neal stopped their progress. "Mr. Taylor, I know you don't like Murph's tactics, but he's right. If Miss Dixon knows anything that could help the sheriff's investigation, the fresher her memory the better."

"Give us a few minutes. I promise, Charlotte will be cooperative."

O'Neal nodded and stepped away from the doors leading to the veranda.

As they crossed the threshold, she broke free from Mac's comforting embrace. Gulping in a breath of cool damp air, she leaned against the railing. The midwinter sun dipped low for an early sunset. How could there be such beauty in the midst of this nightmare?

They stood in silence watching the colors in the west sky bleed from pink to deep purple before blanketing the world in inky black. Stretching her fingers to the left, she brushed against his hand. His palm turned up, and she laced her fingers through his. Her breaths steadied. Calm poured through her weary spirit. Too broken to resist the tug of need pooling in her stomach, she shifted her gaze to his.

He drew her into his embrace. She breathed in his clean, woodsy scent. His arms around her filled her with strength she hadn't realized she'd lost.

"I need to get to Remy. I need to protect him." She rested her head against Mac's broad shoulder. His pulse reverberated against her cheek. "He is my best friend. Often he's my only one."

With feather-light fingers, Mac stroked her back, his touch soothing, sprinkling tingles up her spine. "He loves you. But he isn't your only friend. You have Georgie. Savvy." He stepped back from her, lifting her chin with his forefinger. "You have me, Charlie. You always have me." He brushed his lips against hers.

Tiny bursts of light exploded through her and tamped the darkness threatening to overwhelm her.

Lifting his mouth, he pressed a light kiss to her cheek. "You have me. And we will figure out what happened."

The need for justice darkened his hooded eyes. He would stop at nothing to discover the truth. She sensed the danger emanating from him. But the truth wouldn't set him free.

She knew all too well, the truth could very well lead to his demise. She couldn't allow another person to suffer because of her family. Because of her. Especially not Mac. She didn't know what she felt for him. But if her mother suspected she cared even a little, Charlotte could be signing his death sentence. She shook her head and twisted out of his embrace. Locking her arms across her chest, she stepped to the end of the porch.

The music of the twilight filled the quiet.

"Charlie?" Mac stood behind her.

"My name is Charlotte." She tightened her grip, comforted in the bruising pain she felt stinging her sides.

"Don't do this." Mac's thick fingers clamped on her shoulder, easily turning her to face him. "Don't shut down on me. Don't try to protect me. I can protect myself. Let me protect you. Let me help."

"Help?" She barely restrained a scream. "Like Remy? You want to help? Do you have a death wish, Taylor?"

"Charlie..." He reached for her, but she spun past him.

"Don't." She lifted a hand between them. "Please,

you don't understand. I can't risk you too. I never thought they...she...would come after Remy. But look...my best friend of twenty years is in the hospital, unconscious because I asked him for help. What if he never wakes up? She told me at tea...she told me..."

"What did your mother tell you?"

They both turned at the sound of Murphy's voice. He leaned against a wide column, his arms loosely linked across his chest.

"How long have you been eavesdropping?" Charlotte spat. "Didn't your mother teach you better manners?"

"I'm sure my mother didn't teach me the same lessons as your mother." He pushed away from the column and closed the distance. "Why don't you share some of the wisdom of Stasi Bickford?"

"Special Agent Murphy," Mac stepped between Murphy and Charlotte. "You've walked in on a private conversation. I told you when Charlotte was ready to talk, she would cooperate. She's not ready. Please go back inside and wait."

"I don't think so. The hospital called. Mr. Reynard was transferred to MUSC trauma center. Based on the initial assessment of the scene, and the doctor's assumptions regarding Mr. Reynard's injuries, we believe this was a horrible accident. My guess is Mr. Reynard wandered away from the hubbub after the fire. Maybe he had a few too many, tripped, and fell into the creek. The mud's pretty thick. Your friend likely hit his head, fell unconscious, and nearly drowned."

"An accident?" Charlotte's voice shook.

"Well, we think that's what we are supposed to believe. Is there any reason why we shouldn't?"

An accident?

Could she have jumped to the wrong conclusions? Perhaps neither her mother nor her associates were involved.

The text floated through her mind. Remy wouldn't have been able to send her a text today if he was injured last night. Why would someone steal his phone and make her believe he was out of town? Coincidences were never coincidental.

"I received a text from Remy this morning. He told me he had to go out of town on business."

"Where's your phone?" Murphy asked.

"I think I left it in the kitchen with Georgie and Cole."

He pivoted toward the back door.

"Special Agent Murphy," she called after him.

He glanced over his shoulder.

She sucked in a deep breath. "This has to stop. I'll do anything you need. Please just promise me one thing."

"What's that?"

"Protect Georgie."

24

Mac rested his hip against the breakfast bar of his kitchen. Coffee popped and sizzled to completion as he listened to Charlie answer another of the agents' list of questions.

With the police still tagging and bagging the surrounding property of the plantation, and reporters beginning to swarm, he'd quietly suggested the sisters and the seemingly ever-present federal agents adjourn to his house. Charlie agreed on one condition. She had to see Remy first.

The over sixty mile drive on U.S. 17N to Charleston was slow and silent. By the time they arrived at the hospital Charlotte's standard issue shell was securely in place. Mac ignored her stiff exterior and wrapped his arm around her shoulders. For a moment, he felt her body relax into his, until she saw Remy's mother. Her spine of steel snapped into place as she walked the dozen steps to Mrs. Reynard sitting alone in the stark ICU waiting room.

Charlie wrapped Mrs. Reynard in a tight embrace and the silent tears of both women reverberated through their conjoined frames. Within minutes, Mac followed Charlie and Remy's mother down the sterile hallway to the wide glass walled room Remy would call home for who knew how many days. His swollen face, blackened and yellow, was half covered by a ventilator. A heart monitor beeped in a consistent rhythm offset by the in and out flow of oxygen being pumped into Remy's lifeless form.

Mrs. Reynard slipped from Charlie's embrace and reached for her son's hand. Charlie stepped back from mother and son and wove her arms around her middle. They stood in silence, only the sound of life saving machines to interfere with the chaos of questions surrounding Remy's accident.

Mac wanted to protect Charlie. To save her from the pain he could feel rioting through her.

With a squeeze of Mrs. Reynard's shoulder, Charlie pressed a kiss to Remy's cheek. She turned to Mac. Her eyes were shiny with unshed tears.

"I'm ready." Those were the last words she spoke before she started the FBI inquisition.

Hours later, Mac shook the memory from his mind as Charlie sipped on the sparkling water he'd handed to her after she changed into a pair of his sweats and a Beaufort Bombers t-shirt that dwarfed her lean frame. Perched on the edge of an overstuffed chair, her back elegantly straight, she rolled the glass between her hands, directing her gaze to O'Neal.

The night of the fire, she'd shared most of what Remy had uncovered in her books and some of her worries. But tonight, with each drawn breath revealing a new chapter in the horror story of her life, Mac realized she had only chipped the edge of the iceberg. He was struggling to mask the shock of what she shared with Murphy and O'Neal.

Embezzlement.

Money laundering.

Illegal high stakes gambling.

Suspected human trafficking.

Possible drug smuggling. And now, potentially arson and murder.

How had he not seen what she had been hiding for months...years?

The answer was simple.

He hadn't looked. Hadn't wanted to know.

He, along with nearly everyone in the Dixon clan, had tried and convicted Charlie as the villain in the drama swirling around Bent and his two daughters. Her cold shoulder was a shield of protection for each of them. They were blind by choice.

Cupping a steaming mug of coffee, he glanced toward Georgie sitting cross-legged, leaning against her sister's chair. Charlie's unofficial guard dog against the world.

Georgie didn't try to stifle the horror she felt with each of Charlie's stories. Her face was a mirror into her soul. After years of watching Georgie rescue small lizards and nurse wilting plants back to health, he guessed she wanted to hide her sister in a room for the next six months until Murphy and O'Neal had enough to convict Charlie's mother and her consorts. But Georgie also seemed to sense the separation Charlie needed. Although she was close enough to snatch her sister in a hug, she hadn't touched her once.

"Charlotte, let's go through this one more time."

Nearly two hours into the interview, Charlie asked Special Agent O'Neal to call her Charlotte. She had neglected to give the same courtesy to Murphy.

"Dylan," Georgie leaned forward. "Can't we take a break? It's nearly ten. We haven't eaten dinner. Why don't I make us something?"

"Georgie, I appreciate your concern, but we really do need to make certain we know everything your sister knows before we talk to our boss. She'll want to ensure the paperwork is spotless. One hole in our investigation and years of work will be for nothing."

"Dylan, I think Georgie is right." Murphy spoke for the first time in hours. Perched in the wide window with the lights of the ballfield haloing him, the intense agent catalogued every word, leg cross, and head tilt Charlie made. He was obviously waiting for her to make a mistake.

"Murph…"

"I'm hungry. And you're always hungry. Let's get some fresh air. Allow everyone a minute to stretch our legs. I'm sure Miss Dixon will appreciate a little break."

Charlie nodded and stood with the elegant grace of a decade of ballet training. "Georgie, how about we see what Mac has to cook?"

Georgie bounded to her feet and linked her arm through her sister's. "He always has pasta." She glanced over her shoulder at Mac. "Do you have any vegetables?"

She released Charlie's arm as they wove around the heavy weight bag and into the single line galley kitchen.

Mac pushed off the breakfast bar, walked through the opposite door, and caught sight of Georgie's head and shoulders plunged into the refrigerator. Charlie faced the cabinets and clutched the marble counter. Her knuckles stretched white.

"Georgie, I don't think pasta will do." Mac reached in the back pocket of his jeans and pulled out his phone. "Why don't you go ask the gentlemen what they like on their pizza? Vito's delivers in under twenty. Their number's in my speed dial."

Georgie glanced across to Charlie. She stretched her lips to a soft smile. "Why don't I see if they want to go and take a walk? Vito's is just around the corner." She patted his shoulder when she left.

Mumbles from the living room were followed by the quick sound of the front door closing, leaving Mac and Charlie alone.

Linking his arms across his chest, he rested against the stove and waited.

"She's my mother." Her voice was a dry whisper.

"We don't get to pick our parents."

She twisted to face him. The way her hair fell, barely concealed the yellow and purple bruise from her encounter with the car bomb. Fury simmered in him. He'd like five minutes with the maker of that bomb.

A single tear slid down her cheek and all thoughts of vengeance slipped from his heart replaced by a singular desire to shelter her from any pain.

She smiled against the tears. "But I bet you would have picked yours every day of the week and twice on

Sundays?"

He shrugged. "Doesn't mean they were perfect."

"I'm guessing that Momma Taylor never stole money from your piggy bank? Or your dad never had an affair with the church choir director? Or the FBI didn't think that your family was intimately linked to the Russian mafia?"

"Every family has their issues."

"Seriously, Taylor? That's the best you can come up with? I've been telling the FBI for the better part of two hours, I think my mother tried to kill me, possibly tried to kill my best friend, and is laundering drug money through my art gallery. They believe she is likely tied to an international ring of human traffickers, and all you have to say is my family is as dysfunctional as everyone else's?" She spun away from him. Her bare feet slapped against the hardwood floors as she closed the short distance to the wide expanse of windows facing the ballpark. Hugging her middle, she leaned her forehead against the windowpane. "I used to dream of living in the dugout when I was little."

"Me, too." His reflection was a blur above hers.

"My dad took me to the ballpark everyday between April and September. Stasi hated baseball. She thought it was too American. Too lower class. But my dad loved everything about the sport. His love affair with the game, transferred to me. I wanted to pitch a no hitter. Hit a grand slam to win the World Series. I dreamed of being the first woman in the Show, but after a few weeks of little league I knew I was a better coach than player. I hit clean off the tee, but I proceeded to tell every other little boy how to square up his hips to hit a solid grounder."

"Really? Where were you my junior year when my swing went south, and I couldn't hit a single to save my life?"

She rolled her head to face him. "All in the hips." A faint smile brushed her lips, as she returned her focus to the distant field. "How different would my life have been if I'd stayed with Delia and my dad?"

He closed the distance, leaning a shoulder against the cool glass. "Why didn't you?"

"When my parents divorced, I was too little to really understand. I remember the night we left Colin's Fancy. Mama came into my room; it must have been after midnight because the moon was so bright I could see the circles of black mascara caked against her cheeks. She kissed my forehead and said we needed to leave for our adventure. I asked if Daddy was coming too, and she shook her head. The next thing I knew I was living with my grandparents, and my mother was gone. I don't think I saw her for another three or four months. But my dad never contacted me either. And I did what any six-year-old would do; I adapted. My grandparents became my stability. I don't remember much of the divorce, except one day when my dad came to visit.

"It was right before Christmas. I hadn't seen either of my parents since the night Stasi and I left South Carolina, but there my father was. Standing beside the Christmas tree. The present I was too afraid to ask Santa to bring. He was holding a baseball mitt with a giant green bow in the center.

"I was so excited. I launched myself into his arms. Nothing had ever felt as good as those thick arms engulfing my body. I don't remember much of the visit, but I can still smell the mix of leather, pine, and seed oil that always seemed to linger around my dad. And I can hear him whispering to me how much he loved and missed me.

"I didn't see him for another two years."

Mac's heart screamed. The Bentley Dixon he knew would never have allowed a day to pass without talking to his daughter, let alone two years. But one look into Charlie's glassy eyes dispelled any questions.

"When I finally saw him, I was in the second grade. He came to my school for a parents' day function."

"He came back to New York?"

She shook her head. "I was enrolled at Laramore Academy in Connecticut for most of my primary school."

"You couldn't have been more than eight years old."

"After finishing kindergarten at a day school in Manhattan, my mother felt I would be better suited for boarding school."

Acid that had been on a simmer began to boil in Mac's belly. Eight years old? Abandoned by not one, but two parents? He thought about how he'd spent his second-grade year. Playing little league. Riding in the combine with his dad during harvest. Showing his prize lamb at the county fair. Eating his mom's chocolate chip cookies. He spent second grade being loved and cherished.

Charlie spent second grade abandoned and disregarded.

Swallowing against the wave of nausea, he focused on Charlie's words.

"I didn't know it at the time, but my parents' divorce was final the day he came to visit me at school. He promised I would be able to spend the summer in Colin's Fancy. I'd get to watch every home game from the dugout." The corner of her mouth twisted. "I wanted to believe him, but I barely saw my mother, and despite my grandparents' attempts at normalcy, adults and trust weren't a combination I was used to.

"But that summer he arrived on his own, and we flew to South Carolina. I watched every Bombers home game. Collected frogs from the creek. And met Remy for the first time at the corner of our properties." The wisp of a memory danced across her face, lifting the corners of her mouth. "Remy was so boy and so southern. I loved everything about him from the first moment he shoved his hand into mine to introduce himself. I spent nearly every day with Remy. Swimming. Fishing. Going to ballgames. Playing tic-tac-toe on the back of the church bulletin. He was my best friend. Is my best friend." Her words tumbled from her lips in a choke. A fresh stream of tears poured down her face. "He's my best friend, Mac. Why didn't I protect him?" She slipped to the floor, her body wracked with tears.

Sliding down beside her, he tugged her into his

arms. Her tears soaked his t-shirt. Wrapping his arms around her, he wanted to absorb her pain. Relieve her guilt. But he had no words of affirmation big enough to snatch her from the pit she was tumbling into. *Lord, please help me help her. Let me know what to do.* His prayer cycled in his mind and heart.

With little thought to propriety, he hauled her onto his lap dragging her tighter to him. Sobs wracked her lithe frame, and he began rocking her as if she were a small child. Pressing a light kiss to her hair, he stroked her back in a soothing rhythm.

Her tears slowed. She sucked in a deep breath, exhaling with a low whistle.

Warmth oozed through him with the light touch of her fingers on his chest. He lifted her slightly, forcing her gaze to his. Her eyes were sprinkled with the fresh dew of her pain.

"I'm sorry," she whispered.

"No sorry needed," he said with a quick peck to her forehead. But the brief touch sparked a trill of flashes through his body, awakening a new consciousness of her in his arms. Searching her eyes, he saw the grief retreat, replaced with something he couldn't quite identify.

"If you want to kiss me, Taylor, just put your lips together and go for it."

Her words froze his hand in mid-stroke. Sucking in a deep breath, he gently lifted her from his lap and set her on the smooth floor.

Shoving away from the wall, he stood and placed three long strides between them. What was he doing?

Was he really ready to kiss Charlie? Again. Bent's Charlie? The woman who'd caused him nothing but trouble for the last few months? The woman whom his soul screamed to protect and save? His heart thumped against his chest with the answer: yes.

Scrubbing his face, he snatched a bottle of water from the table and swallowed nearly the entire contents in one gulp.

"I guess that answers my question," Charlie muttered. "It's just a kiss."

The water bottle crumpled in his grip, and he tossed it into the recycle bin by the door. With a quick twist, he closed the three steps separating them, yanked her into his arms, and tilted her chin up. He barely grazed his lips across hers. "A kiss between us will never be just a kiss." His mouth took possession of hers.

She dissolved into his embrace. He drew her tighter against him. The sizzle of lit fireworks tingled through his entire being, ignited by the touch of his lips with hers. Time. Questions. Worries. Death. Pain. Everything slipped from his vision as he melted into her.

Before he fell over the edge of reason and no return, he broke the intimate connection. With a heavy-lidded gaze, he searched her face for answers to questions he was afraid to ask.

"Well…no one would ever call you a liar, Taylor."

A soft tilt to her full lips filled him with an inexplicable joy.

"That was definitely more than just a kiss."

Resting his forehead to hers, his mouth stretched to a wide grin. "We're in trouble, Charlie."

25

Tiny ice chips melted against Georgie's lips as she sipped from the frosted mug of root beer. The tangy sweetness tasted bitter in her mouth as her mind retraced the last few hours, reliving the horrors Charlie revealed with whispered stories. How could she not have known what her sister endured for the majority of her life?

"Penny for your thoughts?" Cade asked. He settled on the barstool next to her as they waited for the pizzas.

She shifted her gaze from the strong-shouldered FBI agent to the dark paneled walls of the corner pizza shop. She'd come here often as a child, taking swinging steps between her parents' protective grips after innumerable home Bombers' games. Her childhood had been loaded with sticky summer nights, sweet as cotton candy, and parents who thought everything she did was angel kissed. But her sister hadn't been so fortunate.

The wet warmth of a tear slid down her cheek, and she felt the gentle touch of Cade as he squeezed her shoulder. Scrubbing her face, she twisted to face him. "I don't think there are enough pennies on the planet to pay for the crazy twists and turns of my thoughts tonight."

"Try me." He tucked a stray piece of her wild hair behind her ear, shooting errant sparks under her skin.

"I just don't understand..." She paused, unable to put into words what she was feeling.

"That's a pretty broad start, Georgie. Do you want to get a little more specific?"

Lifting her gaze to his dark, mossy green eyes, she felt her throat tighten against the words. She swirled her fingers over the warped grain of the bar. Where was she supposed to start? With her sister who'd been the maudlin villain in every Dixon drama for the last fifteen years? Or her father whom she'd thought nearly walked on water but in fact left his precious little girl in the care of the wicked? Or with the sweet man she'd found nearly drowned and still neatly dressed in his New Year's Eve tuxedo this afternoon?

No words would squeak through her lips. Giving words to the revelations of the last twenty-four hours would make all of it real. And she desperately hoped she was in the throes of a horrible nightmare.

He cupped his hand over hers, halting her fingers twisting journey. "It's a lot to take in."

She snorted a strangled laugh through her lips. "You think? My sister just spent the last few hours telling us what she's endured throughout her life. And, that just tops off me finding her best friend swollen with creek water, barely alive. Our house catching fire. Oh, and, Charlie was nearly killed with a car bomb. I'd say 'a lot' is an understatement, Special Agent Murphy."

"Cade. Please. Call me Cade."

Georgie bit her cheek against the warmth pouring through her at the simple permission. "Cade," she whispered. "How can you be so calm? I know she's my sister and it makes her story all the more horrible to me. But how can you take it all in as if...as if you were watching a boring play?"

"What do you mean?"

"I saw you tonight." She tugged her hand from his. "Barely registering a word Charlie said. Just watching her. Waiting for her to make a mistake. Admit it. You think she's involved with all of this somehow, don't you?"

Cade chewed on his bottom lip, but his face remained smooth, unwavering. "Georgie, I don't know what to think about your sister. I want to trust her, but until tonight she hasn't been cooperative. And, as far as Dylan and I know she might be misdirecting us on purpose."

Georgie stood with a start. "How dare you?"

Cade clamped his hand over hers. "Listen. I want to believe her, but it's my job to remain impartial. Your sister's story is...well, let's just say it's more than I thought it would be."

"But can't you see how much pain she's in?" Georgie choked on her words. Tears flooded her vision. Her breath came in short clips. "Charlie's been...protecting everyone...since she was little."

Cade's thick fingers squeezed her shoulder. "Georgie, can you tell me about your mother's death?"

She twisted on the barstool and stared straight into

his eyes, devoid of emotion. "What kind of person are you? Why are you asking about my mother's death?"

"Your sister mentioned she came to visit Mrs. Dixon when she was receiving treatments for cancer. But our records show your mother died in a car accident."

"What are you implying?"

"I just wanted to know about the events surrounding your mother's death."

"You think Charlie was involved. Don't you?"

"I don't know what to think. That's why I'm asking the question. How did your mother die, Georgie?"

She sucked in a deep breath. The images of her mother's mangled body and battered face, so badly damaged her wake was closed casket, flashed across her mind. Georgie had been young, but her father believed she needed to see her mother in death for closure. The tortured memory haunted her through her teens and even today she felt weighted down by the sharp images chiseled into her brain. "She was on her way to treatment. She'd been out of the hospital for a while. I didn't know at the time, but my mother was in palliative care. The doctors agreed to let her live out her final days at home. There wasn't much that could have been done for her. Anyway, Daddy hired a driver because he couldn't take her to treatment that day. The driver lost control of the car. The driver died on impact. My mother died within an hour of arriving at the hospital. Her body was so weak at that point, she didn't have much left in her to fight."

"Based on your sister's story, do you think she had anything to do with your mother's death?"

"No! Of course not. You heard how much she loved my mother. Charlie couldn't be connected." *Could she?*

Cade tugged his gaze away from Georgie. "I think you're right. I just wanted to check my gut. As much as I try to be impartial, I sometimes have a hard time separating my emotions and my logic. This case has pressed my ability to remain neutral to its haggard limits."

Georgie shoved the sudden doubt out of her mind and focused on Cade's words.

"I understand your blind loyalty to your sister. I felt that way about my brother."

"*Felt?*" *Past tense?*

"My brother, Aaron, died. Drug overdose. He was an artist. Free thinker. He made a ton of mistakes and I was always defending him to my parents or making excuses."

She stretched her fingers and cupped his broad hand with hers. "I'm so sorry."

His lips tightened to a thin line. "He was my best friend. The only person who ever seemed to understand him was my fiancée."

"Oh, well, it's good you had her." She slid her hand from his. Regardless of whether the comfort was platonic, or the something more her subconscious began to tempt her with, she shouldn't be touching a committed man.

He twisted to face her. "But I didn't. Not really."

He sighed. "I shouldn't be telling you this."

"We all need to share. If we don't, we will explode with the burdens we carry. Why do you think you didn't have your fiancée?"

A grin, that didn't reach his eyes tugged at his lips. "I found out a few weeks after Aaron's death that Heather was pregnant."

"Oh, well, I guess that happens sometimes."

"Except I'd been at Quantico in training for four months when my brother died. Heather was only two months pregnant."

"Cade, I'm so sorry."

"My brother was the father. Apparently long before I left for training, they started an affair. Brought together by their mutual addiction." He dragged his gaze from hers, shaking his head. "I was so focused on pursuing my dream I couldn't see that I was losing both my brother and my fiancée to a dark world."

Georgie didn't have words to comfort him. The revelations of the past twenty-four hours were too much for the soft and gentle life she'd known. How was she supposed to offer the hand of grace to this man she barely knew? *Lord, please give me the courage and the wisdom to share Your love and peace.* "Cade, sorry isn't sufficient." She sucked in a deep breath. "Were you able to reconcile with your fiancée?"

He shrugged. "I was so angry with her…"

"Justifiably…"

"I don't know about that, but my anger at her and my brother sliced through me. She tried. Begged for my forgiveness. But I couldn't. Their betrayal was too much." He lifted his gaze to hers. A soft sheen of tears glistened. "And my inability to forgive was too much for her. Heather overdosed two weeks after my brother's death."

Georgie stifled shock burning in her throat. She smoothed her hand across his taut shoulders and squeezed.

He swallowed deep, drawing a long breath. "Their deaths motivate me. But they also make me leery of any sad story. Including your sister's."

With a soft nod, she slid her arm back to her lap and tilted her head to meet his gaze in the back-wall mirror. "Well, I guess I'll just have to convince you Charlie's innocent." *Shouldn't be hard. As soon as I convince myself.*

26

Charlotte's steady breath fogged the window, giving the ballpark's lights an ethereal glow. Ignoring the subtle sounds of her sister playing hostess, doling out pizza slices and sodas, she tightened her grip on the window sill. In the distance of a memory, she could hear the sounds of summer.

Cheers, cracked bats, and clean strikes snapped in a catcher's mitt. Her eyes drifted shut and she melted into the innocence of summer days, longing to drown in their delicious sweetness. She could almost ignore the hushed, urgent conversation between Murphy and O'Neal, huddled around Mac's kitchen bar chomping on pizza. They were deliberating her sentence.

Was she a liar or a patsy?

She wasn't sure she knew the answer.

"Charlie."

Hauling open her eyelids, she stared directly into Mac's fuzzy reflection in the window.

"Why don't you come eat some pizza?"

Shaking her head, she settled her gaze back on the ballpark.

"You need to eat something." His words were low and laced with compassion.

Her heart sped. She sucked in two short breaths

against the tears fighting for control of her vision. Spinning away from the windows, she stalked past him toward the front door. "I need some air." Yanking the door open, she slipped on the worn flip-flops in the entryway. She took two tentative steps across the threshold, her feet nearly walking out of the shoes.

"Where do you think you're going?" Murphy yelled after her.

She kept walking. Gaining speed with each step, she tottered on the blacktop-patched brick streets, finding her balance. Lengthening her strides, she began jogging. The flip-flops caught against the dragging fabric of her borrowed sweatpants. With a hopped step, she tugged off each shoe and stretched her legs long.

The night chilled against her heat flushed cheeks. Misty air plastered her hair against her forehead. Her speeding heart paced with the pounding of her bare feet against the slick bricks. Weaving through the deserted streets, she skipped over the rounded curve of the sidewalk, and broke into a sprint down the narrowed walkway to the back entrance of the ballpark.

The gate was secured with a four-inch-thick chain wrapped through the slick wrought iron bars, but she remembered many steamy summer nights when she couldn't sleep and Daddy would bring her to his private sanctuary. Memories floated like cherry blossoms in a spring storm. Wisps of stories, of a time when day games filled the schedule because only God's light would do for His sport and of tall tales of barely mortal men who could make sparks fly with a swing of round bat. The long-hidden memories twisted through her, spikes against the frozen surface of her heart.

Dabbing her cheeks with the back of her hand, she wove through the turnstiles and stopped in front of a long brick wall filled with the names of fallen war heroes. With a tap against a brick marked with a single star in honor of those unknown who gave their lives for the freedoms of the United States, she heard the hollowed promise.

Sliding her slim fingers around the edges, she gently tugged on the brick, releasing silt, dust and the hollow center of her father's favorite hiding place. A single key on a baseball bat keychain slid into her palm. The cool metal warmed in her hands–a calm promise soothing her soul and steadying her heart.

Her bare toes curled against the rough concrete as she closed the small distance between the Wall of Heroes and the entry gate. The key notched against the lock with a click, releasing the gratifying clank of rusted chains against the iron bars. Shoving the bars, she wiggled through the opening and stepped onto the concourse.

Her long strides gobbled the twenty stadium steps to the sunken field below. Tossing the flip-flops onto the manicured grass, she hopped the low fence separating the game from the fans.

Wrapped in a heavy black tarp, the infield waited for the break of spring sunshine through the clouds, but the outfield stretched like a welcome green blanket of soft summer grass. Her toes dug into the dirt as she stretched her legs to begin a slow jog.

Her feet pounded against the packed clay that quickly transitioned to scratchy, winterized grass. Charlotte's pace quickened, creating her own wind tunnel. Stretching her arms away from her sides, the t-shirt transformed to wings, and she felt as if she were flying. Tears slashed across her cheeks as she spun on her heel against the warning track dirt, slowing her pace to a jog.

She dragged a cleansing breath through her nose, her heart slowed to the pace of her steps. Bracing her hands against her lower back, she tilted her head and blinked against the sparkle of the stars pressed into the black velvet sky. A single star raced across the sky before darting into the darkness.

"Make a wish."

She snapped her head toward the dugout. Peace poured through her, blanketing the anxiety and fear threatening to consume her.

With ankles crossed, Mac leaned against the dugout entrance.

"Why would I make a wish?"

Shoving against the dugout bar, Mac's long stride closed the distance between them, meeting her at centerfield. "Shooting star," he said, pointing skyward. "You have to make a wish."

Charlotte laced her arms, hugging her waist with a shrug. Despite the mountain of wishes and hopes she had screaming to be answered, she couldn't focus on one as the priority.

Should she wish Mama wasn't a murderer? A wish for Georgie to be safe? A wish to close her eyes and wake up yesterday, last week, or last year—before her life turned into a made-for-TV movie? She had plenty of wishes, but history taught her not to place hopes on anything but her own skill. Wishes were for dreamers. Her dreams twisted to nightmares. "I'm not much of a wisher."

"If not a wish, then how about a prayer? A simple prayer to the Lord that you and your overly protective sister can make it through the New Year without being arrested."

"What? What's wrong with Georgie?"

"Special Agent Murphy thinks you made a run to your Mama." Brushing hair behind her ear, he slightly squatted to link his gaze with hers. "Georgie hid his cell phone to keep him from calling the police."

"She shouldn't have. I wasn't running." She said with a shrug. "I said I needed air. Just air. Why's everyone so touchy?" Twisting away, she shuffled toward the warning track. "How'd you find me?"

"Didn't take too much deductive reasoning."

His chuckle sent a shiver down her spine. Swallowing against the lump growing in her throat, she spoke to the outfield wall. "Now that you found me, could you leave me alone?"

Mac shifted to stand beside her. "No, Charlie. I'm not leaving."

He stepped onto the warning track clay directly in front of her. "I think one of the major problems is all of the people who've left you in your life actually left when you demanded it." His long fingers squeezed her shoulders. Heat flowed through her with the simple touch. Human kindness. Such an exotic gift.

"I'm not leaving you alone," he said. "I'm not letting you run. I'm not going. I'm here, Charlie."

Tears burned her vision. She didn't deserve his support. She deserved to have Murphy chasing after her. She should be hopping a plane back to New York or California. Anywhere far from Georgie, Mac, Remy, and the family. Maybe she should be in jail. Her family would be safer if she was away. Wouldn't they? Her heart screamed in protest.

Her family. This odd collection of blood relatives and new-found friends was now as vital to her as the air she sucked into her lungs. Somehow, in a few weeks, the people she'd kept at an icy distance for nearly three decades had stitched themselves as a healing cover to the years of agonizing scars slashed across her heart.

Part of her understood the connection with Georgie, Savvy, and the extended aunts, uncles, and cousins. Through the years of friendship, Remy had kept her southern roots close with the sweet scent of night blooming jasmine and a kaleidoscope of anecdotes.

Remy. What would she do if he didn't wake up? He was everything pure and right about her childhood. And he was barely clinging to life because of her.

"Taylor, you should get as far away from me as you can. Look at Remy. He's in the hospital…in the ICU… because he chose to be my friend."

"No, he isn't. Remy isn't in the hospital because of you."

"How can you be sure?" she whispered. Dragging her hazy gaze to meet Mac's eyes, she choked against the surge of grief threatening to drown her in the swell.

"Because you didn't cause his accident."

"But if Murphy is right, my mother is behind..." She couldn't say the words. She couldn't even think them. The possibility her mother was the monster the FBI believed her to be was inconceivable. She couldn't, wouldn't, believe Mama was capable of...

No. Her mother was many things. She was a selfish, neglectful mother, but Charlotte couldn't believe someone she shared DNA with was capable of the atrocities Special Agents Murphy and O'Neal outlined.

Wrapping her arms around Mac's waist, she buried her head in his chest. Every part of her shivered and warmed. His arms tightened around her.

"We'll get through this, Charlie," Mac said with a soft kiss to the top of her head. "Together."

They stood half on the outfield and half on the warning track, her toes burrowed into the thick clay. The mix of rough grass on her heels and cold, soft dirt squishing between her toes settled her broken spirit. The simple memory of running barefoot through the outfield as a child was a gift outlawed at home for fear of fire ants and hidden nefarious creatures in the wide expanse of grass and marsh.

But the ballfield was safe.

At the ballpark she was free. She didn't have to

wear dresses, say the right words, or dab the corner of her mouth with a napkin. Here she could run barefoot as fast as she wanted, scream at the top of her lungs, and Daddy would just laugh and holler at her to steal second. In the sanctuary of baseball, she'd asked him outrageous questions, and he always had an answer. Sometimes quick. Sometimes after a long, thoughtful pause. But she always knew that within the green walls and dirt track of the Bombers' ballpark, answers to the hardest questions could be found. The ballpark was the one place she felt safe. Tonight was no different than the hundreds of summer days and nights she'd run the bases. She'd come for a specific reason.

She needed answers.

"What if..." she whispered into Mac's chest.

"What if your mom is the horrible person the FBI believes her to be?"

Leaning back, she nodded.

He shrugged. "What if she is?"

She pushed away from him with a sigh. "If she is...that makes me..."

"That makes you what, Charlie? I don't see what your mother's crimes, if she's committed any—and we don't know that she has—have to do with you."

"You can't? What they are accusing her of is more horrible than my brain can process. My mother wouldn't have won any mother-of-the-year contests, but she's still my mama. I can't believe she could really be responsible for taking another person's life or orchestrating the laundry list of criminal activities the suits have tied to her, but..."

"But you suspect her of something, or you wouldn't have hired Remy."

"Yes, but, suspecting. Having a hunch that something terribly awful is happening is entirely different from knowing it definitively."

"Then find out."

"How am I supposed to do that, Taylor?"

"Ask her."

Her mouth dropped open. "Did you get one too many concussions blocking home plate? You want me to ask my mother if she's a criminal mastermind who orchestrated the near drowning of my best friend, planted a bomb in my car, and laundered money through my art gallery to support a human trafficking ring. Seriously?"

"How else will you find out?"

"Let the FBI do the FBI's job."

"They've done their job, but you can't believe the evidence they've uncovered. And frankly, I'm having a difficult time believing all of it, too."

"Really?"

"Really. I trust your instincts, Charlie. Even though those instincts can be a little sneaky and tend to be less than forthcoming. You're smart, and you know your mother better than anyone else."

Pinpoint shivers raced through her body.

He believed her?

He trusted her?

How was that even possible?

From the moment she'd arrived in Colin's Fancy

for the funeral and the reading of her father's will, she'd pitted her spirit against his.

And yet, at every turn, he met her anger with honesty and fairness.

He told her when she was being awful, comforted her when she was in pain, and protected her when she was at her most vulnerable. In spite of the litany of crimes associated with her mother, and by association with her, Mac Taylor wasn't giving up on her. His unwavering support merely waited for her to embrace it. If she wasn't careful, she would fall in love with Mr. Cranky-Pants Taylor.

Maybe she should follow his lead and simply start with trusting him. Completely. Could she? "So, just ask her?"

"Everyone is innocent until proven guilty," he said, shoving his hands into his front pockets.

"Sure, but the scales of justice are slanted with the heft of the accusations against Mama. They're tilted so heavily I'm surprised a reality show hasn't been pitched about their weight."

"Innocent until proven guilty. All the evidence against your mother is circumstantial. Granted, its solid evidence. But nothing is concrete."

"Do you ever turn the lawyer off, Taylor?"

"Yes. But I never turn off my desire to see justice served. Your mother deserves justice."

"How can you be so sure?"

"Because everyone deserves justice, Charlie."

27

Cold leather scratched at the back of Charlotte's knees as she slid onto the backseat of the classic, black town car. The driver scurried around the front of the sedan, slipping into the driver's seat.

"Where to miss?"

"Park and 82nd."

Charlotte snuggled into the thick leather, closing her eyes against the familiar graffiti lined path connecting the waterfront of LaGuardia to her beloved Manhattan. She'd hated leaving South Carolina with Remy barely clinging to life. Her best friend needed her, but the only way she knew to help was to return home.

Her return wasn't to her gallery, apartment in SoHo, or the trendsetters of Lower Manhattan. She wouldn't be dining in Little Italy or spending the afternoon reading a book in Washington Square Park. She wasn't returning to her life. She was entering her mother's world in the hope of answers to her never ending questions.

Three weeks earlier, Charlotte and Mac returned to his apartment after her ballpark confession. She'd barely crossed the threshold when Special Agent Murphy began threatening her with obstruction charges, raising his voice several notes above charming. Mac flipped off his lawyer switch, and both Georgie and Dylan were required to keep Mac and Murphy from using each other's faces for sparring instead of the heavy weight bag greeting visitors at the front door.

Murphy's temper quickly simmered with the announcement Charlotte was willing to fly to New York to ask her mother the tough questions and testify against her if the answers were as the FBI suspected. The federal agents' faces flashed relief, but Georgie screamed in protest.

"It's too dangerous." Georgie spat after she dragged Charlotte into Mac's make-shift home office.

"I have to know, Georgie. I have to know if my mother is who these men think she is. My mind believes them. It's logical and their facts are reasonable."

"But..." Georgie filled in the pause.

"She's my mother. Although sometimes it feels as though it's merely a DNA connection, she is my mother and my heart needs to believe she has a moral compass bigger than a cereal puff."

"I can understand," Georgie said, but her words didn't connect with the worry stretched across her face.

What Charlotte didn't say was she could believe her mother's moral compass was so shallow as to involve herself with men who used the depravity of the world to lead a life of luxury. Her mother always chose herself above everything and everyone else in life. Her mother was superficial and self-centered, but could she really be at the center of a criminal organization? Charlotte was about to discover the answer.

"Here we are, miss." The driver's subtle Bronx accent pulled her from her thoughts.

Charlotte glanced out the window and up to the twenty-eight-floor building her grandmother had called home since refusing to return to the familial apartment she shared with her husband, for decades, after his death. Handing the driver a few bills, she thanked him and stepped through the car door opening.

"Hello, Mr. Raymond." Charlotte smiled at the aging doorman who seemed to be always present in her grandmother's building.

"Hello, Ms. Dixon. Will you be staying with your grandmother?" he asked as he lifted her bag and hustled to the front of the building. He propped open the glistening glass door and ushered Charlotte and her carry-on bag through to the spacious lobby.

Glimmering with subtle chrome and low leather chairs, Babushka's new building was a stark contrast to the entrance leading to the six thousand square foot apartment that had been the home of Bickfords for decades. Five years later, Charlotte still struggled with the loss of her grandfather's study and the comfort of his worn leather furniture. When she complained to her grandmother about the sudden change of residence, Babushka's response was simple and final. *"Death is end. I want beginning."*

She followed Mr. Raymond into the elevator and

slipped off her wide-framed black sunglasses. "I'm sorry. My mind was somewhere else. You asked me if I was staying with my grandmother. Yes. But only for a day or so."

"Are you liking...where is it you moved?"

"South Carolina. Yes, but I needed to come home to check on the gallery and Baba. How has she been?" Doormen knew more about the residents of their buildings than a family doctor who spanned five generations.

"She's been doing as well as can be expected. She meets the ladies once a week for cards and tea. And of course she has her duties at the church."

"The church?" Her grandmother had only attended church twice a year, at Christmas and Easter, Charlotte's entire life. Having been raised in post-Revolution Russia, where religion was outlawed in favor of communism, her grandmother had little use for the ritual of the church of Charlotte's grandfather.

"Of course. Your grandmother attends St. Nicholas. She has since she's lived here. I thought you knew. Figured she'd been going there the whole time she's been in New York. Kinda a bit of the motherland, right?"

Charlotte nodded, but the knowledge her grandmother was claiming to attend church for the last five years twisted at her belly. Had Charlotte been so self-focused that she'd missed her grandmother's newfound devotion to God? Or was she fooling everyone else?

The doors to the elevator shut and thoughts of her

grandmother's faith were suffocated in the sweltering heat of the four by six-foot metal box. Mr. Raymond pressed the button to her grandmother's floor and Charlotte swallowed against the growing lump threatening her air.

Soft strands of sweat stretched across her forehead. She gripped her leather gloved hands together releasing a squeak against the gentle music playing over the speakers nestled in the ceiling. Resting her head against the cool paneled wall, Charlotte could hear each click of the lift zooming to its destination. And she began counting the floors as each passed.

Four…

Five…

Six…

Seven…

Ding.

The doors opened with a swoosh revealing her grandmother's gleaming white foyer. Charlotte tumbled into the open space and sucked in a burning lungful of air.

"Are you OK, Ms. Dixon?"

She nodded. Snatching a folded bill from her wallet, she thrust it into his hand.

With a tip of his cap, the doors slid closed, only to reveal her drained complexion in their fuzzy reflection. Pulling a handkerchief from her pocket, she patted her forehead and cheeks, sucking in three more heart slowing breaths.

"May I helps you?" The high-pitched voice held

the rhythm of Eastern Europe, and as Charlotte turned, she recognized the new housekeeper her grandmother hired.

"Hello, Marta." She stretched her hand in greeting. "It's good to see you. I don't know if you remember me. I'm Madame Bickford's granddaughter, Charlotte." She tugged at her gloves and slipped off her cashmere wrap coat, handing both to the diminutive blonde draped in a chambray shirt dress.

Marta nodded and pointed toward the east end of the expansive flat. "Your Babushka id in zee sitting room. You'se expecting?"

"No. But I had some business in the city and my loft is leased out for the year. I was hoping to stay in the spare bedroom."

Marta nodded and turned, her sneakers squeaking against the marble swirled floor.

Charlotte fell into silent step behind her.

The apartment her grandmother selected was draped in the golden opulence she favored in her bedroom and personal study at her previous home. Without her husband's conservative pallor to soften her tastes, Baba's home sparkled like a jeweled encrusted rainbow.

Lifting her free hand, Marta wrapped her knuckles softly against a twelve-foot Christian door with gold set inlays and a gleaming handle, sparkling in the early afternoon sun. With a crack of the door, Marta whispered. "Madame, your granddaughter iz heres."

Charlotte tapped the maid's shoulder and slithered by her into the study with walls lined floor to ceiling in books stacked like neat soldiers on cherry shelves.

"Baba?" Charlotte said. Her voice held a tremor of shock at the sight of her grandmother, draped wrist to ankle in black, a small patch of dark lace covering her brilliantly white waist length hair, twisted neatly in a French knot. When was the last time Charlotte had visited her? Had Baba been in deep mourning without Charlotte noticing?

Baba lifted her gaze to meet Charlotte's, their dark depths flashing surprise. "Dorogoy! Oh, my dear. What surprise! Did I knows you coming for visit?" She stood. The elegance of her decades of training with the Bolshoi Theatre Ballet melted through each wide-armed step toward Charlotte.

Nearly a foot shorter and teetering on ninety years old, Alloochka 'Alla' Bickford was anything but fragile. Snatching Charlotte to her chest, she chuckled. "I care not if I knows you comings. Your face makes heart smile."

Charlotte stepped back from her grandmother. Her lips stretched to a wide grin and all of the acid accusations the agents had been spewing about her grandmother's involvement in her mother's possible criminal activities were neutralized in one Baba cuddle. "Your face makes my heart smile, too."

"Come. Come. We must have zee teas, no?"

"Yes, Baba. We'll have tea."

Baba rang a crystal bell and proceeded to a petite room swathed in cheery yellows. Wide windows with French doors leading to a terrace wrapping the length of the apartment were the focal point of every room. Each piece of furniture in every room faced the expanse of windows. Baba loved the view and wanted every visitor to comment on what a wise decision she had made with her real estate investment. The tiny tearoom overlooked a stunning scene of Central Park stretched out before them and even the low hanging clouds couldn't detract from the beauty of nature in the middle of the concrete jungle.

Baba lowered onto a flowered, high backed chair with thick tufts and stretched her slim fingers toward the matching chair to her left. Charlotte sat, crossed her ankles, and clasped her hands in her lap.

"Tell me. How goes baseball? Do you love more zan ballet?"

"Baba, you know I love ballet, but I have to admit my love of baseball has been renewed."

"Ah, yes. Your baseball." She shook her head. "And everything else iz OK? Your head OK after accident?"

"Yes." Charlotte decided the moment she looked into her elderly grandmother's eyes she couldn't burden her with the weight of the other "accidents" or her mother's unexpected visit.

"You certain, dorogoy?"

"Of course. Why do you ask?"

"Your mama tells me of your friend. Remy? So tragic. Accident on family land. Your pain must be great. You friends long time. All has purpose, no? You find purpose in tragedy. You come home. To family. We help you find purpose."

Charlotte nodded, swallowing against the burning venom rising in her stomach.

Mama told Baba about Remy? Why? Mama hated Remy. Always had. Remy connected her to South Carolina and the Dixons. To a life separate from Stasi.

Sucking in a lung-filling breath, Charlotte rose from her seat and walked to the wide expanse of windows. The chilled early February air pressed against the seams. She cracked open the terrace door allowing the frost outside to battle against the suffocating warmth of the sitting room.

"Ah, Charlotte, you wantz all the cold to freeze you? Close. Close. We must keep warm air." Babushka shouted.

Her words barely registered through the shouts of accusations tumbling through Charlotte's mind. Could her grandmother be involved? Charlotte could barely entertain her distant mother as a character in the FBI's horror story. If her grandmother was...*No. Not Babushka.*

"Ah, the tea." Babushka's lilting voice softened, drawing Charlotte out of her thoughts. "Sit. Sit, myshka."

Charlotte clicked the terrace door in place. The thick carpet muffled her steps back to the chairs.

Marta laid out the tea service and tiny round cakes dusted in powdered sugar.

Sitting in the seat opposite her grandmother, she nodded to Marta who silently left the study. Muscle memory caused her hands to reach for the steaming tea pot, serve her grandmother, and then delicately pour tea into her own cup. The younger always served the elders. Tradition. Family. Bonds that could never be severed. At least not without a very big knife.

Charlotte had such a knife. Was she willing to use it?

28

The tin tap of the winter storm against the triple paned window of Georgie's third floor office fought against the soulful acoustic guitar floating through her desk speakers. The blinking cursor seemed to keep time while taunting her with the pages of contracts she was supposed to read and sign by the end of the day. But her thoughts were at war with the legal phrasing, and the near constant worry over Charlotte.

Her sister landed in New York only two hours ago, but Georgie wished she had chosen any option other than walking into the near certain disaster of a one-on-one meeting with Anastasia.

Cade had promised Georgie that Charlotte would be safe and closely monitored during her entire stay. Georgie wanted to trust his promise.

In the weeks since their first meeting, Georgie thought she'd come to know the heart of the steely federal agent. Through his frequent meetings with Charlotte in preparation for this day, and long chats over coffee, she learned about his family, his love of all things involving Ohio State, and his unwavering passion for justice. Despite her resistance, she liked, even admired, Cade Murphy, but she didn't completely trust him.

Cade still had his doubts about Charlotte's authenticity. He was quick to remind Georgie of Charlotte's slow disclosure of her art gallery's finances and the emotionless mask she wore with every outfit, but Georgie believed Charlotte. Or at least, she wanted to believe her.

She was confident in Cade and Special Agent O'Neal's ability to keep Charlotte safe, but the fact her sister needed two highly trained FBI agents to ensure her safety was the first course of the meal of worry Georgie had been munching on for the last month.

Since the New Year, Georgie's quiet life had been twisted into a tornado of murderous plots, mystery, and mayhem worthy of a Hollywood blockbuster. She'd prayed for so many years to be reunited with her sister. God was definitely working to bring them together. She felt closer to Charlotte every day, and yet her trust of her was straining thin in the light of Cade's accusations. How could her heart's desire cause catastrophe worthy of a national state of emergency?

Charlotte left only hours after the doctor removed Remy's ventilator. Georgie watched from the hall with Mac as Charlotte and Remy's momma held tightly to each other, waiting for Remy's chest to expand on its own.

A few tense seconds passed, but Remy's breaths came, shallow at first but steady. The doctor led Mrs. Reynard and Charlotte from the ICU bay. Remy's ability to breathe on his own was the first step on a long road to recovery, but the doctor was encouraged by his slow but steady progress. The doctor went on to discuss continued concern about swelling on the brain and kidney function, but Charlotte and Mrs. Reynard both looked visibly lighter.

Mrs. Reynard laced her arms around Charlotte's waist. The frozen shield her sister established since leaving Mac's condo three weeks earlier melted into a puddle of soft streaking tears. Mrs. Reynard trembled in Charlotte's embrace. The two women who loved Remy most in the world found solace in the simplicity of human connection and hope in the possibility of his recovery.

Georgie rubbed her temple as the memory pinched her chest. She stood and traced a finger along the path of a raindrop sliding down her window.

Dear God, please continue to heal Remy. And please keep Charlie safe. You are all she has, and she doesn't even know You're there.

A soft knock tugged her from her prayer. "Come in."

Charlotte's administrative assistant, Bridget, slipped through the door, her blonde hair tucked into a tight ponytail and her slim pants hugging every curve of her long body. Something about Bridget's presence chaffed Georgie's sensibilities. She was relatively new to the organization, and Georgie was trying not to judge, but it would be helpful if everything the woman wore didn't need extra inches of fabric. "Yes, Bridget, what can I do for you?"

"Mr. Vasil would like a few moments of your time to walk through the contracts he sent you and there's a Special Agent Murphy on the phone for you. Would you like me to tell him you're busy with Mr. Vasil?" Bridget chomped on her gum between each slowly drawn word, but her lack of decorum could not stifle the flutter of excitement that lifted Georgie's spirit.

"Tell Cole, umm, Mr. Vasil I can meet with him in fifteen minutes. Please connect Special Agent Murphy."

Bridget shrugged and disappeared through the doorway.

Georgie took a few steps and closed the door. Sliding behind her desk, she pressed the flashing red light and sucked in a deep breath. "Special Agent Murphy?"

"Georgie, I thought we'd dispensed with the formality." His voice was low and rich, pouring into her spirit and calming the near constant worry.

"Yes, Cade."

"Better. But unfortunately I'm not calling for social reasons."

"What happened?" An image of Charlie lying in the hospital, head bandaged and unconscious, just a month ago slapped across her vision, and all thoughts of Cade Murphy as anything other than her sister's lifeline vanished.

"Nothing's happened. Your sister arrived in New York as scheduled. She is to contact us when she needs us, but if all goes according to plan, she should be home by noon the day after tomorrow."

Georgie pushed a long breath through her tightly stretched lips. "Good. Good. I have to say I'm as nervous as a long-tailed cat in a room full of rocking chairs."

"Interesting thought."

"Yeah, well, the South has an interesting way of describing emotions. So if this call isn't about Charlie, is it about, umm, something else?" She couldn't stifle the waft from the butterfly wings trembling in the center of her being.

"Unfortunately, I'm calling about the Reynard investigation. I thought you'd want to know. They've just made it public. It wasn't an accident. Mr. Reynard was not intoxicated. The doctors confirmed, he was struck at the base of his skull and then tossed into the creek, with what we can only assume was an attempt at drowning him."

A surge of nausea swelled in the pit of Georgie's stomach engulfing any feelings of anything other than grief. Remy's text message to Charlotte hadn't been a delayed send due to cell phone towers as Georgie had tried to convince her sister. "Someone tried to murder Remy?" She sucked in her bottom lip to stop the deluge of tears threatening to flood her face.

"Yes."

"Poor Remy. How could this have happened? And at Colin's Fancy. I don't understand. Why would someone want to kill Remy?"

"That's something for your county sheriff to determine."

"What? Why aren't you?"

"It's a local matter, Georgie. Sheriff Cambry was generous enough to share an update in the investigation since we were on the scene when Remy was discovered, but it's not our jurisdiction. If they need help, we certainly will be willing to help any way we can, but I have to stay focused on my current case."

"Yes, but…"

"But, what?"

"We don't have much crime here. It's a sleepy community."

"Really? In the week I spent in town, you had a bomb explode, a fire of an unexplained nature, and now an attempted murder. Doesn't sound so sleepy to me."

Georgie sighed. She didn't know why she wanted Cade to help, but she couldn't let the attempt on Remy's life go unsolved. Justice for Remy needed to be served. "It's been a little unexpected, as of late, which is why I can't imagine Sheriff Cambry and his boys are up to an attempted murder investigation. Underage drinking. Illegal poker games. Graffiti in the park. Sure, they'd hit a home run. But murder?"

"Cambry's been trained for cases just like this one. Trust me. He'll want to find the culprit." Static flowed in the silence. Cade cleared his throat. "But I'll let the sheriff know I'll be happy to help in any way he needs."

Relief poured through Georgie. "Thank you, Cade. I can't tell you how much I appreciate it."

"Why don't you show me when I return in a couple days? Dinner?"

The butterflies zoomed in her belly, softening the edges of fear threatening to swallow her whole. "Well, I believe I'd like that just fine."

"It's a date. Let's say, seven the day after tomorrow?"

"Sounds perfect. Just meet me here at the office, OK?"

"Georgie Dixon, you made this cold-hearted federal agent's day."

A giggle bubbled through her lips. She hung up the phone and swirled toward the fogging windows streaked with rain, gleaming like diamonds against the harsh florescent light of her office. She didn't want to think about why or what she felt toward Cade Murphy. Any relationship or even friendship with him would be near impossible. But then again God did like to work in the impossible.

A soft knock and the creak of her door dragged her thoughts from potential outfits and impossible relationships to the present.

Cole Vasil, her friend and coworker who'd been a steady support since her father's death leaned against the door frame. "Good call?" he asked with a smile.

"Yes and no." She stretched her hand toward the chairs across from her desk. "Remy's accident has been classified an attempted homicide. I'm dreading how Charlie will react. She loves him more than a brother."

Sliding onto the chair, he shook his head. "That's awful. Do they know who did it?"

"No, but I'm sure they'll figure it out. But that's not why you're here." She said nodding toward the slim, leather cased tablet tucked against his chest. "You want to talk about those horrible contracts."

The corner of his mouth tilted up. "Shall we?" He

flipped open the case and began outlining the details of a contract for offshore drilling rights near the Black Sea.

Two hours later, Georgie rolled her shoulders and read through the final pages of the contract.

"It all seems pretty straightforward," Cole said. "I just wanted you to know about the few things that seemed out of sort."

"I'll be sure to ask Mac about your concerns. Or would you like to tell him yourself?"

"No, I think he takes your opinions more seriously than mine," he said with a quick wink. Glancing at his watch, he nodded. "It's getting a bit late. You don't want to be driving when you're tired and it's this dark."

Although the night sky had descended nearly two hours ago, her wall clock read only six o'clock and she still needed to review her proposal for the Watershed Foundation board tomorrow. Her only involvement with Watershed Industries, prior to her father's death, had been as a family voice with the company's philanthropic arm. Her proposal to fund a unique music center in an abandoned church a few blocks from the ballpark was one of the last ideas she'd discussed with her father before his disease jumbled his mind. The music center would be an alternative afterschool program for elementary and middle school students. The primary teachers were to be high school students, under the supervision of adults. The Bombers currently had a similar pilot sports program running out of the local recreation center, but many students in need had little interest in becoming the next Beaufort Bomber. There were little boys and girls who shared her love of music and art. She wanted them to have the same opportunities as the athletes. And to ensure her dream, she needed her pitch to be perfect, but perfection would require at least a few more hours work. "I appreciate your concern, Cole, but I need to work through something and want to finish it before I leave this evening." She handed him his tablet.

"Would you like me to wait? There's always more work to be accomplished."

A smile tilted her lips. Cole had the most interesting way of using words. "I appreciate the dedication, but I'll be fine. Enjoy your evening." She swiveled her chair toward the computer desk stretching the length of her wall.

"As you wish." He rose from the chair and tucked the tablet under his arm. "Good evening, Georgie."

"Night, Cole," She mumbled. Her focus locked on her presentation.

~*~

The shrill of her cell phone drew her out of the kaleidoscope of images depicting the future world of the afterschool center. Swiping the screen, she placed the phone on the edge of her desk and clicked the speaker button without looking at the caller ID. "Georgie Dixon."

"Georgiana! I've been worried sick." Savvy's screech twisted Georgie's heart. "You can't not show up with bombs going off and fires blazing on half the plantation. I'm already concerned enough with your sister up North. My heart can't take it, Georgiana. No, it cannot."

Georgie sucked in a shallow sigh and glanced at the large clock centered on the opposite wall. "I'm sorry. I didn't realize it was so late."

"Well, dinner is all but ruined waiting for you."

"I really am sorry. I was..."

"No, I don't want to hear excuses. I heard them from your uncle and your father for too many years to start having them trickle down like DNA memories from your lips."

Reaching for her coat and handbag, she lifted the phone and hurried down the darkened hall to the stairwell. "I'm leaving right this minute. I might drop you because I'm heading to the stairs."

"Don't try that shifty move on me young lady. I know when I'm being given the brush."

"Aunt Savvy, you're breaking up. I'll see you when I get home." Georgie dropped the phone in the pocket of her coat. Resting her forehead against the cool steel door, she released a long sigh. She loved her aunt, but often being the sole focus of Savvy's worry was suffocating.

With a quick hip check to the door, Georgie shuffled into the stairwell. Tentatively, she started down the open crate stairs, her heels sinking into the octagon shaped steel design. As much as she despised this staircase, the metal coffin posing as the elevator to the ground level was one she avoided like the bathroom scale after a two-week vacation. The tap of her shoes echoed against the cinderblock walls as her phone vibrated against her thigh. A smile stretched her lips as she answered. "I'm leaving the office now, Cole."

"I knew I should have stayed to watch over you."

"I'm a big girl." She said, stepping onto the fourth-floor landing. Glancing to her next step, she heard a clink. With a snap of her head, she twisted and went back up the steps. Her heart thumped so loudly in her chest she was surprised it didn't reverberate against the metal stairs. "Hey, Cole?" she asked, lowering her voice to a whisper. "When you left was anyone still in the building?"

"I believe a few cleaning people, why? Is something wrong? Do you need me? I can be right there."

Leaning against the railing, she sucked in a deep breath and willed her heart to slow to a reasonable pace. "Cleaning crew. Of course. Between you and Savvy, I'm jumpier than a grasshopper on a pile of sugarcane." She swiveled and started her slow descent.

Cole cleared his throat.

Her mind must be working on freak out overdrive. She thought she heard it echo. "Cole? Where are you?"

The long pause on the other end of the phone left nothing but the sound of her shoes against the metal grate. She sped her steps. Her heart rapped against her ribs. "Cole?" The clatter of footsteps behind her sent a tremor racing through her spine. A few more steps to the street. She would be OK. Just hustle. At the second-floor landing, she began to run. "Cole, where are you?"

"Why do you ask, Georgie? You know where I am."

She could see the red exit sign flickering just ten steps below her. Tightening her bag to her side, she quickened her pace. The sound of her steps ricocheted against the walls and mingled with heavier footsteps behind her.

Jumping the final five steps to the ground floor, her four-inch heel broke with snap. Pain shot through her ankle, but she limped forward to the door. The threatening thuds closed in behind her. Slamming the metal door open, she shuffled to the side alley that linked the building with the outdoor parking lot Watershed employees were using until the parking garage could be deemed structurally sound.

With each step, pain shot through her leg, but she pressed forward. Her car was only one hundred feet away. She clicked the button to start the engine and her car exploded like a bonfire fueled by gasoline. Stumbling backward, she stared at the orange ball of fury that had once been her vehicle. Shock stunned her in place and Georgie was unable to rip her gaze from the burning embers.

The heavy door rattled open behind her, shaking her from her stupor. She tried to run, but her ankle collapsed under her. She glanced up to the face of her pursuer and calm relief washed over her. "I'm so glad to see you. We need to call 91…"

Smack!

Warmth oozed against her cheek as the last digit

of the emergency number stuck in her throat. Her vision blurred over the familiar face as the world went black.

29

The linen napkin rippled across Charlotte's lap. Crossing her ankles, she straightened the flatware, aligning the fork and knife – like warriors protecting her dinner plate. The din of the restaurant seeped into her consciousness pressing against the screaming fear threatening to swallow her whole.

When her mother suggested a meal rather than their traditional tea, childhood lessons over the dinner table flashed through her body like memory grenades. Did Mama know of Charlotte's plan with the FBI? Could she be setting up her own daughter? Would this be the last dinner Charlotte ever ate? She couldn't worry about how her mother might react. She needed answers and she needed justice.

The pages of missing women connected to Mama's friends Murphy and O'Neal shared with her had eradicated the ability for any true rest in the past weeks. As awful as the gambling, drugs, and money laundering were, the idea her mother could willingly trade human beings as easily as children traded baseball cards terrified Charlotte. Could her own mother be so cruel? And what about Baba? Was Murphy correct? Was her sweet, elderly grandmother aware? Or worse, a co-conspirator? A leader of the corruption? As hard as it was for her to reconcile her mother with the awful deeds...Baba? No, she couldn't imagine.

After leaving her grandmother's earlier in the day, she visited her gallery for the first time in nearly three months. Three new employees and a horrific display by an artist her mother discovered greeted her. The damage of leaving Mama in charge of her passion was evident in each invoice she reviewed and the portfolios of artists stacked in the corner of her office.

She closed the gallery for the balance of the afternoon and sent the new gum-smacking twenty-somethings her mother hired in Charlotte's absence home indefinitely. With a few hours of manual labor and several phone calls to artists she trusted, the gallery was situated. All she could do was pray her mother wouldn't destroy the fixes.

Huh? Had she been praying? Maybe Georgie's love of Jesus was beginning to rub off. What would happen if she started praying for her mother? As if by thinking of her, Mama floated into the room wrapped in a cloud of perfume and chiffon.

She leaned to kiss each of Charlotte's cheeks as she slithered onto the seat just to her daughter's left. "*Malyshka*! My little one, I was so surprised when you called to say you were in the city. Mustn't you stay in South Carolina to adhere to the terms of the will? You don't want *that* woman's daughter to receive all of the money."

"It's lovely to see you as well, Mama." Charlotte twisted the napkin in her lap. "That woman's name was Delia. Her daughter's name is Georgie. And don't worry about the will. There are other, more pressing things we need to discuss."

"Yes, but first the wine." She raised a single hand to the hovering waiter who scurried at the flick of her wrist.

"Mama, you know I don't drink."

"Yes, *malyshka,* but you know I do."

Charlotte rested her slim fingers on her mother's hand. "Tonight, I need you clear headed."

Mama raised her gaze, nearly black as night, and looked at her.

Ice trickled through Charlotte's frame.

"Of course," Mama lifted the glass of water to her lips and swallowed deeply. With a dab of her napkin, her lips twisted to a smile. "What is it you would like to discuss?"

A bead of sweat streaked down Charlotte's back, chased by an artic chill wrapping her in fear. "Mama, I need to know everything."

"What is everything? I have no secrets from my daughter."

"Mama, the gallery..."

"No. We settled that weeks ago over tea," she said with a shake of her head.

"No, we didn't." Charlotte pulled in a deep breath and lifted a prayer, hoping Georgie's God was real. "You know Remy found irregularities in the books. Books you were tending."

"You accuse me?" Mama relaxed into her chair. "Your poor mother? I only worked at your art shop to help you. What do I know of accounting?"

"Mama don't lie to me. Remy found the inconsistencies. Either you are stealing money from the gallery or you are doing something much worse."

Mama lifted a single arched brow. "What could be worse than being accused of stealing from my only child?"

"I don't know, Mama. Why don't you ask those greasy men who seem to flank you everywhere you go these days?" Charlotte said, tilting her head toward the table crowded by the men who'd accompanied her mother to Colin's Fancy.

"They are my protection. You know how dangerous the city can be. Anton ensures I am always protected."

"Mama, Anton Dorokhov is not someone you should be entrusting with your security."

"What do you know of such things? Anton has been a constant support to me. Since I was young, I could count on Anton. He's much like your Remy." She narrowed her gaze and sipped from the glass of wine the waiter had discreetly slid onto the table. "I was sorry to hear of his accident. Such tragedy."

"Don't you dare..." Charlotte whispered.

"Don't I dare what? Console my daughter over the injuries of her dear friend? What kind of mother would I be if I did not comfort you in this dire time? So much loss. First your father, then your house, now your dear friend lies in a coma. Who knows? Perhaps your sister or your aunt might be next."

Charlotte's breath locked in her chest. "If you hurt

Georgie…Savvy…"

"Hurt that girl? *Pfft.* You forget. I am the wounded party." Slamming her open palm against the table, the glasses rattled, threatening to topple. "I've been treated horribly. Locked out of accounts. Accused of stealing from my daughter, when all I've tried to do is be a supportive mother. You should be down on your knees apologizing to me."

"Apologize? Apologize! You've been laundering money through my art gallery to help drug dealers and human traffickers." Charlotte spoke through a clenched jaw. She ignored her vibrating phone in her lap. She'd gone off script. Murphy was likely calling her to put a halt to the 'mission' but she couldn't stop now. The questions swirled with accusations in her chest and she needed to expel them. She needed them in her mother's universe. Charlotte needed to know her mother heard the words from her own lips. She needed to see her face. Her face would reflect a lie or the truth.

"My whole life I've done everything for you." Charlotte sucked back tears. "For a chance to have a taste of your love. I've given up a life with my father. With a woman who truly loved me. All because I wanted your love. Yours, Mama. I wanted you to look at me and not see your mistake, but to see your daughter. But, no, that was too much to ask. Wasn't it? You see me as a pawn. A piece to be used and twisted on a game board. Pulled out when necessary to make a strategic move. Ignored when I get in the way.

"Not anymore, Mama. There's nothing I can do to

protect you. The evidence is clear. You've gambled. You've stolen. You're in the worst kind of debt. You've funded people who are doing horrible things to other people's daughters and sons. But why would you care? You never cared about your own daughter." Tears she couldn't stop streaked down her face, but she ignored her wet cheeks and her phone buzzing against her thigh. "I want to know why. Why did you hate me so much that you would sacrifice me in this way?"

Mama's face drained of color and her hand shook as she lifted the glass of wine to her lips. With a glance over her shoulder, she leaned toward Charlotte. "*Malyshka*," she started with a whisper, her voice a shaky breath of its normal arrogance. "I don't know what to say to these accusations, but I'm disgusted with the thoughts stuffed into your brain. Who have you been talking to? Have you not learned your lessons? Each lie you hear must be countered. You must learn, *malyshka*. Please don't force them to keep teaching."

Charlotte closed her eyes, unable to look at her mother, disgust pouring through her at the sight of the woman who gave her life.

"Ms. Dixon."

The sound of Murphy's voice snatched Charlotte from tumbling into the pit where she teetered.

Fear slashed his face.

"Georgie," her sister's name slipped through her lips with a whisper.

"We don't know. She's missing." His hands were shoved in his pockets, but the unadulterated anger he felt for her mother and her mother's comrades radiated from him like a heater in the middle of Siberia.

Charlotte twisted to her mother. "If anything happens to my sister, I will make it my mission that you never see the light of day again. We are done." Without a backward glance, Charlotte hustled behind Murphy, praying her sister was still alive. She couldn't lose Georgie. Not Georgie.

30

"What happened? Where is she?" The words toppled out of Charlotte's mouth as Cade struggled to keep pace with her long strides.

"I don't know," he said, opening the door to the black sedan he and O'Neal had opted for to observe the mother-daughter dinner.

The dinner? Why had he thought sending Charlotte to confront her mother was a good idea? Cavanaugh was right. He was stubborn and arrogant. And, his arrogance would get someone hurt. Hopefully, that someone wasn't Georgie Dixon.

Charlotte slid in the backseat behind his partner. "Dylan, do you know anything?"

"I'm sorry, Charlotte. Mac called us panicked asking if we'd heard from Georgie."

"How do they know she's missing? Did they try all her friends? Did they call the church? Or that finance kid at the office...what's his name? Cole something? She's with him often."

Cade felt helpless. The call from Taylor shocked both he and Dylan. The stalwart attorney sounded haggard through the spotty cell reception.

Georgie's car imploded nearly an hour ago. The first responders didn't find a body just a charred vehicle leaving few remnants. Surveillance footage from the Watershed building offered minimal clues, but one shimmer of hope. A limping Georgie exited the building moments before the car ignited, but then the footage blacked out. Nothing pointed to whether she was abducted or if she ran.

Based on the last few weeks, Cade knew in the marrow of his bones Georgie was a hostage, but his brain couldn't wrap around the idea of the sweet and funny woman being anything but pampered and beloved. He wasn't sure what he felt for Georgiana Dixon, but the thought of harm coming to her churned his stomach. Stopping his toxic thoughts, he focused on his investigative abilities. Facts, hard work, and sweat solved cases. He hoped this case didn't lead down the path of bad events paving every winding avenue connected to Stasi Bickford. Facts were the only place to start. He shook his head and focused on Charlotte. "There was another explosion. It was Georgie's car."

"What! How are bombs going off in the sleepiest town in the South and no one knows anything?" The steam from Charlotte's rage nearly burnt his neck.

"We know as much as you," his voice sounded broken even to his own ears.

With a flip of the turn signal, his partner glanced at Cade for the go ahead to share. He nodded, unable to deliver any additional bad news. Dylan filled in the details as he drove. "Beyond the video and the investigator's preliminary findings, we are at square one."

"She did this," Charlotte's voice was a murmur

above the chaos crowding their car as they traversed the grid of the Manhattan city streets. "My beloved mother is trying to teach me another 'lesson'."

Glancing in his visor mirror Cade caught the defeated slope of her shoulders as she stared into the streaking city scape.

She's innocent.

With a slight shake of his head, he focused on the road. In the last two years, he never once doubted the multigenerational criminal link of the Bickford women. Every analysis, every bit of evidence, and every hour of surveillance reconfirmed his theory. Despite *bratva* meaning brotherhood, the brains behind this band had to be the beautiful mother, daughter, and grandmother trio. Slam dunk. But in the last few weeks, his theory was reduced to Swiss cheese as he watched Charlotte steel herself against outwardly caring too much for her sister. He no longer believed Charlotte was a co-conspirator. Rather she was as much a victim as the hundreds of missing and dead. Between the evidence she willingly shared and the honest anger she'd expressed toward her mother only moments ago, her innocence was as real as Georgie's belief in her sister.

Fear seeped into the space vacated by his righteous indignation. If he had been so blinded by his need to successfully close the high-profile case, what else had he missed? Did he overlook clear danger in Georgie's world leaving her vulnerable? How much blame would he need to shoulder when they found Georgie? And they would find her. He couldn't fathom any other outcome.

~*~

Charlotte pressed her long fingers against the cool glass of the backseat window.

Georgie was missing.

How had she allowed her sister to be put in danger? For months, years, she'd distanced herself from her father and by extension, her sister, in an effort to keep them safe from her mother's deranged venom. But her sacrifice hadn't mattered.

Remy was barely alive.

Georgie was missing.

What could she do? Who could help her? A single lifeline filtered into her mind.

With a tap of the driver's seat, she asked Dylan to veer from his course to the airport. She needed to make one stop. She could think of only one person who could offer her hope to solve the impossible situation.

31

"Baba, I need your help." Charlotte wasted no time on greeting the housekeeper or being introduced. Her grandmother slowly lifted her gaze from the open Orthodox Bible in her lap to face her granddaughter. The measured twist of Baba's head rooted Charlotte's hasty steps. "I'm sorry to interrupt your solitude, but something terrible has happened and I believe you're the only one who can help me." The shock of seeing her grandmother reading the Bible was eclipsed by her desperate fear for Georgie.

"And the FBI cannot help with your tragedy?" Baba asked with a tilt of her chin toward Special Agents Murphy and O'Neal, hovering outside the entry to the private reading room.

Kneeling beside Baba's chair, Charlotte swallowed against the tears fighting for release. "Baba, its Georgie. Someone's taken her."

"And you should think to come to me for help? Who you think I am, Charlotte? A criminal? How I know of such a crime against the little girl?"

"Of course not!" Charlotte clutched Babushka's frail hand. "But I think Mama…"

"*Nyet!* Stop." Twisting, she looked at the two federal agents. "I will speak alone with my granddaughter. Marta?"

"Yes, madame?" Marta arrived with such expedience; Charlotte wondered if all of her grandmother's conversations were heard in duplicate.

"Marta, please takes officers to kitchens. Give tea and cakes."

Marta nodded.

Visible rejection rippled through Murphy's body, but his partner laid a hand on his shoulder, guiding him to follow the housekeeper to the back of the apartment.

"Baba," Charlotte started, but her grandmother raised her hand and nodded to the open door. With the instruction of dozens of years, Charlotte stood and clicked the heavy door into its frame.

Family conversations, regardless of the nature, were always private. No one, unless of blood, was to hear family business. Charlotte's grandfather was often excluded from the conversations and lessons Babushka had with her. The bonds of blood were greater than the bonds of marriage. Marriage could be dissolved. Blood was forever.

Charlotte padded to the seat angled to the right of Babushka's high-backed, brocade covered chair. With decades of manners hammering through her frame, she sat and waited for Babushka to speak. Silence hovered around the edges of the room, scraping Charlotte's exposed nerves and increasing her question laden anxiety.

"Charlotte, you unwise to come here this night."

"Baba?"

Her grandmother stood and walked to the bank of glass shimmering with the evening light shining from Manhattan's cityscape. Her posture belied her years but whispered of her storied career in the Bolshoi. Clasping her hands behind her back, she surveyed her view as if she were a royal inspecting her queendom. "You know your mother has troubles. But you jumping to conclusion makes worse of bad situation."

"But the situation is only going from bad to worse." Charlotte spewed out all of what she knew about her mother's illegal dealings. From the gambling, to the money laundering through the gallery, to the suspected drug sales, and the horror of human trafficking.

"And you believe Anastasia, my daughter, to be involved in all of this? You believe this of your mother. You think she hurt your friend. Stole moneys from you. Sells drugs to little childrens. Kidnaps womens and sells to mens. For what? Moneys?"

"Baba, I've never known why Mama does what she does. And I don't care anymore. If she's involved in something illegal, she should face the repercussions, shouldn't she? But I don't care about her paying for her crimes. I just want my sister back. All of Mama's choices are connected with Anton Dorokhov. He's the link continuing to feed her gambling problem. To the debt she's accrued with those people. But you have friends in the community, don't you? You know everyone. You know someone who knows something? If you can help Georgie, please help her. She didn't do anything wrong. She doesn't deserve to be sucked into this mess."

"And you do, myshka?" Baba asked, turning from the glass.

Tears burned the edges of Charlotte's eyes, but she fought against the weakness that seemed to plague her since the New Year. Baba would deplore any sign of frailty. Strength was a requirement for all Russians. Regardless of whether her grandmother was involved or if she was unaware of the criminal activities in which Mama was embroiled, Charlotte needed to reflect the strength her grandmother admired. She shrugged. "I was born of her. That is enough to link me to her troubles, no?"

Baba shook her head as she closed the distance between them. Cupping Charlotte's cheeks between swollen jointed fingers, she stared at her granddaughter. "My little one, the Holy Lord Jesus Christ does not ask us to wear the stain of our parents' sins. It is mantle only the devil of this world lays over our shoulders."

Wet streaks burned paths down Charlotte's cheeks. She turned her face, kissing Baba's smooth palms. "The Lord Jesus Christ? Baba, what do you know of the Lord? My whole life you only went to church when you had to...and now you *know* the Lord Jesus?"

Baba's lips stretched thin to a hollow smile. "Even old lady has her secrets, no? Your Papa not like the Orthodox way. He say it all rubbish and icons. I keep my faith silent until he passed. But now, the church she give me comfort. But always the Lord Jesus Christ was near. My mistake was not sharing Him with you and your mama. I not want to upset your Papa. And, yet, the Lord Jesus Christ is near to you, too. For years, I pray in heart. With silence, and the Lord He speaks to my heart. No different than Soviet Union where faith for anything but state was outlawed. Quiet faith is sleeping lion. He sleeps until he roars. You have faith, myshka. Your faith just sleepier."

Her grandmother was a Christian? How could she have missed the signs? What else had she missed in her life?

"Baba, I don't have faith." Tears burned against her eyes. "How can I have faith? Your Jesus, or Georgie's God, neither one will want someone like me. Not with the choices I've made in my life. Not with Mama's choices. How do I not wear her drama like a tattoo, forever emblazoned on my life? I'm Stasi Bickford's daughter. With that comes all of her shame. I can't escape."

"Is it easy to let go of your mother's troubles? Nyet. But you must. She made choices. Now you must own choice of your life."

"But how do I, Baba? Georgie is missing. Remy is barely alive. My life has ripples that are more dangerous than an average person could even imagine."

"But you are no average person. You are granddaughter of Alloochka Anotov who made Secretary Stalin weep with dancing. You have bones built for greatness. Your mother she choose easy path. Silly path. You, Zvezda, my star, you choose hard path.

Make path easier. Ask Jesus help you." Baba's eyes slid closed. Wrapping Charlotte's hands in her tender grip, her voice slipped into her native tongue as she spoke ancient words. "Lord Jesus Christ, Son of God, have mercy on me, a sinner. Have mercy on Charlotte, a sinner. Have mercy on Anastasia, a sinner. Have mercy on little girl, a sinner. Lord Jesus Christ, make haste Your mercies."

Soppy eyes clouded Charlotte's vision, but for the first time in her life, she saw her grandmother. Not as the stoic ballerina who decorated her grandfather's arm or the grandmother who corrected her, but as a child of God. A God Charlotte desperately longed to know.

"Charlotte, are you certain your mother is connected to little girl?"

Charlotte nodded.

"OK. I do what I can. No promises. But you be wary of agents. No person in community help if you allow FBI to intervene."

"But…"

Baba raised her hand covering Charlotte's mouth. "You want sister. No FBI. You must. Blood takes care of blood, myshka."

Kissing Baba on the cheek, she whispered, *"Do svidaniya, Baba. Ya lyublyu tebya."*

"Love you too, little mouse." Baba kissed each cheek and patted Charlotte's hair. "You be safe. May Christ Himself, dispatch His holy angels to protect you. My heart not survive scare for you again. I see if I can help little girl."

Charlotte nodded and rose to stand, slightly dizzy with these revelations about her grandmother, and with fear of once again obstructing the FBI. Good reasons or not, she was struggling with the morality of playing both sides. With two long strides, the space between the chairs and the closed door was gobbled under her feet.

"FBI must go, myshka." Baba's voice floated above the click of the door handle in Charlotte's grip. "Or I not able to help little girl. You do as I say, and I do what I can. You not? Problem out of my hands."

A shudder raced through Charlotte's lean frame fueled by the cold bitterness that poured through her grandmother's sweet voice.

32

"We need to go."

Charlotte's clipped voice snapped Cade from the mental teleplay of excruciating scenarios Georgie could be enduring back to the present. "What did your grandmother say?"

"I said we need to go." The frigid ice wall Charlotte had during their first meeting was slammed back in place. Whatever her grandmother told her closed the door on the focused progress they'd made over the last few weeks. Her concern over her sister's disappearance no longer lingered at the edges of her eyes. Frozen steel replaced any emotion she previously showed.

"OK." O'Neal stood, wiping cookie crumbs from his shirt and mouth. "Marta, thank you for your hospitality. Everything was delicious and you made us feel right at home. Please share our gratitude with Mrs. Bickford."

The housekeeper blushed with O'Neal's generosity. Cade shook his head. With his ruddy face and balding head, O'Neal could charm anyone from a hardened felon to a frightened immigrant. His disarming approach was what made him a lethal interrogator.

"Murph, you ready?" O'Neal lifted a single eyebrow and Cade nodded in response.

"*Do svidaniya*, Marta." Charlotte offered with a nod. Her long strides gobbled the length of the hallway in seconds.

Cade and O'Neal followed behind, with O'Neal continuing to pepper Marta with pleasantries.

Marta pulled their coats from the entry hallway and handed over Charlotte's trench coat.

"Tell my grandmother I will do as she asked, but she must give me what I ask in return." Charlotte gave Marta a narrow-eyed look.

Marta nodded, her eyes shining with understanding.

"Gentlemen," Charlotte said, shoving the door open to the hall. "Shall we?"

Not waiting for a response, she charged toward the elevator and pressed the button with enough force, Cade was mildly surprised the plastic disk didn't fly through the wall to the next luxury apartment building. Riding to the ground floor with only the echo of computer-generated recordings filling the opulent space, Cade stared at Charlotte's tense face and tightly shut eyes. Her hands clutched the edges of the heavy mahogany wood paneling the elevator's interior. Breaths in short spurts. Foot tapping a swift rhythm. Lock tense shoulders.

Awareness dawned on Cade.

Charlotte was claustrophobic.

A compassionate person would try and help the obvious pain unfolding before him. Cade could be compassionate when the situation called for it, but he imagined Charlotte Dixon would spit his care in his face.

The elevator announced their arrival at the lobby and Charlotte hurriedly exited toward Park Avenue. Speaking briefly to the doorman, she clutched his hand in hers. His lips tightened to a thin line as he nodded in response to her words.

The doorman lifted his gaze to Cade, but a shadow seemed to have settled across the jolly man's face. "Sir, I'll have your car brought around momentarily. The front overhang is heated if you want to wait outside." He turned and vanished from the lobby.

"Shall we?" Charlotte asked. Not waiting for Cade or O'Neal, she pushed through to the awning entrance and tightened the belt of her coat against the frigid New York winter air.

"Charlotte," O'Neal started. "Is everything OK?"

"Of course. I have a plane to catch and don't want to be late." She stared into the darkness, huddled in the soft confines of her cashmere coat.

Watching her wrapped in luxury, Cade mentally muttered, but kept his lips sealed in a thin line. *She's warm.* And Georgie could be cold, hungry, injured, or worse. All because she had the misfortune of sharing DNA with this woman. The unending spiral of what-if's pressed at Cade as Charlotte ignored the world around her. "Give over, Miss Dixon." Cade stepped in front of her. "Taylor sent the company jet to expedite your...our...return to South Carolina. There aren't schedules. Just the whim of the wealthy."

Her chin shot up. Her glassy-eyed gaze caught his, tweaking his bruised conscience, but he wouldn't be stopped. "Why did we have to stop to see your grandmother? What does she have to do with Georgie's disappearance? Is she involved with your mother's business? Are you, Miss Dixon?"

Silence. Just the drop of her focus to the roadway beyond them. She stepped around Cade as their sedan hugged the corner and rolled to a stop. Without a backward glance, she slid into the backseat and stared straight ahead.

"Seriously?" Cade muttered. He began to lumber to the car but O'Neal's beefy hand stopped him.

"Lay off, Murph."

"Why should I? Her sister's missing and she's blown the two best leads we have. Why should I give her a pass?"

"Her sister's missing…" O'Neal lowered his voice. "Her best friend is in a coma. She nearly died in a car explosion. Her mother's been stealing from her. And she's turned over evidence against her Mom. She wore a wiretap to try and gain more evidence against her own mother. The average person would crumble under one of those blows, but she continues to fight. Let her fight her way. Don't try and beat her walls down. They'll turn from ice to cold, hard steel."

Cade scrubbed his face with the palm of his hand. "What if we've lost her? What if we've lost Georgie?"

"The more pressing question is what if we lost Charlotte? We may have. You aren't helping us."

Cade opened his mouth to argue, but Dylan's

hand stopped him. "But we'll get her back. She needs us to clear her familial conscience. To right the wrongs of at least one generation of her family. She also needs us to find her sister. And she does need her sister. She won't admit it. But Charlotte Dixon's weakness is her baby sister and she'll do anything for her." Dylan paused as the building valet handed him the car keys. "Regardless, now we've got the grandmother. You did what you needed to do, right?"

Cade patted his empty trouser pocket, crossed his hand over his heart and nodded. While O'Neal chatted about pastries and cleaning products with the housekeeper, Cade excused himself to place microscopic recording and listening devices in the bookshelves that lined the center of Alla Bickford's penthouse apartment. The copy of the expedited warrant approving the surveillance was emailed to him during the ride from the restaurant. The unanticipated stop at the grandmother's apartment was a surprising gift.

When Charlotte agreed to help build the case against her mother, he reached out to his contact in the U.S. Attorney's office in Manhattan and with minimal arm twisting; he had warrants to put both Stasi and Alla under the watchful eye of the Federal Government. Charlotte was aware of the request for the warrant, at least the one for Stasi. Cade and O'Neal didn't share with the beloved granddaughter that they believed her grandmother was likely more treacherous than her mother.

"They're all in place," Cade answered with a nod.

With or without Charlotte Dixon's assistance, he would bring down Anastasia Bickford Dixon-whatever-the-rest-of-her-names-were, and the entire *bratva* in Manhattan. Even if the destruction took a little old lady with it.

33

The city lights nearly vanished in the murk of the Hudson River flowing parallel to the exit out of the Manhattan. Only, a short thirty minute drive to the Teterboro Airport, a drive Charlotte had taken many times with her grandparents to fly back to school or with friends' parents on a trip somewhere her mother wasn't.

Teterboro was the gateway for the elite to travel. Targeted security. Sleek jets. Destinations limited only by the distance the planes could fly and the money spilling from pockets. And today, Teterboro would be how she returned to South Carolina and the growing scrapbook of pain she was creating. Charlotte's vision blurred against the spiraling cables securing the George Washington bridge, but her mind kept sharpening images of Georgie, unconscious, beaten, cold, scared, frightened, broken...alone.

Who could have taken her?

As easy as it would be to blame her mother, Mama looked shocked at the revelation of Georgie's disappearance. But if not Mama, then who? And more importantly, why? Why take a sweet, beautiful young woman? Mopping tears with her fingers, she tried to wipe away the answers fighting to take residence in her mind. But she couldn't let herself register the truth. If her mother wasn't behind the kidnapping, then...

Buzz. Buzz...

The quick staccato of her phone against her thigh pulled her from spiraling thoughts, but the caller ID plummeted the weight in her stomach with a splash.

"Hi, Savvy."

"Hi, Savvy! That's how ya answa the phone? Don' ya know wha's goin' on? Your sista's missin'." Savvy's typically cultured, slow Southern accent jumbled into a quick low country rumble as she spat most of the details Charlotte already knew.

Charlotte allowed her aunt's anger and fear to expel itself through her tirade without interruption.

"When are ya comin' home? We need ya here, Charlie. We all need to work togetha to find your sista."

"Mac sent the plane when he called the security guards travelling with me." With the tenuous status of the FBI's case against her mother, they were unable to share with Savvy her true reason for travelling to New York. Savvy blissfully believed her visit was only to check up on the gallery and visit her grandmother. "I was at dinner when he called and unable to get to my phone. We're on the way to the airport now. We should be home in a few hours."

"Can you call those gentlemen from the FBI?" Her voice slowed to the subtle tone Charlotte had come to find comforting. "The sheriff is on the case and the police are all over Colin's Fancy, just like with Remy...oh, my dear, I'm so sorry..."

"No, it's, OK, Savvy. This is nothing like Remy. I think Mac already reached out to the agents." Glancing at the front seats, she continued. "They may already be on their way." Guilt rose with the bile rolling in her stomach at the half-truths she continued to pour into her relationship with her aunt.

"Good. Good. It'll all be better when you get here. I know you'll know how to find your sister. I just know you will know."

Acid burned at the base of his throat. "Why do you believe I can find Georgie?"

"Because you're sisters. Sisters always find each other. I always knew when my brother needed me. And he always knew when I needed him." Savvy drew a deep breath on the other end. The line went silent.

Charlotte could hear her breath echo to the other line.

"Sweetheart, I know why you stayed away all those years."

Sweat beads pricked her forehead. "What are you talking about?"

"I know. Just know that I know. Anyone who sacrifices as much as you have for your little sister will know what to do. You'll know how to find her. God'll show you the way. Trust Him. I believe in you. Believe in His guidance."

The phone clicked dead on the other end.

Tears slipped down Charlotte's cheeks. If God was her only hope, finding Georgie might truly be hopeless.

34

Ting...Ting...Ting...

Chill seeped into Georgie's bones, permeating every molecule of her being from her numb toes to the backs of her eye sockets where her tears seemed to have frozen in place.

Ting...Ting...Ting...

Consciousness, blessedly, had been in brief spurts, but the soft drip of water against what sounded like a tin pan echoed and drew her to the surface. How long had she been in the tiny root cellar? She assumed her current prison was a cellar. Its muddy mix of broken cement floor, wooden planked shelves, and exposed beams for the sloped ceiling bespoke prior years of rainbow filled jars lining the walls with canned tomatoes, peaches, green beans, and grape jelly waiting for the long winter to come after the harvest of summer.

Swiveling her head she strained to take in the full perimeter of the cellar. A wave of nausea swelled through her frame. Sucking in a deep breath, she tried to slow her heart, but the roll of queasiness continuing to ripple. With another long breath, she struggled to sit against the wall behind her. Both hands were lassoed together. Being bound tugged at her shoulders and made sitting nearly impossible. With each movement, the question of why she was 'captive' seared deeper into her mind. Her last memory was of her car exploding into a ball of flame. And then nothing. Everything was black until the drip.

Her bare heels scraped against the grit and muck mixture masquerading as a floor. Ramming her feet for leverage, slashing pain shot from her ankle and reverberated through every cell as she shoved and scooted until her back rested against the crusty wall. The move showered soot and debris onto her head. Georgie coughed against the fragments falling into her mouth and nose.

Pain whipped through her body.

Her head thumped.

Every joint ached.

The exposed wounds on her hands, feet and face burned with the dirt peppering her skin. But sitting upright had been worth the torture.

The faded daisy chain painted across the crumbling walls and onto the shelves around the room was a slingshot back in time. The paint was chipped and worn but she recognized the childish art. The walls of the root cellar encompassed the last art project she'd completed with her mother before her death.

During a long tornado watch that forced them into the ancient root cellar, Momma kept her focused on perfecting the depth and movement techniques which created the wistful chain of daisies on the walls.

Although, the main house had a large fruit cellar off of the kitchen, she and Momma had been painting by the creek when the storm sirens sounded. The wind had accelerated with the warning sound. Hail and rain whipped around them as they sprinted with their acrylic easel sets, a gift Daddy bought the duo as Christmas 'presence' presents the previous December. Each year he said one present needed to be focused on the gift of being together. The memory warmed her heart, freeing the tears frozen in her eyes.

She was at Colin's Fancy.

She was home.

Worry and fear wafted from her in a haze. This cellar sat steps away from the guest house she shared with Charlie before the fire.

Home?

Dread creeped up her chilled spine consuming the spurt of joy. Her chest tightened. Air seemed to constrict in her throat. Why bring her home? Who would bring her home?

What plan could be successful bringing her to the one place she felt safest in the world?

The one place no one would ever think to look for her.

35

Staring into the hazy sunrise peeking over the charred roof line of the guest house, Mac kneaded between his collarbone and neck.

Georgie had been missing for over twelve hours.

Twelve hours with no note.

Twelve hours with no ransom request.

Twelve hours with no lead other than the scratchy video of her collapsing outside Watershed offices.

Twelve hours after her car exploded in the parking lot.

Rumors were already swirling around town that Bent's girls were cursed. The business brain Bent had cultivated and nurtured in Mac for nearly a decade screamed for the need to bail water out of the sinking ship tied to his daughters. But Mac's heart longed to save his mentor's girls.

He loved Georgie like a little sister. Since the moment she told him to consolidate movements on his throw to second, he'd tucked her under the broad, big brother umbrella. He had watched her grow from awkward teen to young lady in what felt like a blink of his eye. He would walk over hot coals to save her. He just needed to know where she was. He owed Bent his life, and he would find a way to save his daughters.

Georgie and Charlie.

He couldn't explain the invisible connection to Charlie. Mac felt a brotherly affection and protective instinct with Georgie, but with Charlie his desire to save her, to protect her from the world threatening to suck her under, was like oxygen. He couldn't live without her.

When had his feelings for her become a lifeline? Mixed messages seemed to be an art form for Charlotte Dixon. One minute she had an exterior rivaling the best bronze bust in Cooperstown and the next vulnerability poured out of her. It drove his need to protect her with everything in his physical, emotional and mental being. Regardless of what she thought or didn't of him, Mac's heart, his whole person, needed her. He wasn't too proud to admit he needed Charlotte Dixon in a way he'd never thought possible.

Over the last year, he watched from afar as his brother Sean succumbed to the love of his soon to be wife, Maggie, their mutual affection for Christ deepening their romance. But he and Charlie? Even if she wasn't one of the most difficult women he'd ever met, she was his boss, if only on a technicality. And, yet he couldn't deny his uncontrollable desire to protect and pamper her. He wanted to shower her with his love and the love of Christ. He loved her. He loved her and she appeared to barely tolerate him.

He pinched the bridge of his nose, clamping his eyes shut against the ombré marigold sunrise warming the low country morning. Regardless of his burgeoning emotions tangled with Charlie, one fact was undeniably true: Georgie's disappearance was likely intimately connected to his dark-haired beauty.

Somehow Charlie, and more likely, her mother, was at the center of the latest tragedy in a catastrophic set of dominos toppling since the arrival of Bent's prodigal daughter.

But what could be the purpose of kidnapping Georgie?

"They want to hurt me. To teach me a lesson." Charlie's voice floated over him like a whisper.

Pivoting toward her, a sense of peace poured through him, settling in his heart. They may not have a future together, but he trusted there was a purpose to his heart's choice beyond fulfilling Bent's wish for his daughters to find a relationship with each other. And at the moment, his purpose was to comfort Charlie.

He closed the distance between them and wrapped his arms around her gaunt frame. Her arms were laced tightly across her middle, not allowing him to pull her tight. "How are you?"

She stepped out of his protective circle, rubbing her biceps against the chill of the early morning. "How am I supposed to answer that question, Taylor? My little sister, who has never even hurt a bug in her life, is missing. Because of me. Because of my mother. Because..." Her voice broke against the tears streaming down her cheeks. "I don't know how to fix this. I knew the moment I trusted anyone with my secrets, trouble would be quick on trust's heels. First Remy, and now Georgie. Everyone I love is in danger. It's all my fault. I should have kept my mouth shut. Puttered away in

South Carolina. Allowed my mother to ruin the gallery. I could have been a good ostrich. I was for most of my life. Burying my head in the sand. Ignoring the truth. Guarding myself and others against the weakness of my mother. Why didn't they just take me? Why are they doing this? Why is she doing this?"

The weight of her decision to bring first Remy, and then Mac, Georgie, and the FBI into her trust, visibly blanketed her in misery and regret. Doing the right thing often came with consequences most were unwilling to go into debt to pay. Charlie was paying with her very spirit.

Tugging her into his arms, he drew her back, wrapping her shivering body against his chest. Resting his chin atop her tousled hair, he lowered his voice to a whisper. "We'll find her. She'll be home safe and sound, singing in the praise band before you know it." But even as the words slipped out the image of Remy's body kept alive by machines flashed in his mind.

Nothing was certain.

Nothing except the love of God, Mac's love for Charlie, and his desire to bring Georgie home safe. Bent trusted Mac to protect his girls, and he would do anything to ensure they were safe. Even if 'anything' left him with nothing.

36

Charlotte melted into the strength emanating from Mac's embrace. Sealing her vision against the heartbreaking beauty of the warm hued sunrise, she wanted to pretend.

She wanted to pretend today was the start of a glorious day. A day she could use to begin to explore the unexpected desire she felt for the man holding her. A day she could dedicate to joy rather than worry. A day when she could sit in the stands, eat popcorn, and watch the Bombers blow a three-run lead. A day when her biggest concern was finding a partner for Watershed's new series of distribution centers. A day when she could discover a new artist on the boardwalk. A day she could be someone other than the daughter of Anastasia Bickford. A day when she could be anyone else. Anywhere else. But she didn't have the luxury of wistful longings.

Instead of popcorn, partners, and paintings, she had a day filled with palpable fear and panic rising by the minute. Where was Georgie? Was she cold? Hurt? Alone? Alive?

Rubbing her eyes, she shuffled out of Mac's tender hold. She drew in a deep breath and twisted to face him. Salt and pepper stubble shadowed his rigid jaw line, emphasizing the raw masculinity burning under his surface, but his warm brown eyes tugged at her, promised her a safe place to land. Protection from the storms of life. How she longed to settle in the unspoken promise. But she couldn't put another person at risk. Regardless of how much she wanted to lean into Mac Taylor and his island-in-a-storm persona, Baba made her situation very clear. Her circle must be a circle of one. If she wanted Baba's help, and the aid of the ladies tea society Charlotte was certain her grandmother turned to for assistance, she needed to separate herself from Mac, Savvy, and the dozens of police officials who had set up a temporary command center in the dining room of the main house.

How did her life continue to spiral?

"Charlie?" Mac's voice broke through the series of accusations playing on a loop in her mind since Murphy busted into her dinner with her mother.

With a shake of her head, she lifted her gaze to meet the pull of Mac's focus but resisted the silent offer of comfort. "I'm fine. I just want to find Georgie."

"We all do," Murphy said from the door connecting the back porch to the house.

Mac turned to face him. "Do you have any leads? Is it odd that there hasn't been a ransom demand yet? Were the state police able to restore the missing video footage from ballpark?"

Charlotte squeezed his hand. Mac's worry oozed out of him, feeding the panic threatening to overtake her.

Special Agent Murphy shook his head. "Georgie's

only been gone twelve hours, so her kidnappers may still be on the move with her. They may not want to formalize a demand until they feel as though they are safely…away."

The image of her delicate sister hidden and shackled seared her mind. But the thought of what not receiving a ransom could mean was beyond unthinkable.

"As far as the footage, the explosion knocked the video out for a one block radius. But our techs preliminary findings point to the same bomb maker as the hit on your car, Miss Dixon."

A chill chased up Charlotte's spine with the spontaneous recall of being thrown against the cement pylon. Since the accident, she woke nearly every night in a cold sweat with the memory, and now Georgie would likely have the same haunting nightmare.

"Why do they believe the bomb maker was the same?" Mac asked.

"Bombers are like artists. They all have a signature. Most criminals have a 'tell' they don't even realize. That's how we catch them." Murphy tilted his focus to Charlotte. "And I always catch them."

"Good." Charlotte lifted her chin and stared at Murphy. "You catch this guy and you make him pay. No one hurts my family. Whoever this person is, he or she messed with the wrong sisters."

~*~

Charlotte stalked past Cade into the main house.

He sighed and turned to the wide balustrade surrounding the porch.

"She's hurting," Mac said. "You need to start trusting her. She loves her sister. I don't think I realized how much until recently. But Charlie's been trying to protect Georgie, the whole family, from Stasi and the drama connected with her since she was old enough to know the difference between right and wrong."

Cade snorted. "What makes you think Charlotte Dixon has ever cared for anyone but Charlotte Dixon? She cared so much that her best friend is comatose and her sister is missing. That kind of care is catastrophic."

"Listen. I don't know what motivated this vendetta you have against Charlotte's mother, and by association Charlotte, but you have to see that she's been trying to help. Did you ever stop to think how your interference in Charlie's life...your investigation into her mother and her art gallery were the catalysts to her accident, the house fire, Remy's accident, and now Georgie's kidnapping? Glass houses, man." Mac shoved against the railing and headed toward the house. "Watch the stones."

Cade turned his back toward the French doors. Taylor was right. At least partly. Cade had been throwing stones, but they were aimed at his glass house since the call reporting Georgie's disappearance came through twelve hours earlier. If he could go back, stop his investigation, focus on something other than the corruption caused by the *bratva* in New York he would. He wished he had the option. But then again, two years ago when he'd started down this path, if his future-self told his past-self of the destruction attached to his investigation he wouldn't have cared. Nothing would have stopped his insatiable need for vengeance, to destroy the people he held responsible for his brother's death.

He might be able to fool his partner, his boss, and his parents. They believed he was driven by a black and white need to right wrongs and ensure justice was served. But, he knew the truth. In his heart, he wanted vengeance. The Old Testament God he'd heard about when he went to Sunday school as a child may have claimed vengeance for Himself, but Cade felt a longing to enact his own eye for an eye on the *bratva*. And, with sweet Georgie Dixon now missing, and her sister clearly distraught, he questioned whether he had claimed something that was never his.

He stared at the charcoal remnants of the guest house where the two sisters had been living. Had he made the situation worse? If something happened to Georgie would he be able to ever look himself in the mirror again?

"Murph." O'Neal poked his head through the doorway. "You'll want to get in here. We got something."

37

Huddled in the corner, Charlotte felt as though she'd been dropped onto a movie set. The formal dining room was jammed with laptops, police radio scanners, and maps of every county and shoreline along the Eastern seaboard. Every available seat was filled with a menagerie of law enforcement ranging from county sheriff deputies to the South Carolina Law Enforcement Division or SLED. And, of course, the ever-present FBI, including her new bestie, Special Agent O'Neal, who was sipping a cup of coffee, nodding at the information a SLED agent was sharing with him. How was she supposed to follow Baba's instructions and extricate herself from the search for her sister? Dismiss half of the police force in the low country? The idea seemed ridiculous, and yet Baba was clear. If she wanted her grandmother's help, and the help of the ladies' tea society Babushkas, she needed to find a way to separate herself from the team as desperate to find Georgie as she was.

"Hey, Charlotte," Mellie's whispered greeting yanked Charlotte from her spiraling thoughts. With a single shoulder squeeze, her aunt's oldest friend conveyed all of her worry and consolation. When Charlotte arrived at Colin's Fancy the prior evening, she was greeted by Mellie who was the first responder to Savvy's cry for help. Mellie spent the night, soothing Savvy and seeing to the needs of the growing hoard of law enforcement gathered on the first floor of the house. "I need to be getting back to my boys, but you call if you hear anything or if you or Sav need anything, ya hear?" She patted Charlotte's cheek as she turned toward the foyer.

"Oh, I nearly forgot," she said over her shoulder. "Your assistant dropped off some mail needing your attention yesterday evening. Savvy was occupied with the police, so I stacked it in the study. It's on your Daddy's old desk."

Waving a quick good-bye to Mellie, Charlotte closed the door behind her and twisted toward the long hall leading to her father's office.

The door opened with a high-pitched squeak. Few had entered her father's study since his passing. Only the cleaning lady, and Georgie, when she needed to wallow and not let others see. But Charlotte avoided the room entirely, with the exception of Christmas morning.

Everyone in the family had huddled around the kitchen table eating cinnamon rolls and breakfast casserole, and the sheer warmth of familial love chilled Charlotte to the bone. She wandered away from the group, needing air for her lungs and solace for her soul, and stepped across the threshold of her father's private sanctuary with little thought. His scent, a mixture of leather and fresh cut pine, hung in the air like a canopy draping the room in Bentley Dixon. Her fingers traced a long, unseen line across the edge of his desk, over his stuffed bookshelves, and unread newspapers. After her fingers explored his study, Charlotte curled up in one of the two deep mahogany leather chairs angled toward the beveled glass view of the woods connecting Colin's Fancy and the Reynard property. The tears she'd securely locked in a box during the funeral and weeks following released like a spring dam that morning. She'd allowed this room to be the place where she could mourn her father and the relationship she'd never had with him.

And here she was again, lost, with no direction on how to find her sister or bring her mother to justice. She pushed forward into the room, drew in a deep breath of her father's aroma and sank into the odd comfort she found in this space. A comfort she knew she didn't deserve, but one she clung to with the fragments of her life slipping through her grasp.

Embracing the moment of peace, she trailed her glance around the room. Her vision rested on her father's Bible perched on the edge of the reading table. The worn leather was patchy in spots and fringed on the edges. Papers and tabs were shoved, seemingly with haphazard thought, between the binding and fragile pages. Gently lifting the book between her hands, she allowed the cover to open naturally where the pages were marked by a folded church bulletin dated ten years earlier. Tugging the paper from its home she carefully unfolded the yellowing bulletin filled with typed announcements, the order of worship and a sermon entitled, "The Lost and Found". Her father's handwriting was visible across the worn page. Scribbled notes from the message, she imagined. But in the bottom of the bulletin she noticed smudged ink across deliberately scrawled words:

"Prayer for Charlie: Father, find her. Love her. Be with her always. She needs more than I can give. In my weakness she has found strength."

A chill chased a frigid path up Charlotte's spine as her gaze fell from the bulletin to the marked spot in the Bible. Several passages were highlighted with yellow and underlined in black ink, small notes in the margin, but one piece of text was circled in a wobbly line with the simple note: *My Charlie*, in the margin. Her father had circled Isaiah 58:11, *The Lord will guide you always; he will satisfy your needs in a sun-scorched land and will strengthen your frame. You will be like a well-watered garden, like a spring whose waters never fail.*

With delicate fingers, she flipped through the notes and cards stuffed in specific spots. Over two dozen cards had prayers written for her with the notation of Isaiah 58:11 in the place of an *Amen*. A tear cascaded over her cheek and splashed against the open page, damping the black ink highlights. Her father had thought of her. And by the looks of his Bible, his thoughts were more than a passing fancy, but true devotion and longing. He couldn't be with her, so he pleaded to God to step in on his behalf. The hatred mixed with an unknown yearning to be loved and accepted by her father bubbled to the surface. The slow onslaught of tears raced over her cheeks as she hugged the worn book to her chest. "Daddy, help me. I'm so sorry to have quit on you. Please forgive me."

Charlotte didn't know if her prayer was to her natural father or the Heavenly Father she'd been bombarded with from all facets of her life in the past few months. Perhaps her father's prayers for her life had merely been seeds that needed to be watered by a larger circle, because she could now feel love taking root, digging into the parched soil of her soul and challenging her to try and rip Him out.

Breathing in the calm she'd sought all those weeks ago in this room, she closed the Bible and pressed a soft kiss to the binding. "Thank you, Daddy. Please help me find Georgie. Help me forgive Mama."

She laid the Bible on the reading table and glanced toward the stack of mail on her father's desk. The siren call of Watershed Industries pulled her to her feet, and she reached for the thick pile of envelopes. Sorting through the mail, she discounted several pieces from distributors and other business partners as irrelevant for the moment. With a shuffle of envelopes, Charlotte sucked in a deep breath and dropped the stack except a single white envelope.

She twisted the envelope sporting the Watershed logo in the upper left corner. An envelope innocuously waiting for her in a stack of papers from work. An envelope with a broken red 'confidential' stamped across her typed name. Confidential correspondence was always passed in manila envelopes or zipped legal briefs.

Never within corporate stationary.

This note was from the kidnappers. She was

certain of it. Whoever took Georgie was connected to Watershed.

Bile burned through her stomach and raced up her throat. She yanked the wastebasket beside the desk just before her meager breakfast made a repeat appearance.

Wiping her mouth, she snatched the envelope from the desk. Clutching it in her hand she raced toward the dining room. She slid to a stop just outside the door, panting against the burning acid in her mouth and throat. She glanced around the room and tried to figure out who to trust. Where to start?

Mac was chatting with Sheriff Cambry as they leaned over a map of what looked like Beaufort County and the spread of islands dotting the coastline. Georgie could be hidden on any one of those tiny pockets of land. Or north in Charleston. Or New York. Or halfway across the ocean.

Her vision stopped on her FBI tag-a-longs, and she took a slight step toward them just as her grandmother's words rushed through her mind. *"You want sister, you lose FBI. You must. Blood takes care of blood, myshka."*

Could she trust them? She couldn't be certain. And she must be one hundred percent. Georgie's life was too important to risk on her selfish desire to share her burden.

She tiptoed around the mangle of wires connecting all of the monitoring devices and slipped into the kitchen. Snatching a coffee mug from the top shelf, she poured a full cup, sloshing the room temperature brew onto the counter and splashing the mangled envelope.

"Good night," she muttered.

"Well, at least your frustrations are starting to sound Southern." Savvy's low country droll seeped from the breakfast nook.

Charlotte snatched a dishcloth and mopped the coffee. "I can't even seem to pour a cup of coffee anymore."

In the blink of an eye, Savvy's arms were wrapped around Charlotte. The care she'd longed for her entire life seeped through Charlotte in one hug. Tears that appeared to be ever present streamed down her cheeks.

"You listen to me," Savvy's voice was low but fierce. "You did not cause this situation. Any of these situations. Doing the right thing is always the best decision. Sometimes it comes with heartache." She stepped back from Charlotte, squeezing her niece's shoulders. "Your daddy had to make an impossible decision. Fight for you and watch you shredded by your mother or let you go and save his own soul. He fought, just not hard enough. I'm not saying he was right. You should've grown up here. With your family. Friends. He regretted his weakness. Didn't know how to fight your mother. Tried to make amends these past few years. But you didn't, couldn't accept his plea for forgiveness. I understand why. Makes me sad. Made me mad every refusal, but it just makes me sad now. But we can't change the past. All we can do is go into the future with as few past repeats as we can muster." Savvy wiped the tears from Charlotte's cheeks.

"I should never have come here, Savvy. I should

have defied the will. Stayed in New York. Georgie would have Watershed and she'd be safe." Charlotte shuttered her eyes against her aunt's piercing blue inquisition. Twisting out of her embrace, she walked to the window, the feel of the early morning sun warming her face.

"Hush. You're doing your duty. Fulfilling your Daddy's last request. He wanted you girls to know each other. He wanted you to fall in love with each other. To love the business he created. To passionately pursue his baseball dreams. He wanted you to have the joy he had. His girls. He loved you both. Imperfectly, for sure, but love none the less. I hate repeating myself, but you did not cause these situations."

"Really?" Charlotte spat, spinning to face her aunt. "Really? The only reason I jumped at fulfilling the will was the money. The promised salvation to my business. It wasn't some noble gesture to do 'right' by my father. I wasn't coming down here to make nice with a sister I'd spent over a decade keeping at an assured safe distance. I came down here to try and salvage my business. Not to make Daddy's 'girls of summer' bonding dream come true running a baseball team and Watershed.

"I dreamed of being a family with Delia and Daddy and Georgie. But I knew Mama needed me more. Sick twisted need, but she needed more from me than anyone else. And every time I tried to choose this life over a life with her, 'situations', as you keep calling them, occurred. This," she began waving her hands in a circle. "All of this, the car, Remy, Georgie, even the fire. All of this screams of Stasi's jealousy. Granted, the jealousy has escalated from locking me in a closet when I was five so I couldn't see my father or sending pictures of Georgie at day school with a menacing promise written on the back of the photo. But I know my mother. Somehow, she or the people she is associating with are behind all of these situations. I don't know why. She needs the money from Watershed more than I do."

"What do you mean she needs the money from Watershed?"

Charlotte shrugged. "Since I received my trust fund from Grandfather Bickford, Mama has been skimming money from me. Sometimes she asks. Sometimes she demands. Sometimes she just takes. But she always needs money. She has a gambling problem. She likes to play poker, but she's not very good. When I was little, she used to beg my grandfather for money. Screaming and crying at the foot of the stairs. And he would pay her debt, until one afternoon when I was, I don't know eighteen or so, Baba finally said no. No more money. No more 'free ride'. That's when she started skimming from my trust fund."

"You mean stealing."

"I never told her to stop, so I guess I gave permission by omission. When I graduated, I set up the account so that I had to approve every withdrawal. That's when other things started…"

Mac slammed the door open snapping Charlotte and Savvy's collective attention to the doorway. "They think they found her." The curve of a breathless smile tilted his lips.

"Oh, well, praise Jesus!" Savvy shot to standing, wrapping Mac in a swift embrace before shuffling past him into the dining room.

"They found her?" Charlotte stood. Her legs wobbled, but Mac pulled her to him before she could crumble to the floor. "They really found her?" her voice was a whisper.

He nodded. "The harbor patrol called in a sighting of a woman matching Georgie's description boarding a boat in Charleston. Some of the agents from SLED are going to meet the harbor patrol and the Charleston PD to coordinate efforts. The harbor patrol was able to stop the vessel before it made it to the Atlantic. Murphy and Cade are heading to Charleston now. Do you want to go?"

Nodding her head, she opened her mouth to answer but stopped at the vibration of her phone in her back pocket. The caller ID stalled the growing hope in her chest. She paused as she lifted the phone to her ear. "Hello?"

"Good news about the little girl, I hope, *myshka*?"

Swallowing against the thick lump in her throat she nodded with a whispered response. "Yes."

"Good, now those men can go chase after and you be alone. Yes? No need to do police works. You prepare for little girl to return home, no?"

Dragging the phone from her ear, Charlotte lifted her gaze to Mac, hoping her eyes didn't reveal the turmoil churning through her system. "Why don't you go with Murphy and O'Neal? I'll stay here. Wait by the phones with the county guys. Just in case."

Giving her a searching look, his brows drew tight. "Charlie is there something you aren't telling me?" His gaze dropped to the mashed envelope. "What's in there?"

"Just something from work dropped off for me to review yesterday." The lie on her lips was bitter. "I'm exhausted. I should stay here. Wait. It's for the best. Won't be any good to Georgie if I'm all tuckered." She was turning Southern. "Call me as soon as you know anything. OK?"

"All right. But don't leave the house. This may be a red herring. Whoever took Georgie, might still want you, too."

With a tender squeeze of her shoulders, he pressed a soft kiss against her forehead, and she engaged every bit of her eastern European heritage's stalwart strength to resist asking him to stay with her.

"I'll call you soon."

She nodded.

He slipped through the swinging door to the dining room.

With a long exhale, she yanked on her wellies, waiting by the door where she'd stomped them off not an hour earlier. Cracking the door to the back porch open, she stepped into the early morning mist of privacy. The spit of gravel slashed against the air in the distance, signaling the rapid exit of dozens of police and her link to safety. With a sigh, she lifted the phone back to her ear.

"Baba, what did you do?"

"Got you free, myshka. The tea ladies say no moves made until police gone. Now police gone. Moves to be made."

"But...you mean...you don't know about the letter?" She paused. Her mind couldn't grapple the all-knowing tea society didn't know about the envelope clutched in her left hand. "The Babushkas do not know about the letter?"

"What letter? I knows nothing of letter. I do what you ask. I have tea with my ladies. Tea ladies say no police. So I get rids of police. Always best to do what tea ladies say. Work for me. Work for you." She could feel her grandmother's tiny head nod through the phone. "You gets letter? Who from?"

"My assistant dropped off some odd mail at the house yesterday. It's marked confidential, but we don't send confidential notices in this manner. Makes me think that it is not Watershed business."

"What it say?"

Charlotte lifted the mangled envelope to her eye level. "I haven't opened it."

"Why the waitings?"

"I'm afraid. I don't know who to trust, Baba."

"But this letter. Could be nothings. You worried about unknown. Juz like when little. Open letter."

"But if this is from the kidnappers I have to decide. Whether I agree to their demands or allow the police to do their job or..."

"Or what, myshka?"

Or what?

Charlotte didn't like to think what was behind that

choice.

38

"Why did you bring her here?"

The voice echoed in the dark space.

Male? Georgie couldn't be sure. He didn't have a low country drawl. Yet, the sound held familiarity, but her fuzzy mind couldn't place the accent.

Georgie remained still, fighting against the urge to stretch her cramped, pain ravaged body. Hard plastic zip-ties cut into her wrists and ankles transforming her limbs into giant pincushions. She felt the crack of dried blood cupping their indentations. Barely lifting her lids, she tried to see her captor, but her vision blurred against swelling acting as a counterweight.

"I had to be here. It seemed like the easiest place to keep track of the girl and the police."

Shocked awareness flowed through Georgie at the sound of the second captor. The slow, Southern female lilt had been scraping Georgie's spirit for weeks.

Bridget. Charlotte's assistant.

How was she involved? Did Charlotte organize the kidnapping? Had Cade been right? Should she not trust her sister? Tears percolated, but she refused to shed another salty drop for her sister. The sister she'd longed to know and who'd brought nothing but destruction and disgust with every turn.

"Idiot. All was under control and then you do this." The man began to pace just inside the entryway.

"All was not under control." Bridget said with a pop of her gum. "She saw me. I had to do something."

His sigh filtered through the air. "What did Yuri say of this?"

"You know he hates it when you call him by that name."

"I care not about his feelings. What he say?"

"Well, you should care about how he feels. He's the one who has gotten us this far."

The man snorted a chuckle. "And you the one who mess it up, no?"

"I got her attention."

"And now the entire police of the Carolinas are in house. You get all attentions."

Georgie forced her pain-racked body to remain still through the heated exchange, straining to see through her barely open eyelids. In the shadow of the doorway she could almost make out his frame. Maybe six feet, even a little taller. Trim. Definitely male. Short hair? Maybe. *Focus, Georgie.* Knowing her captor would be important.

"Don't worry. As soon Charlotte does her part, this one will be free. No harm will come to Miss Dixon."

"Hmm…if you say."

The echo of shoes against the rough floor paced one of her captor's exits. In opposition Georgie felt the click of heels stepping toward her. Even with her eyes closed, she could feel Bridget hovering over her.

"Why does he think you're so special?" Bridget asked in a mumbled tone.

The sound of Bridget's hands rubbing against each other sent a wave of shivers crashing over Georgie's frame. The shuffle of her steps away from Georgie helped to slow her racing heart. Her breath caught when the steps stopped.

"Huh." Bridget's voice was low. "Maybe you shouldn't find your way out of this hole."

The click of the exterior padlock shifted Georgie's heart into high gear. She forced her eyes open. If she stayed passive, a victim, her life expectancy was low.

Shoving against the floor, she bit her lip smothering the shout of searing pain ripping through her body. Scooting to sit, she stretched as tall as her zip-tied wrists and ankles would allow. Her chest heaved with the force of breaths struggling to find her lungs. The walls seemed closer with each breath, the low rafters nearer her face. Georgie forced her eyes shut, blocking out the shrinking prison. She wiggled to sit with her back against the cool wall of the cellar and tried to slow her breath. Imagining wide spaces. Walking along the Beaufort River. Lying on a raft with the sun warming her cheeks. Cool ocean breeze lifting her hair. Her breathing slowed, lungs filled to capacity. She pushed a slow breath out and sucked another in. The press of the panic attacks she'd faced since her father's diagnosis would not overwhelm her.

She couldn't allow fear and anxiety to swallow her. She needed to find a way to escape–to stop whatever Bridget and her partners were doing. And, it sounded as if her sister was part of the conspiracy. Charlotte may have fooled them all into believing she was trying to bring her mother to justice, but now, what was Georgie to think? Was Charlotte really a savior or a serpent?

Escape was her only option. If she was free, Georgie would know the truth. Sliding her hand against the base of the wall behind her, she tentatively stretched her fingers to find *the spot*. Her great-grandmother had pounded eight nails in the root cellar, long before her daddy was born: four in the walls and four in the ground, each exposed just an eighth of an inch. In the long night of the tornado, Georgie cut her foot on one of the nails in the ground. She remembered wailing when the rusty edge cut the bottom of her foot. Her mother wrapped her foot with a strip of the linen she kept with her to clean brushes and snuggled her close until the storm passed. But when they returned home, her mother demanded her father rip out the nails. Georgie remembered him patting her cheek with a smile, explaining his grandmother used them to dry herbs on twine she twisted through the cellar. She'd pounded the nails herself and only his granny or God would pull them up.

Georgie's finger found the rusted edge of the nail. *Thank you, Granny Dixon.*

Slowly she rubbed the edge of the binding against the nail. Struggling for leverage, the nail sliced her palm sending a streak of burning fire through her arm. With a swift bite of the inside of her cheek she stifled her scream.

No pain, no gain.

39

The last choice was looking better and better.

Stalking across the back lawn towards the charred remnants of the guest house, Charlotte clutched the stained letter and torn envelope to her chest in one hand and clamped the phone to her ear with the other. "What are you saying?" She asked her grandmother.

"Instructions are simple, myshka. You follow. You gets little girl." Baba drew a hissed breath through the phone.

Charlotte read through the typewritten instructions twice to her grandmother. "Baba, this is crazy." Massaging her temples, she shut her eyes against the harsh skeleton of the home she'd shared with Georgie.

"The tea ladies, they say you do what bad people tells you. That how Russia work. That how zez mens works. Theys bad Russia. No compromise. Just do. Letter tells what do. You do. You get little girl. Simple."

"Not simple, Baba. They want me to launder money. They want me to use my father's legacy, his precious ballpark, to make their dirty, rotten money clean. How can I justify one awful deed to rectify a horrific one?"

"Because your blood demands your help. Little girl iz sister, no?"

"Yes…"

"You loves her, no?"

"You know I love her, Baba."

"Then you make sacrifice. Blood cares for blood."

In Babushka's world things were simple. There was right and wrong, but not necessarily legal and illegal. Saving family justified any means. Charlotte wasn't certain Georgie, or Mac, would have the same vision as her grandmother. But none of their opinions mattered. Not really.

"They used my father's company stationary to demand we do the unthinkable. I can't even believe you want me to consider it. It's not only illegal, it is reprehensible, and I can't, I won't do it." Charlotte glanced at the crumpled paper with the ultimatum branded on the Watershed Industries letterhead:

Ballpark = cash.
Your sister for $2 million USD cleaned.
No police.
Police = Death.
$5 million more cleaned by end of summer.

The message was clear.

Pay the ransom. Save Georgie.

Involve the police. Georgie dies.

And the whammy? Use the cash rich ballpark as a way to clean money. Not far off what Remy discovered her mother had accomplished in her gallery. And the similarities only proceeded to further link Mama to Georgie's disappearance.

Regardless, whoever was advising the kidnappers understood the finances of the team well enough to know the initial request was the start-up of cash reserves the ballpark held at the bank, and the balance would be eighty to ninety percent of the ballpark's food and drink revenue for the entire season. The Bombers drew decent crowds which hovered in the top twenty or thirty in attendance each year in minor league ball, but seven million dollars would nearly wipe out all of the funds associated with the concession stands smattered around the concourse, the only primary cash business.

The buyers at the gallery spent significant amounts in each transaction allowing for thousands of dollars, and in some cases hundreds of thousands, to be transferred between accounts with little notice. But the stadium was hundreds of thousands of small transactions, over months not hours. Even if the entire county believed the Bombers overcharged for soda and hot dogs, a week's worth of receipts wouldn't nearly translate to the cash movements of the gallery in a single show.

"Let's say I could manage to get the cash into the ballpark, I could not get the cash back out and past all of the security loops and hooks we have in place to minimize in-house theft. It's a clever idea. Using the American pastime to clean dirty money, but even the thought of helping these criminals, allowing their activities to continue to be funded, well, my conscience can't survive it."

"Charlotte, this iz hard. We all haz difficulty in life. You want little girl back, you follow instructions."

"Baba whoever is behind this is linked to Watershed. They used my father's letterhead. Do you understand? They've infiltrated the family business. Just like my gallery. I feel so exposed. So vulnerable. I can't believe you want me to do something so deplorable. What would your Jesus say?"

"Jesus not in this." Her grandmother's phone disconnected.

Her grandmother was right. Jesus was not in this letter. Or in Georgie's kidnapping. But Charlotte hoped Jesus, Georgie's Jesus, her grandmother's Jesus, Mac Taylor's Jesus, maybe now her Jesus, too, was protecting Georgie and helping to find a solution to the seemingly unsolvable problem.

Unzipping her fleece, Charlotte slid the phone and the letter inside her shirt pocket to keep them dry against the drizzle misting the estate. She wished she could tuck Georgie, Savvy, Mac, and everyone she loved in her pocket. Protect them from the swell of danger threatening to overtake each of them. Swallowing against the tidal wave of fear, she lumbered the remaining fifty yards to the charred guest house.

Hung in the foggy winter morning gray, she could still visualize the warmth she felt in those walls. Even against her will, those four walls had been her refuge.

Her home.

When she'd arrived before Thanksgiving, she

looked at the three-bedroom guest house as a prison. Self-inflicted torture to solve yet another crisis caused by her mother. If she could make it through the year, somehow remain untethered by emotional connections and evade the torrent of unending questions, she would have the money she needed to finally disengage from her mother for good.

Pay off Mama's debt. Regain control of her gallery. Return to New York.

Simple.

But nothing in life was ever simple. Not in her life.

Gliding her fingers along the blistered surface of the front porch, she wondered, what if she hadn't called Remy? Never suspected her mother's lying and stealing? If she had turned a blind eye to the corruption corroding her business? If she'd left the closet door closed? Would she have even accepted her father's death-bed deal? Would Remy be awake? Would her sister be safe, annoying her with non-stop praise and worship music?

Charlotte would give anything to hear her sister singing her "Jesus Music". To have her best friend only a phone call away. To have said good-bye to her father, properly and in person. But choices made were history. They could inform the future, but they could not be rewritten. She could only allow their repercussions to inform her next steps. For Georgie's sake, hopefully her next steps would be wiser than the steps she'd taken in the last six months.

The mist fattened to pellets of sleet, clinging to Charlotte's all-weather jacket and melting through her fleece lined leggings. Chills sprinkled her body, driving a round of breath-stealing shivers to run through her veins. No closer to an answer, she began to plod the swampy overgrowth back toward the main house. Perhaps, Savvy's warm cider or stiff chicory coffee would be waiting and at least warm her body. The fear laced chill seeping into her soul might not defrost for a decade.

The rain-ice mix quickly turned the twenty-minute walk to near impassible terrain. Charlotte sought shelter under an ancient live oak. An old root cellar stood to her left.

Something in the peeled paint and warped boards sped her heart to a sprinter's pace. A vague memory of escaping another of her parents' violent arguments chased across Charlotte's memory. Racing out the back door, shimmying through the propped cellar door, and charging down the shaky steps. The zigzagged lines of drying herbs stifled the air in the tight space, but her nearly four-year-old body wiggled through the maze and found refuge under a crooked shelf not three feet off the ground. With her short arms wrapped around her head and her eyelids sealed shut to block out the echoes of her mother's screams, she didn't hear the cellar door slide shut or notice the light evaporate from the room. But hours later, with no sign of a grown up or air free from the dank must of thyme, oregano, and sage, her tears turned to panicked prayers to the God she'd learned about in Sunday School.

Charlotte didn't know how long she was trapped in that tiny root cellar before Uncle Rayburn found her huddled under the shelves. She remembered his thick arms feeling like steel pillows against her cheeks and the burn of fresh air filling her lungs.

A twig snapped and yanked her from the long-ago memory. Hairs on the back of her neck shot to attention as the feeling of being watched poured over her. Slowly pivoting, her focus darted across the field to the woods and back toward the skeletal remains of her home, but she saw nothing. Not a bird or a squirrel in sight. Sagging against the tree, she sucked in a deep breath wishing she had Mac with her.

What?

She shook her head.

Crazy thought, needing Mac to lean on. Her nerves were too much on edge. She couldn't manage to walk to and from the main house without devolving into a panic. How could she ever think she could handle a multi-million-dollar transfer for Georgie's safety without help?

Pressing away from the moss-covered tree trunk, she stepped toward the main house mentally flipping through the potential plans to help save Georgie. With a glance toward the guest house, she saw a quick flash in the corner of her eye, then a flat board cracked her across the face. Tumbling forward she felt the flesh rip from her hands against the rough bark of the live oak. The wind thrust out of her lungs with the force of her knees landing. She tried to focus on the blurred horizon. Cloudy, with a tinge of red.

Darkness slid like a hood over her eyes. She fought. The darkness won.

40

The wintery mix of rain and sleet crusted against Mac's windshield, lowering visibility to only a few feet on the road ahead, adding to the agonizing frustration from the futile trip to Charleston. The hour and a half drive had slowed to a crawl due to the late winter storm and his mind turned to prayer. But formal words didn't come. He had nothing left but a sorrowful plea to raise. One filled with his desire for Georgie's safe return, and the continued hedge of protection he prayed around Charlie.

The tip to the harbor patrol was clearly a diversionary tactic. But why? What purpose could someone have for pulling them from Colin's Fancy? Had they accidentally come close to finding Georgie? To putting an end to the current crisis? Was she closer to home than any of them thought?

He started calling Charlie as soon as they recognized the couple the shore patrol brought to them weren't connected to the case. Her phone rolled to voicemail. He'd tried nearly twenty times. Something was wrong.

He avoided calling the main house. Fear she wouldn't be waiting for their return rode shotgun with the hope she was drinking Savvy's over-cinnamoned, hot apple cider and waiting for an update from the wild-goose chase.

The concept that both sisters, the two women his best friend had left in his care, could potentially be missing with no leads was incomprehensible to Mac. The desperation in his spirit placed pressure on his gas pedal and he felt his tires spin with the extra speed.

The theme to a popular cop TV show shrilled through his car. His lips twisted in grimaced delight at Georgie's ringtone programming. He pressed his hands-free button to answer the phone. "Yes, Murphy."

"You might want to slow down, Counselor. You won't do anyone any good in a ditch."

"I can't get in touch with Charlie. Her phone keeps rolling to voicemail."

"Have you tried the main house?"

"I don't want to worry Savvy if she's not sitting right beside her."

"Would she have left for any reason?"

"No." Not unless she was following her own hunch to find Georgie. Rescue her sister on her own. If that was true, why hadn't she come to him?

"Do you think she made the call to the harbor patrol?" Murphy's question added another layer of concern to Mac's worry. Pressing the gas pedal to the floor, he prayed for an answer to the spiraling situation. Only God could help Georgie and Charlie.

~*~

"Georgie?"

The whispered voice drew Georgie from her freeze-frame position she'd assumed when the door opened a crack.

"Cole?" Scooting to sit, she squinted to focus on the form moving closer to her. "How are you here?"

He squatted in front of her. His hands shook as they gently stroked her hair and down her shoulder. "Are you OK?"

"I'll be fine." She snapped her wrists apart. The remainder of the plastic binding separated with a crack. Blood from the cuts opened by the scrapes against the nail trickled down her hands, clotting into cracks against her knuckles and palms.

Cole flipped open a pocketknife and slit the matching binding from her ankles. "Can you stand?"

"I can do anything. Just get me out of here."

Cole leveraged his arms under her to help her stand. She wobbled into him but forced her leaden legs to shuffle forward.

Wrapping a long arm around her quivering frame, Cole tucked her to his side and tugged her toward the open cellar door.

Icy wind slammed against Georgie's shaking body. She instinctively snuggled deeper into Cole's embrace, leaning into his heat and strength. Focusing on each step, she shivered with the slap of sleet slashing through the dark. She sucked in a lung-filling breath of the chilly night air and lifted her gaze to the haze of lights in the distance. The main house was ablaze like a lighthouse signaling home.

"Are you OK to walk to the house?" Cole asked.

Georgie nodded. Sucking in her bottom lip, she quickened her pace, breaking from Cole's protective grip. The bolts of pain shooting up from her ankle were annoying, but she wouldn't indulge in the suffering. She was free. She had a mission. She had to discover who was behind her kidnapping. She would do everything in her power to ensure they were never free again.

41

Cade whipped his car to a stop, his bumper nearly kissing Taylor's SUV. Jumping from the car, he hustled to catch the lawyer who was taking the front steps by twos. "Taylor." Cade shouted, but his voice was muffled in the wiping wind.

"Let him go, Murph," Dylan said. "He's got to see if she's in there."

Cade nodded. He also wanted to know if Charlotte Dixon was lounging in the breakfast nook or if she was chasing her own lead. Or something much worse. Hunching his shoulders against the pounding sleet, Cade followed his partner into the house.

The few cops who remained were spread around the large dining room table. From unfortunate past experience, he knew they were cataloguing every lead the team had compiled in the last twenty-four hours to try and determine where Georgie was being held and by whom. And, if the kidnapping, with no ransom note, had twisted into something more sinister.

Cade's worry was outpacing his logic and the systematic compiling of clues.

They had received no direct demands from Georgie's captors. No demands likely led to one outcome. His mind twisted reality with unquenchable hope, his heart unwilling to accept the thoughts his Quantico trained brain was forming.

"Don't go there," Dylan said.

Cade nodded, lifting his gaze to the still swinging kitchen door. With a press of his hand to the thick wood, he stepped into the warmth of the room and the shattered weeping of Savvy Boudreaux.

Wrapped in the wide arms of the family attorney, Georgie's aunt shook with unspoken reality.

Cade searched Taylor's expression.

Charlotte wasn't here, strengthening the theory she was connected to Georgie's disappearance.

"We'll find her. We'll find both of them," Taylor said.

Cade took in the swing of Taylor's gaze, shifting to the frost covered window stretched across the length of the kitchen. He squinted to see what drew Mac's attention and noticed two figures huddled together, moving toward the house.

"Who's out there from our team?" he asked Dylan.

Dylan shrugged and shuffled toward the backdoor peering through the fogged window. "All of our guys not in the dining room are still driving back from Charleston."

Cade tapped Dylan's shoulder, and his partner moved out of his way.

Stepping back into the cold, his breath collapsed in his lungs. "Georgie?" Running to the end of the porch, he sidestepped down the slippery landing and rushed across the back lawn. Her curls swirled wildly around her head, and his heart pounded with the realization his deepest fear was being overridden by his heart's hope. With a sliding stop, barely a breath's distance between them, he placed his hands on her shaking shoulders. "Georgie?"

Tears flooded her cheeks. She fell into his open embrace. Clutching her to his chest, he pressed a gentle kiss to the top of her head. Her body shivered against his and he wished he could absorb the physical pain he could see plastered across her frame.

She pressed out of his embrace and lifted her gaze to meet his. Her face was swollen and red. Flashes of deepening purple were beginning on the edge of her right eye. A deep cut ran the length of her forehead. A quick glance to the hands clasping his, registered the caked blood stretched across her wrists and hands.

"Georgie, where were you?"

"In the root cellar. Near the creek." She lifted a shoulder. "Cole rescued me."

How had he missed Georgie's friend? Cavanaugh would probably demote him to cataloguing evidence for the next decade if she heard about Cade's negligence. Cade took in the lean, shaking form of the young financial analyst, dressed in pressed khakis, button down shirt, and loafers. He couldn't weigh a buck fifty and barely crested Georgie's height. He looked suited to guide leaders on the best mutual fund. How had this guy rescued Georgie? "How did you find her?"

"Maybe we can discuss this inside out of the cold?" Cole nodded toward the house, his hands thrust into his front pants pockets.

Nodding, Cade tucked Georgie against his side, trying to protect her from the pelting sleet and whipping wind. He didn't care how inappropriate Dylan would say his attention toward a victim was. Georgie Dixon was safe. And she was in his arms. He wasn't sure he would ever let her go again, except to hunt down those responsible for her disappearance. For that mission, he could make an exception.

~*~

Walking through the back door, Georgie wanted to drown in the blessed warmth of the kitchen. She'd never been so happy to be suffocated in Savvy's embrace.

"Where have ya been? Half the state's been lookin' for you." Savvy squeezed, sending mind-numbing pain through her left side.

"Ahhh...owww!"

"Darlin', what's wrong? Where are you hurt?" Savvy stepped back from her and began dragging her hands along Georgie's frame looking for injury. "We need to get ya to the hospital. Mac, can you drive in this weather?"

"I'm OK. For now. I need to talk to the police. Doctor later."

"I'm not letting you out of my sight." Her aunt shoved a fist into her hip, her mournful tears all but dry in her eyes, drawing a painful chuckle from Georgie.

"I won't leave the house." She lifted her gaze to

Cade's steely focus. He would only be a glance a way. "I'm safe here. You can go with me to the medical center after I answer what I can. OK?"

"Well…"

"Savvy, she's fine," Mac said.

With a sigh, Georgie slid onto the bench in the breakfast nook. Dylan headed into the dining room, but she wasn't surprised when Mac slid next to her and Cade leaned against the other bench.

"What happened, Slugger?"

She opened her mouth to share the whole story, but Cade lifted his hand. "We will want a neutral party to listen." The implication he was no longer a 'neutral party' helped to warm her better than the cup of hot cider Savvy slipped into her grip. Feeling her blush rise she glanced around the room. Where was Cole?

"Did Cole leave?"

"He went to the restroom," Cade said. "O'Neal's with him."

With a nod, she sipped the cider, the spice burning the cuts on her lips. She glanced toward the backyard and caught the sight of several flashlights bobbing through the winter storm.

"Likely the sheriff, maybe SLED," Cade said. "They'll want to secure any evidence before the storm destroys it."

"Charlotte?"

The wooden spoon Savvy used to stir her cider dropped with a clatter onto the stove, snapping Georgie's focus. Her aunt's shoulders curved forward, shaking with slight tears.

Mac slid from the bench and tugged Savvy to his side, always the comforter.

Cade folded into the breakfast nook, slipping his fingers to cover hers. "Your sister isn't here."

"Did she…"

"No. I don't believe she was connected. I was the one who told her you were missing. No one can fake that kind of devastation. But while we chased a lead to Charleston, she opted to stay here."

"But she's not here now?"

"The tip was a diversion," Mac said. "I've been calling her nearly non-stop over the last two hours. Every call rolled to voicemail."

"She went for a walk," Savvy said. "She was on the phone with her grandmother. I thought she wanted, needed, privacy. Ya know how she puts up that shield. It was shattering around her like a piece of crystal under the foot of a five-hundred-pound pig."

The throbbing pressure building at the base of her skull forced Georgie to close her eyes against the bright lights of the kitchen. Was her sister simply her sister or was she behind the terror of the last few weeks and hours? *Father, Jesus…please help me. Show me what I'm missing.*

The creak of the kitchen door snatched her from her prayer.

Cade got up to share rushed whispers with Dylan and a uniformed sheriff. The urgency of their conversation weighted the room with unheard worry.

"Spill it, Murphy," Mac said.

Cade twisted, ignoring Mac's demand. He

squatted to eye level and held her gaze.

"What is it?" Georgie asked.

"Cole slipped through the window in the bathroom. He's on the run."

"Why? He didn't do anything wrong. He's a hero."

"Is he? He found you. 'Rescued you.' Without any credible leads."

"No. You are wrong. Cole's my friend. He's been nothing but kind." Since the day of the funeral, Cole had been a constant companion, helping her to navigate the troublesome and confusing world of Watershed Industries. He couldn't be connected. No. Not Cole. Not someone she trusted.

"It's not him. It's Bridget. She's the one who knocked me out. She was in the cellar. She was talking to someone else. A man with an accent I couldn't place. Cole must have been walking the property. Seen them and waited to investigate. Yes. That makes the most sense. He must have just found me by accident." She nodded, lifting her gaze to Mac's. "That makes sense, right?"

"Slugger, if he's innocent, why did he run?"

The sound of arguing in the dining room tugged their collective attention.

Dylan slipped from the room, allowing the volume of the fight to pierce the relative solemnity of the kitchen.

The woman's voice daggered Georgie and propelled her through the swinging door. "Stasi?"

Charlotte's mother was screaming unintelligible

words at a sheriff.

"Little girl!" Stasi whipped to face Georgie, violent accusations shooting from her black eyes. "Where's my Charlotte?"

"I don't know."

"You were with her, weren't you? They took you. They took her. They have my baby."

"Stasi," Mac said. His lawyer tone stretched thin over the obvious concern weighing on him. "What do you mean 'they took her'?"

"They wanted the money. I was supposed to get it from her. I wasn't fast enough for them. They rushed. They took you." She twisted to face Georgie. Tears cut ribbons over her painted cheeks. "I didn't know. He's always been patient before. I was able to pay. But now. There's new people. New leaders. I don't know why. I just know they took my *malyshka*."

"Who took Charlotte, Ms. Bickford?" Cade asked.

"Anton. Anton Dorokhov."

Cade nodded to Dylan and snatched his phone from the inside pocket of his jacket.

Dylan placed a gentle hand to Stasi's arm and guided her to sit at the dining room table. "Ms. Bickford, we need to understand everything from the very beginning. Are you willing to tell us what you know?"

"You must find my daughter. They will kill her if I don't get them the money. They've lost patience. Please promise me you will find Charlotte." Tears wracked her frame.

Her fear for Charlotte's well-being seeped through

Georgie. Limping to a chair across from Stasi, Georgie grasped her sister's mother's fingers and squeezed. "Tell them what they need to know. Cade and Dylan will bring Charlie home." Her vision blurred against the tears filling her eyes. Georgie couldn't fully process the last few minutes. Or days. Or months. But she knew a hurting person. And she knew how to stretch compassion without judgment. Stasi would need all the compassion she had left in her person. Charlotte's life depended on how well Georgie could embody Jesus to the woman who had caused her father, her mother, and her sister the greatest pains of their lives. "Start from the beginning, Stasi," Georgie said.

42

Shallow breaths battled against the pounding of Charlotte's heart thumping in her ears. A dark hood cloaked her vision, shrinking her world. Pins and needles raced over her arms and legs in agonizing waves. Cold sweat streamed down her forehead and into her eyes, burning her blackened vision.

One...two...three...

Shutting her eyes against the wall of fabric sheathing her face, she dragged a taut breath through cracked lips and counted.

Counting always helped. Elevator. Airplane. Closet. Regardless of the small space, counting usually helped to ease her tight chest and constricted airway.

Ten...eleven...twelve...

Her heart slowed its pace. The thumping in her ears quieted to a steady drum roll.

Where was she?

How long had she been unconscious?

Was Georgie here?

The ransom note floated into her mind. Why hadn't she told Mac what happened? He would have helped her. Known what to do. *Stop it!* Hindsight was for freedom. Survival needed to come first.

She wiggled her fingers, rocketing streaks of pain

through her body. Short, staccato breaths puffed through tight lips. Her wrists were locked together by a restraint treating her flesh like a Thanksgiving turkey, awakening sleeping muscles with a jolt. She struggled to stretch her toes, the feeling in her limbs limited to stinging numbness. Stifling the scream threatening to bellow from her lips, she chomped the inside of her cheek filling her mouth with the metallic and salt laced taste of her own blood. *Focus, Charlie. Pain. Fear. They live in your heart. Your mind is stronger. You are stronger, Charlie.*

Charlotte could hear her father's dusty southern voice echo in her spirit. How or why her mind landed on the memory of her attempts to learn to ride a bicycle when she was eight years old, she couldn't imagine, but she clung to the coaching moment. She couldn't allow her claustrophobia to disable her. Her father was right. She needed to focus. Her 'where' was most pressing. The how and the why could wait. Drinking in a deep breath, she quieted her mind to listen to the sounds. She couldn't see, but her ears and body could draw a picture. Cold seeped through the building and slithered up her back.

Maybe metal walls? Old brick? A warehouse?

The tin of ice pelted against glass. What warehouses had that much glass? Mentally, she whipped through the docks and industrial locations near Colin's Fancy. But she had no idea how long she was unconscious. She could be anywhere.

Another deep breath in and out. Echoes of water and howls of swirling wind filled the room. Much bigger than she originally imagined. The space felt exposed not tight. She sucked in another long breath, her heart slowing to a crawl. Was she alone in the room? She didn't hear breathing besides her own.

No sounds of movement beyond the storm raging against the building.

Stretching her body, she dragged her long legs against the wooden floor. Her bare feet slammed into a brick wall, reverberating ripples of dull ache over the needles under her flesh. Using the wall as an anchor she scooted forward on her side. The wood scraped against her exposed skin, reawakening the vibrations of pain. Tears burned for release.

"Help me," she said in a whispered prayer.

Mumbled voices floated to her ears. Her heart sped to a rabbit pace. Breaths shallow. She stilled her body. The voices grew louder, and she recognized the spoken words.

Three voices. One female. Two male. All speaking Russian.

Why couldn't it have been French? She'd spent a year in France. Her French was flawless. Even though she'd been exposed to Russian her whole life, she tried to avoid using the language unless she was with Baba. The language was an anchor in her life tethering her to the past. On her best day she needed to mentally translate Russian to English in her mind before she could respond. The conversation swirled around her. Rushed words, but she quickly understood.

Dolg. Debt

Vznos. Payment.

Pogibshiy. Lost.

Lost? What could they have lost?

And she heard, "Anastasia."

Always Mama.

Did they lose her mother?

Korotkiy Devochka. Little Girl.

Georgie. They lost Georgie? Was Georgie free? Was Georgie dead?

Please God. I know You are there. You've shown up too many times these past few months. Georgie loves You so much. Protect Georgie. Please let her be safe.

Charlotte strained to listen, stifling the emotion in which she wanted to drown.

"English, please."

Bridget? Her administrative assistant was here?

"You know I can't follow all of the gibberish."

"You stupid woman. How you call beautiful Russian gibberish? You choose Russia. She not choose you."

"Ugh, whatever."

Definitely Bridget.

"When is he getting here? She has to sign the papers to make this work. I have to get out of this town. She knows who I am."

"Don't rush. You rushing cause problems."

Charlotte recognized the second voice. The smooth, lecherous tone of Anton Dorokhov. Her mother's on-again, off-again boyfriend, and loan shark. He was behind the ransom note. The money laundering. But was Mama complicit? "If you patient. No problem. Just solution. But you impatient. Now we lose little girl. Problem much worse. We have the other one. You take leverage."

"We should just kill this one. Clean up this situation. The gallery. All the loose ends. He has the other one wrapped around his finger. He's her hero. She'll do whatever he tells her. I've been dealing with this one's signature for the last two months. I can totally fake it. Get the accounts transferred."

"We wait. You jump. You cause more problems. We not fix your problems with more problems."

The vibration of heels clicking against the wood floor reverberated through Charlotte's frame.

Please God, keep me still. She steadied her shallow breaths imagining wide spaces. Central Park. The Bombers ballpark. The backyard at the plantation. Her heart slowed, the beats no longer thumping in her head.

"How hard did you hit her, Boris?" Charlotte felt the heat of Bridget's minty breath flow through the hood.

"Name not Boris. Name Vsevolod." The second man's voice was thicker with a heavier accent. His English was not developed. He was pure *Bratva*.

The pointed edge of Bridget's shoe pressed into Charlotte's belly. Tears burned her eyes. Blood pooled in her mouth. But she focused. Her mind was stronger. Pain wouldn't win.

"Whatever. I need my money and I'm not waiting here all night. I need to take a little sail south."

"Relax."

Charlotte's breath caught. A fourth voice. One she

recognized. But from where?

"It took you long enough." Bridget's heels tapped against the floorboards signaling her move away from Charlotte. "You're soaked."

"Unavoidable."

"Do you have solution we discussed?" Anton asked.

"No. The situation turned. I'm compromised."

"We need moneys."

"We will have to discover a different path."

"No!" Bridget said. "I need the money you promised me. I've stuck around in this crummy town for months for this deal. Skimming just wasn't good enough for you."

"Enough. Things changed."

"I want my money."

A single gunshot rattled the windows. The slithered thump of dead weight quickly followed.

The burn of sulfur threatened to choke Charlotte.

"Wrap her in the paint tarp," the fourth voice said. "We'll dispose of both bodies together. The ocean can be their grave."

"We cannot. The other one holds importance. You should let little girl go, but kills this one?"

Let little girl go? Georgie was free. Tears burned Charlotte's eyes. Her heart slowed.

"Everything has changed, Anton. We are no longer safe. The police. The FBI. Everyone is on our trail. We have minutes not hours. She's seen us. She has to go."

"But she one of our own. She only see the woman.

Woman gone. No problem. She will come around. Give big foothold. The art...just beginning. Anastasia say she can make her do."

"Stop. Don't you think I want this to be different? Ms. Nelson's choices exposed us. I will be held responsible for this failure. I must return home. Face Temi. She cannot remain. We will not return to this place."

The thud of heavy footsteps reverberated through Charlotte's frame.

Please God, be with me. Forgive me for not trusting You. For not believing in You. I am Yours. And You are mine. Just as You promised. Forgive me.

Dragging in a deep breath, her lungs filled to the point of aching, but her heart remained slow and steady. "Lord Jesus Christ, Son of God, have mercy on me, a sinner." Words floated through her lips, barely a whisper.

Her eyelids slammed open and she stared into the tightly woven black hood. Cold sweat dried against her temple. The pace of her heart remained slow and steady. Each footstep set a tremor through her body. *Be with me, Lord.*

The light flickered through the weave. A deepening shadow stretched across her vision.

"Take off the hood, Vsevolod. I do not want to make another mistake. I must be sure."

"She the one."

The weight of his steps paced the pounding of her heart, deafening the thick accent.

The scrape of callouses against her neck forced a

moan through her lips.

"Hurry, she's waking up."

How did she know that voice?

"I go fast as can."

The one she thought was called Vsevolod tore away the hood.

The crack of Charlotte's skull against the solid wood floor scattered piercing stabs from the crown of her head to the tips of her toes. Her eyelids slapped shut against the brightness of the room. "Oww…" She struggled to reach the source of her pain, instinctively wanting to rub out the ache with her bound hands.

"Now, now, Miss Dixon. The pain will be gone soon."

The fourth voice chilled her blood. *Cole Vasil.* Georgie's friend. Watershed's newest senior financial analyst. He was a Yuri. One sent to infiltrate. How had she been so blind? Bridget and Cole working together? "How could you?" Charlotte asked, her voice barely a whisper. "Georgie trusted you."

"Yes, well, that was the point."

He squatted in front of her. His hair was damp and his clothes appeared heavy, darkened with the icy rainstorm. But he didn't shiver. Strange. He must be frozen solid.

"If you had just listened." He brushed her hair aside. "I thought this warning was loud enough, but you are stubborn." His chuckle boiled the acid in her stomach. "We thought your mother could convince you. Turn your eyes away. But then Ms. Nelson became antsy. Her patience was never strong. The fire...your friend saw us together that night...and, well, here we are."

"You won't get away with this. Georgie...Mac won't let you get away with any of this."

"Well," he said as he stood. "I don't believe they have a choice in the matter." He raised the gun, aiming it at her head. "Now, at least Georgie will be free of you. If I can't have your father's money, she should have it all to herself."

Charlotte squeezed her eyelids shut. *One...two... three...*

The blast of gunfire rippled through her.

43

She waited for the searing pain. But no new pain emerged. Shouts rang in her ears.

Anton?

Vsevolod?

Others yelling for help. A bus?

Special Agent Murphy?

She lifted her eyelids. Murphy was running towards her with O'Neal close behind.

Murphy knelt beside her. Flipping a pocketknife open, he sliced the restraint at her ankles and the second at her wrists.

Aching warmth burned her fingertips and toes. She pressed her palm against the floor. Pain rocketed through her frame and she slithered into the fetal position. "Georgie?" she asked.

Murphy's lips stretched to reveal bright white teeth. "She'll be fine. We need to get you to the hospital."

Swallowing against the sandpaper lodged in her throat, she nodded. "How did you find…" A fog began to shroud her mind. She needed to know. Her mind fought her body. And her body was winning. Her eyelids felt like twenty-pound dumbbells and she didn't have the strength to lift a feather. She let them win, content to fall asleep on the hard, damp floor. Tremors rattled her frame, as arms slid under her knees and around her back. She seemed to float upward. Her cheek felt a warm, strong chest. An angel? Perhaps she had died, and God had answered her prayer. She was headed to heaven. Tugging against the unseen weight holding down her eyelids, she squinted. The sight of Mac's salt and pepper beard shattered the dam of tears welling in her chest. "It's you. You're my angel."

His lips brushed against her aching forehead. He squeezed her tight to him. A wave of peace washed over her. A smile tugged at her lips as the veiled fog engulfed her.

~*~

Mac swallowed against the mix of burning rage and tender relief as he wrapped Charlie closer to his chest. After being threatened by Sheriff Cambry with disbarment, Mac watched helplessly from behind the barricade of squad cars and a SWAT van surrounding the abandoned church Georgie had hoped to transform into a music and arts education center. The takedown was over in less than a minute, but the sound of the single gunshot reverberated through his frame and aged him at least twenty years.

Thankfully, only one shot was necessary to subdue the scene. A pair of medics dressed Cole's shoulder wound under Murphy's watchful stare.

Mac clutched Charlie tighter.

Anton Dorokhov struggled against the handcuffs Dylan tightened at his wrists and the thug with them shouted something in Russian over and over.

The medical examiner arrived only moments after the mixed force of SLED, FBI, and county sheriff deputies cleared the area. Efficiently, she commanded the scene surrounding Charlotte's assistant, having two other medical examiners shift Bridget's lifeless form into a waiting county morgue body bag. Mac imagined the former assistant would have an autopsy, but unfortunately the cause of death wouldn't be able to explain the chatty blonde's reason for undermining and infiltrating Watershed.

How could he have missed what was happening at the company? Cole had started work as an SFA over a year ago, right as Bent's health truly began to decline. The young man had been so eager and adept, Mac quickly trusted him with a vast array of accounts and the financials for multiple subsidiaries. He was blinded by goodwill and his own need to focus on saying goodbye to his dear friend. If Mac hadn't seen Cole handcuffed to the gurney with his own eyes, he would have struggled to believe Stasi's convoluted story. The fact that Charlie's mother was the linchpin in solving the embezzlement scheme and rescuing her daughter from certain death was beyond surreal.

Charlie shivered in his arms, releasing a soft moan. The metallic emergency blanket crinkled in his hands as he tightened his embrace. The twinkle of colored moonlight reflected off of the blanket, tugging his gaze to the massive stained-glass windows echoing a history steeped in faith. The moon glowed through the colored glass. The evening's storm had passed. He tucked the shiny blanket tighter around her, praying his body heat would help to warm her chilled frame.

"We need to treat her, sir." A medic, with cheeks ruddy from the cold stood above Mac.

Mac nodded and willed his arms to loosen their hold on Charlotte's frail form.

The two paramedics lowered her to a back board and secured her neck with a cervical collar before sliding her onto the gurney for transport. Back to the hospital. Again. Her poor body had endured almost as much trauma as her spirit in the last two months.

Help me Lord. I am failing to protect the one person I have come to cherish most on this planet. What am I supposed to do?

"Do you want to ride with us?" the young medic asked.

Mac glanced at Dylan, who followed the two sheriffs escorting Dorokhov and his associate out of the building. Murphy's wide leg stance and narrowed stare never wavered from Vasil. Justice was being served.

He nodded and took one large step into the back of the ambulance.

44

"Georgie, she needs to rest. You need to rest. I'll stay with her." Mac's whispered voice floated through Charlotte's mind.

"I agree, Georgie. You've only been out of the hospital a day yourself. You need to be cautious," Savvy said. "Remember what the doctor said. Rest. Fluid. More rest. Darlin', you could have died out there in that cellar."

"Yes, I'm aware I could've died. Thank you for reminding me for the thousandth time, Aunt Savvy. But I'm not dead. And, I'm not leaving. You want to leave, go for it, but I am not leaving my sister again. Ever."

Charlotte chuckled. A rattling cough wracked her frame. But there was blissfully no pain. How was that possible?

"You're awake."

Charlotte blinked. Clearing her vision, she caught sight of the greenish blue bruise stretched across Georgie's high boned cheek. "Oh, Georgie." Tears flooded her eyes. "I'm so sorry."

"Hush." Georgie gripped Charlotte's right hand. "This is no one's fault except Cole and his posse."

"But..." Charlotte swallowed against the dryness

consuming her mouth. "You could have died."

"You are as bad as Savvy. Yes, I am fully aware I *could* have died. But I didn't. See..." She stood tall and twirled; her twisted, sandy-blonde locks cascading like a waterfall over her shoulder. She stretched her wide mouth to a grin. "Fully alive. Mobile. And in one piece."

"Thank God." Agent Murphy's deep voice resonated in the tiny hospital room. He leaned against the open door.

The smile Charlotte thought she'd dreamed, tugged the corners of his mouth.

Georgie took two steps into his waiting embrace, tucking her head under his chin. "I didn't think you believed in God."

"You are evidence of the divine, Miss Dixon."

Charlotte shook her head. How long had she been asleep?

"It's been building for a while," Savvy said, as she rested a hip on Charlotte's bed. "You would have thought the two were super glued together the last few days."

"How long? What happened? I can't..." Charlotte's tried to focus, but her brain felt as if it was filled with twenty bags of cotton balls.

"There, there, dear. Mac was right. Rude though the boy was." Savvy lifted an eyebrow toward Mac who leaned against the wall, arms crossed, his own eyebrow raised in rebuttal.

"We should leave you to rest." She patted Charlotte's hand. "The details. The 'who, what, when, where, and why'...well, those can just be discussed another day. Can't they, Special Agent Murphy?"

"I asked you to call me Cade, ma'am."

"And I asked you to leave my nieces alone. We don't always get what we want, do we?"

"Aunt Savvy!" Georgie exclaimed.

Murphy simply tugged Georgie tighter to his chest.

"Well, you'll leave poor Charlotte alone." Savvy squeezed Charlotte's hand and stood. Slipping her square pocketbook to her elbow, she said. "Now, all of you get out. We can see she's quite on the mend. However, my darling niece needs her rest and she won't be shutting those eyes again if any of you are loitering." She leaned down, gave Charlotte a wink and pressed a soft kiss to her forehead. "I'm so glad you came back to us, my dear. You had this old heart worried." With a soft pat to Charlotte's cheek, Savvy turned. "Let's go. I have a pot of beef stew in the crockpot waiting to be eaten."

Georgie gave a little wave, still tucked neatly to Murphy's side. His smile fell to a straight-lined grimace as the two turned and headed into the hallway.

"And then there was one..." Charlotte said. Tilting her head she took in the lean form of Mac Taylor lounging against the wall. With his arms crossed over his worn college sweatshirt and his legs draped in decades' old jeans, he looked ready to paint his bathroom, not about to give her the stinging lecture she knew she deserved. Shoving away from the wall he moved toward her bed.

"I know I should have told you about the ransom note. Baba asked the tea ladies and they said I should try and figure it out on my own. I didn't read it until after you left. But still I was wrong."

Arms crossed, he stepped to the side of her bed but remained silent.

Charlotte felt tears stream over her cheeks. "I wanted to tell you. I just didn't know what to do. I've messed up everything. I shouldn't have come to South Carolina. I should have never accepted the terms of the will. Georgie would have all of the money and none of Mama's 'friends' would ever have tried to cash in on my inheritance."

He leaned forward, placing a hand on either side of her head, and lowered his lips to hers. The touch was soft, barely a kiss, and yet sent bolting electricity through her veins. If the lights went out she could power the city for a month.

Lifting his lips, he rested his forehead against hers, and she felt warmth splash against her cheek. Tears. His. Not hers.

"I thought..." He dragged a deep breath through taut lips. "I thought I'd lost you. The whole way home from Charleston, I must have dialed your number a hundred times and in my gut, I knew something was wrong. You needed me and I didn't know how to get to you. How to help you."

"You aren't mad at me?" She lifted her hand to stroke his neck.

"Oh, yeah. I'm supremely angry with you." He

said, his lips stretching to a grin. Leaning back, he rested his hip on the side of her bed and reached for her hand. "However, I've decided to shelve my anger until you are home from the hospital and the entire situation is resolved."

"What is the situation? I think I know only half of the puzzle. How did they find me? Cole works for Anton? Bridget works for Cole? Oh, Mac, Bridget..." The tears she thought she'd dammed flooded her eyes and streamed down her cheeks. "He shot her. It was so fast. The smell was awful. I remember shooting skeet when I was young, but the smell was like nothing I've ever experienced. She trusted them, him. How could he do it?"

"Let me get this straight. You are crying...for Bridget? The assistant whom I watched make your blood boil simply by walking into a room? Bridget, who we now know has been conspiring to embezzle money from your company? Bridget, who allegedly lit fire to your house and likely caused Remy to be in a coma? You are upset for *that* Bridget?"

"I'm saddened for her. She placed her trust in them. Was it wrong? Of course. But my heart still feels for her. She was betrayed." She swiped her cheeks. "Has anyone claimed her body?"

"I don't know."

"If they can't find her family, I'd like to give her a funeral or at least a small service."

"Are you serious? Charlie, she nearly killed you."

"I know. But she didn't. Everyone deserves someone to celebrate their life even if her life wasn't worthy of a celebration." Charlotte released a sigh. Her eyelids slid shut.

~*~

Five days after her rescue, Charlotte sat with her hospital bed as erect as possible, alone for the first time. The absent pain she'd questioned days earlier had arrived nearly twenty hours ago when she insisted on being removed from a morphine drip. Although she hated the non-stop aches and occasional shooting pain, she wanted, needed, her mind clear of the opioid induced fog when she talked to Special Agents Murphy and O'Neal.

Both had stopped for social visits over the last few days. Neither asked any questions regarding her capture. But she suspected their restraint was Mac-orchestrated.

Each time she woke, he was in the room. Sitting in the chair by her bed, holding her hand or hunched over his laptop, pounding out emails. He chatted with her. Brought her contraband food. Watched romantic comedies with her. Kissed her.

Unlike the first day she woke, he was always dressed ready to do battle in a court of law or preside over the boardroom, but his new accessory of worry seemed to have etched permanent lines on his beautiful forehead. He'd told her yesterday he would be late this morning, his lips drawn in a tight line. She knew he hated being away from her side for even a moment. She wished she had an answer to allay his concern. She also was trying to figure out how to tell him about her encounter, or rather, encounters, with God.

From the prayers said over her by Baba to the ones written for her by her father to the one she silently screamed moments before she thought she was going to die, her heart ached with the transcendence of her new relationship with God.

The creak of the door opening pulled her focus. The corner of her mouth curved. The smell of vanilla and cinnamon announced her sister.

"Well, look at you all clear-eyed and upright." Georgie hustled to her side, kissing her cheek. "I brought you some of Savvy's and Mellie's cinnamon-sugar scones."

"Hide those until I get all her vitals recorded." Her morning nurse, Sally, followed Georgie into the room. She lifted the lid of the leftover Christmas tin. "Those are definitely not on her diet. But they just might be on mine."

Sally was quickly becoming one of Charlotte's favorites in the hospital. The doctors tended to be too clinical. No personal dialogue. They were rightly focused on patching her up and sending her home. The nurses were more frequent visitors, in and out of the room multiple times a day, often once an hour. And since Sally worked days, she'd been with Charlotte during nearly all of her awake hours. In the rare moments Charlotte didn't have a visitor, Sally had made a point to spend time with her. Not simply medical time, but truly caring about her well-being.

"Oh, no. I didn't mean to break any rules. Mac said he's been bringing you treats all week," Georgie said.

"Don't let her worry you, Georgie. The nurses appreciate Mac's illegal food. I believe they have a running buffet in the breakroom." Charlotte winced with the tightening of the blood pressure cuff. She liked her clear mind, but she was coming to understand how people could so easily become addicted to pain-free living.

Sally *tsked*. "Now if the ibuprofen-only is too much, you ask for pain meds. There's no use in suffering. Too much pain will only impede your healing."

"And not enough will impede my thinking," Charlotte said.

Sally completed the twice daily vitals check and made notes in the wall-mounted computer. The nurse asked Charlotte to rate her pain. She couldn't help but glance at her sister who was scrolling through some app on her phone. The purple bruises were slowly fading from her delicate features. Georgie may not be in the hospital, but her pain level must still be high. Regardless of the physical pain, the mental pain of betrayal would run deep for years to come.

Charlotte mouthed a seven.

Sally nodded and typed her response into the computer but left the white board notation blank. "Well, ladies I will leave you to your illegal baked goods. But make note, I counted the number and anticipate an overabundance from you two skinny-minis." Sally shut the door behind her, leaving the sisters in the whitewashed silence of a hospital room mid-morning.

Georgie lifted her gaze to meet Charlotte.

"Why the sad face, Georgie?"

Georgie shrugged.

"Not an answer." Charlotte patted the bed. Her sister scooted in beside her, cuddling to seek comfort she needed. Comfort Charlotte regretted she hadn't provided her entire life. But regrets were for history. She was determined to give her family all the love she'd withheld, showering them to the point of sticky sweetness and greeting card schmaltz. "Come on, Georgie. Today is not the day to find your shy gene."

She puffed a sigh, flapping Charlotte's hospital gown. "I just can't believe I was so trusting. So gullible."

Cole.

Charlotte knew the majority of the story. Taking the bits she'd heard whispered while she faded in and out of consciousness, she connected them with her own pieces and nearly completed the entire puzzle of the last year. The hardest connector piece was knowing the man her sister trusted as a dear friend was actually the mastermind behind the atrocities connected to her mother.

Georgie's heart was naturally open. She was truly Delia's daughter in every kind, generous part of her soul. And aside from Charlotte's treatment of her, she had only known the gift of love reciprocated. Betrayal was a brutal response to the gentle offer of grace.

Charlotte had received this gift exchange too many times to remember, but it was one she wished she could absorb for her sister. "You did the right thing, Georgie." Charlotte stroked her sister's long curly locks. "You gave of yourself. Without hesitation or guile. You were you. Don't let one person's horribleness dim the light that shines in you."

"But when I meet someone new, how do I know I can trust them?"

"You don't. But not trusting them would be a violation of who you were created to be. I understand you wanting to be wary. But God has given you the gift of hospitality and friendship. He wouldn't want you to horde His gift, now would He?"

Georgie sat up straight. Her mouth dropped open ready to catch non-existent flies. "God?"

"Yes, God, Georgiana. God…He…I…well, let me just say that the past few months have been a revelation for me. Life-changing. And I don't mean moving to South Carolina or taking over Watershed. I mean…" She leaned her head back and stared at the ceiling, hoping for God to give her the words to explain the one hundred and eighty degree turn in her life. Baba's prayer once again filled her spirit. *Lord Jesus Christ, Son of God, have mercy on me, a sinner. Lord Jesus Christ make haste Your mercies.* "It wasn't all at once. And yet it was instantaneous."

Charlotte told Georgie about her God encounters from Baba to their father's prayers and beyond. As tears streamed down her sister's cheeks, she felt a matching warm liquid burn a trail down her own.

"Why are you crying?"

"Because," Georgie said, resting her forehead against Charlotte's. "This is what Daddy wanted. I didn't know it. Not really. But this. You and Jesus. This is what he always wanted. He knew you would find him when you found Jesus. You would find your family through your Savior."

She tugged her sister into her arms, her vision clouded by cresting tears. "Oh, Georgie, please forgive me. I've been so horrible. And all you've ever done is love me."

"You are more than forgiven." Georgie pulled away from her embrace. "Charlotte, can you forgive me?"

"For what?" What could her sister possibly need forgiven?

"I thought horrible things about you. I *believed* horrible things."

"I made it pretty easy to believe."

She shook her head. "But I should have known. You were protecting me. Savvy. Mac. All of us. Even Daddy...who should have been protecting you."

Charlotte tugged her sister to her, ignoring the shooting pains zooming through her body. Her heart pressed against the walls of her chest, the force of the light breaking the last of the ice encapsulating her heart. *Thank you, Jesus.* Charlotte leaned back into her pillows, sucking in a shallow breath. The cresting waves of emotion crashed into a rippling pool. Ignoring the numbing pain in her arm, reverberating with each pulse beat, she stretched to sit taller.

Georgie sat straight. "What can I get you? Do you want me to call Sally? Do you need more medicine? What?"

"I'm fine. Just a little tired. Emotional outbursts are not the Russian way. We tend to be stalwart. Suffering in silence."

"Well, you might be part Russian on your Momma's side, but you're all Southern on your Daddy's side, and we are prone to emotional outbursts. Layered in subtext and syrupy smiles. You're just gonna hav'ta learn to cope."

The wide grin stretching her sister's lips warmed Charlotte to the tips of her toes and eased her pain better than any chemical. "Then I guess I better get used to being called Charlie."

45

The tinkle of the sisters' giggling floated down the hall and warmed Mac's heart. In the last five days he had teetered between joy over Charlie's rapid recovery, and terror over what she'd endured and what was waiting for her. The sound of she and Georgie cementing their sisterly bond equalized the teeter-totter of his emotions, a tender balm to soothe the trials of every hour he'd spent away from Charlie in the last few days. He rapped his knuckles against the door. A smile tugged at his lips with the unison, "Come in."

What a picture the Dixon sisters made.

Georgie's long-limbed body, encased in an oversized Bombers sweatshirt and leggings, was cuddled against her equally leggy sister who was sporting less than her standard fashion.

"Well, aren't you a picture for this old heart."

"Mac!" Georgie bounded off the bed, wrapping her arms around his middle. Her exuberance radiated from her being with the power of the sun in July.

His gaze landed on Charlie, meeting her lake blue eyes and reading the longing he felt reflected in his own heart. Patting Georgie's back, he glanced at the darkening bruises on Charlie's cheek and stifled the percolating anger that had been simmering on a steady heat since the day he'd seen Charlie thrown into the cement pylon. His anger at those trying to harm her grew apace with the burgeoning love in his heart. This morning he had been a party to taking real strides to finding justice, a true peace for his righteous anger. Stepping back from Georgie, he closed the distance to the hospital bed in two strides, pressing his lips to Charlie's thankfully cool forehead. "How're you feeling today?"

Her grin stretched wide, cracking her dry lips, but shining brightly through her eyes. "Better, now." She laced her fingers through his waiting hand.

His anger was doused with the surge of unbridled love flowing through him. How had this miracle come into his life? Not three months ago he was frustrated with Bent for leaving the responsibility of his broken relationships with his daughters in Mac's lap. But now he wished with all of his being he could thank his old friend for the gift of the love he found with this woman. As his mother liked to say, God did work in mysterious ways.

Squeezing her fingers, he pulled his gaze from Charlie and smiled at his surrogate little sister. "What have you ladies been doing this morning?"

"Eating sugar and sharing stories. Girlie things," Georgie said. "But I need to be getting back to the house. Savvy will want a full report. I'm not sure how much longer Mellie can distract her from coming down here and making camp on the pull-out sofa." Tugging on her jacket, she leaned forward and kissed her sister's cheek. "Thank you, Charlie."

Charlie nodded, lifting the corner of her mouth. "I'll see you tomorrow?"

"Wild horses couldn't stop me." Georgie gave a little wave and nearly skipped through the door.

Mac reached for the lone chair, scrapping the legs against the floor. Settling onto the seat, he lifted their linked hands to his lips and brushed a light kiss across her knuckles. "How're you really feeling?"

"Tired. Sore. But clearer-headed. Georgie and I had a nice visit. Things were said that needed to be said." She quickly told him of her morning, shyly sharing her newfound relationship with God.

He had suspected her transformation over the past few weeks because of subtle changes in her treatment of the family. The smile in her eyes twinkled when she spoke. As he listened to the joy tripping over her lips, he raised a silent thank You to the One who made all things possible. His prayers for Charlie had been answered with haste. He could only pray the continued hedge of protection around her he had desperately asked the Lord for this morning would be given with the same expediency.

He loved hearing her story laced with tentative excitement. He could see the conversion shining through her, but her background challenged trusting anyone or anything, even the Creator of the Universe. He hated the fact that the story he needed to share would test her newfound faith. Yanking his tie free, he kneaded the small tendons connecting his shoulders to his neck.

She trailed off midsentence and watched him with

clear blue eyes darkening under her hooded gaze. "What happened?"

Why did he have to tell her? He should have left the answers to her questions to the professionals. O'Neal and Murphy were equipped to deal with the ins and outs of what was coming next. His stomach was rolling in anticipation of bursting her current euphoric bubble.

He hissed a sigh and grazed his thumb against her knuckles. The slight, tender touch slid liquid heat through his veins warming his spirit, fanning the flames of desire burning in his belly. How was he supposed to destroy this woman he loved more than his own life?

"Mac, please..." She clasped her open hand around their linked fingers, willing him to raise his gaze to her. "Tell me what happened."

"Do you know how beautiful you are?"

"Taylor, I might have this new relationship with Jesus, but it doesn't mean I don't remember how to be sassy. Tell me what happened."

"Your mother..."

She jerked her hand from his grip, lacing her arms tightly across her middle. "I don't want to talk about her. Talking about her is what got us into this colossal mess. If it wasn't for her, Georgie never would have been kidnapped. Remy would be awake. Bridget would still be alive. People are dead because of her."

"But you are alive because of her."

"What?"

"Stasi is the person who led us to the church. She

knew Anton and his henchmen had you. She also knew about Cole. She was able to give Murphy and O'Neal enough details that they were able to get the police to you in time."

"My mother saved my life?"

He nodded. "As soon as she found out about Georgie, she confronted Anton, but he was already here. She knew you would be taken next. True leverage over her. She must have been on a plane within hours of you leaving New York. She rushed to the house. And gave us everything we needed to find you. No one on Anton's side counted on her love for you. And no one counted on Cole's love for Georgie."

Her head dropped back to the stack of pillows. Although her layers were only slowly being revealed to him, he knew her well enough to recognize her need to process. Closing her eyes, she rubbed her temple, as if to conjure up an image in her mind's eye. Her cheeks glistened with tears streaming over her cheeks. Her breathing came in long, deep drags. Silence hung between them.

He reached inside his jacket pocket and pulled out a plain white business envelope, with her name written in neat letters across the front. Laying the sealed envelope on the table, he could only guess the message lingering inside.

Charlie curved her head toward him, her gaze revealing confusion. "Why would she come here? Why would she risk her life? Risk everything?"

"Charlie, honey, you're her daughter. She loves you."

She snorted. "Funny. She hasn't really been a loving mother in the last thirty plus years. Why did she pick now to start?"

"I don't know, but I know I'm thankful. If she hadn't intervened, you wouldn't be alive."

A single tear fell from her eye and plopped on the pillow. "You really think she loves me?" her voice was barely a whisper.

He imagined the shadow of a little girl waiting in a boarding school hoping one of her parents would come to whisk her away. And neither ever did. Squeezing her hand, he tried to absorb some of the emotional pain Charlotte seemed to have sewn into her soul. "Yes. I know she loves you."

"How?"

"Well, I have two reasons. For starters the whirlwind trip into the face of danger to rescue her baby is one. The other? She's been cooperating with the FBI for the last few days."

"What do you mean 'she's been cooperating'? Is she under arrest? They shouldn't do that. Not after she saved my life."

Mac wanted to chuckle at the quick defense of her mother. Charlie might not realize how deeply entrenched she was in the love she had for her family, but her family motivated every decision she'd made in her life.

"She's agreed to testify against Anton and his entire operation. They've been connected for over thirty years. She knows more than anyone could imagine. She's willing to give up her whole life to ensure you will never be threatened again."

"How do you know all of this?"

"The reason I wasn't here this morning, for which I'm quite sorry. I was in Charleston acting as your mother's counsel."

"What? You're my mother's lawyer?"

He nodded. When Murphy asked him to act as a witness to Stasi's confession, he wanted to politely decline. He wasn't sure he would ever be able to be truly objective where Charlie's mother was concerned. But the why behind Murphy's request twisted his arm to the point of snapping. The Special Agent rationalized, the smaller the circle of people who truly knew what transpired downtown, the safer Charlie would be throughout her life. Murphy and O'Neal moved Stasi to a secure location to outline her testimony. They had also moved Anton, Cole, and Vsevolod to separate holding cells. The three were uncooperative. But Murphy's boss, Senior Special Agent Cavanaugh, was able to work with the U.S. Attorney and kept their arraignment hearings sealed. The agents worked quickly with the information they'd collected over the last two years and combined with the updated insights from Stasi, they'd raided Dorokov's illegal gaming operation, and seized two shipping containers carrying weapons, drugs, and fourteen young women they left port from the New York Harbor. Although no one wanted more drugs or illegal weapons floating in the black market, rescuing the fourteen women, all under seventeen and listed as runaways in the system, was the biggest answered prayer.

"Your mother's testimony will be critical to severely crippling, if not destroying, the *Bratva's* foothold in New York. I was brought in today to help work through her end of her plea agreement."

"Plea?"

"In exchange for immunity, your mother has agreed to testify against Anton and his partners. Since she not only gambled illegally for decades with Anton, but she also orchestrated the money laundering through the gallery, as well as opened additional shady doors for Dorokov, your mother is legally culpable."

Charlotte scrunched her forehead. "But she isn't going to prison?"

"She is getting immunity. And she will be entering the witness protection program." U.S. Marshals assigned to WITSEC had come to collect Stasi this afternoon. She would be moved to a temporary location until the trial, and then they would finalize her move once her testimony was given. Anastasia Bickford would be gone.

"Wait, Mac…if Mama goes into witness protection, I'll never see her again."

He reached for the envelope. Why did he always have to be the messenger?

46

Cade never guessed falling in love would be hazardous. But at this moment he would have rather run "The Yellow Brick Road" at Quantico twenty times in succession, than deal with the danger lurking in his temporary Charleston office.

Lean, legging-encased limbs dangled over the edge of his metal and pressed wood desk. The sight sparked the flame of desire in his belly. His gaze drifted up the legs to an oversized sweatshirt and the tightly laced arms of his personal Achilles heel.

Walking around to his chair, he pecked a kiss to Georgie's cheek. "This is an unexpected surprise." In reality, Georgie in his office was only 'unexpected' and a 'surprise' because her arrival was delayed by about two days by his estimation.

Twisting on her hip, she pressed her hands against the desk, splaying her long fingers wide. "Don't try and 'what a surprise' me, mister. You promised I could talk to Cole. It's been three days since he was released from the hospital. Three days, Cade."

Even when she was angry, he loved the sound of his name on her lips. "Georgie, honey. It's not that simple."

"Well, Cade, *honey*. Why don't you make it that

simple? Five minutes. I just need five minutes with him."

Rage bloomed in his chest, fed by the thought of Cole Vasil being within five hundred feet of Georgie. He leaned back in his metal and vinyl chair as far as his cramped office would allow. Locking his gaze with those ocean blue eyes that seemed to read his every thought, he felt the rage steady to a simmer. She had a right to talk to the friend who betrayed her. To ask the questions to which she likely would receive no satisfying answers. If Cade was being honest, he saw little danger to Georgie being in a room with Cole. The prisoner had been the one to release Georgie. For what reason, he hadn't been able to extract from the man after three days of interrogation, but Vasil did appear to have a soft spot for Georgie. Although with Stasi's extensive testimony the U.S. Attorney needed little else from the three prisoners they'd captured at the abandoned church. But perhaps Georgie could find the closure she needed.

Releasing a sigh, he stretched his hand forward and covered hers with a squeeze. "I will see what I can do."

Her face shined. "Thank you, Cade. This means so much to me."

"I hope you are still thanking me when you're finished."

~*~

Georgie glanced at the sterile walls lining the

undersized interrogation room. Sitting at a wide metal table, there were just two other chairs in the room, a single entrance door and a wide pane of two-way glass.

No natural light. No excess air.

Just white walls, fluorescent lighting, and the stale fragrance of sweat. There were no bars in the room, but prison was stamped on every surface.

Rubbing her forehead, she willed the throbbing headache to ease. The pain had been building all day, but she'd avoided the prescription pain medication given to her at the emergency room five days earlier. She needed to be sharp. Clear of mind, if not free from pain. When she'd chosen to drive to Charleston instead of returning home, she knew she wouldn't leave without the answers she needed. She could barely justify the decision in her own mind, and yet, she somehow convinced Cade talking to Cole was a sane idea.

Since the moment she'd realized Cole was behind her and her sister's kidnappings, the house fire, the bombings, Remy's accident, everything that had happened since her father's death, she had one burning question she wanted to ask him. One question she hoped he would honestly answer. She needed to know what forgiveness was required so she could close the door to the past and step into the future.

The creak of the metal hinges snapped her attention to the lone door as Cole shuffled into the room, his ankles shackled together. His uninjured arm was linked to his waist with a single handcuff attached to a wide chain. The wounded arm was bound tight to his chest in a sling. But despite the chains and the plain prison jumpsuit, he still looked like her Cole.

And with that vision her heart cracked at the loss of her friend.

Cade guided Cole by the elbow to the chair on the opposite side of the table from her. The chains clinked against the metal and a shot of pain rippled across Cole's face as he lowered himself to sit. Leveling his gaze to hers, a slow smile crept to his lips. "This is an unexpected surprise."

A chill tiptoed up her spine at the reflection of cold cruelty shining in the depths of his eyes. "I'm full of them today."

"Georgie, you get five minutes. You're down to four fifty." Cade leaned his shoulders against the cement brick walls of the room. He faced Georgie, but never lifted his gaze from Cole.

"Yes, well, I'm hoping this will only take one," she said. "Cole, did Anton Dorokhov murder my mother?" She could feel Cade's stare shift to her. They hadn't discussed his theory about her mother's death since the night they'd shared root beers and she'd convinced him Charlie didn't have any connection to her mother's death.

"Georgie, cancer took your mother. You told me yourself."

"My mother died in a car accident, on the way to a cancer treatment. My father was supposed to drive her, but he was detained. The brakes gave out on the car. She and the driver both died due to their injuries."

"Why do you believe Anton is connected?"

"Charlotte would have inherited half of my father's estate. She was still young enough her mother would have assumed at least some control. Fifty percent of a multinational corporation was a good motive a year ago when you infiltrated my father's company. I would imagine this was not the first time the thought was floated amongst your group of friends."

Cole shifted in his seat, clanking the chains against metal. "Well, you have developed an interesting theory, Georgie. I may still call you Georgie, yes?"

She nodded. She could almost feel the wheels clicking in his mind. Her heart thumped like a dog scratching an itch. Would he answer her? Did he know the truth? He was young enough he may not have been a party to a scheme concocted over a decade earlier. Her heart knew Cole held the answers to the litany of questions burning in her spirit. Each of those questions hinged on the answer to the first.

But could he be trusted?

Cole was intelligent. He was cunning. And he was an Academy Award winning liar. And yet, she believed she could still trust his answer. Despite everything, she believed, rather, she hoped, he would still give his friend honesty.

"I will answer your query, but I would rather tell you the answer in private," he said, with a glance over his shoulder.

"Forget it." Cade said. "I'm not leaving. You want to spill your guts. You're gonna have to do it with me as your watchdog."

Georgie stretched her hand across the table. "Please, Cole, if we were ever truly friends. Please tell me if Dorokhov had any connection to my mother's death."

His gray blue eyes conveyed his friendship to her; the care she'd so often sought in him over the last year. With the singular glance she knew he held the truth. A truth she was convinced he wanted to share.

"Tell me what you know."

"Lean closer. I will whisper in your ear."

She stretched forward, meeting him over halfway. The thumping of her pulse was so loud in her heart, she was surprised it didn't rattle the metal table. The smooth surface was cool through the worn sweatshirt, but the ripple of goosebumps were not driven by the flash of cold to her skin.

The soft compassion reflected in Cole's eyes swiftly flipped to cold cruelty. He snapped his bandaged arm from the sling and clutched Georgie's throat in his wide grip.

Her eyes went wide. Choking and sputtering, she grasped for a single breath through her slack mouth.

Cade's shouts to release her reverberated off the cramped walls, but did little to deter Cole who dragged her across the metal table, clutching her to his body, a human shield against the thundering footsteps pounding toward them.

Still chained on the left side of his body and at his ankles, Cole shuffled backward, dragging Georgie by the neck. Her feet landed with a thud to the floor.

Scratching at his hand locked around her windpipe, she struggled to suck in a breath. The cinderblock room tilted to the left, Cade's form wavy in her vision. His edges sifted to fog. She heard shouting, but the words were muddled.

Dylan and a female agent slammed open the door, guns raised toward Cole and her.

Cade raised both hands, free of firearms, and slid in front of the agents, placing himself in the target range.

Cole suctioned her body to him. His chained hand clamped his fingers into the soft flesh at her waist. Searing fire radiated from the spot, snapping her back to consciousness. Clawing against the hand clutching her neck, she could feel a spurt of warmth oozing through her sweatshirt onto her back.

With both of her hands, she yanked down on Cole's forefinger with a snap and slammed her right shoulder into his opening wound, checking their bodies into the cement wall. A guttural screech bellowed through Cole's frame, releasing the tension on her neck and waist. She stumbled forward to her knees, landing with a crack. In an instant she was smashed flat to the floor a single gunshot ringing through the room. Georgie tried to cup her ears to block the sound, but her hands were clamped to her side.

The thud of weight thumped near her feet.

A blanket of silence cocooned her, her breaths shaky but steady.

The shuffle of footsteps paced the slowing of her

heart.

Shouting grew clearer. Closer to her cocoon.

"Bus!"

"Medic!"

Words took shape as she felt her body sliding across the floor. Arms wrapped around her frame, cuddling her to a wide chest. Forcing her eyelids open, she stared into the tear-filled eyes of Cade.

He grazed his knuckles over her cheek with a touch as light as a butterfly's wing. Kissing her forehead, he rocked her like she was an infant, murmuring unintelligible words in her ear. His care seeped through her body warming her with sparks of fire tingling under her skin.

Raising a hand to his cheek, she wiped a tear with her thumb. "My hero." Her voice sounded as if she'd woken from a hundred years sleep, but the world was beginning to fade around her and she needed him to hear her. "I love you, Cade Murphy. Thank you." Her hand dropped to her waist and she floated until the darkness pulled her under.

47

Charlotte stretched her fingers against the final glow of the setting sun warming the wide window in her hospital room. Resting her forehead against the glass, she released a slow breath, fogging the surface. Since Mac received the text from Murphy nearly three hours ago, she'd been unable to sit patiently in her bed waiting for news on Georgie. Why had her sister gone to Charleston? What had possessed her to see Cole Vasil?

Answers.

Georgie wanted to know the 'whys' behind Cole's artful deception.

Charlotte couldn't argue with the desire to know the truth. She wanted to understand Mama's about-face as well. How was the most selfish woman Charlotte had ever known willing to sacrifice her whole life to save her daughter? Charlotte turned from the smoldering remnants of God's daily masterpiece and reached for the letter she'd left lying on the end table. She'd read the letter over a dozen times since she'd first opened it early this afternoon. After the initial shock, she tried to process the contents, seeking out the hidden artifice clinging to the simple sentences.

Settling into the stiff one-and-a-half-person

loveseat angled toward her hospital bed, Charlotte held the letter stretched between her two hands. The words blurred to her strained eyesight, but she could almost recite them from memory after hour upon hour of reading.

My Darling CharlotteI wish I could write this letter with joy in my heart, but my pen is filled with regret piled upon regret for the mother I've been to you. You, my malyshka, my baby girl have been the one good thing I've done in my life, but you were the source of that good, not me.

I did not create you, you created you in spite of me and your father.

I regret, most, that I kept you from him. I was afraid you would leave me, choose him and that woman over me, and I would forever be alone. But you were always a good girl and you chose your Mama. Even when I didn't deserve your love and protection, you gave it.

I want you to know that I did not plan for your gallery, or anything in your life, to become involved in ~~Anton's~~ *I mean, my mess, but I saw no other way to solve the problem. As with most of my life I took the easy path. You, malyshka, never had an option for an easy path. You always had a hard road to follow and I only threw more rocks in the path. For that I am truly sorry and beg for your forgiveness.*

Now, I choose the hard path and though I know it doesn't make up for who I've been, I hope you will find it in your heart to forgive me. And maybe, Charlotte, you will be proud of your Mama, who chose you when it mattered.
With my love,
Mama

Charlotte scrubbed her face with her hands. Rereading the letter didn't give her any clarity or direction. Every rational part of her person wanted to rip the letter to threads. Too little, too late. But the six-year-old who could still see the smudged mascara under her mother's sad eyes wanted to run to Mama and hold her until she felt better.

She refolded the letter and stuffed it into the torn envelope. Stretching to stand, she began to pace the small space between the sofa and her door. Thankfully, her IV drip had been removed earlier and she could seek her answers through motion. She may not be able to run, but she was always clearer-headed when her arms and legs were swinging. On her fifth turn of the room, the door to the hallway creaked open.

"I'z coming in. If you not decent, make it so."

A smile tugged at Charlotte's lips. "Baba!" She rushed to stretch wide the door revealing her diminutive grandmother gliding into the hospital room. Snatching her in a hug, she breathed in her floral and spice laden scent. "What are you doing in South Carolina?"

Baba patted her back. Stepping back from Charlotte, she lowered herself onto the edge of the chair Mac had vacated four hours earlier. "I came to see if you were alive. You like to be near exploding t'ings since you move away. I never knows if you are alives. I must see for self. My heart iz happy you are alives. But if you nots gets in the bed, you catch cold and die. And I makes long trip for nothings." She swatted her hand in the direction of the hospital bed and Charlotte gladly conceded.

"Now I see you OK, why not tell my whys you pace, hmm? Wear hole in floor? You drop through. No good for healings."

Charlotte curled to her side, snuggling her head into the scratchy hospital linen stretched across the pillow and faced Baba. How could she ever have thought her grandmother would have been involved with her mother's drama? "It's Mama..."

48

A grin tugged Mac's lips into a curl with the soft chatter floating into the hallway from Charlie's room. Pressing the door open with his wide palm, the ever-present exhausted tension stretching his shoulders seemed to ease in an instant as he took in the idyllic picture of Charlie with her grandmother.

Alla Bickford was a stunning woman. Not stunning for her age. Simply stunning. She sat on the edge of the chair he had called his second home for the past five days. Her ankles were crossed and tucked, barely grazing the floor. Stark white hair was twisted in a neat knot at the base of her neck. Her spine appeared as if she had a metal rod melded to her frame. Draped in black silk, topped with a fur stretched across her shoulders, she looked to Mac as if she was holding court, deigning to give the joy of her presence to her subjects. And her number one subject was curled on her side, head resting on a folded arm gazing at her grandmother with loving peace exuding from her.

"Excuse me ladies, may I interrupt this party?"

Charlie flipped over to face him, her lips stretched wide. A sparkle sizzled in her eyes warming him to his core. "How's Georgie?" Charlie pushed herself up to sit. Her eyes shuttered for a moment and she sucked in a slow steadying breath.

Mac closed the distance between them in two strides. "Whoa, honey, you OK?" He stroked her back and hitched his hip onto the edge of her bed.

She nodded, lifting a finger. "Georgie?"

"She'll be fine. A little bruised up, but fine. She should be halfway to Colin's Fancy by now. Murphy swore he would escort her personally. And, I imagine, Savvy will stuff her so full Georgie won't move from the house for a week." Lacing his fingers through hers, he gave a soft squeeze. "How are you? Are you sure you should go home tomorrow?"

She nodded. "I'm fine. Just a little bruised up, but fine." She gave him a wink and a soft nod to her grandmother. "Mac Taylor, I would like to introduce you to Alloochka Antonov Bickford, my Babushka. Baba, this is my Mac."

My Mac...

His heart burned with Charlie's words as he shuffled around the end of her bed. "Mrs. Bickford, it is an honor to meet you." He stretched his hand forward to her, thankful the tremble he could feel shudder through his body didn't reverberate through his fingers.

She nodded and placed her four fingers across his forefinger. Diminutive but strong. He lifted her hand to his lips and pressed a soft kiss to her knuckles.

"The pleasures to meet 'my Mac' iz mines." She nodded shifting in her seat to focus on Charlie. "Dorogoy, you getz betters." She stretched to stand, lengthening her body with the grace of an eternal ballerina. "I go home. Much to consider. You come visit, no?"

Charlie nodded. "As soon as I can."

"You follow heart. Not time to be Russian. OKz?"

A cloud seemed to douse the joy reflected mere seconds earlier on Charlie's face. "I will think about it, Baba."

"Goodz." With a nod, she twisted to face Mac. Clamping her long fingers against his jaw her dark gaze pierced his. "You takes care of my baby. She all I have. Now she yours."

"Yes, Ma'am."

Loosening her grip, she patted his cheek, with the faintest smile tugging on her lips. "Charlotte tells me you loves Jesus and the baseballs."

He chuckled. "Yes…"

"Goodz. All goodz. Must go." She leaned over Charlie and pressed a soft kiss to her cheek, whispering something in Russian Mac couldn't understand. But the unspoken language of love translated to a soft trickle of tears streaming down Charlie's face as she gripped her grandmother's hand. "Please stay, Baba. You could come back to Colin's Fancy. Eat too much of Savvy's food. Meet Georgie. Wouldn't that be nice?"

Alla patted Charlie's hand. "Another day, dorogoy. Today must return to home. Much to do. You come see me when you betters. Bring 'My Mac' to your New York."

"Yes, Baba. I will. I promise."

"*Ya lyublyu tebya*," Alla said, with a kiss to Charlie's palm.

"I love you, too, Baba. Be safe."

Alla nodded, wrapping the fur stole tightly around her ramrod straight shoulders. Her soft footsteps closed the distance to the doorway in seconds, but she seemed never to move. With a glance over her shoulder, she nodded again to Charlie and then to Mac. A slight sheen glistened in her eyes. "Take carez. *Spokoynoy nochi*." With a raised hand she turned and glided through the doorway, her spicy, floral scent lingering in her wake.

Mac glanced down at Charlie. Her palms were pressed against her eyes. Tears shook her frame, echoing through Mac's spirit.

Resting against the edge of her bed, he drew Charlie into his arms.

~*~

The feel of Mac's gentle embrace poured strength and peace into Charlotte's spirit. Drawing in a deep breath, she tried to settle the tremble shimmering through her frame. The seemingly ever-present tears slowed and she wiped her cheek against Mac's soft sweater. The heat from his body seeped through her pores, warming her skin, but her heart remained shaky and frozen.

Pressing away from him, she settled into the hospital grade pillows and looked into his deep brown gaze. The etched lines of worry and concern stretched across his forehead. The burn of acid bubbled in her stomach and pulled her hands to her lap. Clamping her bottom lip between her teeth, she dropped her gaze to the twilight shining through the far window. A new night with endless possibilities. Possibilities strewn with dangers she was all too aware were real. Choices needed to be made. Was she able to face the dangers? The choices?

"Hey," Mac said, tenderly clasping her jaw in his hand. "Where did you go?"

"I'm here." She shook her head and looked into the kind comfort of his chocolate brown eyes. "It's just tough to see her go."

"Did you tell her about Stasi?"

Swallowing against the rising bile, she nodded.

"Was she as surprised as we were?"

"Baba's hard to read, but I think she's proud of Mama. Proud her daughter made a good choice." She reached for his hand resting beside her, lightly floating her fingers over his wide knuckles. "I told her about you...about us."

"I see. 'My Mac'?" He raised a single eyebrow.

Heat burned against her neck and chest. "Are you OK with the title shift?"

"I might miss the scowl and 'Taylor', but I think I can adjust."

"Oh, the scowl and 'Taylor' can come back with a snap, buddy."

He leaned forward and pressed a gentle kiss to her lips. Tingles of electricity rippled through her frame from the simple touch.

"I think we can think of a better way to use those lips than a frown." He rested his forehead against hers and she felt his deep intake of breath.

"I'm sorry, Mac. All of this hasn't been fair to you."

He sat back on the bed and laced his fingers through hers. "No. It hasn't been fair to me. But all of this hasn't been fair to you, either."

"She's my mother. Her choices…"

"Aren't yours. I know your side of your relationship with God is just starting, but His relationship with you has been eternal. He died for your sins and Stasi's. He didn't sacrifice so you could inherit your mother's guilt. You have to let her baggage go. It was never yours to hold in the first place."

She nodded.

Faith seemed so easy in her head. She knew God loved her. She even could reconcile He had forgiven her. That He had taken away all of her sin and guilt. And if God had forgiven her, how could she not do the same for her Mama?

49

"Knock, knock."

At the soft lilt of Georgie's voice from the doorway, Charlotte lifted her hooded gaze to the alarm clock on her bedside table: 7:46 AM. Better than six in the morning, but still her bubbly, early rising sister was pushing the bounds of familial grace. The ache surrounded her head like a halo but didn't make her feel like much of an angel. "Unless you have black coffee and a cinnamon roll, you will need to return in an hour." Charlotte said, stuffing her face into the fluffy down pillow.

"I have both!"

Georgie's steps creaked against the old floorboards. The aroma of chicory coffee mixed with the spicy sweet roll lifted Charlotte's head from the pillow. Her sister lowered a wide breakfast tray on to the white duvet, filled with two coffee mugs, a tall carafe, and barely enough room for the half dozen rolls teetering against the edge.

"Georgie, there's just two of us. Do you want us to go into a sugar coma?"

Georgie chuckled. "The thought is kind of appealing."

Charlotte reached for the carafe and sloshed coffee

into her mug, feeling the caffeine perk her system through the intoxicatingly rich scent. Taking a tentative sip, she snuggled against the pillows stretched against the four poster bed and lifted an eyebrow to her sister.

"But," Georgie sighed. "We have some business that needs to be resolved."

Pinpricks raced along the back of Charlotte's neck. What had Georgie and Mac found while she had been recuperating? Charlotte reached for a cinnamon roll. "Lay it on me." She sank her teeth into the toothache-inducing sweetness, allowing the empty calories to be the filter for Georgie's message.

"Cole was siphoning funds from several different entities, but the majority were taken out of the funds supporting the Watershed Foundation. He was deftly recording the donations, but the funds were transferred to a shell corporation with the outward appearance of being able to properly distribute resources to designated charitable organizations. The corporation is a known front for Dorokov and his partners. Despite what appeared to be healthy books, the Foundation is nearly bankrupt."

"Oh, no, Georgie." She laid her roll on a plate, wiping her sticky fingers on a napkin as she reached for her sister's hand. "The music and arts program?"

Georgie shrugged. "Until we are able to reestablish the Foundation with clean books and cash flow, approved by the IRS, the program will be a non-starter."

The cinnamon-sugar syrup turned to tar in Charlotte's mouth. Georgie should not be suffering for her family's mistakes. "I'm so sorry. We will find a way to get the program started. Maybe other benefactors? People in Beaufort County?"

Georgie shook her head. "I think we should just focus on stabilizing Watershed and having a winning Bombers season. The need for an afterschool program isn't going away. But right now we should focus on our family. Our business."

Charlotte yanked Georgie into a hug, the fading bruises at her neck burning her vision. "I'm so sorry for everything, Georgie. I don't deserve you or Savvy or anyone. This is all my fault."

Georgie gently disentangled herself from Charlotte. "Stop." She cupped Charlotte's cheeks in her hands. "Stop blaming yourself. Believe it or not, you are not in control of the entire universe, Charlotte Dixon."

Resting her forehead against her sister's, Charlotte sucked in a deep, cleansing breath. "That's a hard lesson for me to remember. It's harder for me to believe."

Settling back onto the bed, Georgie clasped Charlotte's hands between hers. "Forgiveness is the most difficult thing we are asked to do as Christians, because true forgiveness cannot coexist with lingering guilt. Charlie, you have to forgive yourself. Did you handle the situation perfectly? No. But did you have the best of intentions? Yes. Every decision you've made, since finding out about what was happening at your art gallery, has been about protecting the people you love. Your error wasn't in trying to help. Your error was in trying to fix things by yourself. You are not being asked by God to do penance for your mother's sins. And He is not asking you to flay yourself with the whip of guilt for the next thirty years to earn His grace for your own sins. He already sacrificed enough for you to have forgiveness. You have to take the big, difficult step to accept His grace."

"This seems to be a reoccurring message from Mac and my grandmother."

"Maybe three times is truly a charm and you will accept you are loved and forgiven? Do not keep wallowing in what can't be changed. Instead look to what can be made new and whole in the future."

"How did the younger sister come to be the wiser sister?"

Georgie lifted a shoulder. "Age does not parlay wisdom."

"Touché."

Georgie poured a mug of coffee and lifted it to Charlotte in a salute. "To new beginnings."

Charlotte lifted her own mug. "To new beginnings."

They clinked cups and sipped the warm, dark coffee. The bitterness of the dark roast melded with the remnants of the cinnamon roll in Charlotte's mouth creating the perfect balance of flavors. A harmony of what her life could be. Strength and kindness melded together.

She listened to Georgie discuss the coming weeks of meetings with different government officials to clear Watershed of any wrongdoing associated with Cole

Vasil and Anton Dorokov. Charlotte's heart seemed to swell five sizes bigger as she listened to her sister. Her meek Georgie, who six months ago could not decipher the difference between a balance sheet and a box score, exuded serene confidence as she outlined the multipoint plan to shore up the security breaches in the company and ensure the growth of Watershed.

Her sister didn't need her anymore. Watershed would be well managed with or without Charlotte at the co-CEO helm. The knowledge relieved her lingering doubts. The decision she made in the hospital after reading her mother's letter took root in her spirit. Now, could she make the ultimate sacrifice? Could she be like Jesus?

50

"The jet will be leaving at noon tomorrow to head to Florida. We will have one extra seat if you have anyone you want to invite." Mac looked across his desk at Georgie, who stared out his office window toward the ballpark. Closing the folder, he placed it in a matching stack on his desk. "What gives, Slugger?"

"Huh?" Georgie shifted her gaze to face him, but her eyes were cloudy.

"What's the worry of the day? It isn't Murphy, is it? If he hurt your feelings, I will make him wish he'd never set foot in South Carolina."

Georgie chuckled. "No. Cade is fine. We are more than fine. And you really should start calling him by his first name. He has one, you know."

Cade? He could try. "OK, if it isn't you and your...friend. What's bothering you?"

"Have you noticed Charlotte has been working overtime since she returned to the office? She has barely been out of the hospital a week. It's like she's trying to make up every hour she's missed in the last two weeks in a few days. I know we are ramping up for the season, but it's Sunday and we are all in the office. Do you know why?"

He reached his hand to knead the knot forming in

his shoulder muscle. "I'm not sure. But my best guess would be she's trying to get back to normal. Whatever normal is for this group."

"But she shouldn't be working so hard. She's had so many traumatic things happen to her...both mentally and physically. Don't you think she should take it easy?"

Mac glanced at the greenish-yellow marks still visible at Georgie's neck and wondered the same about her. "I think work gives her something to focus on."

Georgie picked up the Johnny Bench autographed baseball his father gave him for his thirteenth birthday. His stomach flipped on its side. "Slugger, I love you like the sister I never wanted, but if you smudge that baseball, love will take a backseat."

She gently returned the ball and laced her arms across her middle. "I understand wanting to focus on anything *but* what she's endured or what her mother is currently enduring. I get it, but I'm afraid she'll break. She's tough, but she's not as tough as she thinks she is. No matter how many conversations we have, it always seems to be weighted with a sense of guilt Charlie can't or won't release. That's just not healthy, Mac."

"No. It's not. But I'm not comfortable talking about your sister behind her back. When she is ready for help, she will ask. You need to trust God is working through her. He will help her find her way."

Georgie nodded and stood to exit his office. She opened the door and smiled over her shoulder. "My plus one's name is Cade Murphy. He's wrapping up a few things but should make it back down in time to make the flight. He's got pretty high security clearance so he shouldn't cause a problem when he's vetted." She sauntered out of his office.

Mac twisted his chair to face the ballpark, increasing the pressure as he kneaded the muscles connecting his neck and shoulders. His little Georgie was quickly growing into a full-blown woman. He blew out a slow steady breath. "When did that happen?"

"About six months ago."

Mac swiveled and his stomach dropped.

Charlie leaned against the doorframe of his office draped in a high neck, soft pink, sleeveless blouse tucked into a formfitting navy-blue pencil skirt skimming her too long legs to just above her knees. His gaze raked over her form to the four-inch high stilettoes she favored. "You'll break your neck in those things."

She slipped into the room and lowered onto the edge of the visitor chair. "Nope. I can run a fairly fast forty in heels. Men's flip-flops might be a different story."

He couldn't help the chuckle, despite the agony of that particular memory. "What gives me the great honor of a visit? I thought you were going up to Charleston to see Remy."

"I am. His mama said he squeezed her hand yesterday."

"Ah, Charlie, that's wonderful."

She nodded. "I wanted to discuss the itinerary for Florida before I headed out." She laid her folder on the desk. "I need to arrange different travel."

Mac felt his brow furrow. "Why? We're all leaving tomorrow. Stella booked us a block of suites in the hotel closest to the training facility. We have two days of practice games where you can pick apart every prospect we, and the big-league team, have on our rosters. To me it sounds like your little slice of heaven in Florida." Mac had been counting the hours until they could enjoy the carefree warmth of Spring Training days. The sweet relish and mustard combo hot dog had his mouth watering for over a week. His emergency cell phone pinged in his desk, dragging his thoughts from the welcoming sunshine and popcorn only hours away.

He held up a finger to Charlie as he pulled out the antiquated flip-phone he kept specifically for family emergencies. "Sean? What's wrong?"

"Where've you been? I've been trying to get you for the last twenty-four hours." His brother's panic stretched through the phone.

"My phone was dead, and I left the back-up at work. Hold on a second." He placed his hand over the bottom of the phone. "I'm sorry. Can we talk about this in a minute? It's my brother."

Charlie nodded, and if he were a betting person, he would have doubled down on a wave of relief washing over her. "I'll just leave you to it." She rose and closed the distance to the doorway. With a glance over her shoulder, she lifted a smile, but the gesture didn't quite fill her eyes as she exited.

The door closed with a soft click, igniting a

burning desire to slam the phone closed and run after Charlie. Something wasn't right.

"Mac...bro? Are you there?" Sean's shaky voice drew him back to the phone pressed to his ear.

"What is it?"

"It's Sprout."

Mac's eyelids slammed shut against the glare of the midmorning sun. "What did he do this time?" His little brother, Joey, was one of the best centerfielders Mac had ever seen play the game. He also managed to hold the title of the biggest moron.

"He was in an accident. It's bad."

His pulse quickened as he listened to Sean relay the details of his little brother's latest mess up. And it was bad.

"Is he conscious?" He listened to the additional details of the near-death car accident. His brother had been using something to dull his endless cycle of pain and was now looking at extensive rehab. His mind began to flash through the variety of rehabs where he'd sent both ball players and executives. "I have a place in mind. I'll make a call." Mac rolled through the details of moving his brother to South Carolina. He would have to delay his trip to Florida, but he couldn't worry about the work-play excursion of spring training baseball. His baby brother needed him.

Family came first. Always.

~*~

Charlotte slid onto her white leather, high back

desk chair and swiveled toward the stadium.

Bombers Stadium. The place of her childhood comfort and her adult longing. She drew in a deep breath and bowed her head. *God...Jesus...Not really sure how these conversations are supposed to start. I know I've asked more than my fair share lately, but I was hoping you could watch out for Georgie, Savvy, Baba, and my Mac. Continue to help Remy heal. I'm not sure how my decisions over the next few days will impact them, but I'm afraid I will hurt them once again. I know they always have You. They all love You more than I could have ever imagined. Please be near them, Lord. Please.* With an exhale, she lifted her lids and stared out at her greatest dream. The morning sun glinted off the wrought iron gates. "Daddy, if you can...watch over them too. I'm sorry I couldn't do what you asked. I hope God lets you know I'm sorry. And I love you." She knew what she needed to do.

Family came first. Always.

A single tear splashed her hand as she stacked four long, plain white envelopes together and placed them in the center of her desk.

The top one simply said: *Mac*

51

The cramped clerk's office had thick faux mahogany wood paneled walls lined with unorganized rows of photos, awards shouting far-flung successes ranging from 'best new employee' to bowling league champs and bulletin boards stuffed with every take-out menu and dry cleaning coupon Charlotte imagined existed in the five boroughs.

Less than eight miles by car to her childhood residence, and yet she might as well have been a continent away. Her view as a child was of Central Park and the gentle whispers of Upper East Side luxury. As an adult, she had the hipster-chic of SoHo rhythm surrounding her. She knew her city by the sounds and the sights, but the gritty world of law and justice hummed a tune off pitch and raw to her spirit. The mixture of postmodern grandeur and intimidation built on part of the historic Five Points, what once was one of the worst slums in America, seemed fitting. The halls of blind justice were helping to redeem the country from the clutches of the modern mafia on the playground of the original gangs of New York.

Glancing out the window to the surprisingly quiet Pearl Street, she pressed her hand against the cool glass, offering a silent prayer of thanksgiving she was able to be in this place today. Despite her unsettled state, Charlotte was confident she made the right choice in coming to New York.

The preliminary hearing for Anton was today, and likely would stretch into tomorrow. Mama was being called by the U.S. Attorney to confirm the depositions she'd given to Dylan and Cade. Despite the swiftness with which the hearing had started, Cade had informed Charlotte today was only the beginning of what would begin a multiple months', potentially years', long process of bringing the New York City *Bratva* to some semblance of justice.

The Assistant U.S. Attorney assigned to the case was as giddy as a schoolgirl when she met Charlotte early that morning. The evidence Cade, Dylan, and their team had curated over the last two years, coupled with Mama's corroboration of specific events and dealings, allowed for the swift transition from arraignment to the preliminary hearing. The A-USA believed a plea deal was probable. One she promised would ensure Anton and his cronies wouldn't see the sunrise in Little Odessa for the rest of their lives.

Charlotte was proud of her mother's choice to testify against the man who had been her protector, benefactor, lover, and ultimately, her tender vulnerability for decades. But her mother's uncharacteristic choice caused a knot of worry to grow in Charlotte's belly since she read her letter over a week and a half ago. Up to today, she had the letter, Cade's reassurance, and the U.S. Attorney's excitement to confirm the radical change in her mother. Her heart and her mind were struggling to believe the transformation of Anastasia Bickford.

The same woman who had twisted her life in knots giving and withholding her love as if it was a carnival toy, only won by the most skilled and tenacious of champions, was supposedly sacrificing the luxuries of her life to ensure her daughter's safety and the dissolution of the Russian mafia.

Charlotte wrapped her arms around her middle. A slight chill seeped through the pane, reminding her winter very rarely recognized March as spring in New York. Thankful for the oversized cashmere turtleneck and wool pants, she cupped her hands around her mouth and blew warmth into the icy cavern they created.

The creak of the door opening behind her pulled her from her endless prayer, and her heart sped at the vision entering the office.

Mama was led into the room by Cade, but the air of superiority infusing her every move throughout Charlotte's life seemed to have evaporated. In its place she saw an aura of humility draping her mother. For the first time in Charlotte's memory, her mother was dressed age appropriate. Her mound of over-processed hair was tamed into a twist at her neck. She wore a black wool suit, with a high neck, silk blouse, accessorized with her debutante pearls. The clothes hung loose, beautifully tailored. She looked professional. Cool. The air of the Upper East Side floating on the scent of expensive perfume. But no amount of tailoring could hide the flurry of expression in her dark eyes when she caught sight of Charlotte. Love. Fear. Trepidation. Anxious joy.

All of the emotions Charlotte had coursing through her own frame reflected in her mother's gaze.

"Charlotte? What are you doing here?" She started forward her arms lifted, but she quickly let them drop to her sides as she halted her steps.

Charlotte swallowed. "I wanted to see you, Mama. To talk to you. I read your letter. I wanted to tell you thank you for…" She glanced at Cade who had laced his arms over his chest and leaned against the overstuffed bookshelf to the left of the door. He lifted an eyebrow and gave a subtle nod.

"For saving my life." Charlotte wrapped her arms tighter, tugging her wide sweater into an accordion fold across her chest.

"Oh, *malyshka*, of course. I'm so sorry…" Tears glistened against her mother's deep-set eyes, twisting Charlotte's heart with the echo of memories. Her mother always begged for forgiveness with tears.

Charlotte drew in a cleansing breath. "Mama, I wanted to talk with you for a little bit. Agent Murphy arranged this time for us." She glanced to Cade who stretched tall, twisting to the door. "We will have a meal. Talk. If that is OK with you?"

Mama snapped her hands to her mouth sucking in delight. "Charlotte that is more than I could have hoped."

Nodding, Charlotte closed the few steps to the door and accepted the take-out bag from Cade filled with lunch she doubted she would be able to swallow.

But food made talking easier. Less formal. Less an interrogation.

"If you need anything," Cade whispered into Charlotte's ear. "Dylan and I are right outside." He clamped a hand on her shoulder and gave a soft squeeze.

"Georgie's a blessed woman," Charlotte said.

The slightest pink hue tinted Cade's cheeks before he retreated into the hallway.

She opened the bag and allowed the garlic and tomato infused aroma to roll through her body. "Mmm, I love caprese pasta." She set the bag on the desk, clearing a small spot for a makeshift table. Placing two brown recyclable to-go containers on the emptied desk, she reached in the bag and pulled out plastic ware. Nodding toward the chair opposite hers, Charlotte said, "Mama, won't you join me?"

Her mother lowered onto the chair, the shadow of the once much lauded debutante lingering. Reaching for one of the boxes, she nodded. "Thank you. This smells divine. The food hasn't been Manhattan quality in the last few weeks." Her head shot up and she glanced at Charlotte. "Not that I'm complaining. The Marshals taking care of me have been lovely. They really have."

Charlotte reached her hand across the desk and squeezed her mother's clenched fist. "It's OK, Mama. I miss Manhattan food, too."

Mama's shoulders softened. A slight smile graced her lips. "I never thought I'd see you again. I promised myself if I ever did, I would be better. No complaining.

Or whining. Or making you feel...feel less than loved. I'm so sorry it took you being in danger for me to realize what a horrible mother...person I was. Am." She shook her head and twisted the wrapped plastic ware between her hands. "I never thought the situation would escalate to where it did. Your grandfather tried to get me to quit gambling. And when he died, I was able to stop. For a few months, but the draw to the game. To feel the exhilaration of the bet. The lure was too strong for me to resist. I'm weak, *malyshka*, but you know, don't you? You always have."

Charlotte looked at her mother.

The woman deprived her of a relationship with her father. Unabashedly stole from her. Twisted and misshaped her love for decades.

Saved her life.

Charlotte wanted to hate her. She wanted to rail at her for all of the injustices. But all she could see was the scared mother, with mascara shadows, who dragged her from her bed to flee South Carolina. And the scared mother who raced to South Carolina to save her life. The bookends of their relationship. She didn't want those to be the opening and the closing chapters. Charlotte wanted more. She wanted a relationship with her mother. She wanted to be a daughter. Not a caretaker. "I forgive you." The words slipped through Charlotte's lips. More of a whisper than a bold proclamation.

Mama snatched her hand and squeezed with such might, Charlotte winced.

"Oh, thank you. Thank you." She lifted Charlotte's

hand to her lips and brushed a soft kiss across her knuckles. Warm, wet tears slid over their linked fingers. "I could never have expected...I hoped...but..."

Charlotte cupped her free hand around her mother's. "It's OK, Mama. We can start over."

A wide smile stretched Mama's lips. Her eyes sparkled with looming unshed tears, matching the ones Charlotte was desperately trying to keep from spilling over her cheeks. Charlotte squeezed her mother's hands.

They could start over. But their new beginning would mean the end of everything else.

~*~

Twilight stretched over the city. Charlotte lifted the mug of tea to her lips as she watched the transition of evening roll through, announcing the close of business life and the start of social. Pin pricks of light popped up like lightning bugs on a hot summer night. Her mind numbly flipped through the countless nights she'd armed the alarm, securing the locks on the gallery, before strolling to meet friends for a casual drink or dinner. In reflection, they were acquaintances, more than friends. She now knew what real friendship was. And with that real friendship, she had found home. And surprisingly, home was not in Manhattan where she had spent years of her life.

Home was a baseball park in a town so small it didn't make the county map.

Home was a rambling, centuries-old, drafty house complete with a pushy aunt, a nosey sister, dozens of second and third cousins, aunts, and uncles, and one fine man who was a conduit of all of God's grace.

"Why not you brings My Mac to your New York, dorogoy?" Baba asked.

Her grandmother's reflection marched alongside hers in the floor to ceiling windows.

Meeting her gaze, Charlotte shrugged. "Mac is helping his brother. He was in an accident."

"Is he OKz?"

Charlotte nodded.

"Why you not with him? You supports one you loves, no?"

"Baba, Mac needs to take care of his brother by himself." *And I couldn't do what I need to do if I saw Mac.* Charlotte turned away from the waking city and padded to a high back chair angled toward the brocade loveseat. Lowering on to the plush surface, she set her mug on the end table and scrubbed her face.

"She not your responsibility."

A shudder rippled through Charlotte's frame. Squeezing her eyes shut against the tears, she let out a steadying breath. "How can she not be? She's my mother. She saved my life. Does a life not equal a life, Baba?"

Her grandmother perched on the edge of the loveseat beside her. "She is mine. But she is her decisions. Her decisions not your decisions. You not owe her life. She your mother. She give life. She no choice but save life. That what mamas do. If I could save Anastasia, I would. But she must save self."

Charlotte dragged the back of her hand across her cheek. Lifting her gaze, she painted the image of her grandmother on the canvas of her mind.

Shock of white hair. Black brocade suit. A single white gold band stretching nearly to her knuckle on her left ring finger.

Charlotte tried to burn the image into her heart. "Baba, I've decided I'm going with Mama."

"What? Why?"

The tears threatening to overtake her flooded her vision. "I don't want my ending with her to be this...today. We had so many tense, awful years. I want a chance."

"A chance for what?"

"A chance for a real mother. A relationship that means something more than fear and trembling. Is that too much to ask?"

Baba shook her head. "But to have this chance, means you close door to all others, yes?"

Sucking in a shaky breath, Charlotte nodded.

"Anastasia would not want."

"But she will be all alone."

"She has chance to start new life. No more Anastasia. But better."

"Won't you miss her?"

"Of course. But Russians, we say good-byes. I say good-bye to Motherland. I say good-bye to husband. I say good-bye to daughter. We Russians bear tragedy. It honor to be sorrow. You Russian. You say good-bye." She patted Charlotte's hands. "You say good-bye to

Anastasia. You spend life sacrificing for her. You need live life. Not sacrifice."

"But I will never see her again."

"No."

"How can I let her go, now that I finally found her?"

52

The quiet of the early morning chaffed Charlotte's frayed nerves. Crossing and uncrossing her legs, she glanced across the narrow hall adjacent to the secluded courtroom where Cade and Dylan sat.

Dylan appeared every bit a man of leisure, with his folded *Post* propped against his crossed legs, his chubby fingers gliding against the words on the page.

Cade hunched over a pint-sized book. His forehead rested against his palm. His fingers were firmly stuffed in his short hair. His lower lip clamped between his teeth. No steely-edged special agent in sight.

Swiping her thumb against the smooth surface of her phone, she sipped her second latte, wishing she had something more distracting to read than work emails. Even having Cade's present state of confusion would be a welcome respite from the heavy weight of waiting.

The second day of her mother's testimony began promptly at eight in the morning. They shared a quick coffee, before Charlotte watched her slip into the courtroom for the closed proceedings. With the muffled click of the doors, the countdown clock ticked silently in the back of her mind.

She narrowed her focus on the contract outline for a new port acquisition, but the backlit screen blurred in her vision. Sliding her phone onto the smooth bench, she closed her eyes. She'd lost count of how many times her eyes closed against the world in the last two days. *"Father, help me know. I'm new to this faith thing, but I'm trying. I'm trying to be faithful to You. To this gift You've given to me in the new relationship I've found with Mama. But, leaving with her I leave the home You've given to me. Georgie. Savvy. Remy. Mac...Help me have the strength to do Your will, rather than my own. Amen."*

With a deep sigh, she lifted her lids and caught a glimpse of long legs stretched out alongside her. She let her gaze drink in his lean body before glancing into the welcome dark depths of his eyes. "What are you doing here?"

Mac drew her to his side and tears flooded her vision. The heat from his chest warmed her cheek through the soft cotton of his pressed shirt. His fingers barely touched her arm in a soothing caress, but the contact shot wild fires burning through her frame.

He was here.

Mac had come to her. When she needed him most, he came. Without being asked. How could she not love this man? How could she leave him? Drying her cheeks with the back of her hand, she sat straight. "Hi," her voice barely registered a whisper.

A small tilt of his lips deepened the dimple in his cheek. "Hi." He pressed a soft kiss to her cheek. "How're you holding up?"

She shrugged, sucking in a deep breath willing the

tears to retreat. "It's been a long couple days. How's your brother?"

Mac kneaded the space between his neck and his shoulders. "He's been better, but I think Sean and I have him convinced to get the help he needs. He's not quite ready to own all of his choices, but I'm praying he will take the time to not only heal his body, but his spirit as well. Baseball might be over for him, but he still has a lot of life left to live. Superstar Joey Taylor might be done, but Joe Taylor can be whoever he wants to be. He won't be famous, but he can have something different. Sprout will have to find his way. It's an amazing opportunity. A chance to start a new life. Something better."

"She has chance to start new life. No more Anastasia. But better."

Baba's words pounded inside Charlotte's mind. Could she rip the gift of starting fresh away from her mother? Could she willingly throw the gift away for herself? "Mac, can we go somewhere private to talk?"

His whole body tensed, but he nodded and extended his hand to her. Nestling her fingers in his wide grip, she nodded toward the empty office where she'd met her mother before the sun rose this morning.

The room was tight. The aroma of the coffee and rolls she shared with her mother clung to the walls. The vision of Mama sipping her coffee and daintily eating a pastry as she regaled Charlotte with the tale of her morning commute with her assigned U.S. Marshals guarding each of her steps, warmed Charlotte's spirit. She had a happy memory with her mother. An odd thought. The happiest memories with her mother included law enforcement and her mother's admission she was connected to horrific crimes. Charlotte was pleased their lives together wouldn't only be marked by disappointment and anger. Could she give up the potential of future happy memories with her?

"Charlie..."

She glanced over her shoulder.

Mac's arms were laced across his chest. His hip rested against the table, allowing his long legs to stretch wide in front of him. He exuded calm assurance, but she knew the litigator was ready to pounce.

Matching his posture, she rested her shoulder against the door, and wrapped her arms tight across her middle. Opposite of the calm she hoped to project, her mind sputtered and slogged through the words she wanted to say. The questions she needed to ask. She wanted his reassurance. Leaving with her mother was the right course of action. She needed him to say abandoning Georgie would be OK. She longed to know her future wasn't a pinpoint of happiness swallowed up by a lifetime of regret.

"Charlie," His voice was low, the sound of rumbling thunder on a warm spring evening. "I read your letter."

Fear rippled through her frame. "You did?"

He nodded. Closing the tiny gap between them, he placed his hands on her shoulders and met her gaze. "Don't do it," his words were a whisper.

Mac flooded her vision. Wide shoulders. Graying

temples. Tiny lines at his eyes. Kind eyes. *My Mac.* Raising her palm to his cheek, she stroked the day's growth of salt and pepper stubble coating his chin. "I just found her. The mother I've always wanted. How do I let her go?"

"You just found us. How can you let us go?"

Her entire body shook with the force of her ache. She wrapped her arms around his waist, longing to find her center in him. His grip slid from her shoulders and tightened across her back, lengthening her against his lean body. Pressing his lips to her cheek he whispered, "Please don't do this to us. I can't breathe without you. How can I live without you?"

Charlotte tightened her arms, trying to burrow deep into him. When she wrote the letters to Mac, Remy, Georgie, and Savvy, she was letting them go of their obligation to her. They would have better lives without her. Her life would be less, but she could take comfort in knowing the lives of the ones she loved would be better. She had been carrying a similar letter in her purse for Baba. She hadn't had the courage to leave it for her last night. Saying goodbye was easier when done from a distance. Being up close and personal yanked her well concealed emotions into the fray. Leaving face to face required courage she didn't possess.

"I love you." She said, through broken breaths. "I love you so much. But how do I choose between loving you and helping her?"

"You choose *you*, Charlie. For the first time in your life, you choose *you*. Your mother has chosen herself her entire life. This is her journey. Not yours. Don't allow her decisions to eradicate the life you've created. If you choose her, you lose everyone."

"But everything that has happened...Remy...the fire...Cole...all of it is because of me. How can I stay knowing the chaos I bring? Georgie, Savvy...you...You all deserve far better lives than ones attached to someone like me." She stepped out of his embrace and swiped at her cheeks. "All I have done is bring chaos and destruction with me."

"Charlie, you've brought love. To me. To Georgie. To Remy. To Savvy." He stepped back and lifted her chin, forcing her gaze to meet his. "I won't lie to you and tell you it was sunshine and roses. You were, are, a challenging woman. But every obstacle you placed between you and the family, between you and me, was done as an outpouring of your love. Even writing those stupid goodbye letters was your way of trying to protect all of us. And yourself. I don't know why you feel the need to punish yourself for other people's choices, but you can stop being a martyr now."

Pivoting from him, she stomped to the side wall. "I am not being a martyr."

"Yes, you are. You've been a martyr your whole life. You can stop now."

She whipped around. "How dare you? I've been trying to keep my family and friends safe. You have some nerve, Taylor."

"Ahhh...there she is. There's my Charlie."

Burning anger fizzled to embers in an instant. "I don't know what to do."

Mac stepped to her, forcing her to look up to his six foot three inches. "Yes, you do."

"I do?"

"You have to say goodbye. You have to let go so she can let go. Live the life she couldn't."

Live the life she couldn't.

Peace poured over Charlotte with the softness of summer rain. She nodded. She had asked God for direction and He seemed to be shouting through two of the most important people in her life. God had given her these precious moments with her mother, not as a motivation to stay, but as closure to walk away. She needed to say good-bye to Mama, because God had a new journey she needed to start with this man. A journey including a whole new family in South Carolina.

53

"I'll be home by Friday," Charlotte said.

"And you aren't changing your mind?" Georgie's typically soft, rounded words came through the phone clipped with a tinge of fear.

She glanced at her slim fingers linked loosely between Mac's wide ones. "I promise. I will explain everything when we get back home."

"We? Who's we?" There was the little sister she'd always wanted. Nosey. Pushy. And Annoying. Charlotte couldn't be happier. "Control your inner Austen, George. Or would you like me to start poking at you, Mrs. Special Agent? I saw that Bible Cade has been twisting his brain in a pretzel to understand."

A muttered cough pressed through the phone into Charlotte's ear.

The crack of the courtroom door sliced through the hustle of the hallway. "I have to go. It looks like the hearing is breaking for the day."

"I love you, Charlotte."

"Love you, too. Tell Savvy I'll be home soon." Slipping the phone into her purse, she stood.

The two Assistant U.S. Attorneys in charge of making the case against Anton Dorokhov and his crew exited the courtroom deep in discussion. Neither prosecutor broke their strides as they passed the group.

Dylan hustled after them, pacing his gait with theirs.

Charlotte intently logged every head nod and shake. The older A-USA tucked a stray hair behind her ear and the younger, barely shaving attorney straightened to appear nearly two inches taller.

Dylan's natural ability to build camaraderie broke through their tough exteriors.

She wondered if Dylan's super power would uncover details in favor of Mama or against her.

Dylan shook both of the A-USAs' hands and pivoted back toward them.

The warm lifeline of Mac's strong grip tightened around her fingers.

"Her testimony's complete. For now."

"Can I see her?"

"The Marshals are moving her to another temporary location today. I'll make a call. See if we can connect you."

"Dylan." Charlotte clutched his hand. "I need to say good-bye."

He nodded. Lifting his phone to his ear, he separated himself from the group.

"What if I can't see her, Mac?"

"You'll always have your last visit."

"But I didn't know it was the last."

"We never do." He pressed a soft kiss to the top of her head. "But we can be thankful when the last memory is a good one."

Charlotte thought back to coffee with her mother and a soft warmth spread through her chest.

Dylan slid his phone in his pocket, shaking his head. "I'm sorry, Charlotte."

"We can't arrange a meeting?" Mac asked.

"Not today. She will need to testify during the trial. There might be a chance then, but I think it is highly unlikely. I'm sorry."

Charlotte nodded. "I'm ready to go home." A new chapter needed to begin.

Dylan and Cade took the lead, with Mac and Charlotte following through the hallway down to the entrance on Worth Street. Mac called for their town car as they stepped through the front door. The cacophony of whistles, horns, and shouting voices vibrated through her being. The music of the city was no longer a welcome harmony, but a rowdy dissonance between her old and new life.

All three men had their phones pressed to their ears, as the quartet closed the dozen steps to the street. Tightening her grip on Mac's hand, she stretched her gaze along the lower Manhattan thoroughfare. Bike messengers, yellow cabs, creeping city buses, all crawled, sometimes with halted journeys, carrying hundreds of people by the majestic building. They had children. Spouses. Bills. Favorite restaurants. Busy jobs. Worries she could understand. And many she never would. No one maneuvering this street knew or cared about the life altering moments she experienced over the last two days. They were living life. A smile tugged at her lips. She looked forward to joining them.

"Our car was waiting at Foley Square. He's pulling around," Mac said, as he slid his phone in his pocket. "That's a nice look. Haven't seen one of those crack that pretty face of yours in a while."

"It's a beautiful day."

Mac leaned forward and pressed his lips to her cheek, branding her with the gentle touch.

Her cheeks burned with heat reflecting the pure light of hope flaming through her. Pressing a breath through her lips, she glanced at a series of three black SUV's idling on the corner. A flurry of activity drew her attention to the side entrance of the courthouse, and she watched as two oversized men in U.S. Marshals' jackets hovered over a small woman as they jogged to the waiting vehicles.

"Mama?" She whispered. Sliding her hand from Mac's, she hustled toward the corner waving. "Mama? Mama, wait…"

The lead Marshal opened the back door of the middle SUV, guiding the small, dark haired woman into the backseat. He followed her in, and then closed the door.

"Wait!" Charlotte screamed.

The caravan moved onto the street.

"Please…"

BOOM!

Charlotte propelled backwards, scraping her left side as she slid to stop. Pushing to her knees, she wobbled to stand, facing the explosion. "NO! MAMA!"

The middle SUV, engulfed in flames, was swarmed by federal, state, and local first responders.

"Charlie." Mac tugged her to his chest.

"Mama...Mac, she was in the SUV."

54

The funeral was graveside. Only Charlie, her grandmother, and Mac attended. Her grandmother's priest officiated. No mourners. No flowers. No music. No body. The explosion left only ash and soot. And dozens of unanswered questions.

With the final prayer, Alla thanked the priest and laced her arm through her granddaughter's crooked elbow.

Mac followed behind Alla and Charlie to the waiting limousine. He listened to the melancholy tones of their Russian heritage as they spoke words he could not comprehend but the sentiment he understood all too well with the loss of both his mother and father.

The driver opened the rear door to the limousine. Alla slid in with traces of the Bolshoi infusing each movement. Charlie followed.

Mac couldn't help but admire the practiced grace with which she folded her long body into the waiting car. A sharp pitched scream snatched him from his wondering thoughts and sped his feet down the slope to the waiting car. Shoving the driver out of his way, Mac dove through the doorway. "Charlie!"

Landing on the wide floorboard with a thud, knocking the wind from his chest, but not the fear from his veins, he flipped to his knees and stared at Charlie who was embracing Georgie.

Georgie merely lifted a single brow to match the soft twist of her lips.

Pushing himself to sit on the open bench, he kneaded the muscle at the base of his neck. "Do not scream when there are shooters, bombers, and mobsters running lose and wreaking havoc."

Both sisters chuckled.

"Yes, sir." Charlie saluted. "From now on I'll reserve my screams for violent attempts on my life, near disasters, and all around natural crises. Is that fair?"

Mac bit the inside of his cheek, pooling blood in his mouth, but the metallic taste was preferable over the words he wanted to shout at Bent's daughters.

Alla winked at Charlie. "Your My Mac is good man, myshka. He run to crisis. No teasing."

"Yes, Baba."

"Mens don't appreciate womens humor. They too sensitive."

~*~

Two hours later, Charlotte carried a tray of empty teacups and delicate china plates littered with scone and sandwich crumbs from the elongated tea her grandmother hosted for their surprise guests to the kitchen and Marta's waiting hands.

Georgie, Cade, Dylan, Savvy, and Mellie flew up to support Charlotte and her grandmother. They let them have their privacy at the cemetery, but in true southern tradition, a spread of treats, casseroles, snacks, and food laden in butter and sugar covered every surface of Baba's kitchen.

Charlotte was astounded by the extreme kindness. No one, aside from her grandmother and Mac, knew Mama as anything but an accomplice to an international crime syndicate and yet they came to celebrate her life.

The clank of silver against china drew Charlotte's focus.

Mac balanced a small stack of plates in his left hand, while cradling her grandmother's prized teapot in the other.

"If you drop that teapot, Baba knows places in Siberia they will never find your body."

"Har, har." He handed her the pot and slid the balance of the dishes on the last open spot on the counter beside the sink. "I used to help my mom when she had her café. I can balance plates and bowls with the best of them."

"So, when you're fired because you break the heart of the co-CEO, you have a back-up plan." Charlotte leaned her hip against the wide breakfast table.

Mac closed the distance between them and rested his hands on her shoulders. "If I break her heart, I promise I will fix it."

"Good to know."

"And if she breaks mine?"

She leaned forward and pressed her lips to his. "I

have a lifetime supply of mending just waiting for you."

Epilogue

THREE MONTHS LATER...

"That was a strike! Ump, you better get some glasses if you're gonna call games here." Charlotte dropped her cupped hands from her lips, gratefully accepting the ice water from Mac's extended hand.

"As a former strike-ball expert, that was definitely a ball."

Her lips pinched to a pout. "Don't mess with me, Taylor. We're down by two in the bottom of the fifth. If I have to get in the ump's head, I will."

"She takes this all very seriously." Cade's intended whisper to Georgie floated over her left shoulder.

"You have no idea. It's easier to agree." Remy said. His chrome and black cane and slow, slightly slurred speech were the only remnants of the terrible accident six months earlier.

"Hey, Special Agent man, if you don't take baseball seriously, you don't take life seriously," Charlotte mumbled.

"See what I mean?" Remy said.

Mac lowered onto the seat to her right, draping his arm over her shoulders. "We are only a month into a very long season, Charlie."

She leaned forward, resting her elbows against her knees, hiding her broad smile. She couldn't remember the last time she was this content. This truly happy.

Over the last three months, thanks to her mother's pre-taped testimony, dozens of Anton's partners had been arrested, some already tried and convicted, for the hundreds of crimes they had committed in the United States. The RICO trials would begin in the fall, but based on what Cade and Dylan had been allowed to share, their cases were airtight. The demons who had tortured hundreds of thousands directly and indirectly would be brought to justice. Finally.

With each update, the pride she felt for her mother's final choice nearly burst through with the brightness of the sun at midday.

As the case closed, Cade asked for a permanent transfer to the Charleston Field Office. He asked Savvy and Charlotte for their blessing in his asking Georgie to marry him over a week ago. Now, Charlotte was on pins and needles every time she saw her sister's name pop onto her phone screen. If Murphy didn't ask her soon, Charlotte was going to shove him onto one knee on the way out of church on Sunday.

Her phone buzzed in her pocket, drawing her attention from the poorly called game. "Charlotte Dixon."

"Hi Charlotte, its Dylan. Sorry to bug you during the game, but wanted to give you a heads up. You should be receiving a package at the ballpark today. It's from me. It's safe."

"OK."

"Don't be worried. I just wanted to ensure it wasn't accidentally thrown out as a suspicious package. Thought the ballpark would be the safest place for delivery. Have a good one."

"Weird," she whispered.

Mac leaned forward. "What's weird?"

"That was Dylan. He said he sent a package to me. Here. At the ballpark."

He tugged a white business envelope from his shirt pocket. "That he did. Jimmy had it delivered to security, but Cade gave me a heads-up this morning. I stopped by the security office after I was finished with the new port contracts. Cade told me Dylan's been temporarily reassigned. I don't think we will see him for a while. I think he's working with Maggie's Uncle Jack."

She snatched the envelope from him. Measuring the length with her fingers, she peeled back the edge, ripping through paper made soft in the late spring humidity. Hurried handwriting scrawled across three pages. Flipping to the end, she saw the signature, "Mama."

Her heart thumped, nearly rattling her chest. She whipped her head toward Cade, who lounged with his hand over Georgie's shoulder, his opposite hand laced fingers with hers. His vision focused toward the field.

"Charlie, sweetheart, what is it?" Mac asked. His tone hushed seeming to sense the fear she felt oozing through her skin.

She quickly read through the letter, the words a blur in her vision.

Her mother was safe. She couldn't say where. The explosion had been a quickly thwarted plot attempt by one of Anton's men, the same bomb maker who had attacked her. The U.S. Marshals swiftly responded to the threat with a convincing piece of theater.

Mama apologized for the hasty exit, but wanted Charlotte to know how much she loved her.

"She's alive." Charlotte's voice was barely a whisper. She handed the letter to Mac.

He scanned the letter and then refolded the pages, shoving them into the ripped envelope. Tugging her to his side, he whispered, "You will have to destroy this letter."

She nodded. The lump in her throat was too thick to allow for words.

They watched the sixth inning in silence. She was content to have the comforting sounds of the ballpark announcer's game day chatter fill the giant holes of question filling her being.

The traditional seventh inning stretch had fans in the Bombers' stands unfolding from their seats and screeching about rooting for the home team. She watched arms slung over shoulders throughout the stadium and a warmth flooded the icy chill that had crept into her soul with the letter.

Her mother was alive.

She could only pray the transformation she had seen in Mama three months earlier would take root and she would one day see her mother again in the arms of Jesus. The hope would be enough.

Charlotte glanced to her left and caught the glint

of sparkle on Georgie's left hand. Grabbing Mac's fingers, she squeezed. "Taylor, he did it! He proposed. Finally!" She turned to face Mac, a smile stretched across her heart.

Mac lowered to a single knee in front of her as the final strains of 'Take Me Out To The Ball Game' flitted through the air.

"What are you doing?"

Mac popped the hinge on a tiny ring box. A perfect square cut solitaire shined back at her. "Murphy stole my thunder and my idea, but I thought the seventh inning stretch was the perfect time to propose to my girl of summer. Charlie, love of my life. Pain in my side. Gift from heaven, will you marry me?"

Tears flooded her vision. She nodded.

Slipping the ring on her finger, he pressed a light kiss to her lips. Applause rocketed through the ballpark. She glanced at the centerfield screen. Their faces were twenty feet tall and the words, "SHE SAID YES" scrolled under the image.

"No taking it back now." He chuckled.

"You are stuck with me for all of your summers."

A Devotional Moment

But the tax collector stood at a distance. He would not even look up to heaven, but beat his breast and said, 'God, have mercy on me, a sinner.' ~ Luke 18:13

For centuries, the words of the tax collector have been prayed by Christians in a prayer known as The Jesus Prayer, or the Prayer of the Heart. For Christians, acknowledging our sins and asking for forgiveness is the way to show humility and to rely on God. In acknowledging that Jesus is the Son of God, we express our faith. We come in humility, confessing that we are sinners and unworthy, but He's given us grace! We are forgiven if our heart is truly contrite.

In **Girls of Summer**, the protagonist learns that her actions lead to disaster, so she pushes everyone away in an attempt to protect her family from evil forces bent on tearing them apart. But her family, driven by God's tender grace, work together to bring her peace. Her experience with God leads her to The Jesus Prayer, faith, and absolution.

Have you ever found it difficult to rest in a place

of peace? It's important to take time to pray, but not only to pray, but to call to mind any sins you may have committed during that day. Remember sins can be done in thought, word and actions. God will forgive you for anything. All you have to do is ask. While some may think that since He'll forgive you (or has forgiven you) that you don't need to confess sins or even bring them to mind. But, there is something wonderful that happens when you do confess your sins to God, even when you already believe He'll forgive you. And that something wonderful is that they are brought to light so that the evil one cannot use them against you. Once you've given the sins to God in a tangible way that can be grasped by human senses, even if guilt or shame try to bring you down, you will know in your own self that you are forgiven and that God has removed that guilt or shame. What is brought into the light cannot harm you. So confess your sins to God on a daily basis. Clear your conscience, receive mercy and forgiveness. When you do, you'll receive power to overcome evil and the grace to live with a peace-filled heart.

LORD JESUS CHRIST, SON OF THE LIVING GOD, HAVE MERCY ON ME, A SINNER. IN JESUS' NAME I PRAY, AMEN.

Thank you

We appreciate you reading this White Rose Publishing title. For other inspirational stories, please visit our on-line bookstore at www.pelicanbookgroup.com.

For questions or more information, contact us at customer@pelicanbookgroup.com.

White Rose Publishing
Where Faith is the Cornerstone of Love™
an imprint of Pelican Book Group
www.PelicanBookGroup.com

Connect with Us
www.facebook.com/Pelicanbookgroup
www.twitter.com/pelicanbookgrp

To receive news and specials, subscribe to our bulletin
http://pelink.us/bulletin

May God's glory shine through
this inspirational work of fiction.

AMDG

You Can Help!

At Pelican Book Group it is our mission to entertain readers with fiction that uplifts the Gospel. It is our privilege to spend time with you awhile as you read our stories.

We believe you can help us to bring Christ into the lives of people across the globe. And you don't have to open your wallet or even leave your house!

Here are 3 simple things you can do to help us bring illuminating fiction™ to people everywhere.

1) If you enjoyed this book, write a positive review. Post it at online retailers and websites where readers gather. And share your review with us at reviews@pelicanbookgroup.com (this does give us permission to reprint your review in whole or in part.)

2) If you enjoyed this book, recommend it to a friend in person, at a book club or on social media.

3) If you have suggestions on how we can improve or expand our selection, let us know. We value your opinion. Use the contact form on our web site or e-mail us at customer@pelicanbookgroup.com

God Can Help!

Are you in need? The Almighty can do great things for you. Holy is His Name! He has mercy in every generation. He can lift up the lowly and accomplish all things. Reach out today.

Do not fear: I am with you; do not be anxious: I am your God. I will strengthen you, I will help you, I will uphold you with my victorious right hand.

~Isaiah 41:10 (NAB)

We pray daily, and we especially pray for everyone connected to Pelican Book Group—that includes you! If you have a specific need, we welcome the opportunity to pray for you. Share your needs or praise reports at http://pelink.us/pray4us

Free eBook Offer

We're looking for booklovers like you to partner with us! Join our team of influencers today and periodically receive free eBooks!

For more information
Visit http://pelicanbookgroup.com/booklovers

How About Free Audiobooks?

We're looking for audiobook lovers, too! Partner with us as an audiobook lover and periodically receive free audiobooks!

For more information
Visit
http://pelicanbookgroup.com/booklovers/freeaudio.html

or e-mail
booklovers@pelicanbookgroup.com